LINEAGE OF CORRUPTION

COVENTRY SAGA BOOK 7

ROBIN PATCHEN

JDO PUBLISHING

For Laurel, Micah, Melissa, Chris, and Kat.
Thank you for letting me walk alongside you on your writing journey.
The Lord has great things in store for you.

CHAPTER ONE

Josie Smith contemplated felony assault—would any jury convict her?—and not for the first time on this doomed adventure.

She glared at the back of the head in front of her. Bentley Kent's hair was prematurely graying, and unlike when they were together years before, he no longer bothered to hide it. Maybe he thought it made him look more distinguished, gave him a bit of gravitas. He wouldn't be wrong about that.

But all the dignity in the world wouldn't help them out here.

"It can't be much farther." He tossed her a smile over his shoulder, but she wasn't buying it. He was all decked out in hiking gear, from the rugged flannel shirt—still creased from its packaging—to the brand-spanking-new boots. He wasn't an outdoorsman, but she hadn't thought twice about joining him today. Trails snaked all over this side of the mountain. It should have been fine.

She hadn't figured on their leaving the trail, though. He'd claimed he wanted to show her something. Considering it was nearly dusk, she assumed he'd found a remote spot on Mt.

Coventry to watch the sunset, but if they didn't reach it soon, they'd miss the show. Either way, they'd have to get back to the trail in the dark.

She stepped over a fallen branch and slipped on the wet leaves on the far side, barely keeping herself from falling. "Bentley, I think we should return—"

"No, no. It's just ahead. The directions are very clear."

"Directions?" She froze. "You mean you haven't *been* here before?"

"Not technically." He looked back at her, eyebrows lifted.

"It's getting dark." People went missing in the White Mountains all the time, sometimes for days. It was June, and though it had climbed into the high seventies, as soon as the sun set, the temperature would drop. "We don't want to get lost."

Rather than give Bentley the chance to argue, Josie started hiking back to the trail. With any luck, they'd reach it while it was still light enough to see.

She reached the fallen branch and stepped over it, but her foot landed in a hole and twisted.

Pain stabbed her ankle and shot up her leg.

She tumbled to the damp forest floor.

"Josephine!" Bentley stumbled over the uneven ground and crouched beside her. "Are you all right?"

"It's *Josie.*" She pushed the words past clenched teeth. That he refused to use her adopted nickname in her adopted hometown was the least of her problems at that moment.

Bentley helped her to a sitting position. "What hurts?"

She rotated her foot until another sharp jab stopped her. "It's my ankle." He reached for it, but she flinched. "Don't touch it."

But, just like he used to, he ignored her words, eased her jeans up and her sock down. "It's swelling. We need to get you to a doctor." Bentley helped her up, but even the slightest pressure on that foot was unbearable.

She slumped back to the ground. "You're going to have to go for help."

"I can get you out of here. I'll carry you."

Bentley was a lot of things—handsome, clever. She knew he worked out. But there was no way he could carry her over the uneven ground to the trail and then all the way down the mountain.

And he knew it, despite the bold words.

"Call for help," she said. "They have people trained for this."

He looked around as if there might be another option before pulling his phone from his pocket. "There's actually service up here."

His incredulity irritated her. This was New Hampshire, not Siberia.

He made the call and then slid his phone back into his jeans pocket. "I'm going back to the path to wait for them so I can show them the way."

"Great." She'd just sit on the damp ground, alone in the woods, and try not to freeze to death. Or be eaten by a bear.

She and Bentley had gone on a lot of dates in the past. This was shaping up to be the worst, and that was saying something.

At least an hour passed—an hour of shivering and praying for rescue while the sun disappeared beyond the trees—before she heard his shout. "Josephine?"

"Over here," she yelled. Based on the frantic tone in his voice, he'd lost her. No wonder it had taken so long.

Finally, a flashlight beam crossed over her. "Stay here, sir." The other man's voice was familiar. "I'd rather not have to carry you both out."

Surely, surely it wasn't *him*.

What were the chances?

A moment later, the man crouched at her side. She couldn't see much of him in the darkness, but she didn't miss the jacket he wore, the *Search and Rescue* emblem sewn on it. "Sorry it took so long. Your friend's not exactly a tracker. It's your ankle?"

Maybe he wouldn't recognize her voice. It was dark, after all. "Uh-huh. I don't think it's broken."

He leaned back and studied her. "Josie?"

"Yeah. Hi."

"It's Thomas," he said. "You probably can't see my face."

She couldn't, but she could picture it. Deep-set brown eyes, dark hair, strong jaw covered by a beard that was just the other side of *I didn't have time to shave*. She had a lot of good-looking customers. This one was drop-dead gorgeous—if someone were attracted to his type. Which she wasn't.

He was in full-on rescue mode. He poked at the injury, eliciting a gasp. "Sorry. You may be right, but sprains can be just as painful as breaks, sometimes worse. Here, take this." He held out the flashlight. "You're going to have to light the way, okay?"

She took it. "I can do that."

"Good. Wrap your arms around my neck so I can lift you."

"You're not going to *carry* me?"

"Do you have a better idea?"

"Is that really how you handle this sort of thing? I'd imagined..." Some sort of contraption to get her down the mountain.

But they were deep in the woods, far from the trail. Unless he could levitate her, she didn't see another way.

"Truth be told," he said, "we'd normally come in pairs and put you on a stretcher, but a toddler wandered away from his campsite on the lake, and most of the team has gone to find him. I was on my way there when the call came in. I figured I could handle this myself."

"So I'm keeping you from finding a lost kid?"

"You're no less important. Besides, I was halfway up when I heard they found him."

Thank goodness for that.

"You ready?" When he leaned close, she had no choice but to wrap her arms around his neck. He lifted her as if she weighed no more than a child and settled her against his chest.

Oh boy.

It was strong and broad, and she resisted the urge to nestle into his warmth—so comforting after the cold bracken. His intoxicating scent had her inhaling. Pine and sandalwood and man.

"Light the way, Rudolph."

Despite the aching ankle and the embarrassing situation—or maybe because of those things—she chuckled as she aimed the flashlight ahead.

Bentley crashed through the brush toward them using his cell phone flashlight to illuminate the way. "Josephine, are you all right?"

"Just glad you guys are here."

Thomas said nothing as he picked his way carefully on the uneven ground. When they were back to the trail, he asked, "What were you two doing so far from the path?"

Bentley answered. "A guy told me about a lookout where we could watch the sunset."

Josie felt more than heard a low growl in her rescuer's chest. "The path leads right to it. Everybody coming up here in the evening is looking to see the sunset."

"The guy at that restaurant said to turn off at the big boulders."

"There are no boulders near here."

They'd reentered the path higher up than where they'd left it, so a few minutes later, Bentley—stubborn as always, more so when he was wrong—pointed as they passed. "The boulders are right there."

Josie moved the flashlight to cross over rocks about the size of a coffee maker.

Thomas laughed. "If those are boulders, a house cat might be confused as a full-grown tiger."

"It's a relative term," Bentley snapped.

Thomas mumbled, "Not *that* relative." Louder, he said, "I recommend that, in the future, you don't stray from paths unless you're with a trained guide."

Josie agreed heartily, but she didn't say so.

Bentley ignored him.

They walked a long time in silence. The path was empty now, the smart hikers having left long before. She had no idea how far they were from the bottom when Thomas spoke again.

"Sir, why don't you hurry ahead and get your car. Park it near the trailhead."

Bentley turned to her. "Will you be all right without me for a few minutes?"

The thought of finally getting off this mountain and into a warm, cozy car appealed more than she should say. "Go ahead."

After a wary look at Thomas, Bentley jogged down the path, his light bouncing ahead of him.

Thomas sighed. "If he trips and falls, I'll come back for him."

"He'll be fine." She hoped.

"Just out of curiosity," Thomas said when Bentley was out of sight, "how many times do you think I've asked you out?"

She'd been hoping his professional veneer would hold. "A couple."

"A *couple*? A lot more than that."

"Maybe you should have taken the hint and given up."

"Oh, I quit believing you'd ever say yes and started using the conversations to build up my immunity to rejection."

"Glad I could be of service."

"I'm curious, though. What is it about *Bentley*"—his emphasis on the name came with attitude—"that earned him a yes?"

Rather than delve into her psyche to come up with a legitimate answer—or at least an answer that would satisfy Thomas— she simply shrugged. "He's smart, well-educated, well-mannered."

"And I'm not?"

"I don't know you. I've known Bentley a long time."

"So you decide which men to date based on how long you've known them? If you met the man of your dreams tomorrow, you'd reject him out of hand because the chronology didn't work out?"

Ignoring him seemed easier than trying to justify herself.

Thomas's steady footfalls on the dirt path were barely discernible over the nightly orchestra of crickets and frogs.

"I figured it out," he said. "Guy with a name like Bentley's gotta have money. You're a gold digger."

"You know nothing about me."

"I know more than I did an hour ago."

"No, you don't. And the fact that you think you do..." She clamped her lips shut before she finished the sentence.

"What? Am I wrong?"

"Completely. And let's be honest. Your question isn't really, 'Why did you say yes to Bentley?' Your question is, 'Why did you say no to me?'"

Another few steps of silence, and then, "And what's the answer? I mean, for the sake of my education and personal growth, I'd like to know why a beautiful woman like you would flat-out refuse to have dinner with a humble guy like me."

"Humble. Ha."

He chuckled but didn't defend himself. "I mean, Bentley got you into this mess. If I could give you one little piece of advice, don't go into the woods with a guy who can't get you back out."

"And...that's why."

He slowed, then came to a stop to look down at her. His face, though shrouded in darkness, was just inches from hers. She had the irrational desire to press her hand against his stubbly cheek and lean in.

She looked away. "Are we just going to stand here?"

"Maybe I need a break."

Though he'd been carrying her for at least twenty minutes, he wasn't even out of breath. She doubted he was tired but couldn't figure out how to say so without stroking an ego that needed no more stroking.

"Explain, please," he said. "What about my advice was so objectionable?"

"I don't date politicians."

A beat of silence followed her words. Then, "If I get whiplash from this conversation, who's going to carry you to the parking lot?"

"You're running for mayor."

"How did you...? I haven't announced that yet."

"I hear things."

He started walking again, though more slowly than before. "Two questions. First, what does that have to do with me giving you advice?"

When she didn't respond—because how could she defend her flippant remark?—he moved on. "Two, the mayor hadn't even resigned the first time I asked you out."

"You act like a politician."

"How so?"

"You know, all the greeting people by name and smiling at everybody."

"You mean being friendly?"

"I mean...forget it."

She prayed he would let it go.

A few moments later, though, he said, "You never answered the first question."

"Are you serious?"

"About wanting an answer? Yes. And I'm not above using the fact that I'm literally *rescuing you* from your current date."

"You're not my type."

"What type is that?"

"Your whole alpha-male thing."

"I'm an alpha male? Okay." He walked a few steps. "An alpha male is a guy who takes charge, a leader, right? I guess that describes me, but you don't know enough about me to know that."

"It's not just that. It's all the working out and..." How could she explain herself without...actually explaining herself?

"You're offended by my strength? Because at the moment, one might think you'd be grateful, all things considered." He tossed her up a few inches, eliciting a gasp, and then caught her without missing a step. "Of course, as an alpha male, I generally prefer to drag my women by their hair, but I left my club at home."

"Lucky me." She infused her words with all the sarcasm she could muster.

"Seriously? I could just leave you here, you know."

"But you won't. You'll do your job."

"It's not my job, Josie. I'm a volunteer."

She would have realized that, if she'd given it any thought at all. He almost always wore a suit when he came into her coffee shop, and his hours were pretty regular. Neither of those would be true of somebody who worked for search-and-rescue.

And he had come to her rescue after dark on a Friday night. Didn't he have anything better to do? A date, maybe? A guy with his face and body wouldn't want for willing females, present company excluded.

"I didn't mean to offend you," she said. "I'm sorry. And I am grateful."

"You're welcome." He walked a few steps. "So, why don't you date alpha males?"

"Has anybody ever told you you're annoyingly persistent?"

His chest rumbled with his laugh. "Maybe. More than once."

She wasn't going to explain her history with men to him.

He walked in silence a few moments. What in the world could he be thinking? She'd always figured he was like so many men she'd met—all shine and no substance. Kind on the outside, conniving beneath the pretty exterior. This conversation—the longest in their brief acquaintance—made her question that assumption.

"If you ever decide to dump your boyfriend—"

"He's not—"

"Just tell him that you chose him because he's not an alpha male. That would do it."

She imagined what that conversation would look like and conceded that Thomas was probably right. Bentley might not be the type of guy to volunteer for search-and-rescue, but he was comfortable being in charge. He came off as a deep thinker, but when push came to shove, he made his opinion known and often figured out a method to get his way.

Was Bentley a closet alpha male?

Her father was powerful, thanks to the office he held, but he was also gentle and tender, deep-thinking and curious. He was an academic, nothing like this guy, all bluster and brawn.

Whatever the label, she knew what she wanted in a man—someone smart and well-read. An intellectual. What she wanted was absolutely not what Thomas had to offer, no matter how safe she felt pressed against his chest.

CHAPTER TWO

Thomas Windham berated himself for his stupidity.

He should have carried Josie down on his back. It wasn't that he hadn't considered it, either. It was that...

No need to name it, though he could. *Stupid. Ridiculous.*

And label himself... *Glutton for punishment.*

His problem now as they neared the parking lot wasn't that he was winded. His half-full backpack weighed more than this woman. But after dreaming about her for months, after seeing her almost every single day, after being rejected by her nineteen times—and yes, he'd been counting—now, to have her so close, her face barely inches from his, her scent, vanilla and coffee, filling his nose...

It was its own distinct form of torture. And still, he dreaded the moment he'd have to set her down and send her away with *Bentley.*

Really, God?

He could practically hear an Almighty chuckle.

It's not funny.

Though, rescuing the woman who'd rejected him *nineteen times* from her current date...

Okay, it was a little funny.

They were getting close to the parking lot. Once he had a better look at her ankle, he'd turn her over to her beta-boyfriend and watch her ride away.

So, he might as well make it an even twenty.

"You say Bentley isn't your boyfriend?"

"He's not."

"Then how about you let me take you to dinner? There's this great place..."

She laughed, the sound somehow as beautiful as it was degrading.

Thick skin. He'd continued to ask her out in order to build up thick skin. He'd probably need that when he lost the election which, all things considered, felt like a foregone conclusion.

He'd expected Josie to turn him down again, but to laugh?

"I'm sorry," she said. "I'm so sorry. I'm not laughing at you. I'm laughing at this whole"—she gestured to the woods with the flashlight—"bizarre situation. I mean, what are the chances you'd be the one to rescue me?"

"I take it that's a no?"

"It's not you."

"Sure it is." He kept his tone light, as if she hadn't just stabbed him in the heart. "But, if I can survive a woman literally laughing in my face as I carry her off a mountain, I can survive anything. Which means, my skin is thick enough."

Bentley stood silhouetted against the lights in the parking lot of the trailhead. They'd been spotted. He started jogging their way.

Thomas lowered his voice so the guy wouldn't hear. "I promise, I won't ask again."

"I truly am sorry. I didn't mean—"

"Josephine!" The man sounded frantic. What, had he thought Thomas might steal her away? "Hurry, hurry!"

Thomas said, "What's the—?"

"What happened?" Josie called.

As Bentley neared, Josie aimed the flashlight beam toward him, and Thomas caught terror in the man's eyes.

He asked, "What's going on?"

"She needs to get in the car, now." Bentley's gaze scanned the surroundings as if threats loomed all around.

Thomas started jogging, and Bentley kept pace at his side.

"What happened?" Josie asked again.

"There's been an...attempt."

Josie gasped. "Oh, my gosh. Is he—?"

"Reports are spotty, but they say he wasn't hit. We gotta get you somewhere safe."

What were they talking about? Something was very wrong. There was still the matter of her ankle, though. "She needs X-rays."

Bentley's eyes widened, but he didn't slow. "Okay, okay. We can—"

"It's just a sprain," Josie said. "If it's not better tomorrow, I'll go to the emergency room."

Thomas said, "We just need—"

"If you think it's okay." Bentley directed the words to Josie. "We'd be wise to wait until we know what happened."

They ate up the remaining twenty yards or so in seconds, and Thomas set her in the front seat of the BMW idling at the trailhead. "I'll meet you at your place."

Bentley was halfway to the driver's door when he stopped. "You know where she lives?"

Thomas looked over the top of the car. "Above the coffee shop."

The man's eyes narrowed. "And you know that how?"

"Is it a secret?"

Josie called, "Just get in the car, Bentley. We need to go."

Bentley glared at Thomas. "We don't need your help."

"You have crutches in your trunk, do you?"

"Uh..."

"An ace bandage? Medical training?"

"Get in the car!" Josie yelled.

"Fine," the man said. "Bring those over."

As if Thomas wouldn't have without the guy's permission. Not only did Josie need them, but Thomas was going to figure out what had these two so spooked.

Bentley slid into his driver's seat. "Close your door and lock it."

He was talking to Josie, ignoring Thomas.

Josie looked terrified, and Thomas had the urge to grab her hand and squeeze it, to infuse her with strength. But she had *Bentley* for that.

"See you in a few," Thomas said. "Be safe."

He closed the door, and the lock clicked.

The BMW tore through the nearly empty parking lot and turned toward town.

Thirty minutes later, with crutches in his hand and his medical pack over his shoulder, Thomas climbed the exterior staircase to the apartment above the coffee shop, mentally kicking himself. He should have followed them here, carried her inside, and then gone home for the crutches. How had she gotten up the stairs? He pictured her walking, putting weight on her ankle.

Stupid.

He reached the door and knocked.

A moment later, it swung open. Bentley said, "Do they have any leads?"

"Uh..." But Bentley had earbuds in his ears. He stuck his head out the door, looked around, and then backed up.

Thomas stepped into a living room a little smaller than the one in his condo, which was to say, tiny. It held a sofa, a club chair, a narrow coffee table, and a TV mounted on the wall. Behind the sofa was a table surrounded by four chairs. The door beyond that led to the kitchen. Small as the apartment was, it was cozy and decorated well with a few houseplants, a mirror leaning by the door, and pictures on the wall. It wasn't just a place to live. Josie had made this a home.

He'd wondered over the previous few months if her stay in Coventry was temporary. If that was the reason for her continually rejecting him. Apparently not.

Josie was on the couch, swollen ankle propped on pillows, gaze riveted to a news program on the TV. She had a phone pressed to her ear. "Carlyle, I just need to talk to him for one... Yes, I understand that, but..." She sighed and tipped her head back, catching sight of Thomas.

He propped the crutches against the wall and set his bag beside it, then slid the coffee table out of the way and crouched beside her foot.

Since both she and Bentley were on the phone, he set to work examining her ankle. It wasn't misshapen—a good sign. She'd complained of pain, not numbness, another indication it wasn't broken. But Bentley had said she couldn't put weight on it.

Which might indicate a fracture.

"Two minutes," Josie said. "I just need to know he's all right." She waited, and Thomas did, too, turning his attention to the muted television. He read the closed captioning.

...attempt on Senator Davis Harrington's life. At this point, the suspect is at large. The DC police chief...

"Put my mother on the phone then." Her eyes widened.

"Examined for what?"

Thomas's heart hammered. Whatever was happening, it was bad. Very bad.

A moment later, she blew out a relieved breath and collapsed against the cushions.

Thomas forced his gaze away from her face. Whatever she was dealing with was more pressing than her ankle.

If he could alleviate her pain and get her ambulatory until she could get an X-ray done, he would.

"I'll wait." She caught his eyes and added, "It's not like I'm going anywhere."

She was trying to put on a brave face, but he didn't miss the tears dripping down her cheeks. Whatever was going on, it scared her, badly.

As long as she was on hold... "You need to tell me where it hurts, okay?"

She nodded, and he pressed his fingers against the smooth skin over her lateral bones.

She barely reacted.

But when he shifted to the soft skin beside them, she flinched.

"Right there. That's the spot."

He pressed more here and there, but nothing elicited the reaction the ligament had. He sat back on his heels. "I'm pretty sure it's a sprain, but you should still get it X-rayed. It's not worth risking serious long-term damage."

"Can it wait?"

"Tomorrow at the latest."

She started to say something else, then closed her eyes and spoke into the phone. "Thank God, thank God you're all right. And is Mom...?"

Tears spilled down Josie's cheeks, and she lowered her chin to her chest and wrapped her free hand around her stomach. "Is he going to be all right?" She listened, then, "God was looking out for all of you."

Thomas turned away to give her a modicum of privacy. He watched the scene on the television. Somebody had fired at the senator. His bodyguard had pushed him down and taken the bullet, but the captions reported that the man was stable.

"Does Carlyle have a theory?" A pause. "A bodyguard? I don't think I need... Nobody knows me here." She leaned her head back. "I'll think about it, Dad."

Bentley approached, drawing Thomas's attention.

Josie focused on him. "I promise we'll talk about it."

Bentley muttered, "We'll more than *talk* about it."

Josie probably hadn't heard that. If that wasn't alpha-male behavior, Thomas didn't know what was.

The second she ended the call, Bentley said, "There's nothing to talk about."

"You're right. There isn't."

Based on their tones, they weren't in agreement. Thomas stayed on his knees beside the sofa.

Talk about awkward.

Bentley stomped away, and Josie sighed. "So, I can go tomorrow? To the ER?"

"Tomorrow *morning*. I'm gonna wrap it." He grabbed an ace bandage from his backpack. "You need to ice it for twenty minutes every hour when you're awake. And keep it elevated."

She nodded to the pillows where her foot was propped up. "We knew that much. We've been busy dealing with this"—she tipped her head toward the TV—"or we'd have thought about ice."

Did she have to use *we*, as if she and Bentley were a team? Hadn't she said he wasn't her boyfriend?

This was definitely not the time to analyze that relationship.

Thomas was careful not to hurt her as he wrapped her

swollen ankle. "You'll need to stay off it as much as possible."

"Okay."

When he had it wrapped, he said, "Swing your feet to the floor, and I'll get the crutches."

She did as she was told while he grabbed a crutch and adjusted it. Then, he helped her up. She wasn't tall—maybe two inches above five feet, nearly a foot shorter than himself. He put the crutch beside her, comparing the height, then shortened it even more—maybe he should have brought the children's pair—and tucked it under her armpit.

"How's that feel?" Before she could answer, he said, "One second." He lifted the grip higher for her short arms and tried again. "Now?"

Bentley's voice rose in the other room. "How can you be sure?" And then, "Obviously, it's a threat."

Thomas didn't like the sound of that.

Josie tucked the crutch under her arm and slid her hand around the grip. "It's good."

It looked right. "Sit and..." He helped her down, then pulled an ice pack from his bag. He snapped it to release the cold and set it on the wrapped ankle. "Twenty minutes, then into the freezer with it." He grabbed a couple more ice packs and set them on the coffee table. "You'll probably want to get better quality ones from the drug store."

"Thank you for doing this," she said. "I think we've ventured pretty far outside your search-and-rescue duties."

"It's not a problem." He grabbed the second crutch and adjusted the height and grip.

"You're obviously prepared, though," she said.

"I buy them used and keep them in my pickup. Sometimes, people return them to me. Sometimes..." He shrugged. "Unfortunately, I wasn't driving the pickup today, so I had to go home first."

"Why?"

"Wasn't I driving it? I was out—"

"No. Why do you keep used crutches in your truck?"

He leveled his gaze and deadpanned, "For such a time as this."

She smiled.

"We're usually called because people get injured. I like to help."

"I didn't realize search-and-rescue volunteers had emergency medical training."

"The basics. In my case, I worked as a paramedic in college." Still did, when they needed him. They didn't have enough trained paramedics in town.

Her smile faded when she focused on the television again.

"Senator Harrington is...your father?" he guessed.

She nodded. "Nobody knows that, though. It's important to me that it stays secret."

"I won't tell." He looked up to find her studying him through squinted eyes. "Who's Carlyle?"

"His chief of staff."

"And they think you need a bodyguard?"

She shrugged.

"Your boyfriend was worried—"

"He's not my boyfriend."

At the same time, the man's voice came from behind. "Fiancé."

"*Ex*-fiancé," she snapped.

Okay, then.

Thomas cleared his throat in the silence. "They're worried that whoever did that might come after you?"

She glared over Thomas's head another moment, then nodded.

"Why do you think—?"

"Looks like you're done here," Bentley said. "Thanks for your help."

Thomas stood and found himself a lot closer to the irritating man than he'd ever wanted to be. Rather than back away, he stepped forward.

Bentley stepped back.

Stupid, but Thomas took the little victory. Bentley was with Josie, had been *engaged* to her, and, if Thomas guessed right, hoped to be again.

All Thomas had done was carry her off a mountain.

And now, as Bentley had pointed out, his work was finished.

"You ever walked on crutches, or do you need—?"

"I can teach her," Bentley said.

She glared at her *not*-boyfriend before focusing on Thomas. "In high school, I injured my knee playing field hockey."

"A veteran, then." Thomas moved the coffee table back into place, snatched his bag off the floor, and dug a business card from the outside pocket. He held it out to Josie. "Call me if you need anything."

Josie took the card. "I appreciate—"

"You give your card to everybody you carry off the mountain?" Bentley asked.

Just the beautiful ones.

And those who don't have anybody reliable *to depend on.*

But he didn't say that, just kept his gaze on Josie as if Bentley hadn't spoken. "I'm glad your father's all right. Be safe."

He swiveled, marched past the ex, and stepped out the door.

Bentley was a jealous jerk, but he'd done his best to protect Josie. Thomas would give him credit for that, if never out loud.

But what bothered him as he climbed into his car and drove away was one niggling question.

If the senator was safe, what did her father, Carlyle, and Bentley think she needed protection from?

CHAPTER THREE

Josie kept her smile pasted in place on Monday morning as customer after customer came into her coffee shop and saw her not behind the counter, where she spent the bulk of her life, but seated on the couch in the dining room, her MacBook on her lap, her swollen foot propped on pillows.

If she had any room for the comfy sofa in the kitchen, she'd have had her employees move it there. Alas, the floor space in the kitchen was about as big as a walk-in closet, and her apprentice, Kinsley, was having enough trouble getting all the pastries baked and into the display cabinets without having to dodge a loveseat.

Instead, Josie tried to get some work done in the dining room amid constant interruptions.

"Oh, my!" A seventy-something woman—mocha latte with almond milk—spotted her. "What happened to you?"

"Sprained my ankle on a hike," she said for the seven thousandth time since they'd opened an hour earlier.

"Oh, dear. I'll pray you get well soon." The woman patted her shoulder and continued to the line, where Marcel, the barista, would take her order and fix her coffee.

The line was longer than Josie ever wanted to see it, but two people were doing the work of three.

Her foot *would* be better by the next morning. She hoped, anyway.

It was interesting to see Cuppa Josie's from this side of the counter. She was proud of what she'd created after she'd left her former life. She'd tried to keep the original charm of the old downtown Victorian she'd purchased. The artwork on the walls had been crafted by local artists. Each piece was for sale, and whenever one sold, the artist would replace it with another.

Josie's favorite item in the room was the clock in the shape of a teapot hanging behind the counter. Her mother had bought it for her when Josie announced her crazy plan to open a coffee shop. Her parents didn't understand why she'd left DC, but they'd always supported her.

Though there were a handful of café tables spread among the three rooms that made up the dining area—originally a living room, a parlor, and a dining room—she'd furnished much of the space with vintage chairs and love seats. The pieces weren't fancy or expensive. They were cozy and invited guests to get comfortable.

Her customers did just that. A crew of old men came in a couple of days a week to drink coffee and play cards. Multiple female friend groups met here regularly after they dropped their kids at school or the local church for mothers' day out. Older women congregated here after meetings of their charities and political organizations. Two ladies' Bible studies met in the smallest of the three rooms on two different days, and a men's Bible study met there every Friday at seven a.m.

When Josie first opened the café a few years before, it was a one-woman operation. She did all the baking and all the coffee-making, coming in at four-thirty every morning and staying open through lunchtime. But her customers kept asking her to extend the hours. Now, she had seven employees, and they were open from six in the morning until nine at night, ten on Fridays and Saturdays. The only exception was Sunday, when she opened at the regular time but closed at ten a.m., which gave her —and her employees—just enough time to make it to the ten-thirty service at church.

She'd left a life she couldn't handle any longer and come to Coventry all alone, not even bringing her name with her. She'd built a business she loved here. She'd built a life.

A life she wasn't willing to give up.

No matter what her father or her ex-fiancé said.

The bell over the door jingled, and Thomas entered. Today's suit was light gray, and he'd paired it with a royal blue shirt that made his brown eyes pop.

Her heart did a little flip at the sight of him, her body remembering being held against his chest as he carried her down the mountain. Remembered the concern in his gaze when he'd crouched by her sofa, tending to her ankle and listening to her end of that terrifying conversation.

He scanned behind the counter, then the room. When he caught sight of her, he headed her way.

As usual, he not only greeted everybody who made eye contact with him, but he called them each by name.

"Hey, Marcy."

"How you doing, Bud?"

"Hey, I saw you got a new truck, Ed. That thing have four-wheel drive?"

Everybody smiled at him, talked to him, and seemed a little happier because he'd graced them with a kind word.

Classic politician. He remembered everybody's name and acted as if he cared about every person he met.

Josie's father sincerely cared about people, but he'd always been the exception to the rule in political circles, a combination of an absentminded professor and a brilliant statesman, but not the kind of guy who felt comfortable schmoozing or playing the quid-pro-quo game of politics.

She could see Thomas fitting right into that role.

He got the attention of Marcel, the barista, who gave him a thumbs-up. Meaning he'd get his order started even though Thomas hadn't waited in line.

She glared at Marcel, but he was too busy to notice.

Thomas grabbed an empty chair, one of the few she kept lined against the wall for folks who wanted to squeeze in one more, and pulled it near. "I've been worried about you. How's the ankle?"

"Improving slowly." She closed her laptop and slid it onto the coffee table. "Thanks again for all your help Friday night. I'm not sure what we would have done if you hadn't come by."

"It was my pleasure." He held her eye contact a moment, then seemed to force his gaze to her foot. "What'd the doctor say?"

"It's a sprain, just like you thought. He told me to stay off it as much as possible."

"I can see you're taking his advice."

"It was easier on the weekend. Looking at that line... It's killing me."

Thomas glanced at the people waiting to order, then lifted his hand to greet someone across the room.

"Do you know everybody?"

He turned back to her, shrugging. "I tend to remember faces."

"And names," she said.

He conceded that with a nod and leaned closer, lowering his voice. "How's your family?"

"Everybody's safe, thank God."

"I've been watching the news. Is it true what they're saying about—?"

"Not entirely." She looked around, but nobody was listening. If they kept their voices low, nobody would be able to hear them over the din of the conversations, the hiss of the espresso maker, and the overhead music. "They caught the guy. He claims to have been working alone, but that hasn't been confirmed."

Thomas's eyebrows rose over those pretty brown eyes.

Did he have to be so gorgeous?

"What do they think, then?"

Not that Thomas deserved an explanation, but he'd been so kind to her Friday night, and she hadn't exactly returned the favor. Bentley had been downright rude. The entire situation had been awkward, made more so by the fact that Thomas had asked her out—again. And she'd laughed in his face.

The memory of that moment brought heat to her cheeks that she hoped didn't show. She hadn't meant to be unkind. The thought that this hunky, gorgeous man really wanted to go out with her...that he'd ask her out while rescuing her...

It had felt ridiculous.

But she'd hurt his feelings. He'd tried to hide it, but she'd seen the truth of it in the set of his mouth. And still, he'd gone out of his way to help her. And sat beside her now seeking more information, not because he was nosy but because he really cared.

Maybe she was getting sucked into his little charisma bubble like the rest of town. Still, she owed him.

"It has to stay between us."

He blinked and sat back. "You can trust me. Case in point, does anybody know who you are?"

"No."

"I've already proved I can be trusted, Josie. And I've already promised not to ask you out again. I hoped...I still hope that, after Friday, you and I can be friends."

Friends?

Aside from her best friend, Shelly, who lived in the DC area, Josie didn't have many of those. Maybe Bentley, though until the previous week, they hadn't spoken in nearly three years. That relationship was awkward at best—him trying to win her back and her working very hard to keep him in the friend zone. There were acquaintances she exchanged small talk with at church, her employees, her customers. But friends? In Coventry?

She must've waited too long to respond because he sat back. "Or not." And then he laughed. "I guess I'm not done building my thick skin where you're concerned." He pressed his hands to his thighs and started to push to his feet.

"I'm sorry," she said quickly. "Sit, sit." He did, eyeing her warily. "I'd like to be your friend."

He nodded. "Okay."

"There's this bill they're trying to get passed."

"I know about the health care bill, and I know your father is refusing to vote for it, and without his vote, it won't pass. I know he's been under incredible pressure, and I know the authorities believe the shooter was someone who thinks your father stands in the way of all that's good and right in the world."

"You're well informed."

"I still get the newspaper, and every once in a while, I glance at something besides the funnies."

She couldn't help the smile. "Then you know my father's not about to back down. Throughout his career, he has never once voted for any bill that expands or funds abortion. He's made a lot of compromises, but he refuses to compromise on that."

"I admire his steadfastness. Lesser men would have buckled

to the pressure. I can't imagine what it's costing him to go against the party."

Thomas understood more than most. Her father had faced a lot of opposition, but no opponent had ever proved as powerful —or as ruthless—as some people associated with his own political party.

Thomas's head tilted to the side, and he leaned a little closer. "You don't think the party had anything to do with the assassination attempt, though. Right?"

"We don't know. Dad's had death threats before, but an actual attempt? Somebody's trying to either force him to vote for the bill or remove him from office so his successor will. If Dad resigned or were"—she swallowed the word that came to mind —"gone, the governor would appoint somebody more pliable. More of a typical politician, which my father is not."

"I assumed that, considering your disdain for the profession."

"Believe me, I come by it honestly."

He looked like he wanted to say something about that. But he shook his head and seemed to change tact. "And Friday night, I overheard... Your father wants you to get a bodyguard?"

"He's overprotective, but nobody knows where I am." As she'd been saying to Dad and Bentley for three days, ad nauseam. Her brother, Alton, had agreed to a bodyguard, but he had a wife and children to protect, and everybody knew where Alton lived and worked. Josie's situation was different. "I left public life and legally changed my name. I've done my best to make myself impossible to find."

"Why?" As soon as the word was out of his mouth, he shook his head. "Sorry. Not my business. I'd love to know someday, but right now... Your boyfriend is from that life, right? He knows."

Bentley wasn't her boyfriend, but she saw no point in saying that again. "I can trust him."

"I wasn't saying you couldn't. Just that there's at least one person who could give your whereabouts away. Is there anybody else?"

"My best friend knows where I am. My family, of course. But they won't betray me. Besides, I really doubt I'm in any danger. It's not as if I can get my father to change his vote."

He sat back. His lips pressed together. What did that expression mean? That he disagreed with her? That was her guess, but he didn't say so.

The bell over the door had jingled a few times since Thomas sat down. She hadn't bothered to look at customers coming in and out, but when Thomas's back stiffened, she turned that way.

Bentley made his way through the long line and to their side.

"Hey, Beta," Thomas said.

"It's Bentley."

"Sorry. I knew it was something with a B."

Beta. As in, not *alpha*. She glared at Thomas, but he wouldn't meet her eyes, though his lips twitched.

Bentley leaned down and kissed her on the cheek. It was not an expression of affection but of possession, which was confirmed when he shot Thomas a triumphant look. "What are you doing here?"

"Getting coffee and chatting with my friend. What are you doing here?"

Bentley ignored him, settling on the arm of the couch by her shoulder, so close that she tried to shift away without being obvious about it. "How you feeling?"

Crowded. "Why don't you get yourself coffee?"

"I will in a minute."

"I think Marcel's got mine made." Thomas pushed to his feet. "Let me know if there's anything I can do, okay? For the foot and...anything else."

"I will." She wouldn't, but Bentley's attitude was getting on her last nerve. "Thanks."

Thomas moved to the counter, where of course, his coffee sat waiting for him. He handed Marcel cash and headed for the door, greeting at least four people by name on his way out.

Bentley watched through the window until he was out of sight. "What is it with that guy?"

"What is it with *you?*"

He moved to the chair Thomas had vacated, thank heavens, and Josie adjusted herself on the sofa. "Oh, come on, Josie. You're not blind. The guy's obviously interested in you."

"I know."

Bentley's eyebrows rose, dipping behind the rogue hair that fell no matter how much gel he used to keep it back. "What do you mean, you know?"

"He asked me out a couple of times."

"You've been *on a date* with him?" His volume rose, and a couple of people turned their direction.

"Keep your voice—"

"I can't believe you didn't tell me that." Though he was quiet, his words were vehement. "That whole time he was with us, and you two—"

"I didn't say yes."

He sat back and blinked. "Oh. You didn't?" A smile crossed his lips. "I'm sorry. I shouldn't have jumped... You and I have just been so on-again-off-again."

They hadn't been. They'd been on, almost married, and then off. She'd barely spoken to Bentley in years, and once he'd resigned himself to the fact that she wasn't changing her mind about their breakup, their few conversations had revolved around her father. But Bentley knew all of that. She saw no reason to remind him. It seemed his feelings for her hadn't waned. "Thomas isn't my type."

Bentley smiled. "You're right. You always were a good judge of people."

Was she? She wasn't so sure. She was beginning to think she'd judged Bentley all wrong.

And Thomas too.

Kinsley approached, the apprentice's apron covered in flour. Heavens, the girl even had a little in her hair.

"What's up?"

"I'm sorry to interrupt." She held out a recipe. "I've never made croissants from scratch. I'm a little confused."

Josie took the recipe but spoke to Bentley. "Why don't you get your coffee? I have work to do."

He was still smiling as he made his way to the end of the line. Unlike Thomas, he'd have to wait and order like all her other customers.

She was going to have to let Bentley down, again. She hated that, but in her defense, it wasn't as if she'd invited him to invade her hometown or her life. He'd just shown up the week before declaring his decision to rekindle their romance as if she had no say in the matter.

She turned her attention to Kinsley. "Sit down, and I'll talk you through it."

CHAPTER FOUR

As Thomas went about his work, made the calls he needed to make, and handled fires as they cropped up, Josie's image hovered in the back of his mind.

That was nothing new. He'd been drawn to her since the first moment he'd seen her. How she'd been in town for years but he'd only discovered her a few months past, he had no idea. He used to go to The Patriot for coffee, so he'd never bothered with Cuppa Josie's, though it was right next door to his office. The Patriot had been in town forever, its owner a friend. And he never minded the walk—just two blocks. In fact, he'd always welcomed it.

And then he'd seen Josie on the sidewalk one day, and there was something about her.

Ridiculous. It wasn't that she was drop-dead gorgeous. She was attractive, but he knew lots of attractive women, though they were almost all spoken for, most married to, or about to be married to, his closest friends. One by one, each of the guys he hung out with had paired up with a knockout while Thomas had watched from the sidelines. He was a little tired of playing usher at other people's weddings.

He felt like an old bachelor—the male equivalent of a spinster. Not that he'd ever say that out loud.

So when he saw Josie the first time, he hadn't waited a moment. He'd followed her into her shop, found her on the far side of the counter, introduced himself, and invited her to dinner.

She'd promptly turned him down.

And now, thanks to her disastrous hike Friday night, they were friends.

He was glad for that much. Based on everything he'd heard Friday and learned over the weekend, Josie might be in more danger than she wanted to admit, at least to him. Maybe, with his new *friend* status, he could help keep her safe.

He just had to figure out how. And though he didn't have any answers, he had a place to start. He grabbed his cell and called Dylan.

"O'Donnell Investigations."

"It's Thomas. I have a question about finding people."

Dylan was one of the guys who gathered at Braden's on Monday nights to watch sports. He and his wife attended the same church as Thomas. Dylan was a private investigator, and his specialty was finding lost people.

"Who are you looking for?" Dylan asked.

"Nobody. I'm trying to figure out how hard it would be to track a person down after she changed her name and moved."

"Legally changed her name?"

"Yeah."

"Pretty easy if you know where to look."

"Even if the name is really generic, like Smith?"

"If this Smith woman has the same social security number as she did before, then yeah, still easy. If someone wanted to find your Smith, he could do it. It would just take time and money."

The money was irrelevant. The people trying to get Senator

Harrington to change his vote had deep pockets. "How much time?"

"Couple of hours, maybe a day or two."

"That fast?"

His worry must've carried in his tone. "Not what you wanted to hear?"

"What I expected, though. Thanks, man. See you tonight?"

"I'll be there."

As he hung up, the phone rang in the reception area, and his assistant answered. A moment later, she called through the open door, "It's Derrick. Says it's important."

Of course it was.

He pressed the flashing button on his desk phone. "This is Thomas."

"We need to get these platform statements finalized this week. And photos for the literature."

Derrick was Thomas's campaign manager, one of the locals who didn't want Greg Farley to remain mayor. After the previous mayor, Brent Salcito, had been arrested for attempted murder and a whole bunch of other crimes and Farley had been named interim mayor, Derrick and a little cadre of Coventry leaders had convinced Thomas to run for the office against Salcito's right-hand man, promising all the help and support he'd need. Not that any of them had experience with this sort of thing, but Farley didn't have Coventry's interests at heart.

The more Thomas knew about the guy, the less he liked him. So, he'd allowed himself to be roped into this doomed campaign.

"How about I come by your office this afternoon?" Derrick suggested.

Thomas's small insurance agency was more cramped than ever since he'd hired two more underwriters, but it wasn't as if he wanted to rent another space for campaign headquarters.

They weren't very well funded as it was. He could meet the guy at his condo, he supposed, but that was a good ten minutes out of town, fifteen if there was a lot of traffic, which there always was June through August.

And then the other problem he'd been mulling over converged with this one.

"Let's meet at Cuppa Josie's," he said. "Four o'clock?" He happened to know that the shop was pretty dead between three-thirty and five-thirty, despite all the tourists in town. He and Derrick could meet there, and he could work on his campaign and keep an eye on his new friend at the same time. Maybe, God willing, he and Josie could build a relationship. Even if it would never be romantic, at least he could help protect her.

Not that she'd want his protection. Which was why this was the perfect solution.

"That's a great idea," Derrick said. "The locals all know that place, and your association with it will remind people that you've been in town your whole life, separate you from Farley."

Not exactly what he'd been thinking, but he was glad to have a good excuse for what he wanted to do.

"In fact," Derrick said, "you ought to have all your meetings there, where you can shake hands and meet people. Be seen, you know?"

"If you say so."

"See you there at four o'clock."

That he would. Thomas would be there early. He'd need time to convince Josie that this was a good idea.

CHAPTER FIVE

Josie had moved from the main dining area to the back room when the rush hit that morning. She'd been reclining on the long sofa, her injured ankle propped on throw pillows, when Thomas had arrived—again. He'd asked if he could come to Cuppa Josie's for his campaign meetings, which would be held weekly, at least.

Not that she minded the business, especially at her slowest time, but did she really need Thomas's presence, his very unavoidable *self*, in her shop all the time? It was bad enough that he came every morning.

The man who'd spoken to her wasn't the rugged rescuer from Friday night. Though she'd seen the guy five days a week for months, now she knew the finely toned muscles that lay beneath his suit. Close enough to feel his chuckles in his chest, his breath on her skin.

Before Friday, Thomas had been like a pesky fly, asking her out twice a week, always with that charming smile and charming disposition. She'd had no problem turning him down. She'd figured him for a mid-level worker bee at HCI, the local clothing factory.

She'd grown up in a city in the South, where a person's name—especially an old, revered name like hers—meant something. Meant *everything* to some people. And then she'd moved to DC, where she'd made a name for herself. As her father's assistant, she'd walked the halls of Congress. Greeted heads of state. She'd even met the president. She'd been invited to the hippest parties and rubbed shoulders with people who wrote policies that affected lives. She'd been powerful.

Though she loved Coventry, she'd never imagined herself dating any of the locals. They were...*ordinary.*

Which made her the worst kind of snob.

Yet, here was this man, handsome, gentle, and caring, and she couldn't swat him away like a pesky insect anymore.

Thomas, seated at the club chair by her feet, quirked that expressive eyebrow. "If it's a problem, I can come up with a different solution."

"No, no. Of course you're welcome here whenever you want." She swung her feet to the floor. "I'll just move back—"

"Don't go. There's nothing you can't hear, and you're probably getting a lot more work done back here than you would be out there."

She'd agreed, and ten minutes later, here she still sat, trying to ignore the meeting on the far side of the room.

But she couldn't help herself.

They had no idea what they were doing.

"I was looking online," his campaign manager said, "and it seems we need to get your platform out there. Your big issue is keeping outsiders from coming in and gobbling up swaths of land to build resorts, right? Most of Coventry's tourist establishments are owned by locals, and we want to keep it that way. So that's what all your literature should focus on."

Was he kidding? Thomas couldn't run for mayor on one issue.

She must've scoffed because both the men looked her way.

Whoops. She hadn't meant to make her thoughts known.

Thomas's lips tipped up at the corners, but the older balding guy with the bad comb-over and the keg-sized belly—Derrick, she thought—scowled. "You have something to add?"

"Nope. Sorry."

She returned her attention to her laptop, but she couldn't focus on her work. Instead, she opened her browser and researched local political issues.

Thomas's big issue was important, but what about education? According to the local paper, parents had been battling the school board about curricula they deemed inappropriate. And there were the problems of overcrowding at the elementary school and the need to update the town's ball fields. Little league may not be a huge issue for unmarried and childless businessmen, but for parents with school-age kids, having clean bathrooms and a safe place to play mattered a lot.

Then there was traffic. She was lucky she didn't have to drive to work, but she heard the complaints and saw the steady stream of cars outside her shop, and that was nothing compared to the traffic on Main Street. The town desperately needed to widen the roads and add a few stoplights.

There were myriad issues that needed to be addressed in the platform.

Thomas's opposition knew that. Greg Farley's platform made sense. If outsiders came in and built multi-level resorts on the lake and in the mountains, those resorts would pay boatloads in property taxes, which would fund the many needs facing the town. Farley's campaign platform addressed every issue she'd found and more.

Not only that, but based on the header image on his website, Farley had a wife, four adorable children, and a golden retriever with big floppy ears. Everything about the guy screamed *family man*.

She jotted her thoughts in her notebook. Farley was slick. Based on what he'd put together, he'd be hard to defeat.

But not impossible.

At the table, Derrick said, "We'll get your photo on the sidewalk outside your office, remind people who you are. Just your name recognition alone..."

She snickered, and the men looked at her.

Derrick started talking again, but Thomas held up his hand to silence him and addressed Josie. "I'd love to hear your thoughts."

"Trust me, you wouldn't."

He stood and settled on the arm of the chair by her feet. "You have more experience in politics than both of us combined, so trust me, I would."

Derrick's scowl disappeared. Now, he seemed more curious than anything as he turned fully in his chair to face her.

Before he could ask how that was, Thomas's eyes widened. He faced his friend. "Josie worked in politics, back in the day."

If "back in the day" meant three years before, then that was true.

Derrick stood beside Thomas and looked down at her. "Really? Where? Which—?"

"A few campaigns over the years. I have a little experience." *A little* being relative, that wasn't untrue.

"What do you think?" Thomas asked. "I'd love to know."

"If you depend on your name recognition and your single issue, you're not going to be defeated, you're going to be decimated."

"Tell us how you really feel," Derrick said.

She met the man's eyes but nodded toward Thomas. "He did ask."

Unlike his friend, Thomas didn't seem offended at all. "Go on."

She glanced at the notes she'd been taking. Not that she'd ever intended to share them, but she'd always been good at politics. Very good. Which was one of the reasons she'd quit.

Because success in politics often meant cutthroat tactics, and she didn't want to be that person anymore.

She ripped the page out of her notebook and handed it over.

Thomas read it quickly, gave her that one-eyebrow-hitched look, then handed it to Derrick.

All irritation slid from the man's expression as he perused it. "You're hired. Although, I should explain that it's not exactly a paid position."

"And I should explain that I'm not exactly interested."

"What? Why not?" Derrick yanked a chair from a nearby table and sat near her head, forcing her to shift to see him. "You obviously know what you're doing, and we could really use your help."

She turned and lowered her feet to the floor. "I don't do politics."

Derrick waved the paper. "Obviously, you do. Look, maybe if we get enough donations, we could—"

"It's not a matter of money."

"What is it a matter of, then?"

"I just said, I don't do politics."

Derrick turned to Thomas. "Would you say something?"

Thomas watched her for a long moment, eyes narrowed as if trying to read her mind. Then he turned to his friend. "Let's meet back here tomorrow. Three-thirty"—his attention shifted to Josie—"if that's okay with you."

"You're welcome, but I can't promise it'll always be this quiet." Though there were customers in the main dining room and the smaller front room, this back room was empty today. "You'll rarely have this much privacy."

"That's all right," Thomas said. "We have nothing to hide."

Definitely a political rookie.

He ushered his friend out the door, and she returned to her reclining position. The sooner her ankle healed, the sooner she could get back to her real job.

Maybe she'd opened Thomas's eyes to what he needed to do. She'd promised herself she'd never get involved in another political campaign, but she hadn't gotten involved, not really. Just offered a little friendly advice.

Josie had just returned her focus to her work when someone appeared at the door of the small dining area.

Thomas stepped back into the room and settled in the armchair he'd been perched on a few minutes before.

"I thought you'd left."

"Just needed to tell Derrick a few things. I wanted to talk to you privately, and I didn't want him browbeating you. You think I'm persistent, but I have nothing on him. He's the reason I got roped into this thing."

"Roped, really?" She allowed her disbelief loose on a laugh. "I've never met a candidate who didn't secretly relish the opportunity to run."

He sat back, the picture of casual. "You have now."

"Then why do it? Does Derrick have something on you?"

He laughed, then seemed to realize she was serious.

Unfortunately, she'd seen it all.

His smile faded. "No, he doesn't 'have something' on me. This isn't Washington."

"Almost every powerful politician started right where you

are today, though admittedly, most have more experienced people helping them."

"I have zero desire to run for any other office. Mayor is as high as I ever intend to go, and honestly, if anybody else would step in—"

"So why are you running? Because you were browbeaten into it?"

He leaned forward and propped his elbows on his knees. "I'm running because I don't want to see my hometown become nothing but a tourist trap. We appreciate tourism here, as you know, but we want to keep Coventry's money in Coventry. And we don't need a bunch of huge conglomerates in town. Thanks to the HCI factory, we have plenty of jobs and plenty of revenue."

"And yet, the traffic is terrible, the elementary school is bursting at the seams, the town parks and fields are in desperate need of an upgrade—"

"Thanks to the previous mayor's mismanagement, you're right." He sat back and gestured vaguely toward the town. "We don't need Marriotts and Hiltons littering the shore of Lake Ayasha to fix those problems."

"They would, though," she said. "With their property taxes, there'd be plenty of money."

"There's already plenty of money. The money just needs to be managed properly."

"So your problem is that you don't want your hometown to change."

"No." He stood and paced to the opposite wall, then turned and leaned against it. "This isn't about nostalgia, Josie. It's about protecting my neighbors. Again, I have nothing against big resort towns. But those big resorts bring in thousands of strangers. Some of those strangers are great, but not all."

Despite his defensive posture, his tone went from conversational to something else, something powerful and passionate. She suddenly understood why they'd asked him to run.

"Tourists bring their own set of problems. You have to have experienced that, right? People on vacation drink more than usual. They drive on our roads, usually narrower and windier roads than they're used to. They get into wrecks. They bring drugs to town."

"Uncross your arms," she said.

He squinted, fanning slight lines around his eyes. His lips opened slightly. He looked, despite the tiny wrinkles, like a confused little boy.

He was adorable. But adorable wouldn't win elections.

"You need to work on that look. You can be confused, but you don't want to show it."

His face blanked—no smile, no anything.

She sighed and sat up straighter. One thing at a time. "It's harder when you don't have a podium to know what to do with your hands. Gesture. Worst case scenario, leave them at your sides. But you should never, ever cross your arms. I don't care if you're about to freeze to death, those arms stay uncrossed."

A slow smile spread on his face as he did as he was told.

"Go on," she said. "Tell me more."

He chuckled. "I've lost my train of thought."

"You're going to need to deal with interruptions, Thomas. Try to find the train."

He took a deep breath. "We have tourists now, but they stay in the B-and-B and the campground or one of the few small hotels. Right now, we're attracting families. Big resorts will attract different sorts. And again, there's nothing wrong with those sorts. They're great, and if there's a town that's struggling to survive, I'd encourage them to court the Marriotts and the Hiltons of the world. But we're not struggling to survive. We have a huge corporation in our backyard. And don't think those things aren't related. These big companies want to come to Coventry because of HCI, because they know the local services will be taken care of by the local business, so they won't have to invest any of their profits to make it work. They'll keep their money for themselves. Trust me, unlike with HCI, those profits won't stay in Coventry or benefit our people."

He paused to take a breath.

"That was good. Impassioned. You've told me what you *don't* want for Coventry. Now tell me what you do."

His mouth opened, then snapped shut.

"You want to be known for what you're for, not what you're against. I mean, all your opponent has to say is, 'He's against change, but he has no plan.' And he'd be right."

Thomas sat again. "Is my candidacy doomed?"

"Do you want it to be?"

He didn't answer immediately, just rubbed the back of his neck.

She'd met her share of idealistic politicians like Thomas. They always went into office with grand plans. In her experience, they either didn't win a second election or they lost their conviction. But there were the rare exceptions. People who were so passionate that, rather than bending to others' ideas, they were able to convince people of their own.

Thomas might be that sort.

Finally, he spoke. "I've never run for any office in my life, not even student council. This wasn't my dream, and it still isn't. But if Farley wins, our shoreline will be rezoned, hotels will be built, and Coventry will forever change. I don't want that. Most of the people I talk to don't want that."

"If you want to win, you can. But you need a plan. You need to explain why, if there's plenty of money, these issues haven't been addressed. And you need to get past your name recognition."

Again, that narrow-eyed look of confusion—which could be construed as suspicion—crossed his face. "I thought name recognition was good."

"You know what happened to Jesus when he went home to preach in Nazareth? He had name recognition, and they tried to throw him off a cliff."

Thomas shook his head. "Let's hope it doesn't come to that."

"The locals see you as a nice guy who volunteers with search-and-rescue, who's some sort of businessman. But they don't—"

"Some sort of businessman? Do you really not know what I do?"

"How would I?"

He laughed, the deep sound filling the room and pinging a weird response inside her. She wasn't sure how she'd made him laugh, but she had the irrational desire to do it again.

"My office is right next door."

She imagined the buildings on either side. One was a house like hers with a nail salon on the first floor. She assumed he wasn't a manicurist.

The other was an insurance agency. She could picture the sign out front. *J.T. Windham & Associates.*

"You're an insurance salesman?" She could see that.

He leaned forward, held out his hand, and said, "Jeremy Thomas Windham, insurance agent."

She slid her palm against his, ignoring the way her body responded. "Pleasure, Jeremy."

He scowled and pulled back. "Thomas. My dad is Jeremy."

"So you own the place."

Not a mid-level worker bee, but an entrepreneur. That truth elevated him slightly in her mind. She really was a terrible snob.

"Being a business owner gives you a level of authority," she said, "but it doesn't qualify you to be mayor. Some of your responsibilities will be similar, but most will be quite different. And people see you as the friendly fellow who knows their name. That's great, but until they also see you as somebody who can deliver on his promises, they're not going to trust you with their town."

"What do I do?"

"We'll get to that. I'll give you pointers, but I'm not agreeing to work on your campaign."

"Okay." The man's face showed his every emotion. Based on the way he was fighting a smile, nodding solemnly, he obviously thought he'd hooked her, despite what she said.

Josephine Harrington wouldn't have been able to resist.

But Josie Smith could.

She ignored that irritating expression. "The most important question is about HCI. If you polled their officers, what would they say? Are they for the resorts or against them?"

"Against. I mean, I think, anyway."

"Were any of them among the people who asked you to run?"

His lips slipped into a frown. So...no.

She liked the way every thought showed on his face. Lethal for someone running for office, but she liked it.

Before he could speak, she said, "If they're against you, I don't see how you can win. The other side is going to be well-funded. I mean, assuming those big hotel chains want into Coventry."

"They do."

"Then you're going to need money and lots of it. Your first step is to reach out to HCI corporate and see if you can get a meeting with the CEO."

He smiled. "I'm pretty sure I can. We're friends."

"That's good. If you can secure his support—"

"*Her* support. Chelsea O'Donnell, formerly Chelsea Hamilton, owns the company. Her husband and I are buddies."

Right. Josie had heard of Chelsea Hamilton and the trouble her family's company had had a few years back. It'd made the national news, and she'd followed the story because of her family's connection to Coventry. Her mother's parents were from Boston and had owned a second home here, where they'd vacationed when she was a kid. Which was how she'd chosen it when she'd been looking for a place to rebuild her life.

She'd always loved Coventry, the small town, the friendly atmosphere. The idea of the charming little Lake Ayasha being surrounded by resorts didn't sit well.

"That's perfect," she said. "Call her. If you can't get financial backing from HCI, you might still have a fighting chance. But, if they're against you—"

"I'm sunk before I even start swimming."

"Unfortunately, yeah."

"I'll do it." He shoved the old, heavy coffee table away with his foot and slid his chair a little closer. "There's something else we need to talk about."

"Look, I made a decision a long time ago not to get involved in politics again. I'll be happy to give you advice now and then, but that's as far as it's going to go."

"Not about that. About your father."

She leaned away from him, pressing her back against the sofa cushion. "That's not your concern."

"I thought we decided to be friends."

"Well, yeah, but—"

"I concern myself with my friends' safety. I don't like when people I care about are in danger. And, frankly, I tend to get involved if they are. It's what I do."

"Thus, search-and-rescue."

"And the volunteer fire department. And I sometimes work

with the local EMT service when they're short-staffed. I should probably seek help"—his lips tipped up in an almost smile—"but at this point, I prefer to be helpful."

She liked his play on words. "It's really not necessary."

"Chelsea O'Donnell is a friend of mine, as is her husband, Dylan. He's a private investigator, and his specialty is finding lost people. He does a lot of work looking for runaways, who tend to leave very few clues behind. We're talking about kids with no credit cards, usually no jobs. They're hard to find, and he almost always finds them, so he knows what he's talking about."

She had an idea where this was going and didn't want to hear it. Because she wanted to believe she was safely hidden in Coventry. That her father's enemies couldn't touch her there. That her anonymity was secure.

But for all his talents, Thomas didn't read minds. "I asked him how hard you'd be to find—"

"You told him who I am?"

"I didn't give your name, just the generalities—a woman who changed her name to something common and moved away. He said a good investigator could find you in a matter of hours."

Hours?

She swallowed the fear that rose to her throat.

"As much as you want to believe you're safe here, Josie, you're not. You should take your father up on his offer of a bodyguard."

"I'm not going to do that."

"Jo—"

"I don't want anyone to know who I am."

"They wouldn't have to. You could have your father hire a woman, tell everyone she's your sister or your cousin or something."

"Who goes with me everywhere? Who carries a gun? No,

it'd be suspicious. I'm trying to fly under the radar here. And besides, they caught the guy who took that shot at my father. He wasn't working for anyone or connected to anything."

"Maybe," Thomas said.

"The authorities have checked him out. There's no conspiracy, no grand plan to take my father out if he doesn't do what he's told. And even if there were, Dad's the one in danger, not me."

"How can you be so sure?"

"Because that's not how it works. They'll do everything in their power to get him to vote for that bill, but they won't attack his family. I've been in politics a long time, and I can tell you those kinds of things never happen."

"Your boyfriend seems to think—"

"He's not my boyfriend."

And there Thomas's face went again, showing pleasure at her pronouncement. "Speaking of Beta-boy, does he have a chance?" Thomas asked. "He's obviously here because he wants to win you back."

Josie considered the question. Bentley had shown up a week earlier with exactly that goal—to win her back and return her to Washington. But he'd claimed that if he couldn't get the second, he'd take the first. She wasn't buying it. Bentley loved politics, thrived on the political intrigue of Washington. He'd never be happy in central New Hampshire.

He wasn't lying to her, at least she didn't think so. He was lying to himself.

Even if he could be happy there, he wasn't the man for her. Years before, they'd gone from working together to eating together to sleeping together as if it were a natural progression. He was older, more experienced, and powerful. She had no idea why he'd chosen her, though she'd been flattered. She was beginning to understand why she'd chosen him. They were both passionate about the same things. They fought on the same side. They were together all the time. And he was *there*. Though she'd lived in the city and had hundreds of so-called friends, she'd hardly had anybody she could confide in. With Shelly busy with a new boyfriend or jet-setting around the world, Josie had felt incredibly isolated.

Bentley had been convenient.

But shared beliefs and convenience did not a strong marriage make.

And they didn't even share the same beliefs anymore, not since she'd rededicated her life to the Lord.

So, the answer to Thomas's question was obvious, but he wasn't the person she needed to tell.

"You should tell him." It seemed Thomas *was* a bit of a mind reader. "Much as I dislike the guy, he's obviously devoted to you."

"I will. Soon."

"Which means you'll have one fewer person in town who knows who you are and how much danger you're in."

"I'm not in danger."

"I have a pretty good instinct for this kind of thing, and I'm afraid you are. So, if you refuse to get a bodyguard, do me a favor and keep your eyes open for threats. Don't go out at night without an escort. If you need someone to take you anywhere, don't hesitate to call me."

She started to speak, but he held up his hand. "Not as a date, as a protector. Okay?"

No, it wasn't okay, but she didn't see the point in arguing. "If I feel like I'm in danger, I'll call you."

He scowled, but he let it go and stood. "I'll see you tomorrow. You have my card if you need me."

He walked out of the small room, leaving her alone with her thoughts.

Was he right? Was she in danger?

Surely not.

Dad's enemies might go after him, but they wouldn't attack his children. Politics was an ugly business, but it wasn't *that* ugly.

CHAPTER SIX

Thomas finished at the gym after work, showered, and changed into khaki shorts and a polo. Maybe he should put the suit back on.

This felt weird.

He'd been friends with Dylan for a couple of years, but tonight as he walked toward Braden's house for their weekly get-together, his heart rate kicked up like he was a kid in the mail-room hoping for a promotion.

Before he reached the walkway, a car approached.

Dylan parked and climbed from his SUV. Good. Thomas could do this without an audience.

"How you doing?" His redheaded friend walked up the driveway and stuck out his hand, which Thomas shook.

"Looking forward to Carly's cooking."

"She's got a gift," Dylan said. "Her food's even better than The Patriot's."

Through the open window, James called, "Heard that."

Dylan yelled, "You should be in the kitchen trying to learn something."

Laughter carried into the warm June evening.

Dylan started toward the door, but Thomas said, "Can I talk to you a sec?"

He turned his head. "This about your call earlier? The elusive Ms. Smith?"

"No." He lowered his voice. He didn't want all his friends hearing this. "It's about the election."

"Oh." Dylan shifted to face him. "What about it?"

"I'm wondering if you and Chelsea, or the company, have chosen who to... Are you planning...?" He really should have thought about how to ask this before he got here.

"You want to know if you have our support."

"Yeah."

"We want what's best for Coventry. Though we would like to see more hotels in town, we aren't in favor of Farley's plan."

Thomas hadn't expected that answer. Until Josie had floated the possibility today, he'd thought his friends would naturally be on his side. "Why do you want to see more hotels?"

Dylan glanced at the door. The guys' voices and the hum of a basketball game carried through the windows. "The company entertains colleagues from time to time, and they'd do more of that, maybe even bring retail buyers to town for tours, but they're limited in what they can do because of the lack of rooms. The B-and-Bs don't exactly cater to business people. The hotels are small and, frankly, kind of dingy. HCI's not about to put people up at the campground. They own a couple of houses near the office, but they're small and limited. New hotels would really help."

Thomas nodded as he spoke. "I'm not against new hotels. I'm against huge resorts that'll bring more people than Coventry can handle. I'm against out-of-towners coming in and sucking out as much money as they can."

"I know what you mean. And neither Chelsea nor I want to vote for Farley. Just the fact that he worked so closely with a murderer looks bad, and the more we know about what Salcito was up to, the less we like the guy. Farley can't have been ignorant about Salcito's lining his pockets with taxpayer dollars. But not everybody in town knows all that. You'd be wise to tell people what your plan is. Your opponent is way ahead of you."

In Thomas's defense, he'd only decided a couple of weeks before to run. He hadn't even officially announced it, though word had gotten around.

Farley'd been running since the mayor was arrested in February, even if not officially. And as interim mayor, he had a leg up.

"HCI won't be supporting or funding Farley, then?"

"I don't speak for HCI," Dylan said. "You need to talk to my wife about that. I'm just telling you what the two of us think. But HCI is a big company with a strong board, and they might have a different take on this altogether."

The words settled like a rock in Thomas's gut, but he smiled. "I'll call her. Thanks for the insight."

CHAPTER SEVEN

J osie sat in the passenger seat of Bentley's BMW, which idled at the curb, and glanced at her coffee shop. She wished she were in there, alone, instead of out here with Bentley. "I'm sorry. I just don't think—"

"We had something great."

"Did we? Because that's not how I remember it."

He blinked in the darkness. Unlike on the main drag through town, High Street didn't have a lot of streetlights, so his face was illuminated only by the glow of the dashboard.

She should have refused to go to dinner with him. She'd tried to back out, but he'd been insistent, and she'd known this conversation would take time. Bentley wasn't one to give up easily.

They'd been discussing the fate of their relationship for an hour. He'd told her in countless ways how perfect they were together.

He'd told her how they believed the same things.

He'd told her how much he loved her.

But did he, really?

"Josephine—"

"It's Josie."

"No, it's not." He blew out a breath and took her hand. "It's not Josie. You're not this person, this owner of a dinky coffee shop. You're a brilliant political strategist. You've been given a gift, don't you see? You don't belong here with small-town people. Those people don't have any idea who you are."

"'*Those* people'?" She hated that she'd caught herself thinking something similar earlier in the day. She'd considered Thomas one of *those* people. As if she were somehow above the locals because of her family's name and power.

"You know what I mean."

"That doesn't mean you're right." She pulled her hand away. "Look, Bentley, you want me to be something I'm not."

"No, I don't. I want you to be who you are. Who you were born to be. And you'll never be that when you're stuck here north of nowhere. Come home, Josephine. Your father needs you, especially now."

Dad had never once asked her to return to her position as his assistant in DC. But did he need her? Had he not asked because he didn't want to pressure her?

"You know he'd never tell you that, but he does," Bentley said. "Nothing's been the same since you left. You were the moral compass of the staff, your father's voice when he wasn't there. Now, we're floundering, trying to figure out what he wants, which direction to go. We need you."

"My father was in politics long before I worked for him. He'll survive. And I'm sure the staff is happier without me."

"Not happier, and not nearly as effective."

"I can't do it, Bentley. I can't."

"Okay. Okay." He looked beyond her a moment. When he met her eyes again, she saw pleading in them. "I need you."

"You're doing just fine without me."

He let out a humorless chuckle. "You have no idea what

your leaving did to me. You have no idea... I love you. I imagined us together, forever. I've tried to move on. Believe me, I've tried. I've dated other women. But it never works. Nobody knows me like you do. And nobody knows you like I do."

She couldn't argue with that. Bentley had seen her at her best—and at her worst. And he'd loved her through it all. Maybe she'd been wrong to discard him along with the job. Even still, that didn't change the geography problem.

"I'm not moving back. This is my home now."

He stared at her for a long time. "I'll move here."

"No."

"Josephi—Josie, I want to be with you."

"You want to be with me in Washington, the way things were before. But I'm not the same person. I won't go back."

"I'll give it all up for you. I'll resign from your father's staff."

He would resign? Give up everything he'd ever dreamed of? For her?

Were his feelings really that deep?

She'd loved him. But their relationship had been so intricately connected to their work on her father's campaign and in her father's office. When she decided to leave politics behind, it had only made sense to leave Bentley behind as well.

Maybe that had been a mistake.

"There's still the issue of my beliefs." One of the biggest reasons she'd decided she couldn't make things work with him was his lack of faith. How could she marry a man who wasn't a Christian?

"I'll try," he said. "I don't understand your whole, you know, Jesus thing, but I'll go to church with you. I'll try to learn."

"Really?"

"Don't you see?" He took her hand again and pressed it against his chest. "I love you, Josie. I love you, and I want to be with you. Say we can be together again. Please, just...just try."

The earnestness in his face, the pleading, shocked her. Did he really care so deeply for her?

She hadn't known.

And she didn't know what to do about it.

"I'm not ready to get involved again."

He dropped her hand and faced forward.

"I'll think about it. In the meantime, you should go home."

His gaze snapped back to hers. "You're kidding, right? You really think I'm going to leave you up here by yourself with all that's going on?"

"My father needs you."

"Your father wants you to be safe, and he trusts me to make sure that happens."

"What?" She must have misunderstood. "What are you saying?"

"He asked me to stay. He wants—"

"I thought you came because you wanted us to get back together."

"I do, absolutely. I've wanted that for years. But after Friday, he wants me to stay and make sure you're safe."

She dropped her head against the headrest. After all of this, and Bentley still didn't plan to leave?

Not that she was trying to get rid of him, but...

Yeah. She was trying to get rid of him. She needed to think, and she needed to do so without his hovering all the time.

She needed distance to know her own heart. Did she love Bentley? Could she?

Should she?

Oh, Dad, what are you thinking?

"He's worried about you," Bentley said, as if he knew her thoughts.

"I'm fine." This conversation needed to end now. She wasn't about to go another ten rounds with Bentley about her safety or their relationship or anything else. She grabbed her purse from the floorboard, slid it over her head, and opened the car door.

Before she'd stood and gotten herself balanced on her good foot, Bentley'd come around and yanked her crutches from the backseat. He held them out to her. "I'll walk you up."

She was way too frustrated to rest. "I'm going to the café."

"You need to stay off that ankle."

Anger surged and sent her heart racing. She took a deep breath before she spoke. "I'm a grown woman, Bentley. I am perfectly capable of knowing what I need and what I don't." And her ankle didn't hurt, not that much. It was getting better every day.

Ignoring him as he walked beside her, she hobbled to the front door, thankful she'd installed the handicap ramp, then pulled her keys from her purse and let herself in.

Bentley started to follow, but she stopped a foot inside and craned her head back. She'd turn completely if not for the stupid crutches. "Thank you for dinner."

"I was hoping—"

"I don't want to talk about this anymore. I'll talk to my father about relieving you of your babysitting duty."

Hurt filled his expression. "That isn't what this is."

"I know." She sighed and crossed the dark dining room into the kitchen, where she flipped on a light.

He followed but stopped before entering her domain, standing in the space between the public area and the private. That was their problem, wasn't it? They'd mixed the two.

Maybe they should never have been more than friends.

But they had, and they'd fallen in love. When she'd broken off their engagement, her heart had crumbled. It'd taken years to get over him. Now he was back, and she didn't know what to do. "I never wanted to hurt you."

His head fell forward. A long moment passed. When he

met her eyes again, his expression was carefully blank, all his new wrinkles smoothed for the moment. "I'm not leaving until the senator calls me back to DC, but I'll keep a professional distance until you make up your mind."

"I'd appreciate that."

He took a step back. "I can wait until you're ready to go up."

"I can maneuver the staircase. I've done it twice today already."

His lips stretched into what might've looked like a smile to one who hadn't known him as well as she had. "Lock the door behind me."

He crossed the dining room and disappeared into the night.

As soon as the door jingled closed, she followed and locked it then returned to the kitchen to start on the muffins for the morning.

Baking relaxed her. Maybe after a batch or two, she'd be able to rest.

Thirty minutes later, she was about to slide two tins of banana-nut muffins into the industrial oven when a car alarm blared.

She moved into the small dining room that overlooked her driveway. Flashing lights reflected off the building next door. Though she couldn't see her car from that vantage point, it had to be the one causing the trouble.

What in the world?

After snatching her keys, she crutched her way out the front door, down the handicap ramp, and between her building and Thomas's insurance agency next door. The space was just wide enough for her car and a stockade fence, which separated her yard from his.

What would have set her car alarm off? Was it a short, or maybe a small animal? She clicked the button, but the alarm kept blaring. She'd been needing to replace the battery on her key fob for weeks. She hobbled closer to the car and clicked the button again. When she was within a couple of feet, the alarm cut off.

The blessed silence helped her blood pressure, which had spiked at the sound. All was well in the quiet night.

She turned to hobble back to the door.

But a man stood on the driveway between her and the handicap ramp.

She gasped and froze, nearly losing her balance on the crutches.

He said nothing, just stared at her.

She braced herself. "Who are you?"

He took a step toward her.

Another person came into view on the street. She couldn't make out much in the darkness, but it looked like a man. She called, "Hey!" Hoping he'd help her. Hoping the second man's presence would scare away the first.

But the second person stalked slowly toward her.

The men were together.

As they got closer, she realized they both wore masks.

They'd set off her alarm. They'd planned this.

She crutched backward until she bumped into her car. How far could she run on her sprained ankle? And to where? The small yard behind her property was fenced in. Even if she could get to the gate before these guys, she'd lose precious seconds getting the gate open, getting inside, closing it again.

And there was no lock.

No, that wouldn't work. She'd be trapped either way. At least here, there was a chance someone would see her.

She had no weapon, just her keys. And the crutches. Maybe she could swing one, take one of the men down.

It might buy her a second, but could she get to the street, or back inside?

Maybe she was overreacting. Maybe this was nothing. Maybe she could talk her way out of it.

"What do you want?"

They didn't answer. Either she was dealing with two mutes, or she was under attack.

The men continued inching toward her. One lifted a phone. Light flashed.

Was he taking her photograph?

She sucked in a deep breath and let out a bloodcurdling scream.

The men halted.

And then one of them laughed.

CHAPTER EIGHT

When the car alarm went off, Thomas had rubbed his eyes. Though all he'd wanted to do tonight was hang out with his buddies and then get a good night's sleep, after his conversations with Josie and Dylan, he'd realized two things. First, he really did want to be mayor to protect his town from what Farley would do to it. And second, a lot of work needed to be done—and fast—if he was going to have a shot.

He'd bugged out of guys' night early and returned to the office, where there were fewer distractions than at his condo. He'd been studying the issues Josie'd jotted down and trying to come up with his own ideas, which had made him realize how poorly prepared for this he was. Rather than try to fudge and guess his way through, he'd compiled a list of people he needed to talk to. He needed to know more about just about everything that went on in Coventry. Fortunately, he had enough friends and contacts in town that he ought to be able to gather the information easily.

The car alarm had silenced, and he'd returned to his work when he heard the scream.

A woman's scream.

He stood so fast, his chair rolled back and crashed into the wall. He bolted out the front door.

Where was the threat? He peered up and down the street but saw nothing and nobody.

Then, remembering which direction the alarm had come from, he hurried toward Cuppa Josie's.

He peered down the driveway between their buildings.

In the darkness, he made out the shapes of two men facing the other way. Though he didn't see anybody beyond them, he had a bad feeling Josie was on the other side.

Thomas was strong, but he wasn't trained in combat, and for all he knew, they were armed.

What should I do?

He backed up and made his way between the houses on his side of the fence, dialing his cell as he did. When the operator picked up, he whispered, "Intruders, 116 High Street. Hurry." He shoved the phone into his jeans pocket, guessed where Josie would be standing, and scaled the stockade fence, wincing at the creaks in the quiet night.

He peeked over.

On the other side, Josie was leaning against her sedan, favoring her injured ankle. She held one crutch in two hands like a baseball bat. The other was lying on the pavement beside her.

Looked like she didn't plan to go down without a fight.

She wouldn't have to fight alone.

He launched himself over, dropped to the ground, and stepped in front of her, barely noticing her shocked gasp. He snatched the other crutch to use for a weapon.

"You guys lost?" Somehow, his voice sounded casual and unconcerned, despite the fear pounding in his chest. There was no way he could take on two men by himself. And if one of them had a gun, even a knife...

How could he protect Josie? Could he hold these guys off until the police arrived? Would they get there in time to save her, if Thomas were injured or killed?

Images of what could become of her flashed through his mind, mingling with other images of a different woman. Not this time. Not again.

He'd fight them. They might get to her, but they'd have to kill him to do it.

But as all those thoughts jumbled in his mind, the masked men backed up a step.

"Police are on their way," Thomas said.

Neither of the intruders said a word.

Creepy.

If they'd been trying to hurt her, surely they could have. A good minute had passed since she'd screamed.

No, if he were to guess, he'd say this was about intimidation.

They stared past him, at Josie, for a protracted moment that had his pulse pounding.

And then they turned and walked away. As soon as they hit the sidewalk, they broke into a sprint.

Thomas turned to find Josie wide-eyed with terror. She dropped the crutch just as he scooped her up. He jogged toward the exterior staircase.

"It's locked," she said. "Go to the café."

He ran that way, up the steps, and inside. After settling her on one of the sofas, he locked the door.

And then he stopped and breathed.

In and out.

She was safe.

They were all right.

As soon as his fear dissipated, fury took its place. He rounded on her in the dark dining room.

"Do you have a death wish?"

Her eyes were wide, her lower lip trembling.

"Seriously? It's ten-thirty at night. Pitch black. And you can't even run! Are you out of your mind?"

"I don't... I just thought... My car alarm..."

He let out a frustrated grunt and turned away.

He had to calm down.

He was scaring her, and considering how terrified she must have been before, that wasn't helping anything.

He turned back to find her watching him with those wide eyes.

He flipped on the overhead lights, brightening the space. The chairs had been turned over on the tables, presumably so somebody could mop. The room seemed smaller without the crowd, the sounds of people chatting, dishes clattering, machines beeping.

Josie huddled on the sofa, looking terrified.

"I'm sorry," he said.

"I d-d-didn't think." Her teeth chattered. She was trembling, her skin pale, her lips taking on a bluish tint.

He looked around the silent space. He'd been here enough to know...

He stepped into the back room, snatched two throw blankets from the basket she kept by the fireplace, and returned to her side. He lifted her injured foot onto the sofa, put a couple of pillows beneath it, and then tucked the blankets around her. He didn't have to do an examination to know she was in shock.

"It's okay," he said. "We're safe. Just don't ever..."

He didn't need to explain the obvious. She knew now, though that could have been a very expensive lesson. He took her cold hands between his and rubbed. "You're safe now. It's okay. Did you get hurt? Your ankle? Anything else?"

Her head shook so quickly that he wondered if she was answering him or trying to jar herself out of her fear.

He understood that. Even though the thugs had run and the danger had passed, adrenaline pumped in his veins.

What would have happened if he hadn't been next door?

A few minutes later, a siren's wail carried through the walls. Just when its volume reached an unbearable level, it cut off.

Thomas unlocked the front door as Zack Tyler walked toward him. Thomas knew most of the guys on the police force from his work with SAR, the fire department, and the EMTs. Not to mention that he'd gone to school with a few, including Zack.

They had not been friends.

The uniformed cop paused a half-second at seeing Thomas there.

"Where's your partner tonight?" Thomas asked.

"Stomach flu. What happened?"

"Come on. I'll let Josie fill you in."

Zack stepped past Thomas into the café and approached Josie on the couch. She made a move to sit up, but Zack waved her to a stop. "You're fine like that, ma'am. Officer Tyler."

"Josie Smith."

"Can you tell me what happened here?"

Josie explained about her car alarm going off and how she'd hobbled outside to silence it. How she'd turned to find two men in her driveway. How they'd been walking toward her slowly.

Thomas could picture the scene, could hear terror she was trying to mask in her voice as she described it.

"And then," she said, "one of them took photos of me."

"What?" Thomas pulled one of the chairs down from a table and sat. "I didn't see that."

Her gaze shifted to him. "I think they heard you coming.

The one with the phone shoved it in his pocket a second before you hopped over the fence."

Zack asked, "Why would they take your picture?"

She shrugged, though the answer seemed obvious to Thomas.

He gave her a look intended to convey *tell him who you are or I will.*

Josie pretended not to see it.

Before either of them answered Zack's question, Bentley burst into the room, out of breath. He scanned the space until his gaze landed on Josie. He pressed his hand to his chest. "Thank God. Thank God you're all right."

Zack and Thomas had both stood when he walked in. Zack said, "Who are you?"

Bentley regarded Josie a long moment, probably checking for injuries, before he turned to the cop and held out his hand. "Bentley Kent."

The cop shook it. "What are you—?"

"How did you know?" Josie's tone radiated irritation. "Were you watching me?"

"No, no." He started to cross the room, but Zack stopped him with a hand on his chest.

Josie said, "It's okay. He's a friend."

Zack didn't seem inclined to move out of the way until Bentley lifted his cell phone and angled it for the cop to see.

"Where did you get those?" Zack said.

"They were emailed to her father. He sent them to me and asked me to check on her."

"What?" Josie shoved the blankets off and lowered her feet to the floor. Her lips were no longer blue. "Why you?"

"You weren't answering your phone," Bentley said.

She tapped her pockets. "It's in the kitchen. I want to see what he sent."

Thomas grabbed the blankets and tossed them on a table so she wouldn't get tangled.

When she went to stand, he offered his hand and helped her to her feet. Everybody else was standing. He understood the need to feel on equal footing.

Zack stepped out of the way, and Bentley handed her his phone.

Thomas peeked over her shoulder and saw the images as she scrolled through them.

Josie, leaning against her car, crutches beneath her armpits.

A few snaps of her dropping one, lifting the other.

One of her holding it like a weapon.

There were more as the photographer closed the distance between them.

In each, Josie's eyes were wide. She looked terrified. But also determined.

The images had been zoomed, so it looked as if the assailants stood nearer than they really had. Eventually, if Thomas hadn't hopped over the fence, they would have gotten that close.

He should have attacked them from behind. He should have made an effort to get a look at their faces. He'd been focused on protecting Josie, but now he knew they'd never meant to hurt her, only to scare her—and her father.

Josie tipped back, bumping into him. He gripped her waist to keep her from falling. "Let's sit back down, okay?" He helped her settle onto the sofa, catching a glimpse of the worry in her eyes before he turned to Zack and Bentley. "Let's all sit."

Zack pulled an armchair close and did, but Bentley seemed too keyed up. He marched around the grouping of chairs until he loomed over her. "What were you thinking, going outside by yourself?"

"I know." Her voice was timid. "It was—"

"You could have been killed."

"I under—"

"Do you have any idea what that would have done to your family? To me?"

Thomas was about to shut the jerk up, but Josie beat him to it.

"I understand what could have happened." Fire blazed in her eyes, the timidity gone. "I don't need you to spell it out for me."

Thomas looked away so nobody would see his smile, but he must've failed because Bentley changed tack, pointing at Thomas. "And what's this yahoo doing here?"

Thomas squelched the urge to snap that finger off at the joint.

"What, did you double-book yourself?" Bentley asked Josie. "Two dates in the same night? Let me guess—the second I dropped you off, he showed up."

Thomas stood and stepped nearer. "You'd better shut your mouth before somebody shuts it for you."

Bentley glared. "Is that a threat?"

Zack pushed himself between them. "Both of you, sit down or take it outside." He looked from one to the other. "And if you choose the latter, you'll find yourselves in front of a judge tomorrow." He focused on Thomas. "I don't care who you are."

Thomas took a step back, then resumed his seat, kicking out his legs as if he hadn't a care in the world, though it took effort to unclench his fists.

But it wasn't only Bentley he was angry at.

He was angry at himself. He'd been trying to protect Josie, but he'd failed. The guys had gotten her photo and escaped without a scratch.

Bentley collapsed onto the sofa beside Josie.

She focused on Zack, who prompted her with, "So they were taking your picture..."

"And then Thomas jumped over the fence and stepped in front of me. He scared them away."

Bentley's gaze snapped up. Thomas might've expected to see anger there, but the man surprised him. The jealousy from earlier had been replaced with what looked like gratitude, though the look faded fast.

The guy might be a jerk, but his feelings for Josie seemed genuine.

Zack shifted to Thomas. "Tell me what happened from your perspective."

He explained the events from when he first heard the car alarm to when the guys took off.

Zack turned back to Josie. "What did they look like?"

"They wore masks," she said. "And I barely saw more than silhouettes. The first guy was taller than the second, I'd say maybe six feet, six one?" She looked at Thomas for confirmation.

He nodded.

Zack said, "We'll get his description in a minute."

"The second guy, the one who took the pictures, was a few inches shorter. The taller one was thin, almost lanky. The shorter one, stocky, like he worked out."

"What were they wearing?"

"Their clothes looked black in the dark. Black pants, long-sleeved black shirts. Black ski masks."

"Did you see any hair? Eye color?"

She shook her head. "They were too far away, and it was too dark."

"And you're sure they were both men?"

"Both men. I'm sure of it."

Zack turned to Thomas. "Anything to add?"

He closed his eyes and allowed himself to return to the moment. From the front, Josie's description was spot-on.

From behind...

"The taller one was over six feet. He had long hair, light-colored. It was sticking out below his mask in the back. He was thin, but I wouldn't say lanky. He had broad shoulders and thick legs. The shorter one was probably five-ten. No hair sticking out. Definitely worked out."

"What about their voices?" Zack asked.

"I didn't hear them speak," Thomas said.

Josie said, "The taller one laughed, but they didn't say anything."

"No strange cars on the street?"

Josie shook her head. "I didn't notice."

"Me, either," Thomas said. "When they left, they ran. If they started an engine, I didn't hear it. But I was focused on getting Josie to safety."

Zack turned to Bentley. "You said that you and Ms. Smith were on a date tonight? Did you pick her up?" At Bentley's nod, he asked, "Notice anything unusual when you dropped her off?"

"No, nothing."

"Wait a minute." Thomas focused on Bentley. "You two were out tonight, in your car?"

"You have a problem with that?"

"Funny how Josie's car was here all evening, but nobody tried to break into it—or lure her out—until you'd dropped her off. How did the bad guys know she was home?"

Rage blazed behind the man's eyes, but Thomas didn't care. "What are you trying to say?"

"I'm not *trying* to say anything, Beta. I'm saying Josie was perfectly safe until you showed up in Coventry."

Bentley started to stand, but Josie grabbed his arm, her glare pointed at Thomas. "This isn't Bentley's fault."

"How did those two thugs know you were home?" He turned back to Bentley. "Somebody tipped them off."

Bentley said, "You'd better shut—"

"That's enough, both of you." Zack's cop voice brooked no argument, and Thomas clamped his lips shut. But that didn't temper his suspicion.

"Were the lights on?" Zack asked Josie.

"In the back," she said. "Not in here."

He nodded slowly. "It's possible they got lucky—saw your car and assumed you were here. Or they were watching the place."

The thought sent all new fears racing through Thomas's veins. He looked out the big picture window that faced the street. Was somebody out there, watching, even now?

Zack shifted to Bentley. "When you dropped her off, you didn't see anybody?"

"The block's pretty deserted." He turned to Josie. "It's not safe here. You know that now, right? I mean, most of these businesses are abandoned at night. Except maybe"—he tipped his chin toward Thomas—"everybody else lives in real houses." Then he turned to Thomas, and Thomas braced for a shot.

But Bentley's tone softened. "Not that I'm not glad you were here."

Maybe Thomas was wrong to suspect the guy. He seemed genuinely concerned for her safety. Either that or he was a superb actor. If Bentley could be magnanimous, Thomas could too. "I don't live here either. I was working late." He hated to agree with Bentley, but the guy wasn't wrong. He turned to Josie. "You're pretty secluded here at night."

"This is my home." Josie sat up straighter. "I'm not leaving."

Bentley said, "Then it's time for—"

"Not now." She turned back to Zack. "Do you need anything else?"

The police officer's gaze flicked among them and settled on Thomas. "What am I missing?"

"Not my story."

The officer turned to Josie. "The more we know, the better we can protect you. Obviously, somebody's trying to scare you and your father, right?"

She nodded but added nothing.

"Do you know why?"

"I do."

"Are you going to tell me?"

"I'm not because it's irrelevant. Suffice it to say, I wasn't hurt. I don't think anybody would hurt—"

"Oh, come on!" Bentley shot to his feet. "Are you kidding me? Even after this?" He held out his phone, showing the picture of her, wide-eyed and terrified.

"Nobody hurt me," she said.

He paced away, muttering obscenities under his breath.

Josie watched him as he darted among the café tables across the room.

Again, Thomas found himself in the unfortunate position of agreeing with the man. He kept his voice low, going for gentle. "You thought nobody knew where you were. Obviously, you were wrong."

She looked at him, swallowed. "They're just trying to intimidate my father, scare him into doing what they want."

"Who is your father?" Zack asked.

She shook her head.

"Josie," Thomas said, "you're not safe here at night by yourself. You either need to relocate to a safer location or hire a bodyguard."

Behind him, Bentley said, "There is no *safer* location." He stomped back toward their little group. "You need protection. I've already talked to your father, and he's sending someone—"

"You had no right."

"It wasn't my decision," Bentley said. "Your father made it for you. If you have a problem with it, take it up with him."

Her gaze flicked from one man to the next, but nobody was going to stand with her on this.

Zack said, "Ma'am, I wish I could tell you that the police will protect you, but chances are good that, if there's a next time, it'll go down like tonight did—us showing up after all the excitement is over. Maybe you'll still be standing, but"—he shrugged—"unfortunately, I've responded to a lot of calls that ended up much worse than this one. If you're in danger and your father's willing to pay for a bodyguard, I recommend you take him up on the offer until these guys are caught."

"You think they will be?"

"We'll do our best. In the meantime, I'll feel better, and I know your friends will, too, knowing you aren't alone. Take the protection."

Thomas prayed she'd do as everybody recommended because it wouldn't matter if tonight's thugs were caught. If the people behind what happened here were as powerful as Josie believed, they had money and lots of it. There would always be more thugs to hire.

"Fine," she said. "I'll take the bodyguard. I just need to come up with a good story."

Thomas blew out a sigh of relief.

But a bodyguard could only do so much.

Josie wouldn't be safe until the health care bill was voted on or the people pulling the strings were compelled to stop.

Which meant Thomas would be sticking close, whether she wanted him to or not.

CHAPTER NINE

After a short conversation with her parents the night before, in which she'd promised to keep a bodyguard with her until the vote, Josie had fallen into bed and slept surprisingly well, if not for enough hours.

She'd awakened before dawn, read her Bible, and was showered and dressed by five o'clock. Tired as she was, the pastries were not going to make themselves, and the day before, she'd told Kinsley she could manage the early-morning baking herself. Fortunately, in all the activity, she hadn't exacerbated the injury to her ankle. It was much improved.

After Officer Tyler had left, Thomas had retrieved Josie's crutches from the driveway, and then Bentley had helped her up the stairs.

And refused to leave.

As she crutched out of her bedroom, he sat up from his space on her couch, yawning. "Is everything all right?"

"Go back to sleep," she said. "I'm just going down to start for the day."

"You need help?"

"Nope."

He seemed to debate the issue, then burrowed back under the blankets she'd found for him. She was surprised he didn't insist on joining her, but it wasn't necessary. The bakery was locked up, and Kinsley would be there in an hour.

It was sweet, Bentley's desire to protect her. And after the night before, she no longer felt it was unnecessary.

She was stubborn, but she wasn't stupid. And she definitely didn't have a death wish.

Making her way down the narrow staircase, one hand on the railing and the other holding both crutches, she was pleased at the lack of pain in her ankle. This had been harder the day before. She took it slowly and made it to the bottom and into the kitchen without injury.

She flipped on the lights, propped the crutches against the wall, started the first pot of coffee, and set to work on her daily offerings, finding peace in the rhythm of baking.

She'd refrigerated last night's unbaked muffins, so she took them from the fridge and slid them into the oven. She was rolling out dough for turnovers when she caught something moving in her periphery. She spun toward the opening between the kitchen and the dining room, gasping and gripping a silicone scraper as if it were a knife.

Thomas stepped in, hair mussed. He wore soft flannel pajama pants and a T-shirt, no socks.

"What in the...?" she said. "Why are you...?" She'd had her share of strange and scary dreams the night before, and Thomas had appeared in more than one, though never as the *scary* part.

Was this another dream?

But no, she was definitely awake.

"Your boyfriend didn't tell you?"

"He's not my... Tell me what?"

"I slept on the sofa out there. I was worried, and... I'm sorry. I didn't mean to scare you."

"Bentley knew?"

"Of course. You'd already gone up, but he said he'd check with you."

"He had to go to the hotel and get a few things. I was in bed by the time he got settled, and he probably didn't want to bother me."

That explained why Bentley hadn't insisted on coming downstairs with her. That he'd trusted Thomas to protect her said a lot.

That Thomas was here, this man she'd barely known a week before... That said a lot too.

"I was just hoping for coffee." Thomas's lips quirked when he added, "Don't have my wallet though."

She smiled at that. "I owe you one—or maybe free coffee for life after last night." She hobbled toward the cups, but he beat her there.

"I'll get it. You go back to"—he waved toward her work station—"whatever that's going to be."

"Apple turnovers. I don't have any espresso made for your Americano."

"I think I'll survive." He filled a cup with coffee, sipped, and turned to face her.

She was still watching him.

His eyebrow quirked, and she shook her head. "Sorry. I'm so tired, and having you here is a little..."

"I can go back out there."

"No, I didn't mean..." She turned back to her work. "The muffins will be done in a couple more minutes. They're really good fresh out of the oven. Unless you need to go. You probably have stuff to do."

"I'm not leaving you alone. When someone else gets here, I'll head out."

She understood Bentley's protectiveness. They'd known

each other for years, and he worked for her father. Dad expected Bentley to keep her safe.

But Thomas had no reason to stay except an overactive protective instinct. Had he always been like that, or had something happened in his past, something that made him protective?

She wanted to ask, but she wasn't the deep-probing-questions type. Because asking them invited them to be asked in return, and the last thing she wanted was to share her own secrets.

He was quiet. Though she longed to peek at him, she kept her gaze focused on the dough as she rolled it out.

She was starting to think he'd slipped back into the dining room when he spoke again.

"Are you always at work this early?"

"Pastries don't actually bake themselves."

"So what was it about opening this place? Are you a coffee aficionado? Or were you in it for the baked goods?"

She glanced at him. "What do you think?" Though she didn't look again, she could feel his gaze on her.

After a moment, he said, "Based on how you pour yourself into what you're doing, and that you were baking muffins last night, I'm guessing this was about the baking."

"Baking relaxes me. I've taken a number of classes over the years, just for fun. So when I decided to quit my job, baking seemed like a good alternative."

"Quite a change from politics."

She chuckled. "I went from a job that left me so stressed that I could barely sleep to one that relaxes me. I went from a position where I could rarely make anybody happy to one where, if I do it right, I can make just about anybody smile. Before I had to deal with conflict on a daily basis. Now, conflict is rare and can usually be solved with free muffins. Why would I ever go back?"

Her timer dinged, and she glanced up in time to catch his expression. He was looking at her as if she were a puzzle that needed to be solved.

She started for the oven, but Thomas beat her to it. "Let me. I'm glad your ankle is better, but don't overdo."

She handed him the oven mitts. "Set them there." She pointed to the workstation closer to the front.

He did, then grabbed the two tins of blueberry. "These go in, yes?"

"Thanks." After he closed the oven door, she said, "Feel free. Banana-nut. I can plate it if you—"

"I got it, if you don't mind." He helped himself to a plate and fork and worked one of the muffins from the tin. He took the first bite and smiled. "You're right. Delicious."

She set her timer. "Glad you like."

"How are you so skinny? You can't weigh a hundred pounds."

He'd now carried her not once but twice. He was as familiar with her weight—though obviously guessing low on the number —as she was with the width of his chest and the strength of his arms.

She wasn't about to correct his assumption, just laughed and returned to the dough.

He was quiet, and she was too as she worked. The next time she glanced his way, she saw that strange, curious look on his face.

"What?"

"Just... I know what you're saying about this job. It's probably much less stressful than what you did before. But I'm guessing you were pretty good at politics."

"I'm good at this too."

"Okay."

"You disagree?"

He made a show of taking another bite of muffin and swallowing. "I do not disagree. You're a fabulous baker. And barista. And probably business owner."

She felt a *but* coming.

"Not that you have to explain yourself to me," he said, "but if you're that good at politics... I just think we need people like you, people with strong values, in Washington. I mean, if all the good people open coffee shops, then who'll be left to run the cities and states, the country?"

"That's the problem, though," she said. "Once people get into positions of power, most of them lose their values."

"I don't believe—"

"That's because you don't know." She folded the dough and rolled it again. "You're running for office because you want to do something good. You want to protect your town from outside forces you think will harm the people here. You have high ideals. But once you get into office, you're going to find it's really hard to hang onto those ideals and keep your job. So what do you do? Do you willingly give your office to the next guy, a guy you don't trust as well as you trust yourself? Or do you compromise to keep power? If the first, then you're out of politics. Maybe you made a difference, maybe you didn't, but you're done. You go on with your life and trust the town or the state or the country to someone else. But if you compromise... That's when it starts to get interesting."

She cut the dough into rounds.

"Because that first compromise turns into a second, and a third, and after a while, you no longer remember the values that had you running in the first place. And the people around you... Oh, they're even worse because they don't have to answer to anybody. They're pulling strings and seeing what unravels."

She plopped a round of dough into her turnover mold and spooned apple filling onto it, the repetitive task barely drawing her attention.

"Your staff, your cronies...they don't have to face voters. They don't have to defend themselves. And their actions...their actions are hidden, not just from voters but from you. Nobody tells you what's going on. That way, you'll have plausible deniability. And maybe you won't even know what's been done in order to get you reelected or to get your programs passed."

Josie's father didn't know all the things his staff had done to keep him in office. All the things *she'd* done.

If he knew...

She hated to consider what he'd think of her.

"You'll be on one of those Sunday shows," she said, "smiling at the hosts, telling people what you believe, and voters will buy it because, maybe in your case, it'll be true. Meanwhile, behind the curtain... You'd be shocked to learn what's going on behind the curtain. If you knew, you'd realize that you'd compromised your values, whether you meant to or not."

She plopped a turnover onto her baking sheet beside the rest. "Here at the shop, somebody wants to know what goes into the dough, I'll tell them. It's simple. Flour, sugar, baking powder, baking soda, salt, butter. Loads of butter, which might not be good for you, but it's not going to get anybody killed."

She pinched the edges of her turnover and added the next round to the mold.

Her heart was pounding as if she'd just run a race.

What was she doing?

What was she *saying*?

Thomas was leaning against the counter, watching her with wide eyes.

"Anyway, I'm just saying..." She swallowed hard.

It had to be fatigue that had released the torrent of words.

Fatigue and fear, knowing her old life was catching up with her. Maybe what had happened the night before had nothing to do with what she'd done back then. Still, evil begat evil. Hate begat hate. Lies begat lies.

It was time for a reckoning.

CHAPTER TEN

Based on the horror on Josie's face when she looked at Thomas, he guessed she'd forgotten who she was talking to.

He smiled, though probably too late to mask the worries her words had unleashed.

"Sorry," she said. "Sorry. I didn't mean..."

"You don't owe me an apology. You obviously know a lot more about this than I do."

"But that doesn't mean..." She plopped another turnover into the weird metal tool and crimped the edges. "Not every politician compromises his ideals. My father hasn't. I mean, he's had to make compromises over the years, of course. That's the business of being a senator. They have to give a little to get a little. But he hasn't compromised on what matters."

"Which is why all this is happening," he said. "If your father would vote for the bill—"

"Exactly." Her lips pinched closed, and her brown eyes filled with torment.

"What happened, Josie?"

When she met his eyes, her lips were no longer pinched but slightly open, her eyes bright with fear. "What do you mean?"

"You were obviously speaking from experience."

She went back to her task. "I've seen it all."

A sufficiently vague answer.

But he didn't call her on it. She had enough on her plate without feeling like she had to explain herself—or defend herself—to him.

"You think if I become mayor, I'll lose my values?"

Her shoulders lifted and dropped. "I don't know you that well."

"But you wouldn't be surprised."

"Mayor of Coventry isn't exactly a position of great power."

"Meaning?"

"Meaning I don't know. I've only ever been involved with national politics, so I don't know what happens in small-town America. Once people get to the national stage, things are different. They're different. Or maybe..." She shook her head. "I don't know. It's possible I'm jaded."

He chuckled. "Wow, you think?"

A smile played at the corner of her lips. "Maybe more than jaded."

"Maybe enough jade to make a nice necklace," he said, "and matching earrings."

That made her laugh. Goal accomplished.

Though he wasn't feeling amused. "I don't want to compromise who I am or what I believe."

"Then don't."

Her words had him doubting himself. "How do you recommend I stop that from happening?"

"Know the people in your inner circle, and be sure you can trust them. Be sure they're looking out for your best interests, but also that they're not the win-at-any-cost type. Because there are some costs you don't want to pay."

"If you were in my inner circle—"

"No."

"Come on. You could help me...and Derrick and anybody else who volunteers. Not just to do all the...the things, but to stick to our values."

She brushed the turnovers with melted butter.

The timer dinged. He started that direction, but she got there first, limping slightly. She carried muffin tins to the table near him. Then she slid the turnovers in.

She was very efficient at this baking thing.

She hobbled back to her counter. "How do you know I can be trusted?"

"Are you kidding? Did you hear your little lecture? You obviously care about this stuff."

"You've already failed your first lesson."

He let out a chuckle that even he didn't believe.

"Anybody can talk a good game, Thomas." There was no amusement in her expression. "It's not about what a person *says*. It's about what they *do*. It's about who they are when nobody's looking."

"I trust you to say and do the right thing. I trust you to be the same person whether somebody's looking or not."

"Why?"

"Because...because you're trustworthy."

"Based on what?"

He set his plate on the counter behind him. "Based on..." But there was no good answer to that. He hadn't seen her in action. He heard her impassioned words, and she had no reason to lie to him. But words were all he had. "Okay, I see your point. But how am I supposed to ever know anybody that well?"

"That's the problem. How can you?"

"Are you saying I can't?" Irritation sharpened his words. "Is this a riddle I'm supposed to solve? Another test?"

"Unfortunately, no." She swiped her workstation and grabbed a clean bowl and a measuring cup. Then she stopped what she was doing and met his gaze. "Truth is, Thomas, I don't have an answer for you. I don't know how you're supposed to separate the power-hungry from the humble. The people who'll say anything from the people with integrity. If I knew that, maybe I'd help with your campaign. Heck, if I knew that, maybe I'd go back to Washington."

And then she mumbled something under her breath, something he didn't quite make out. All he caught were the words, "As if I weren't one."

One *what?*

But he didn't ask. Josie's guard was back in place. No more insights for now.

Not into politics. Not into her.

He cared more about the second than the first.

"I hate to mention it," he said, "but I've now rescued you twice."

Suspicion lurked in her squinting eyes. "I thank you for that."

"Some might say you owe me." He tempered the words with a smile so she'd know he was kidding.

"You're better at playing politics than I'd guessed."

"Come on. I could really use your help. And it would give me a good excuse to hang around more, which I'm going to be doing anyway, until your father casts his vote."

"I don't need your protection."

He let his facial expression show his amusement at her statement, which was ridiculous, all things considered.

"I don't need it *anymore*," she said. "Dad hired me a body-guard. She'll be here later today."

Though Thomas would have preferred a big, burly man, a woman could do the job.

"Can I at least ask you questions now and then?" Thomas was probably pressing his luck, but he'd press until she shut him down for good.

She seemed to mull that over as she watched the water in her bowl foam.

Oh, yeast. She was making bread.

He wasn't a complete novice when it came to baking. He'd watched his mother make her share of muffins and bread over the years.

"I guess," she said. "I do owe you."

He laughed. "You don't owe me anything, Josie. We're friends now. Friends help each other. And I could really use your help."

She measured a cup of flour, then dumped it into the yeast. "I'm glad we're friends." Her expression turned almost shy. "In all the years I've been in Coventry, I haven't made any of those."

He would take friendship with Josie. For now. But eventually, he hoped for more.

Not just her political skills, either.

CHAPTER ELEVEN

Josie had her foot elevated on the sofa in the back room of the café after lunch that afternoon. Her ankle had held up well while she'd baked that morning, but it was aching now. She hoped she hadn't overdone it.

The bodyguard had arrived during the lunch rush. Josie wasn't sure what she'd been expecting, but the six-foot-tall blonde with the knockout body wasn't it.

The woman could have been a model, except she wasn't stick-skinny like so many of those airbrushed women on magazine covers. No, if Lake—her last name, Josie thought, but the bodyguard hadn't shared her first—ever found herself on the cover of a magazine, it would be one of those fitness glossies. Josie could imagine her wearing a shiny workout outfit, her long hair in a ponytail. She'd be sporting boxing gloves and a huge smile.

Assuming the woman smiled.

Lake probably wouldn't appreciate the image if Josie shared it. Which she wouldn't. Lake didn't seem the chatty type. She stood with her back to the wall, her gaze darting from the door to the main dining room to the door to the restrooms to the windows outside.

"Could you please sit?" Josie asked.

"No, ma'am."

The *ma'am* sounded foreign in that thick Boston accent.

At least the back room was empty for the moment. The lunch crowd had gone, and it would be hours before the dinner crowd would file in. She'd started Cuppa Josie's as a coffee and pastry shop but had expanded over time. She'd begun by offering a few lunch specials. Now she served a full deli menu through the dinner hour every day.

"I was sort of hoping you could relax a little so people would assume you were a friend," Josie said. "But that's going to be hard if you insist on standing the whole time you're here. And if you refuse to engage in conversation."

Lake spared her a glance, though it exhibited about as much emotion as a gravel driveway. "I was under the impression that your life was in danger, in which case, I need to remain standing and keep vigilant. If you're looking for a friend, there are more effective ways to find one."

"That's not what I..." Was the woman really so clueless? Her father had assured her that Lake came highly recommended, that she had the experience and expertise needed to keep Josie safe. If Josie complained, he'd just send somebody else. At least Lake was a woman. The last thing Josie needed was another man telling her what to do. Between Dad, Bentley, and Thomas, she had quite enough of those.

She'd texted her best friend before she'd gone to bed the night before to catch her up on everything going on. Shelly'd responded in her usual high-drama way. She'd even tried to call, but Josie'd brushed her off, saying she was going to sleep and she'd call her today.

She needed to do that. Shelly would probably worry herself

sick until they spoke in person. Though Josie loved Shelly—they'd been friends since preschool—conversations with her were rarely relaxing.

To Lake, she said, "I just don't want the world to know I have a bodyguard."

"Yes, you do," Lake said. "If they know I'm here, they'll be less likely to come after you."

"If I moved a chair to that wall so you could sit—"

"I'd move it back," Lake said.

Well, this was going to be fun.

"Let's go to my apartment." Josie wasn't getting any work done anyway. The few people who'd stepped in looking for a table had taken one look at Lake and stepped back out. Attractive as she was, Lake wasn't doing her business any good.

She'd left her crutches in the kitchen, so she limped to the inside staircase and made her way up. She settled on the couch in her apartment while Lake checked out the space to make sure the bogeyman hadn't gotten in while they'd been downstairs. When she was finished, she positioned herself by the exterior door. Wise, considering Josie was the only person to use the interior one, and there were locked doors on both ends of the narrow stairwell.

Josie grabbed her laptop. She'd focus on her work and try to ignore the six-foot blonde standing against the wall.

She wanted to figure out who was coming after her and find out a way to stop them. There *had* to be a way.

Before she'd even begun the research, footsteps sounded on the outdoor stairs, which led into her apartment. When a knock sounded, Lake peeked out. "It's Mr. Kent."

At Josie's nod, she opened the door.

Bentley passed the bodyguard—they'd met earlier—and settled on the chair beside Josie, where he opened his laptop. "How's your ankle?"

"Better. Did you arrange the meeting?"

He glanced at his watch. "We have a conference call. I'm glad you're already up here." He navigated to the conferencing program. A few minutes later, the images of her father and Carlyle filled the screen, each in his own box.

Though he was only fifty-nine, Carlyle's hair and beard were completely silver. He had striking blue eyes in a rather ordinary face. Ordinary, but he comported himself as a powerful man, which somehow made him seem more handsome than he was.

Dad, on the other hand, was dashing. His hair was still brown, though it was graying at the temples. Funny how that only made him more attractive.

"I'm here with Josephine." Bentley sat beside her on the sofa so the camera would show them both.

Carlyle said, "Glad to put eyes on you, Josie." It wasn't hard for him to use her nickname. Josie'd known her father's chief of staff for as long as she could remember—since way back before she'd moved to DC and started going by her full name. He was the perfect behind-the-scenes kind of guy. His voice was more nasal than soothing, and she doubted he could garner votes himself if he chose to run for office. But he was one of the smartest men Josie'd ever met, which made him perfect for the role of chief of staff.

"How are you, darlin'?" Unlike Carlyle, Dad's voice could boom through rooms and demand attention. The more volume he put behind it, the more passionate he seemed. That same voice could sound calm or vehement, gentle or urgent, and in every situation, it was deep and trustworthy. At that moment, the concern in her father's tone wrapped around her like a hug. Even though he was on the far side of the screen, just seeing him made her feel comforted and loved.

"I'm okay, Dad. The bodyguard is here." Josie glanced at

Lake, who seemed to not be listening. "She's not going to blend in. Everybody's going to know I have security."

"Can't be helped, I'm afraid." Josie had worked hard to lose her Southern accent, but Dad had lost none of his over the years. "Your safety is more important than your anonymity."

Maybe to him. "I've built a life here. I'm trying—"

"Nobody needs to know you're related to the senator," Carlyle said. "Come up with a story people will believe."

"You want me to lie?"

"Not *lie*." The man's tone conveyed his every thought, and at that moment, Carlyle thought she was being ridiculously naïve. "Just misdirect."

So, *lie*. And what story could possibly explain Lake?

Bentley shook his head, telling her to let it go. "We need to figure out who was behind last night's attack."

"It wasn't an attack." They hadn't come near enough to even touch her, much less attack.

"Only because of Thomas Windham," Dad said. "Speaking of...Carlyle?"

"He's clean, no record, no—"

"Wait." Josie's voice was louder than strictly necessary. "You looked into Thomas? Why?"

Carlyle answered, no hint of apology in his voice. "Bentley thought it seemed awfully coincidental that he just happened along when you needed him."

She glared at the man in her living room. "He works next door."

"It was after ten. What was he doing there?"

"Working."

"Or so he said." Bentley gentled his voice to a condescending tone she hated. "I didn't start suspecting him until this morning. Last night I was so grateful he was there that I didn't think about what it might mean. But now—"

"You're crazy," she said. "Thomas didn't do anything wrong."

Carlyle said, "I agree, Josie. It wasn't a bad idea to check him out, but there's no reason to think he's working against us. In fact, he's made a number of contributions to pro-life causes over the years."

"How did you...? Why would you—?"

"I have a guy," Carlyle said.

She knew about Carlyle's *guys*. She'd worked with a few of them over the years. Carlyle was good at what he did—protecting her father and his interests. But he could be ruthless to get what he wanted.

"Better safe than sorry," Bentley said. "And you have to admit, Thomas has been hanging around an awful lot."

"We're friends."

Bentley studied her as if he were trying to see beyond her simple explanation to something else. But there was nothing for him to see. There was nothing between her and Thomas but friendship. She'd shut that other option down.

After their conversation that morning, after all the time she'd spent with him in the previous few days, a tiny part of her was sorry about that.

"I agree that we can trust him," Dad said. "I understand he's running for mayor?"

"He is," Josie said.

"Against the incumbent," Carlyle added. "He has a tough battle ahead of him."

"He's a longtime Coventry native," Dad added.

Why would Dad bother to learn so many details about her neighbor? This conversation had suspicion thrumming in her brain. What were they up to?

"Knows everybody," Dad continued, "and he's obviously got a soft spot for you, Josie."

"What are you getting at, sir?" Bentley asked.

"We need all the allies we can get up there," Dad said.

"I'm thankful Windham was here last night, but Josie has a bodyguard now." Bentley's tone was dismissive. "She doesn't need that guy."

Lake didn't react to their talking about her as if she weren't in the room.

"I'd sure feel better if I could come up there and see you," Dad said. "Then we could assess the situation and better see about your safety."

"I'm safe here, Dad." Her parents had never visited her. They'd wanted to, but she'd feared their arrival in town would broadcast Josie's identity. Now, with a bodyguard, with her life in danger because of her father's position, she wasn't sure she could keep it secret much longer.

Not that anybody in Coventry would care about the daughter of a Southern senator. It wasn't as if Dad were a celebrity, though he'd become more of a national figure since the recent election. Their party held only a functional majority in the Senate, and Dad had gone against them more than once, keeping laws from being passed or even coming to a vote because he withheld his support.

As the lone lawmaker in their party willing to stand up to a president trying to ram through a bunch of policies he thought would be bad for the country, Dad was recognizable, his name well known and repeated on news channels and in papers every day.

Which only made her anonymity more precarious. Not that she minded her father's prominence. She just didn't want to be pulled into the fray again.

Carlyle said, "I've got an update on Friday's shooter. Investigators are convinced he was acting alone."

"Considering what happened last night," Bentley asked, "how can that be?"

"They think the two incidents are unrelated."

"What do you think, Dad?"

"It didn't make sense to me, either," he said, "but the investigator convinced me that the fellow who took that shot at me Friday isn't connected to anyone in power at all. He's mentally unstable and has a mountain of medical debt and believes the health care bill will save him from having to pay it back."

"Which it wouldn't, right?" Josie asked.

"The bill's proponents are hinting that it would wipe out people's medical debts and keep them from mounting more," Dad said, "but there's actually no provision that would grant that or even encourage costs to go down.

"No, most of the money in the bill is pork. Fancier hospitals in wealthy communities, funding for a handful of pet projects in districts that'll get the incumbents reelected and line the pockets of their biggest donors." Dad continued as if he were speaking to reporters or constituents instead of his own family and staff. "It's a huge money grab camouflaging as a health care bill."

A knock sounded. Lake opened the door, spoke to someone, then closed it again. "Thomas Windham is here to see you."

Her father said, "Good. Good. Let him in."

"Dad—"

"—Senator," Bentley said, "we need—"

"I want to talk to the man who saved my daughter's life."

Neither Josie nor Bentley bothered arguing. She nodded to Lake, who swung the door open.

Thomas zeroed in on her and Bentley on the couch together. "I didn't mean to interrupt."

Josie's little one-bedroom apartment had never seemed so small. "We're on a conference call," she said, "and they want to talk to you."

Thomas's eyebrows hiked. "Uh, okay." He moved closer and stood behind the sofa to face the screen.

"Dad, this is Thomas Windham." To him she said, "Thomas, my father, Senator Davis Harrington."

Thomas focused on the screen. "Honored to meet you, sir."

"Honor's mine, young man. Have a seat there. We'd like to talk to you."

Josie scooted closer to Bentley, and Thomas sat on her other side.

Well, this was cozy.

"Carlyle Nichols," Carlyle said. "We wanted to talk—"

"Before we get to all that..." Dad said.

All that? What were they talking about?

Had they planned this?

"I wanted to personally thank you for protecting my daughter last night. Way I understand it, you put yourself between her and danger, unmindful of what might happen to you."

"It wasn't..." Thomas seemed to rethink what he'd planned to say. "I'm glad I was there."

"Well, I am too," Dad said. "I understand you weren't in the armed services, right? And you're not a police officer?"

Thomas glanced at her, confusion as clear on his face as his brown eyes. "No, sir."

Poor guy had no idea what he'd just walked into.

Josie guessed. "Thomas is on the volunteer search-and-rescue crew here in Coventry, and he's a volunteer fireman as well. And sometimes he helps out with the local EMTs, right?"

"Yeah." He drew out the word, confused, maybe suspicious.

"Wherever you learned it, son, you've got a real protective streak in you." Dad's voice held admiration, something she didn't hear often from her father. "I like that. Like it a lot."

"Okay." And then, almost as if it were a question, "Thank you."

Bentley blew out a loud, exasperated breath.

Dad either didn't hear it or ignored it. "Carlyle, why don't you tell Thomas what we were thinking."

"We had sort of a trade in mind," Carlyle said.

"Wait," Josie said. "What trade?"

Carlyle ignored her. "We understand you're running for mayor. I doubt you know this, but Josie's got a brilliant political mind."

"I had surmised that, yes," Thomas said.

"You're a protective sort," Carlyle said. "If it were up to the senator, he'd hire a whole team of bodyguards to protect her, but Josie won't hear of it. We had to practically arm wrestle her to get her to agree to the two she's got."

Two?

"We were thinking that Josie could help you with your campaign and you could stick close, help keep her safe. What do you think about that?"

Whoa. What?

"No," she said. "Absolutely not."

Thomas ran a hand through his hair and shook his head. "I'm sorry, but I won't be able to accept Josie's help on my campaign."

Dad said, "Listen, son—"

"—Look here," Carlyle said.

Bentley laughed. Under his breath, he muttered, "Idiot."

Josie just turned to the man beside her and stared. Hadn't Thomas asked her for her help that very morning? Maybe her little speech had gotten through to him. Maybe he didn't trust her.

The thought should have brought relief, not this prickly defensiveness.

"You don't understand what we're offering," Carlyle said.

"It doesn't have to be anything formal," Dad added.

The men in her life continued to talk, but she ignored them, trying to figure out this man beside her. What was going on in his head?

Thomas held up his hand, and everyone quieted. "Senator, I would love to agree to this. Heaven knows I could use Josie's help. She taught me more in a thirty-minute conversation yesterday than I would have learned in years of study. But I asked her for her help, and she refused."

Would he use that against her now? She hadn't taken him as the petty sort. Not that she wanted to work on his campaign, and not that she wanted him to help protect her. But that he'd refuse...

"Now, son..."

Thomas lifted that hand again, and her father nodded for him to continue.

"If I were to agree to this, I know Josie would do her very best to uphold her part of the bargain. And I need her help, but I refuse to force it."

"She doesn't mind," Carlyle said. "Do you, Josie?"

Thomas looked in her direction, his curiosity and frustration clear.

The man needed to learn to mask his feelings.

He wanted her help, and he realized he needed it. He was refusing because he respected her wishes.

She'd called him an alpha male. In her definition, that made him the kind of guy who'd go to any lengths to get what he wanted. The kind of guy who was powerful and knew it.

She was surrounded by alpha males. Her father, Carlyle, Bentley, all using their power and positions to get what they wanted. That they wanted to protect her was beside the point.

And Thomas, when offered exactly what he wanted on a

silver platter—and the opportunity to impress a powerful senator to boot—refused in deference to her.

She'd been wrong about him. Very wrong.

Rather than answer Carlyle's question, she said to Thomas, "This isn't your problem."

Thomas turned back to the screen. "As to protecting Josie, I'd already planned to do that. I don't need to be incentivized. And I don't expect anything in return."

Dad's eyes shifted into that studious look Josie knew meant he was confused and unsure but trying to hide it.

Carlyle said, "Well, I think you're a fool to turn her down, but if you're willing to keep your eyes out for our Josie, we'll take your help. You'll need to back off all your other volunteering duties for the time being."

"I think that's enough," Josie said. "Thomas doesn't owe me anything, and he certainly doesn't need to rearrange his life on my account." To him she said, "I'll be fine. I have Lake over there." She gestured to the Venus statue against the wall. "And Bentley's not going anywhere for a while."

Hurt crossed Thomas's expression, as clear as if he'd spoken his pain aloud. "I'd like to hang around, too, make sure you're all right. I even moved a few things over from my condo so you won't be alone on the street at night."

Bentley stood. "That hardly seems necessary. I'll be staying here."

"No, you won't." This was getting ridiculous. "I don't need any more babysitters." Josie gestured to Lake. "My new bestie and I will do just fine. Right, Lake?"

The blonde looked their way. "I never turn down help, ma'am. If it were up to me, there'd be a team of guards to protect you. I'd rather work with pros, but if this is what we've got..." She lifted her shoulders in a *you take what you can get* gesture.

"All right then," Carlyle said, "it's settled. Bentley, sit. Now, let's talk about what we know."

Josie sneaked a glance at Thomas, who settled in to listen as if this hadn't been the weirdest conversation he'd ever been a part of. As if he got yanked into meetings by US Senators about protecting virtual strangers on a daily basis.

He caught her looking and nodded, no smile.

She'd hurt his feelings, this man who'd already done so much for her, who was evidently willing to do so much more. She'd make it up to him, and she knew precisely how to do it.

CHAPTER TWELVE

Thomas had received a strange call from Senator Harrington's office, asking him to go to Josie's apartment. He'd questioned the woman on the phone, but she hadn't known anything else about it.

He'd figured the senator wanted to thank him for protecting Josie the night before. He'd never guessed he'd be asked to keep her safe in exchange for her help on his campaign.

But how could he put her in that position? It had been clear by her reaction that she'd had no idea what her father and Mr. Nichols planned. Bentley hadn't known either.

Josie shifted, moving her injured ankle to rest it on the coffee table. Thanks to his short-sleeved shirt and her pretty sleeveless blouse, when her arm brushed against his, he felt the warmth of her skin.

It was distracting enough that he tried to inch away. Unfortunately, the sofa wasn't that big.

Mr. Nichols—Carlyle—moved the discussion to theories about who was behind the events the night before. "There's a whole bevy of folks who have a lot to gain if that bill gets passed."

"I talked with Nannette this morning," Senator Harrington said.

Josie leaned close to Thomas and whispered, "Nannette Parker, Senate—"

"—Majority Leader," he supplied just as quietly. "I figured."

Josie looked impressed, but Nannette wasn't the most common name in the world. And the woman had been in politics since the cooling of the earth's crust.

"What'd the crypt keeper have to say?" Bentley asked.

"Nothing you wouldn't expect," the senator said. "That she has no idea who was behind what happened last night and that the quickest way to resolution would be for me to vote yes on the bill."

"Do you believe her?" Bentley asked.

The senator shrugged. "Do I think she hired thugs to intimidate Josie? No. Do I think people working on her behalf might have done so? Maybe. They're running out of time."

Josie leaned close and whispered, "Everything changes come November. We'll probably lose a bunch of seats in the Senate, and then—"

"I understand." Thomas kept his voice low. He wasn't lost. He was intrigued.

"She's not above dirty politics," Carlyle was saying. "The woman's got more skeletons than Arlington Cemetery. If these attacks are coming from her—"

"I don't know," the senator said. "Nannette's a lot of things, but she has a family of her own. Attacking mine opens up hers, and I don't think she'd risk that. She's passionate about what she believes, but I don't think she'd go so far as to threaten my daughter to get my vote."

"That's pretty naïve," Carlyle said.

"Not naïve." Josie inserted herself into the conversation for the first time. "If it got out that Senator Parker was using devious tactics against members of her own party, she'd lose her position. Parker loves nothing more than being in command." Josie shook her head. "No, I don't see it. She'll do everything in her power to get you to vote her way, Dad. If you don't crumble under the pressure, she'll make sure you have a well-funded opponent in the primary."

"The party's planning that," the senator said. "I've burned my bridges with party leadership already this session. I can't see rebuilding them."

"But you've got two years before you have to worry about that," Josie said. "Meanwhile, she'll try to shame you, twist your arm, do whatever she can to get you to vote her way. But at the end of the day, it's more important to her to be the leader— majority or minority—than to get any one bill passed. Parker is all about Parker. She won't risk her job for this or any other bill."

Carlyle seemed to weigh her words, nodding slowly.

The senator beamed with pride. "I miss having you around, Josie-girl."

Thomas caught the soft expression she was giving her father. It morphed into a serious one before she spoke again. "What about party leadership?"

Carlyle fielded that. "The party's out for blood. Again, the question is, would they stoop this low? Would they risk the stain if it were to come out?"

There was a moment of contemplation, but nobody could answer the question definitively.

Finally, Josie said, "I'd be surprised if anyone in Washington is behind last night's threats. Let's talk about who else stands to gain if the bill is passed."

Carlyle, Bentley, and Josie threw out names and debated them. Heads of corporations, heads of political organizations, lobbyists. They debated who had the most to gain by the passage of the health care bill and who would be most likely to sink to sinister tactics.

The senator listened but offered little input.

Thomas, of course, had nothing to say. He should probably excuse himself. He had work to do, after all, a business to run. But his associates could keep the office running smoothly without him. He made less money because of all the help he hired, but it gave him the freedom to volunteer whenever help was needed.

Right now, Josie needed his help. And honestly, he was curious. He wanted to know who would come against her. He needed to be prepared. Not that the blonde standing guard at the door couldn't handle it. Maybe she could.

But if Josie's enemies were as well-funded as these people seemed to believe, a couple of bodyguards weren't going to cut it.

"And of course," Carlyle said, "There's Mitchell."

Josie stiffened. "Jude Mitchell?" She turned to Bentley. Neither said anything, but the room hummed with tension.

Carlyle didn't seem to pick up on it. "That's right. You two had dealings with him before."

There was a beat of silence before Bentley spoke. "Back during the election. He's ruthless."

"I remember Jude," the senator said. "His dad and mine used to play golf together, back in the day. We lived in the same part of town. He and I never hit it off, even though our families were friends. What makes him ruthless?"

Silence greeted the question. Thomas resisted the urge to lean forward to look at Bentley and Josie and their unspoken communication.

Bentley answered. "It's a long story. Suffice it to say, he's not above using underhanded tactics to get what he wants."

"He's a physician," the senator said, "if you can call it that."

Thomas asked, "What do you mean?"

Josie said, "I'm not sure he's practicing anymore, but when he was…" Her voice trailed. She blew out a long breath. "He's an abortionist."

Thomas cringed at the ugly word.

"Owns clinics all over the South and Midwest, and he's looking to expand." The senator's lips twisted in what could only be disgust.

Bentley leaned forward to speak to Thomas. "The health care bill would offer federal funding to build new abortion clinics in the poorest neighborhoods across the country."

Josie's explanations were slightly irritating. Bentley's had Thomas squelching the urge to punch his smug face.

"I know. I can read."

Josie raised an eyebrow at Thomas before turning back to the screen. "Mitchell hates me, and the feeling is mutual. What happened last night? I wouldn't put it past him."

"But how did he find you?" the senator asked.

Finally, Thomas had something to offer. "I asked a private investigator I know about that. He figured a good PI could find her in a matter of hours."

"So much for your anonymity," the senator said.

"Mitchell knowing where I am doesn't matter," Josie said. "It's the locals I don't want knowing my identity."

The senator's lips turned down at the corners, and his eyes softened. "I'm sorry my position has made your life so difficult."

"This isn't about you, Dad. It's about me. It's about who I was turning into."

"What does that mean," he asked. "What were you turning into? As far as I could tell, you were a brilliant strategist. I loved having you on my team."

"There are things you don't know."

"Like?"

She shook her head.

Her father regarded her for a long time while Carlyle and Bentley looked away.

They were probably thinking the same thing Thomas was, that they'd rather be anywhere else than witnessing this awkward exchange.

Carlyle broke into it with, "So, let's say it's Mitchell. What can we do?"

Before any of them could answer, a knock sounded at the door.

The bodyguard opened it and peeked out.

She closed it and turned to Josie. "Shelly Sanders to see you."

Josie jumped up. "Shelly's here? Let her in."

The bodyguard did, and a petite, slender woman with pale blond hair stepped into the room, eyeing Lake. "Who the—?"

She cut off her question before she finished it.

Josie scooted past Thomas, and the two women hugged. "How are you here?"

"Are you all right?" Shelly held Josie at arms' length and studied her. "After your call, I just had to see for myself that you're okay."

"I'm fine. I'll tell you everything, but"—Josie gestured to the screen—"we're in the middle of a meeting."

Thomas stood to greet the newcomer.

"I'm sorry. I didn't mean to interrupt." Shelly approached the sofa. Her gaze landed on Thomas and stayed there a long moment before it slid away. "Bentley."

"Shelly."

Not long-lost besties then.

Shelly continued to the back of the sofa and faced the screen. "Senator, Mr. Nichols. It's good to see you."

"I'm glad you're there, Shelly," Senator Harrington said. "Josie can use all the friends she can get right now."

Shelly hooked her arm in Josie's. "I plan to stick to her side like glue."

The look that crossed Josie's face was a combination of happiness and horror. Thomas barely resisted the urge to chuckle.

"If you don't mind heading back to my bedroom," Josie said.

But Carlyle spoke before Shelly. "I think we're about done here. Y'all contemplate what we were discussing and get back to us. You agree, Senator?"

"That's fine."

"Fair enough," Bentley said.

The senator added, "Take care, sweetheart," and ended the meeting.

Thomas turned his attention to the women standing beside the sofa.

"Thomas, this is my oldest and dearest friend, Shelly Sanders."

She stuck out her hand.

He shook it. It was small, like everything else about her, except, he guessed, her personality. She was cute and bubbly, like a thirty-year-old cheerleader, and wore a hot pink dress that showed more cleavage than one generally saw on a Tuesday afternoon in Coventry.

She gave him a wide smile. "It is *very* nice to meet you."

Beside her, Josie sighed. "And you know Bentley."

The woman went from bubbly cheerleader to angry she-bear. "What are you doing here?"

"Same as you, checking on Josie."

"She's fine. I'm here now."

They engaged in a staring contest as if there were prize money involved.

Josie hobbled away. "You two are going to have to come to a truce."

Shelly pulled a set of keys from her pocket and held them out to Bentley. "Why don't you go get my luggage?"

He glared but, after a glance at Josie, said, "With pleasure."

A blatant lie, but nobody called the man on it as he passed the bodyguard and pounded down the steps.

"Well," Thomas said, "much as I'd love to hang around—"

"I'm so sorry you got pulled into all of this," Josie said. "You have better things to do than worry about me."

"Not *better* things, but more pressing things, considering your friends are here."

Shelly looked between them. "I'm going to go use the bathroom. You two just..." She waved between them and giggled before flitting down the hall.

"She's...unique," Thomas said when she was gone.

Josie laughed. "Wait until you get to know her."

"I'm glad she's here. And, just to be clear, I'm not at all sorry that they asked me to help protect you. I'm honored."

"I didn't know they planned that."

"If you had, I'm guessing you'd have tried to stop them."

"Not that they would've listened to me."

"I picked up on that too." No wonder Josie was defensive around powerful men. She was surrounded by them, and they didn't exactly take her desires into consideration. "Anyway, I'm glad to help, but I better go. Derrick's probably waiting for me downstairs."

"About that—"

"Don't. It's fine."

"I want to," she said. "I'm going to work on your campaign."

"You don't owe me anything."

"And you don't owe me anything, yet you're helping me."

"Because we're friends."

"Which is why I'll be helping you too. Because we're friends. Okay?"

He'd be an idiot to refuse. "Whatever you can do, I'll take it."

She smiled, and the expression sent his stupid heart fluttering like he was the captain of the math club talking to the homecoming queen.

"You've been working on your platform?"

He nodded, wishing he'd done more. "I spent the morning talking to people about issues I don't fully grasp."

"Smart. You and Derrick put together your ideas today. You and I will go over them. Maybe this evening. Depends on what Shelly has in store for me."

"That sounds ominous."

"Trust me, when Shelly's involved, it always is."

From down the hall, Shelly yelled, "I can hear you!"

"I know. That's why I said it." Josie lowered her voice and leaned in. "Pray for me."

Thomas was still laughing as he stepped out the door, passing Bentley on the way. The bodyguard scowled at both of them. Apparently, they needed permission to enter and exit.

Josie wasn't looking, so he and Bentley didn't pretend to be cordial.

Josie might see Thomas as a friend, and he was trying very hard to see her the same way. But Bentley knew the truth, and Thomas wasn't about to deny it.

CHAPTER THIRTEEN

Josie turned her attention to her friend as she returned from the bathroom.

"What in the world are you doing here?"

Shelly plopped on the sofa. "After what happened last night, how could I not come? I'm worried about you."

Josie took the chair catty-corner to her, but before she could speak, Bentley came back in. He set a suitcase—not an overnighter—against the wall.

"Anything else, Your Majesty?" he asked.

"Be nice," Josie said.

Bentley pressed a smile on his face that looked about as authentic as Mr. Potato Head's. "Sorry, sweetheart."

She was not his sweetheart, and he knew it. He'd used the term of endearment to irritate Shelly.

"It occurred to me as I was hauling her highness's trunk up the stairs that you don't have a guest room. Is she staying here?"

"Uh..." Josie turned to include her friend in the conversation. "Actually, Shelly—"

"The couch'll work. That's where I slept last time."

Lake cleared her throat, and everybody turned to her. "I plan to stay on the couch. We have a room at a hotel—"

"We?" Josie asked.

"My partner and I. Our understanding from your father is that this enemy will wait until you're alone to attack, so you should be safe in public. At night, one of us will be here at all times." She nodded at Shelly. "Sorry for the inconvenience."

The woman was clearly not sorry, but who was going to argue with her?

Shelly heaved a dramatic sigh. "I can get a room. Do you think there are any available?"

"Probably not," Bentley said. "I had to pull strings for mine. The place is booked solid."

"She got one." Shelly nodded to Lake with another dramatic sigh. "I guess I'll just sleep in my rental car."

"You can stay with me," Josie said. "I have a queen-size bed. It'll be like our sleepovers when we were girls."

By the scowl on his face, Bentley didn't like that idea. "Lemme see what I can do. If I can make something work, I'll come back for that." He glared at the suitcase as if it were to blame for all his problems.

"Thanks, Bentley," Josie said, "for everything."

He closed the space between them and lowered his voice. "You'll be okay by yourself?"

"I'm not by myself. I have Lake, and now Shelly."

"Don't let her talk you into doing anything stupid. Do what Lake—"

"I can hear you," Shelly said.

The woman practically had sonar.

Josie scooted past him toward the door. "We'll be fine." She reached to open it, but Lake stepped in, shooed her away, and then inched it open. When she deemed it was safe, she opened it wider.

"Fine." Bentley leaned in and kissed Josie on the cheek.

She shouldn't have allowed the intimacy, but she didn't want to make a scene. "Let us know about that room."

He looked like he wanted to say something else, but he kept his lips clamped shut as he walked out.

The tension in the room lessened considerably when Lake closed the door.

Josie turned back to her friend. "I'm thrilled you're here." But praying a hotel room would be available. Shelly was a night owl, and Josie needed her sleep. If Shelly stayed with her, Josie'd have to fight to get into bed at a decent hour, which she needed to do in order to be in the kitchen downstairs before dawn every day.

Now that Bentley was gone, her friend's trademark smile was back. "I should have warned you I was coming. I wanted it to be a surprise."

"You accomplished that." Josie moved into the tiny kitchen and called through the open door, "Hungry? Thirsty?"

"Yes and yes." She slipped into the room and leaned against the doorjamb. "Are you limping?"

"I sprained my ankle last week. It's much better, though." In fact, she hadn't thought about it as she'd been moving around her apartment.

"Just a snack," Shelly said, "since it won't be long until dinner."

"I don't have a lot, but we could go to the café and grab a couple of cookies."

"That's all right. Crackers?"

Josie found the box and set it on the table in the living area, followed by flavored water for Shelly and iced tea for herself. Facing Lake, she said, "You need anything?"

The bodyguard shook her head.

Josie slipped into a chair, and Shelly followed suit. "So, seriously, what are you doing here?"

"Why does there have to be another reason? I wanted to make sure you're all right."

Josie let her expression show her skepticism, and Shelly sighed. "I needed a break from the job and Washington and...everything."

The real answer must be the elusive *everything*. "What's going on?"

She shrugged, breaking the club cracker into tiny pieces on a napkin. "I had an argument with my boss. Nothing huge, but we have different visions for one of our clients, and I might've gotten a little exuberant with my objections."

Shelly worked for a political consulting company. Where Josie was good at crafting messages, Shelly was brilliant at putting together the visuals. She managed photo shoots and logos and fliers and yard signs...anything to do with a candidate's public image. "You didn't get fired, did you?"

"Nothing like that. But he wanted me to take time away."

Josie'd known her friend long enough to know how to wheedle information out of her. It just took asking the right questions. Shelly was usually dying to share, even if she knew she shouldn't. It was one of the reasons that, though she'd longed for a job in politics like Josie's, she hadn't been cut out for it. Too many secrets she was terrible at keeping.

"And did something happen that caused you to disagree with your boss? Something with the job?"

"No, no. It was nothing like that."

She didn't miss playing twenty questions with her friend. "Something outside the office then? A disagreement with your family?"

"The family's fine."

"A boyfriend?"

Shelly's blue eyes brightened. Bingo. "He's so amazing, Jo."

"You haven't told me about this one."

"Oh, you'd *love* him. He's absolutely wonderful. Strong and handsome and powerful."

Powerful. That could mean a lot of things. Shelly'd dated her share of *powerful* men. Another word for them—abusive. She was incredibly attractive, but she'd always been drawn to the kinds of guys Josie wouldn't look at twice. Good-looking but also controlling and manipulative. Men who used her not just for her looks but for her trust fund.

Shelly was Josie's oldest friend, and for many years, they'd been as close as sisters. They'd both given their lives to Christ in middle school, and they'd both drifted away from their faith in college. But where Josie had rededicated her life to Him a few years back, Shelly had kept drifting. Now, though Josie still loved her friend, they didn't always see things the same way.

Shelly gushed about her new guy. "He's very successful. He has money of his own, so he doesn't need mine. In fact, he pursued me before he knew who my father was. He loves me for me."

"I can't wait to meet him."

Shelly pressed her hands to her chest. "You're going to love him, Jo. He's just *perfect*. And you know what else? He goes to church! Like, every single Sunday. I even went with him a couple of times."

"Really?" She tried to keep the incredulity out of her voice. "That's great. Do you like his church?"

"Sure. It's fine. Different from where your family went when we were kids. More modern, I guess. I love the music. And the messages... I used to think church was all about God telling me what to do and what not to do, but I'm starting to see what you've been saying for so long—that God wants me to behave not for Him but for me, you know?"

Josie leaned closer to her friend and took her hand. "I do know. He's like...like the kindest Father. He only wants what's best for us."

"I'm starting to realize that maybe, if I'd done things His way instead of my own over the years, I wouldn't have gotten myself into so much trouble."

Hope bubbled like a spring in Josie's heart. She'd been praying for Shelly for so long.

For years Josie had figured she was the only Christian Shelly had in her life. Unlike Josie, whose parents were believers, Shelly's parents never bothered to attend church. The only time Shelly ever went was with Josie and her family.

"What's his name?" Josie asked. "Anybody I know?"

"Jay. I'm sure you've never met him. He's sort of well known, so we're keeping our relationship on the down-low right now. He's divorced, and he has a custody hearing coming up. He doesn't want our relationship to cloud the issue. He's the best father, really."

"I take it he's older than you?"

She shrugged. "A few years. He married young. Now he's a single father, and that takes precedence over me."

Josie knew her friend well. "That's gotta bother you."

But Shelly just shrugged. "He has a vacation home, and he took his kids there for a month. It's awful, him being gone, but I totally understand that they have to come first. And then this thing happened with you. It seemed like... Is it weird to think maybe God orchestrated it so I could be here?"

Wow. Shelly had matured since Josie had seen her last. Josie stood to hug her friend's shoulders. "Not weird at all. I think you might be right."

Shelly toed the vacated chair. "Enough about me. Sit and tell me about the hottie."

"I assume you don't mean Bentley."

She mimed gagging. "Please. He's about as hot as a broken toaster."

"Don't hold back, Shell. Tell me how you really feel."

Her friend giggled. "What is he doing here, anyway?"

Josie shrugged. "He wants us to get back together."

"You're not going to, are you?" She looked as horrified as if Josie had just admitted to falling in love with a kangaroo.

Josie'd gotten over Bentley in the years since she'd left him. Now that he was back, she didn't know what to think. Sometimes, when he looked at her just so, she remembered what they'd had together. They understood each other. They appreciated each other's gifts.

But he was as much a part of the DC landscape as the Washington Monument. Could he be happy apart from that? Or would he spend their lives trying to pull her back in?

Shelly was watching her, so she answered truthfully. "I have no plans to."

"I'd have to kill you if you were, and you know how much I like you. That would ruin my whole week."

Josie couldn't help but laugh. "What do you have against him, anyway?"

"He's just...not for you. You changed when you were with him."

Josie had changed, but she couldn't blame Bentley for that. She'd become so steeped in the culture of Washington that she'd begun to take on its color and flavor. That wasn't Bentley's fault, it was hers.

"You two were like this scary power couple—you and him against the world. You were so serious, working all the time, never resting, never laughing. You weren't happy when you were with him."

Josie started to protest, and then she let herself hear what her friend was saying.

Shelly wasn't wrong.

Much as she wished she could deny it, she and Bentley had been like that. Everything in their relationship had been about winning. Taking on the bad guys and bringing them down. And they'd done it well.

At first, Josie'd managed to hang onto herself and her values. But after a while...

Memories of those last few months in Washington assailed her, filling her stomach with acid. Would that she could go back and do everything differently.

"It wasn't just that, though," Shelly said. "If I thought you loved him—and he loved you—I'd have been all for it. But it wasn't about love with you two. It was about power. It seemed from the outside—and don't get mad, okay?—but it seemed like you were using each other more than loving each other. It was just...weird."

Shelly, Josie's flighty, flaky friend, had seen beneath the veneer others never knew was there. She'd seen the truth long before Josie'd recognized it.

Even now, Shelly put words to what Josie'd felt back then. And what she feared now.

She gripped her friend's hand. "You're incredibly insightful."

"I just see—and hear—more than the average person."

Both true. The woman had superhero senses.

Shelly continued. "Which means I didn't miss the hottie. Tell me about him."

"Thomas. He's a customer who's turned into a friend." She told Shelly about the sprained ankle and how he'd brought her the crutches. And about how he'd jumped between her and danger the night before.

"Oh, my gosh!" Shelly said. "He saved your life!"

"It wasn't that dramatic."

"You don't know that! And then carried you inside?" She collapsed back in her chair and fanned her face. "Mamma mia, what a hero."

Josie kicked her lightly. "Get a grip, goofball."

"Ow!" She held her leg as if Josie's tap had been painful. "You trying to kill me?"

"Keep it up."

Shelly laughed, and Josie joined her. With all the stress in her life, it was a joy to have a friend to share everything with.

"What was he doing in the meeting with your dad?"

"You wouldn't believe it." She told her friend how Dad and Carlyle had blindsided him, offering him Josie's expertise in exchange for her protection. "I know Thomas well enough at this point to know he can take care of himself. He didn't feel pressured into taking their deal, even though they were most definitely pushing him. But that they did it without even consulting me..." She was still angry about that. Not surprised, though.

She'd forgotten how forceful her father could be. Living away from him, it was easy to remember him as the guy in the library surrounded by books like an absentminded professor. Today, she was reminded of Senator Harrington, the man who was accustomed to getting what he wanted and not afraid to use any method to do it.

Not that she could blame Dad. He'd grown up in a political family. His father'd served in the Senate before running for governor—and winning. His grandfather had spent more than half his life in Congress, rising to leadership. She'd loved and respected her grandfather. She knew her great-grandfather had done good things too.

But she wasn't proud of everything they'd done, particularly their fight against civil rights reform and school integration.

Dad didn't think like them, but he was part of a legacy. Some of that was impressive.

Some of it shameful.

All of it—her family's political legacy—she wanted nothing to do with.

"So you're going to help with Thomas's campaign?" Shelly asked.

Her question sparked an idea. "How long are you staying?"

Shelly smiled. "As long as you need me. And before you ask, I'll do whatever you and the hottie need."

The song "Matchmaker, Matchmaker" from *Fiddler on the Roof* might as well have been playing in the background. Josie didn't want to think about what lengths her friend would go to push her and Thomas together.

The thought should have brought anxiety, perhaps even a stern warning.

Instead, she found herself fighting a smile. She yanked Shelly from the chair and hugged her tight. "I'm so glad you're here."

CHAPTER FOURTEEN

The weather was perfect the following Saturday afternoon. The sky was bright blue and dotted with puffy white clouds. The temperatures had reached into the low eighties—a little warm for Thomas's taste, especially in his suit—but the tourists loved it. Families sunbathed on the beach while kids splashed in the calm water of Lake Ayasha.

Thomas was chatting with old friends in the grassy park near the sandy beach when Josie's silver sedan slid into a parking space. He said goodbye and hurried that direction. He'd offered to pick them up, but she and Shelly—and two body-guards—had gone to Plymouth that morning, so they'd agreed to meet him there.

The masked intruders Monday night had marked the first event of an interesting week. Tuesday, after the conference call with the senator and Carlyle, Thomas had met with Derrick to get on paper his opinions about the various issues facing Coven-try. That evening, Josie had organized his rambling ideas into straightforward statements in such a way that they would resonate with voters.

He'd just watched in awe.

The rest of the week, he'd made calls and ginned up support. He'd talked with Chelsea Hamilton, Dylan's wife, to learn about her short-term and long-term hopes for Coventry. They weren't so different from his. By the time he left that conversation, he felt confident in Chelsea's support—and that of the board of directors of HCI.

As he crossed the park, he thanked God for Josie's help. He was miles beyond where he'd been the previous weekend, all thanks to the woman he was rushing to meet.

By the time he got to Josie's sedan, Lake and her partner, Donley, were standing on either side of the car. Donley was tall and built—more NFL tight end than linebacker—but obviously powerful.

Thomas smiled at the guy. "How's it goin'?"

Donley's serious disposition didn't change at all, but he did open the driver's door.

Josie stepped out, thanked her bodyguard, and grinned at Thomas. "You look great."

It was his best suit. He usually chose colored shirts, but Shelly had told him to wear white.

There'd been no room for Shelly at the hotel down the block, so Thomas had offered her his condo for the duration of her stay. He'd moved a few things into the apartment over his insurance agency, where he'd lived before his business had taken off. It was old and dingy, but it was close to Josie, which was all that mattered.

When he'd gone to his condo on Thursday to grab more clothes, he'd discovered that Shelly hadn't had any trouble making the space her own. She wasn't exactly the tidiest person he'd ever met, and her things had been scattered everywhere.

But she was Josie's friend. And, according to Josie, she was also extremely gifted. Thomas was going to be the recipient of her gifts today, which was why they were meeting at the park.

She'd gone through his closet—he was still recovering from the thought of that—and decided that none of his ties were suitable.

Which was the reason for their trip to Plymouth that morning. He'd told them he could buy his own clothes, but Shelly had insisted.

Now, she joined them in front of the car and held out a sack. He peeked inside and found a dark red tie.

"Put it on," she said. "If it doesn't work, I got a blue one too."

"What if I wanted to wear green?"

She looked horrified. "You're running for office in the United States of America. You want to wear green, move to Ireland."

Chuckling, Thomas slipped off his jacket and handed it to Josie, then lifted his collar and put the tie on.

He wore ties almost every single day, so knotting the thing without a mirror was no trouble.

Still, Josie approached and straightened it for him, her cool fingers searing heat through the thin fabric of his shirt.

He met her gaze and held it. "Thank you."

Pink filled her cheeks as she stepped back. "You look perfect."

He'd take perfect in Josie's eyes.

Shelly said, "The photographer's meeting us..." Her gaze roamed the space. "There he is." She led the way into the park.

Thomas followed, Josie at his side. Lake walked on her opposite side, and Donley brought up the rear as they crossed beneath trees and around picnic tables and grills to the area farthest from the beach.

A huge golden retriever bolted their direction, and a little boy followed, calling, "Reb! Come back."

Thomas grabbed the dog's collar and crouched as the kid ran up.

"Thanks for catching him." The boy held up a leash. "He got away before I could clip it on 'im."

The whole group had paused. Josie and Shelly were smiling, but Donley gave him the evil eye. Who wouldn't help a little boy catch his dog?

"Why don't you do it now, while I've got him?" Thomas asked.

The kid did, clicking the leash in place.

"What's your name?" Thomas asked.

"Connor."

Thomas held out his hand, and the kid shook it, though his grip could use a little work.

If Thomas ever had a son, he'd teach him how to shake hands.

"Thomas Windham. Nice to meet you." He bent to pet the dog. "And this is Reb, I take it?"

"Uh-huh. Rebel. Daddy and me are trying to train him, but Mom says he's dumber than a bag of kibble."

Thomas chuckled. "I bet you and your dad will straighten him out." He looked at a couple he assumed were the kid's parents. He lifted his hand in a wave, and they waved back. "Good luck with your training."

"Thanks!" The dog took off, dragging Connor behind him.

Thomas nodded for the group to continue. "Sorry about that."

The bodyguards glared, but Josie wore a soft smile that made his insides do a funny little flip.

They reached the photographers—there were two, which felt ridiculous—and spent hours trying to get the perfect shots for the fliers and website.

Stand this way, fold your arms, don't fold your arms, smile, don't smile, look serious, wave...

And if that weren't bad enough, people gathered to watch.

And chat. And tell him he had their support—or he didn't, and why.

He kept stopping to talk to people, because, as important as these photos were—and Josie assured him they were important —talking to voters seemed more so. And he was much better at dealing with people than he was mugging for the camera.

By the time they were done, Thomas was rethinking the whole run-for-mayor idea. But the way Shelly was beaming as she flipped through the images they'd captured, he figured it'd been successful.

"Well done." Josie walked beside him back across the park. Shelly had lingered with the photographers, promising to walk to the café when she was finished. Lake stayed in front of them, Donley behind.

Scents of grilling burgers and dogs filled the air, making Thomas's stomach growl. A glance at his watch told him it was dinnertime.

"I feel like an idiot," he said. "Why would these people vote for me after seeing that?"

"Hey, mister!" The boy from earlier ran up to them, the dog on the leash at his side. "Wanna see a trick?"

"Love to, Connor." Thomas turned his attention to the dog. "Did you learn your manners, Rebel?"

The dog panted in front of them, its tongue hanging out.

Connor said to the dog, "Rebel, sit."

The dog seemed to contemplate it for a moment. And then it lowered its rump to the ground.

Connor gave him a treat, the dog gobbled it up, and the boy beamed.

"Wow!" Thomas high-fived him. "Good job."

"Thanks. See ya!" He took off toward one of the picnic tables, where his parents were setting out a feast for their little family.

"And that's why," Josie said.

He turned to her. "Why...what?"

She laughed, slipping her hand in the crook of his arm as they continued walking.

He was relishing the feel of her beside him while she explained. "You just asked why people would vote for you after that. We staged this whole thing, guessing how you'd react to the people here. And you did just as we hoped."

That had all been for show?

They better not think he was going to put up with *another* photo shoot. "What do you mean?"

"They got great posed shots of you, no question. But the best pictures are the ones the photographer took when you were talking to voters and kids. Do you know how many people introduced themselves to you today?"

He'd lost count. A lot.

She watched him for an answer, but he just shrugged.

"At least fifty. And yet you still remember the name of a seven-year-old boy—and his dog."

"That's my thing. I always remember names. How do you know how old he is?"

"I talked to his parents. They're going to vote for you, by the way."

"Oh. Huh."

"It's not just names," she said. "You were talking to people you'd just met about subjects you'd known next to nothing about a few days ago, connecting with them, making them feel like they were the most important people you'd met all day long. You've got a gift."

"I like people," he said. "That's not a gift. It's just...it's who I am."

She smiled, shaking her head. "That's why you're going to win."

He stopped. "You really think I have a chance?"

"If we do our part with the message, the website, the fliers, and you do what you did here until the election, no question."

Wow.

He'd agreed to run because nobody else wanted to do it. Because somebody had to stand up to Farley. But he'd never really thought he could defeat the guy.

Josie's confidence in him... It changed everything.

They started walking again, not in any hurry.

This was the first time he'd been alone with Josie since Monday night. The bodyguards were always there, but Bentley and Shelly had been too.

He didn't know when he'd get another opportunity to ask this. "Tuesday, during the conference call with your father, you seemed upset at the mention of that doctor's name—the one you said was an abortionist. Jude Mitchell, right?"

Her expression dimmed as if the sun had gone behind the clouds. "Yeah."

"There's a story there," he guessed.

"We bumped against each other in Dad's last primary race."

"What happened?"

He caught a hint of sadness in her eyes. "It's a long story."

A story she wasn't going to tell him.

They reached the road and crossed to the other side. "You need a ride?" she asked.

"I walked down. I'll take a ride back, if you don't mind."

"Not at all."

Lake checked over the sedan while Donley loomed nearby. Then they stepped away as Josie climbed in. Thomas wasn't sure how she'd managed to talk the bodyguards into following in their own car, but once Josie and Thomas were settled in the front seat of hers—a car so luxurious, it put his to shame—the bodyguards walked to their black SUV parked in the space just behind.

Josie talked about the fliers and literature Shelly would put together with the photographs they'd just gotten, but Thomas's mind wasn't on Josie's words so much as her voice, her presence beside him.

And what she was saying. That he really might be mayor. A crazy thought, but Josie knew what she was talking about, and she seemed to think it was possible.

He'd do everything she said and try his very best not to screw it up.

CHAPTER FIFTEEN

Cuppa Josie's was seven blocks west and one block north from the park.

One might think Josie could manage to travel eight blocks without getting a ticket, but the red-and-blue lights in her rearview mirror told her otherwise.

"I'm being pulled over."

"What'd you do?" Thomas asked.

"No idea." She was tempted to wait for the intersection so she could get off Main Street, but there were spaces in front of the library, and she didn't figure the cop would take kindly to her ignoring them.

The police cruiser stopped behind her. The bodyguards parked behind them.

Josie watched in the rearview mirror as the bodyguards stepped out of their SUV and walked forward, prompting the cops to jump from the cruiser.

Josie rolled down her window, but she couldn't hear the conversation, though she could see it was heated. She started to open her door, but Thomas gripped her arm.

"Just stay in the car."

"But maybe I should—"

"Just stay in the car." Thomas's smile had been replaced by a tight expression, and worry lines fanned from his eyes.

"Do you know what's going on?"

"No idea. If it's nothing, then it's nothing. If it's something, you're better off not making them think you're a danger."

A danger?

What in the world?

She found her driver's license, car registration, and proof of insurance. She couldn't remember the last time she'd been pulled over and had no idea what the police officer would ask for.

Her heart thumped, but she had no reason to worry. She hadn't done anything wrong. Had she not come to a complete stop at the sign? Had she forgotten to use her blinker?

Passersby were watching the scene unfold. Josie'd stopped within full view of the two restaurants on Main Street. And her car—a Cadillac she'd bought when she still lived in DC—didn't exactly blend in.

One of the cops approached her window. She recognized him as a regular customer at the café. His normally friendly manner was missing. "Could you step out of the car, please?"

Step out?

Did cops usually ask people to step out for minor traffic violations?

Were they mad about the bodyguards?

No, that didn't make sense.

Thomas leaned across her. "Hey, Rich. Looks like you recovered."

The cop, who seemed a little younger than herself, looked confused.

"It was a stomach bug, right?" Thomas asked. "Zack

responded to Josie's call Monday, but you weren't there. Said you were sick."

"Right. Yeah, I'm fine."

"What's going on?"

"Step out of the car, please." He focused on Josie. "Both of you."

She left her documents on the center console and did as he asked.

The officer she'd met Monday, Zack Tyler, directed them to sit on the sidewalk, a grim expression on his face.

Lake and Donley took up position behind them, but Josie feared the bodyguards couldn't protect her from whatever this was.

"I don't understand," Josie said to Officer Tyler. "I wasn't speeding. I don't think I broke any laws."

Tyler said nothing.

Beside her, Thomas muttered, "I don't have a good feeling about this."

"You know these guys. They're your friends. What are they doing?"

He shook his head and pressed his lips closed.

Telling her to do the same.

Another cruiser pulled up.

While Officer Tyler watched over them, three cops searched her car.

She felt sick to her stomach as she watched.

This was the first day she'd driven it since the alarm went off on Monday. Had the assailants done more than just set it off? Had they broken in?

The new cops searched the front and back seats.

Rich dug in her trunk.

And came out with a little baggie filled with...

Oh, no.

She didn't know what those pills were, but she had a few guesses.

Thomas lurched to his feet. "Her car was broken into a few nights ago. Somebody must've planted that."

"Sit. Down." Zack Tyler said.

Thomas sat again. He shot her a wide-eyed look of fear.

This was bad.

Very bad.

When the search was complete, Officer Tyler said, "On your feet, Ms. Smith."

While she stood, the police officer addressed Thomas. "I could take you in, but I've known you a long time, and I don't think you had anything to do with this."

"*She* doesn't have anything to do with this," Thomas said. "Her car was—"

"I was there," Officer Tyler said. "I know what happened."

Thomas turned to her. "Don't say anything. I know you did nothing wrong, but there's something going on. Just wait until you get a lawyer, okay?"

Josie nodded, but the idea that she might talk to them... What could she say? She had no words.

"Who should I call?" Thomas asked.

She could barely focus.

The police officer was watching her.

"Josie," Thomas said, "who should I call?"

The question registered. "Bentley. Call Bentley."

Tyler stepped behind her and took one of her arms.

Cold steel wrapped around her wrist.

"Sorry, ma'am." Officer Tyler said the words quietly, only loudly enough for her to hear. "We got a tip, and we had no choice but to follow it." His voice was louder when he continued. "You have the right to remain silent..."

CHAPTER SIXTEEN

Thomas stood beside the bodyguards and watched as the cruiser pulled away from the curb, Josie in the backseat. *Handcuffed* in the backseat.

Then he turned to Lake. "I need a ride."

"Let's go."

The three of them jogged to the SUV.

The group was silent for the short drive to Bentley's hotel. Lake had barely shifted into park when Thomas hopped out.

He didn't have Bentley's phone number. If the man wasn't here, then Thomas would have to call Carlyle, who'd sent his number and the senator's after Thomas had agreed to help protect Josie.

He approached the front desk. An older man with gray hair stood on the opposite side. Thomas flipped through his memory bank, remembered being introduced to the guy once at The Patriot. "Bob, right?"

The clerk nodded. "Have we met?"

"James Sullivan introduced us." He forced his tone to remain cordial while his insides thrummed with tension. "Could you call Bentley Kent's room and tell him Thomas

Windham is here to see him?" He never assumed that people remembered his name. He'd found most didn't. "Tell him it's an emergency."

Bob punched in the number. It was a long, torturous moment before the clerk relayed the message.

Thank God Bentley was there.

Bob hung up. "He'll be right down."

He'd barely finished speaking when feet pounded on the staircase behind him. This wasn't an overlarge hotel—just three stories, six rooms on each. There was an elevator, but he doubted it could be faster than running.

Bentley was definitely running.

He pushed through the doorway. "What happened?"

"Come on." Thomas marched outside. No need to have this conversation in front of Bob.

Bentley followed, and they both climbed into the back of the waiting SUV.

As soon as the door slammed, Bentley said, "Where's Josie?"

"She was arrested for drug possession ten minutes ago."

"What? How could you let this happen?"

Thomas resisted the urge to punch the guy. "What should I have done? Beat up the cops and told her to run?"

Bentley took a deep breath. "Right. Okay." He snatched his phone from his pocket and dialed.

A tinny voice came faintly through the phone.

Bentley said, "I need to speak with Carlyle. Now." He glanced at the cell's screen. "Crap. It's the senator." To Thomas, he said, "You have his number. Call him."

Thomas did, and a moment later, he heard, "Senator Harrington."

"Senator, this is Thomas Windham. Josie was—"

"Arrested. I know. I just got the pictures."

Thomas tapped Bentley's shoulder to get the man's attention, speaking to the senator. "Pictures?"

Bentley's eyes closed, and he dropped his head against the headrest.

"I'm trying to reach Bentley," the senator said.

"He's here. He's on the phone with Carlyle."

"Okay, good. Tell me what happened."

Thomas climbed out of the car, looking around to ensure nobody was nearby, and relayed the events.

"The drugs were planted, of course," the senator said.

"Monday night, when her car alarm went off," Thomas guessed. "We assumed they set off the alarm just to get her outside. But obviously..." He could kick himself for not investigating.

Stupid.

He'd been so caught up in his work, in *himself*.

And someone he cared about had paid the price.

Again.

"I'm sure Carlyle's already securing her an attorney." The senator, so confident when they'd spoken Tuesday, sounded shaken. "These charges won't stick, but this wasn't about the charges. It's about the scandal."

"What do you mean? You said something about pictures?"

"I got them a few minutes ago. Someone photographed the whole thing. You two sitting on the sidewalk. The cops standing over you. The bodyguards. And then Josie being handcuffed."

"Did they come from the same number as Monday's photos?"

"No, but that's not surprising. Whoever this is doesn't want to be found out."

"Tell me the angle. Where were they taken from?"

"Looks like..." There was a pause. "The person was standing

across the street and down a little...would have been to your left."

"Send them to me, would you?"

"Sure."

Thomas waited until they came through and studied them. He pictured where they'd been, where the photographer must've been standing—in front of the little souvenir shop beside The Patriot. He remembered the people who'd been there. There were a few he'd met, but most were strangers. Tourists, he guessed, based on their attire.

But there'd been one guy. Slender, over six feet. Wearing a red baseball hat.

Phone up and aimed.

"I think it was one of the guys from Monday night. The tall one."

"What did he look like?" The senator sounded optimistic for the first time in their conversation.

"I didn't see his face. He wore a cap low, and we were a considerable distance away. And his phone blocked my view." If only Thomas had noticed the man's presence. He'd been so focused on the cops and Josie that he hadn't thought to look at bystanders.

Again...stupid on his part.

"I'll ask the bodyguards," Thomas said. "Maybe one of them got a better look."

"Good thinking," the senator said. "This is another intimidation tactic." The man's words came slowly, accentuating his Southern accent. "They want me to vote for the bill, and they're telling me they'll stoop to any level to get it done. We can hire her bodyguards, but Josie still won't be safe. They can get to her. They can ruin her. And they can get to *me* through her. They think— accurately—that I'll do just about anything to protect my daughter."

As frustrating as this situation was, there hadn't been that many pills in the little bag. If that was all the police had found, then she'd be charged with possession. It wasn't nothing, but it wasn't intent-to-distribute, either.

The people behind this, whoever they were, could have done more damage if they'd wanted to. So this was a warning shot.

"Sir," Thomas said, "are you saying you're considering supporting the bill?" Thomas had no right to ask the question, but he couldn't help his curiosity.

No. It was more than curiosity. As much as Thomas wanted Josie to be safe, he didn't relish the idea of this upstanding senator voting in favor of something he disagreed with so vehemently.

Something that would use Thomas's tax dollars—and everybody else's—to fund more abortions.

It was one thing to have abortion be legal. He hated that, but its existence wasn't on the table.

It was an entirely different thing to force people who were morally opposed to the practice to *pay* for it.

And to line the pockets of a bunch of bigwigs who didn't give a rat's behind about the people whose lives would be altered or destroyed as a result of their policies.

"Supporting the bill?" The senator's voice sounded strong as he repeated Thomas's question. "If I have to send Josie somewhere safe for the duration, then I will. But I cannot...I will not support a bill that throws hundreds of millions of dollars toward abortion. I think Josie understands that."

"As do I," Thomas said. "There are things worth fighting for."

"That's the truth. Thing is... I knew when I ran for office that I'd be putting myself in a lot of battles. It never occurred to me I'd be tossing my daughter in the ring. It'd be one thing if the foe would attack head-on. This is..."

"She's strong. She can handle it." But even as Thomas said the words, he worried. When this tactic didn't work, what would their enemies try next?

Behind him, the car door slammed, and Bentley rounded the car, hand outstretched. "Lemme talk to him."

Thomas didn't appreciate the order but said, "Bentley would like to speak with you."

"Good, good. Put him on."

Thomas handed the man his phone but stayed close to listen.

"Carlyle hired a local attorney," Bentley said. "He's on his way to the station, and he's working on getting the number for the county prosecutor."

Thomas said, "I can get you her number."

Bentley's gaze snapped to him. "Hold on, Senator." He held a hand over the phone's mic. "You know the county prosecutor?"

"She's an old friend of the family. But I'll need my phone."

Bentley lifted the phone again. "Senator, Thomas believes he can reach the prosecutor. We'll get back to you when we know more." Bentley ended the call and returned Thomas's phone.

Thomas texted his mother.

Got an emergency. Need Sheila Robicheaux's number ASAP.

Why?

He didn't feel free to explain this situation to her, so he just said, *Please?*

A moment later, the contact information came through.

He thanked his mother, then tapped the contact and showed it to Bentley.

"Text that to Carlyle. You have his—?"

"Yeah." Thomas forwarded the prosecutor's number to Carlyle.

Then he dialed it himself.

Three rings later, the line connected. "Sheila Robichaeux."

"Ms. Robichaeux, this is Thomas Windham."

"You're not a kid anymore. When are you going to start calling me Sheila?"

"Old habits die hard."

"What can I do for you?" Her tone was friendly and accommodating. He hoped it would stay that way.

"I need your help. On Monday night..." He told the prosecutor the basic facts of the situation without sharing who Josie's father was.

She listened, added nothing, until he ended with, "She's been arrested."

"You're saying you think somebody planted the drugs?" she asked.

"I'm certain of it. I know this woman personally. You probably know her too. She owns Cuppa Josie's."

"I know her face. But lots of people use drugs."

"Not Josie. Somebody tipped the police off. If those were her drugs, how would that somebody have known they were in her car?"

"An ex-friend with an ax to grind?"

"In this case, there's more going on than meets the eye."

"What does that mean?"

How much should he tell her? "Could we meet?"

"I have a date."

Thomas didn't say anything, just waited.

She sighed audibly into the phone. "Where are you now?"

"I'm headed to...my office." He met Bentley's eyes, and the man nodded. "I'll be there in two minutes."

"On High Street, right?"

"Right next door to Cuppa—"

"I'll be there in ten."

After Thomas ended the call, Bentley said, "Well?"

"She's on her way. We probably ought to call the attorney."

As they climbed back into the bodyguards' SUV—the two had stood awkwardly beside them as if unsure what to do without anyone to guard—he directed them to his insurance agency just down the block.

With any luck, they'd have this managed and Josie out of jail in a couple of hours.

If the police decided to hold her, she'd be stuck in jail until she could be arraigned—in two days.

CHAPTER SEVENTEEN

At least Josie was the only person in the holding cell that evening. Coventry was a small enough town that she figured the jail was empty most of the time. There was a bed and a thin mattress, and though they looked clean, she was too hyped up to sit.

Furious.

They'd gone too far. Whoever'd done this, they weren't fooling around.

Well, they'd taken on the wrong target this time. She knew all the tricks in the book. She'd played more than her share. When she figured out who'd framed her, she'd make them pay.

Really?

Ugh. It was either her conscience or...Him.

She sighed and sat on the side of the bed. *What do You expect me to do?*

There was no answer.

Which didn't surprise her. She was on the right side of this battle. She was supporting her father, who was standing up against a terrible bill.

She wasn't going to let them win. If that meant she had to

get down in the dirt to fight them... Well, she'd gotten dirty before.

Dirt washed off.

Does it?

That voice again.

It was accurate, unfortunately. The last time she'd played dirty, things had gotten out of hand.

There was a reason Josie'd left Washington and vowed to never go back. Though her sins had not been exposed, she knew what she'd done.

God knew.

And yes, the dirt washed off, but not because of Josie's actions.

Her sins had been washed away by the blood of Christ.

She knew that. She did.

She just wasn't sure how that knowledge should inform what she had to do next.

The uniformed officer who'd locked her into the cell returned through the heavy door.

"Let's go," he said.

"Where am I going?"

He didn't bother to answer.

Josie followed the man into a small room, where her belongings were returned to her. Then she was led to another door. The police officer opened it, and she stepped...

Outside.

Bentley, Thomas, and a woman she'd never met were standing beside the bodyguards' SUV.

Before she could process that, Lake and Donley took positions on either side of her.

"To the car, ma'am," Lake said.

As she walked, her gaze locked with Thomas's. "What happened?"

"Ms. Smith?" The woman beside him held out her hand. "Sheila Robichaeux. I'm the county prosecutor."

Josie shook her hand. "Can you explain what's going on?"

Her father must've pulled serious strings to get Josie out so quickly.

"Thomas is a friend of the family," the prosecutor said.

Thomas? Not her father?

Ms. Robichaeux continued. "He told me about the incident Monday night. Based on the fact that you have no criminal record and your car was broken into, our office decided not to pursue charges."

The weight of uncertainty lifted and floated away. Unfortunately, the trauma and the anxiety wouldn't dissipate so easily. "Thank you."

"I do wonder, though..." The prosecutor's gaze flicked to the bodyguards, then to the men at her side. "There's obviously more to this than a prank. What's going on?"

Josie started to answer. "It's sort of a—"

"—This isn't the time," Bentley said.

Lake's voice overshadowed them both. "We need to get you someplace safe."

"My office?" Thomas suggested.

She'd never been inside his office, but it seemed a better idea than the café, which would still be filled with dinner guests at that hour.

Anxiety had kept her hunger at bay in the jail, but it was roaring back now. The lunch she and Shelly had shared in Plymouth had long since burned up.

Shelly.

Josie'd promised to meet her back at the apartment. Her friend was probably frantic.

"Ma'am," Lake said, "in the car please. Now."

Five minutes later, Josie stepped into Thomas's insurance

agency. Like her café, this had been an old house. Except for a glass front door and the prominent sign over it, it still looked like a house, but the inside had been completely remodeled. Beyond a reception area, offices lined both sides of the building. With the refinished hardwood floor, white woodwork, freshly painted walls, and tasteful artwork, it felt both luxurious and cozy.

She'd assumed his business was successful. This office told her that her assumption had been spot-on. She could imagine what the place would be like when his employees filled all the offices, the phones ringing, customers coming and going.

Impressive.

But it was eight-fifteen on a Saturday night, and the offices were empty.

Thomas led the way to a conference room, probably once a dining room, which she guessed because the layout was similar to what her building's had originally been.

She was just settling in a chair when somebody pounded on the front door.

On the way, Josie had called Shelly, who had indeed been worried. Josie popped up. "I'll let her in."

The look Donley gave her had her sinking to her seat.

"Better yet, why don't you?"

Without comment, he stepped out. A moment later, Shelly burst into the room. "Omigosh, omigosh!" She yanked Josie to her feet and hugged her. "Are you okay? I was so worried. I called your phone about a million times, but you never picked up."

"It couldn't be helped." Josie caught her friend up on what'd happened, which only heightened Shelly's anxiety.

"You were *arrested*! What the—?"

"It's okay. I'm okay."

On the far side of the long table, Bentley said, "We don't

have time for your drama, Shelly. Either sit down and be quiet or leave."

"Bentley!" Josie shot him what she hoped was a scathing look. "Knock it off."

Then she caught the smug look Shelly sent him.

They were both ridiculous.

"I ordered dinner for everybody," Josie said. "If you don't want to sit in on the meeting, you could walk next door and pick it up for us."

Shelly pulled out one of the rolling upholstered chairs and sat. "I'll stay. Maybe Bentley can get it."

Josie resumed her seat, closing her eyes to pray for patience. She didn't have the energy for their bickering.

Thomas's hand slid over hers on the table. The look he gave her—eyebrows up, chin lowered, communicated his question. *You okay?*

She nodded, thankful for his gentle presence at her side.

Sheila Robichaeux sat at the end of the table. "My date is waiting for me. I'd like to know what's going on here."

The woman had to be in her late fifties, maybe early sixties, so the word *date* surprised Josie, but not everybody was married and settled.

Bentley swiveled to her. "Can we trust you to keep this confidential?"

"I have been known to keep my share of secrets," Ms. Robichaeux said. "Just keep my position in mind."

The woman's loyalty lay with her employer, the county. But Josie had nothing to fear there. She'd broken no laws.

Bentley looked at Josie, who decided that this woman, this friend of Thomas's, could be trusted. "My father is Senator Davis Harrington."

The woman's eyebrows rose to her hairline. "Oh. Oh. He's in the fight of his life right now."

Oh, good. She knew. "That's what this is about," Josie said. "Whatever side you stand on, he should have the right to vote his conscience. Somebody's trying to compel him to support the bill, and they're using me to do it. Thomas told you what happened Monday night, right?"

She nodded.

"Both times, my father's gotten photographs almost immediately."

"You're being threatened," the prosecutor said.

"Not bodily."

Over the prosecutor's head, Lake's eyes tightened around the corners. She clearly didn't care for the distinction.

Bentley said, "They framed you, Josie."

"I know that. I'm just saying—"

"If I hadn't gotten to you the other night..." Thomas's pause was just long enough for her to jump in.

"I'm just saying that, so far"—she met Bentley's eyes—"it's mostly intimidation tactics." She turned to Thomas. "Though we have no idea what they would've done if you hadn't shown up."

The prosecutor was nodding. "And you don't know who these people are?"

Josie recognized the expression on Bentley's face. He didn't want her to say.

She tended to agree. "We have theories, but nothing concrete."

Ms. Robicheaux faced Thomas. "And how are you connected to all of this?"

"I'm a friend," he said. "I'm helping to keep Josie safe, and she's helping me with my campaign."

"The thing is..." The prosecutor scanned the people. "You're trusting me with your stuff, so I'm going to trust you with this. It can't leave the room."

At nods all around, the prosecutor turned back to Thomas. "You need to win this race. Farley isn't to be trusted. In fact, one of the reasons I moved so fast is because I assumed that whatever was going on with your friend was related to you."

"Me?" Thomas looked stunned.

"I wouldn't put it past him to use your girlfriend to make you look bad."

"She's not his girlfriend," Bentley growled.

Thomas's gaze flicked to Josie, probably waiting for her to agree with Bentley. Josie didn't bother because it didn't matter. What mattered was what she was saying. "You think he should distance himself from me," she clarified.

Ms. Robichaeux nodded. "If you're mired in scandal, he will be too. Can you help on his campaign in the background? In a less public role than what you guys did at the park today?"

"Absolutely."

Thomas spoke to the older woman. "How did you know—?"

"It was all over social media," Ms. Robichaeux said. "And Josie's face was in more than one of the photos. And then her face was all over social media because she was arrested in front of the whole town. Your association with her has already hurt you."

He sat back, mouth half open.

"I'm so sorry," Josie said. "It never occurred to me this could come back on you." To the prosecutor, she said, "I'll keep my distance. I can still help on the campaign. Thomas'll just have to stay away from me."

"Forget it." He swiveled to face her. "I promised to protect you."

"I have Lake and Donley and Bentley. You can't risk your candidacy—"

"Your safety is more important." Thomas stared at her, hard, as if trying to read something behind her eyes. She guessed what he was looking for—some indication she wanted him to leave.

Or maybe the opposite, that she *didn't*.

Truth was, the idea of keeping her distance from Thomas was about as comfortable as that jail cell had been. She'd come to depend on him. She enjoyed his company. She wanted him nearby.

But she wouldn't be the reason he lost this race.

She hardened her expression. "I don't need you."

He hardened his as well. "I made a promise to your father. Whether you want me around or not, I'm not going anywhere." He turned back to Ms. Robichaeux. "I'm going to do the right thing, which means standing by my friend, and I'm going to trust God with the results. If I'm supposed to win this race, then I will. If I lose, then I'll trust God's sovereignty in that as well."

His words pricked at the deep places in Josie's heart. She wanted to have that depth of faith.

At the same time, she wondered... Was Thomas being very wise or very stupid?

After the prosecutor left, Josie called the café and asked her employee to deliver their dinners. He did right away, and they ate at the conference table.

Lake sat at the far end of the conference table to scarf down a salad and sandwich while Donley stood watch near the door.

Thomas shoved his paper plate away and took out his phone. When Josie glanced that way, she caught the image of herself and him on the sidewalk.

"Those were sent to Dad?"

He leaned closer. "Your father forwarded them to me." He flipped through the photos, which captured the events from the time they were pulled over until the cruiser turned the corner, Josie visible in the rear window.

Thomas asked, "You didn't happen to notice anyone across the street, did you?"

"I was focused on the guys searching my car. Did you see someone?"

Thomas described a man who sounded a lot like the taller of the two who'd threatened her Monday.

"Did you see his face?" she asked.

"Wish I had. His cap shaded it."

Feeling far too comfortable so close to Thomas, Josie turned away and caught sight of Shelly beaming. Despite all the craziness of that afternoon, it was clear Shelly's mind was on romance, and she approved of Thomas.

Across the table, Bentley was watching, too, an entirely different expression on his face. His eyes were narrowed, his lips pressed closed. His Adam's apple bobbed.

Thomas walked to the end of the table and bent to show the photos to Lake. "See the angle? The guy was probably standing in front of the souvenir shop by the restaurant. Any chance you saw him?"

Lake wiped her mouth with a napkin. "Six one, probably one ninety. Wore blue jeans and a gray T-shirt. Red cap and sneakers. I took him for a tourist. He was taking pictures, but so were a lot of people."

"You didn't happen to notice where he went?"

"Sorry, no."

"Too bad *you* weren't paying attention, Thomas." Bentley barely spared him a glance as he tossed out the words. "You'd seen the guy before. If only it'd occurred to you to keep your eyes open."

"Gosh, if only you'd been there, Beta. I'm sure you'd have handled it so much better." Thomas stood up behind Lake. "But you decided protecting Josie was less important than your afternoon nap."

"I was working. And my name is *Bentley*. You'd think in your business, you'd have learned to remember people's names."

"Do you two mind?" Josie said. Thomas's whole *Beta* thing was getting on her nerves.

He shot her an apologetic look that she didn't believe for a second.

Bentley didn't even bother with that.

Thomas started toward Donley, who spoke before he crossed the room.

"I saw the guy." The bodyguard focused on Josie. "After you were taken in, the man walked to the next block. He had blond hair sticking out the back of his cap. I think he climbed into a white hatchback."

"Wow," she said. "I'm impressed."

The nearly silent bodyguard just nodded.

Josie knew very little about the people who'd been hired to protect her. Quiet and serious as they were, the more she knew them, the more she trusted them.

"Not exactly a typical villain car," Bentley said. "What kind of man drives a hatchback?"

"Fathers," Thomas suggested. "Guys who need to haul sporting equipment or tools. People who are environmentally conscientious and don't want to drive gas-guzzling SUVs but need cargo space."

"Yes, I'm sure that's it." Bentley's voice was laced with sarcasm. "An environmentally conscious goon. He probably plays polo on the weekends. Those polo mallets can be unruly. Thanks for your input, man. Really helpful."

Shelly giggled. "This is fun."

By the irritation on Donley's face, he disagreed entirely.

Josie was with the bodyguard.

"One assumes," Donley said, "that he's been watching, waiting for you to drive your car so he could alert the police."

"The tip." Josie ignored the other two men in the room.

"Did anybody see him at the park?" Donley asked.

Josie hadn't, and she doubted Thomas had found a moment to notice anyone but the people crowded around him. But Shelly...

Her friend's smile faded. "Actually, you say he wore a red cap?" She was focused on Lake. "Sort of dark red?" At Lake's nod, Shelly closed her eyes. "Yeah, I saw him. He was on the edge of the beach, sitting on a picnic table."

Thomas's head tipped to one side. "The beach is a good hundred and fifty yards from where we were standing."

Josie said, "Shelly has remarkable senses."

"Okay." Thomas sounded skeptical. "But I mean, the human eye can only see so far."

Shelly said, "There's a dead fly on the floor in the second office on the right, against the wall beside a paper shredder."

"You can't be serious."

She gave him an unmistakable *try me* look.

Thomas disappeared out the door.

The group waited in silence until he returned a moment later, smiling. "Wow. I can't decide if I'd like to have your senses or not. Do you see every speck of dust?"

"Unfortunately. It's a curse more than a blessing." Shelly turned to Josie. "The guy was just sitting there. I noticed him toward the end of our session. He might've been there longer." Her shoulders lifted and dropped. "My focus was elsewhere."

"Was he watching Ms. Smith?" Lake asked.

Shelly shook her head. "Not that I noticed. Even if he had been, we were making a scene. Lots of people were watching. We were pretty far away, though. He couldn't have seen much."

Lake stood and threw her trash in the can by the door. She

took up Donley's position, and he grabbed a sandwich and settled in her seat.

They were like a well-oiled machine, these two.

Donley unwrapped his sandwich. "So either he'd been watching you all along, just waiting for you to drive your car, or he had a way of knowing when you were driving it."

"Meaning?" Bentley asked.

"I wonder if there's a tracker on it."

Josie leaned back in her chair. This got more fun all the time.

"We'll check it out, ma'am," Donley said. "I assume it's been impounded?"

"Oh." She hadn't thought once about her car. She looked at Thomas.

"That's what Zack told me," he said.

Shelly cleared her throat. "You'll need to call the station. They'll tell you where it is."

"Why am I not surprised *you* know that?" Bentley said.

"Listen, you little—"

"Please, you two." Josie breathed through her exasperation. "Give it a rest. Okay?"

"Sorry, Shelly. I didn't mean anything by it." Bentley tossed out the casual reply.

"No worries," she answered just as breezily. "I would expect nothing less."

At that, Bentley actually smiled.

Josie'd forgotten how much they despised each other. Maybe she'd blocked it out like one might a trauma. Selective amnesia.

"Ma'am," Lake said, "this was why we cautioned you against today's events. You were in a public place surrounded by unknown elements. Anything could've happened. I'd say you got off pretty easy."

"Easy?" Bentley faced the woman standing against the wall. "She was arrested."

"She wasn't shot. She wasn't kidnapped. She wasn't harmed." The woman's gaze landed on Josie. "Next time, you might not be so lucky."

Those words hung in the room, oppressive in their accuracy.

"Have you two nailed down any more information about who's behind all this?" Thomas glanced at Bentley but focused on Josie.

Bentley fielded it. "Based on what we know about him"—his gaze flicked to Josie's, and she nodded for him to continue—"we presume Jude Mitchell."

"Why?" Thomas asked. When Bentley's eyes flashed, Thomas lifted his hands in a gesture of surrender. "Not saying you're wrong. Just wondering what led you to the conclusion."

His expression softened infinitesimally. "Josie and I had a... situation with him in the past. He didn't come out of that well."

"That clears it up. Thanks, man." Thomas turned to her. "Anything to add?"

She couldn't blame Thomas for his irritation. He wanted to know what they were up against.

It wasn't his fault that she and Bentley didn't want to tell the story.

She could tell part of it, though.

"My father's views have been shifting steadily away from the party for years. Or, more accurately, he would argue that the party has been shifting away from him and his values. Not just his, but those of his constituents. Often, he ends up opposing the party line. The party usually lets him get away with it. They'd rather keep the seat than risk him voting with them and putting the seat in jeopardy."

"You're saying that, when the party has the votes to pass their bills, they don't expect him to join their side," Thomas said. "They want him to get reelected, which means not going against his constituents' wishes." At her nod, he added, "Which worked fine when the Senate wasn't so narrowly split."

"Exactly."

"But not everybody in the party was on board with that plan," Bentley said. "Senator Harrington had a strong opponent in the primary in his last election. Mitchell threatened to throw his support behind that opponent."

"Mitchell is well known and well respected in my state," Josie said.

"And well funded," Bentley added. "If he'd supported the other candidate, a rabidly pro-choice feminist, the senator probably still would have won, but he'd have depleted his resources to do it. Getting beat up in the primaries only weakens a guy when the general election comes along. It would have made him vulnerable."

"Makes sense."

"So," Bentley said, "we found a way to *encourage* Mitchell to keep his mouth shut and his money to himself."

Thomas looked from Bentley to her. "What did you do?"

"It's not important." Bentley answered before she could, which was good.

She had no intention of giving him the details.

Those details churned her stomach.

They were the reason she was living in New Hampshire instead of DC.

They were the reason she owned a coffee shop instead of working on her father's staff.

They were the reason Josie could no longer pretend her father's situation didn't affect her. She'd washed her hands of Washington, but grime didn't wipe away so easily. Mitchell'd been biding his time, and now she had no doubt he was relishing this opportunity to get revenge.

And that was the reason Josie had to jump back into the fight. Until she found ammunition to use against Mitchell, she would be vulnerable. And so would her father.

Bentley was the only one present who understood. Shelly, her oldest friend, Thomas, her new friend, and the two bodyguards... Josie and her father weren't the only ones who needed to be cautious. Those who chose to stand with her would land in Mitchell's cross hairs.

Which meant, until she could find a way to bring Mitchell down, everybody in this room was vulnerable.

Because of her.

CHAPTER EIGHTEEN

The photo shoot at the park had alerted everybody in Coventry that Thomas was running for mayor—not that it'd been much of a secret before. News traveled fast in the little town, and after the former mayor was arrested for kidnapping and attempted murder—and a thirty-year-old unsolved mystery—everybody was suddenly interested in politics. Thomas had been fielding questions all over town. From clients at his office. From fellow diners at The Patriot. Some guy had even approached him in the locker room at the gym after his morning workout. Nothing like trying to have a serious conversation about elementary school curricula while wearing nothing but a towel.

Ms. Robichaeux was right about people's perception of Thomas and his relationship with Josie, but with Josie's help, he'd managed to get an article printed in the local paper that covered both her arrest and the reasons the DA had decided not to press charges.

That had helped...some.

Whether it helped or not, he wasn't going back on his promise to protect Josie. If it hurt him in the election, so be it.

It'd been over a week since the arrest, and nothing else had happened. But he didn't think for a minute that her enemies had given up. And Josie didn't seem to believe that, either. Before and after their daily campaign meetings, he'd caught her poring over her laptop, trying to find a connection between what had happened to her in Coventry and Jude Mitchell. If she'd found anything, she hadn't shared it with Thomas.

The bodyguards had located no tracker on her car, which meant the man in the red cap had been watching her. And Thomas hadn't noticed him. Nobody had.

It was just before three o'clock on Monday afternoon when Josie followed Lake into the café's back room and settled beside Thomas at the table near the cold fireplace, dropping her over-size purse on the floor. Though he would prefer to sit with her on the cozy sofa on the other side of the room, the bodyguards had asked Josie to stay away from the windows. This was the safest spot in the café's dining room.

"You're not limping," he said.

She lifted the offending ankle and turned it in a circle. "All healed."

"That's good news. Where's Shelly?" Lately, Shelly had joined her more often than not, and always for their campaign meetings.

Bentley had flown out of town a few days prior. Not surprising how much more Thomas enjoyed life when the guy wasn't around.

"I've got the afternoon off," Josie said.

"Shelly and Bentley's bickering has gotta get on your nerves."

She gave him a closed-mouth, eyebrows-lifted look that had him squirming.

Maybe he shouldn't be throwing stones where bickering was

concerned. "I'll try to knock it off. But your ex is eminently dislikable."

"He's not," she said. "He's brilliant and talented and, most of the time, pretty charming."

Her words burned like scalding coffee. "If you say so." Apparently, she didn't buy the mild response, so he figured it wouldn't hurt to add the question that begged to be asked. "If he's so great, why is he your *ex*-fiancé?"

"He belongs in Washington, and I'm never going back."

Was she saying that, if Bentley would move to New Hampshire, she'd get back together with him?

Did she still care for the guy?

Because Thomas's feelings for Josie were only growing with all the time they spent together. And Bentley obviously wanted her back.

Somebody was going to have his heart crushed.

She was studying him. Hopefully his thoughts hadn't been broadcast on his face.

"I really wish you'd stop calling him 'Beta.'"

"Golly, I wouldn't want to hurt the guy's fragile feelings."

"His feelings aren't hurt. He's tougher than that. It just makes him think you're a dolt."

"I don't care what he thinks of me."

She held Thomas's gaze, no smile there, no amusement. Apparently, *she* cared. If Thomas wanted to have a shot, he should probably do as she asked.

"Fine. No more 'Beta.' Though I have to admit, I've been waiting for him to ask me why I call him that."

"He won't. Not because he's not curious but because he refuses to give you the satisfaction."

Thomas would behave exactly the same way.

"Where is he anyway? Off on some grand adventure?"

Josie lifted one shoulder. "We've both been trying to gather intel on Mitchell. He didn't tell me who he was meeting, but it's related to that." She glanced at the time on her phone. "I thought Derrick was coming today? Don't you and he usually meet on Mondays?"

"He's happy to step aside and let you be in charge."

"Really?" She seemed genuinely shocked. "I thought he'd be offended at my presence."

"He was only helping because he knew I didn't know what I was doing. He's got a business to run, so if we don't need him..."

"Did you show him what we put together? The platform? The fliers?"

The man had gushed his praise. "He approves."

"Huh." She seemed perplexed.

"What?"

"It's just rare for people to take a backseat when there's power involved."

Thomas couldn't help his laugh. "This isn't DC. If I win this race, I'll have tens and tens of dollars at my disposal."

"Not that little."

He shrugged. "I'm going to get paid peanuts. It's a part-time job. I'll be inheriting a boatload of problems and debt, thanks to Salcito's mismanagement. It's not as if people are fighting over this job."

"Farley wants it badly enough."

Thomas's amusement faded. "Farley's planning to get rich with his own investments—and maybe kickbacks. I'm just trying to protect my town."

She smiled at him, a sweet expression which he'd come to understand meant she was impressed, and his heart hitched.

"We need to talk about your announcement," she said. "Most everybody knows you're running already, of course, but you need to create a media event to make a formal announcement. A presser or—"

"I was thinking I'd do it at Liberty Fest. Fourth of July is two weeks from today, and the festival will begin on Sunday. There's an opening ceremony, where the town officials welcome everybody and give speeches."

"Can you get on the agenda?"

"It's run by the Chamber of Commerce, and I happen to be friends with the president. She's supporting me. I talked to her a couple of days ago, and she said she'd be happy to give me a few minutes."

"How well attended is that opening ceremony, though?" Josie asked.

"There usually aren't that many tourists there yet, but everybody with booths will be there. Everybody with a stake in the festival. People who own businesses and run nonprofits, not to mention lots of town employees who need to be there for various reasons."

Josie was nodding. "I see what you're saying. It won't be a lot of people, but they'll be the people you want to reach."

"Exactly. I'll have the rest of that day and all of the next—all the Liberty Fest events—to reach everybody else. I've rented a booth at the festival and plan to walk in the parade. I sponsored the fireworks, so my name'll be attached to that. There's always a fancy dinner the night of the third—a fundraising event for the year's project."

"Project? What do you mean?"

"You've been to Liberty Fest, right?"

"The café's taken part in the tasting—"

"That's right. You provide iced coffee."

"And tea. But other than that, I'm usually here, manning the store. We get a lot of business that week, people who need a break from the heat."

"Every year, the chamber surveys the community and chooses a local nonprofit to support."

"Oh, yeah. I filled out that survey."

"This year, it's the youth center. They're hoping to expand into the storefront next door, add a game room, table tennis and pool tables. It'll be a place for local kids to hang out. The chamber sells tickets, provides a fancy catered dinner and dancing. The person who runs the charity, in this case, Cassidy Sullivan, will get up and give a speech to explain the organization. People will write checks. The whole thing benefits the charity, and at the same time, the locals get to have a fun night."

"I've never been, but it sounds like a great event," Josie said. "How could you use it?"

"I've been asked to introduce Cassidy and the youth center, which will give me the opportunity to discuss the needs of Coventry. I bought a couple of tables, and I'll invite a handful of my supporters. It'll be another opportunity to shake hands with people, get my picture in the paper."

"Farley will be there, of course."

"He'll be at all of this stuff," Thomas said.

Josie smiled. "You've got this all figured out. I don't think you need me at all."

He laughed. "Ha. I couldn't do any of this without you. I do think you're rubbing off on me, though."

A throat cleared, and Bentley entered. "Sorry to interrupt."

Great. The guy was back. Thomas had hoped he'd get caught up in Washington and never return. Still, he forced an amiable expression. "Bentley."

The man's eyebrows hiked. "Thomas." Then he looked at Josie. "Thought I'd find you here."

"We're in a strategy meeting. You need me for something?"

"Got information."

"Maybe we can talk about it—"

"Come on in," Thomas said. "If you don't mind my hearing it."

Bentley squinted and studied him as if looking for the catch.

Thomas was trying very hard to propose a truce without actually proposing a truce. Maybe if he made the first move, Josie would be impressed.

He'd do just about anything to impress her—even make nice with her ex.

Bentley pulled up a chair and joined them. "Did you learn anything about Mitchell?"

"A little," Josie said. "He's at a conference in Europe some-where." She shifted to Thomas. "Are you sure it's all right if we—?"

"Please." He hadn't asked what she'd been up to, figuring she'd tell him when she was ready. "I'd like to know what you've learned. So he's out of the country?"

"That doesn't mean he's not behind all this," Bentley said. "He has people."

"Makes sense," Thomas said, eliciting another curious look from the guy.

She pulled her laptop from her bag and opened it. "I can't find any connection between Mitchell and New Hampshire except the abortion clinic he owns in Nashua."

"This far north?" Bentley rubbed his chin. "He's expanding."

"I did a deep dive on the high-level employees there but found nothing concerning," she said. "I hired someone to look into Mitchell's finances. It looks like he's been buying up real estate in poor areas of the nation's larger cities where abortion will most likely remain legal. Not just New York, LA, and Chicago, but Sacramento, Denver, Las Vegas, Boston... He's purchased commercial property in twelve markets, and my source tells me he's in negotiations on another three. Altogether, he's on the hook for over a billion dollars in those properties."

Thomas whistled. "Holy smoke. How much money does this guy have?"

"The abortion industry's a cash cow," Bentley said. "For him—and a lot of people with a financial stake in the game—it's not about 'reproductive rights.' They're fighting for their right to rake in millions." He turned his attention to Josie. "If this bill doesn't pass this session, it'll be years before there's another chance. The slightest downturn in the economy before he unloads those properties... Mitchell could lose big time."

With a billion dollars on the line—not to mention what the man stood to gain if those commercial properties became his latest abortion clinics—Mitchell had all the incentive he needed to come after Senator Harrington. And Josie.

Josie snapped her laptop closed. "But knowing that doesn't help us stop him."

"Exactly," Bentley said. "Which is why I reached out to a contact at his organization, and she said—"

"Wait," Josie said. "What contact?"

"Someone I met a few months ago. Name's not important. We were at a fundraising event. After a couple of drinks, she started talking about the guy. I guess he's got quite the reputation for unseemly behavior."

"Meaning?" Josie asked.

"He's a little too familiar—and handsy—with his female employees. When women complain, their accusations are brushed aside. This woman told me that after she filed a complaint with HR, people she worked with—*women* she worked with—pressured her to retract her statement. Said that he does so much for women's rights that he should be afforded a little grace."

"Oh, come on," Josie said. "Someone actually said that to her?"

"More than one. She feared her job was on the line. Her reputation. There were no overt threats, but it was impressed upon her that if she didn't retract her statement, she'd have trouble getting another job."

"So the guy pushes for more abortions—to fill his own coffers—and then uses that as an excuse to sexually harass women?" Thomas couldn't keep the disgust from his voice. "What a pig."

Bentley barely glanced his way, but he nodded.

"What exactly does this woman do?" Josie asked.

Bentley shook his head. "Sorry. Can't say."

Josie's eyebrows hiked. "Okay. Tell me more about her."

"She was putting out feelers for a new job. I talked her into staying, told her I could use her help."

"She agreed to spy on her employer?" Josie asked.

He shrugged. "She really dislikes Mitchell."

"Or she really *likes* you."

Thomas wished he could see into Josie's thoughts, know what she was thinking. Her words, her tone—they didn't give enough away.

Bentley held her eye contact. "My affections are elsewhere."

"I wonder if she knows that."

"She does."

Josie studied him for a few moments, leaving Thomas to feel like a third wheel. He needed to get this tricycle back on track.

Because he wasn't about to slink out the door.

Thomas asked, "Everybody knows you work for Senator Harrington, right?"

Bentley's eyes narrowed.

"What if this woman got friendly with you to feed you misinformation?"

"It's not like that."

Josie looked from one to the other, her gaze settling on Bentley. "Thomas asks a good question, Bent. Are you certain?"

He held her eye contact, and something passed between them.

Thomas's jealousy spiked. He hated their connection. Hated how well they understood each other.

Seemingly satisfied, Josie asked, "So what did she have to say?"

"Mitchell's fighting mad about your father's refusal to support the bill. He's been breathing threats, Josie." Bentley lowered his voice. "Dangerous threats."

The expression on Bentley's face made Thomas's heart thump hard. "Like what?"

Bentley spared him a glance. "Like he knows what's important to the senator." He trained his gaze on Josie again. "He knows *who's* important to him."

Before the words settled, Josie said, "We already know he's willing to come after me. He's already shown his hand."

"He's not going to give up. He has until the session ends, meaning months, to get your father on board."

"Dad's not going to change his mind."

Bentley stood. "You and I should continue this conversation upstairs." To Thomas he added, "I'm sure you have work to do. You two can strategize later, right?"

Thomas rose. "I'll join you." He turned to Josie. "If that's all right."

"Yes, of course." She started for the inside staircase, the bodyguard by her side.

When her back was turned, Bentley shot Thomas a look that might've left a bruise, but Thomas forced a smile. If they were going to keep Josie safe, then they'd need to work together. He could do it, for Josie.

And if it meant he got to spend more time with her, all the better.

~

Since Bentley'd taken the spot beside Josie on the couch, Thomas chose the club chair catty-corner from her. When they were all settled, he spoke first. "What are you afraid this guy's going to do?"

"There's no telling." Bentley focused on Josie. "I wouldn't put anything past him. I honestly think... Your life could be in danger."

Thomas's stomach flipped at the words, but Josie scoffed.

"Oh, please. Mitchell's not going to have me killed. As if Dad would give in to his demands at that point. We have to keep his endgame in mind. He wants to get Dad to vote for the bill. Killing me wouldn't do that."

"Unless your father thought you were just the first. There's your brother and his family, your mother... And we both know..." Bentley eyed Thomas, then pressed his lips closed.

"Know what?" Thomas asked.

"Stay in your lane," Bentley snapped, keeping his eyes on Josie.

Thomas had to force himself not to toss the arrogant prig out the second-floor window.

But Josie seemed to take Bentley's side. Her voice was kind when she said, "We have history with Mitchell. He has good reason to target me."

"What reason?"

Bentley and Josie eyed each other but said nothing.

Lake was standing in the corner, and though her expression gave little away, Thomas caught a hint of frustration cross her features.

Both of them were trying to keep Josie safe. Having to do it in the dark didn't sit well. But Josie wouldn't tell him anything with Bentley in the room.

"Fine," Thomas said. "So Mitchell dislikes you, wants to target you." He addressed his question to Bentley. "Why do you think that means he'd actually harm her?"

Bentley spoke to Josie as if she'd asked the question. "You already know he's staked a fortune on getting this bill passed. There's a reason my contact retracted her statement. She's close enough to him to have seen how he deals with enemies. She wasn't only afraid for her job. She was afraid for her safety. According to her, he's still smarting over what happened... before." Bentley's lips screwed up, and his face reddened. "Even though you and I both know it was mostly *my* plan, he blames you. And he's looking for revenge."

Josie's face paled. "It was *our* plan."

Bentley ignored that. "Which is why..." He flicked a glance at Thomas. "Does he really need to be here for this? I think we should—"

"You can trust Thomas."

"I don't." Bentley heaved a breath. "I told your father this morning what my contact told me. We agree it's time for you to consider hiding. You and I could—"

"Forget it." She stood. "I'm not leaving."

Thomas stood as well. "Are you really using this as a ploy to win her back?"

Bentley glared. "As important as your desire is to date my *fiancée*—"

"I am not your fiancée."

Bentley flinched at her words but continued speaking to Thomas. "Her safety trumps—"

"Okay, wait a minute." Thomas lifted his hands and forced his frustration down. He faced Josie. "Let's take Bentley out of the equation." He met the other man's eyes, challenging him to argue.

Bentley nodded for him to continue.

Thomas settled back in his chair and waited for Josie to do the same. "Let's say we could find people to keep the café running while you're gone. When this is over, you can come back to it, resume your life here."

"I refuse to hide," Josie said.

"Then don't." As much as it pained him to agree with Bentley—and the idea of Josie being gone hurt even worse—Bentley wasn't wrong. "Take an extended trip. You and Shelly go somewhere out of the public eye, off the radar. Kick off your shoes and rest."

"For six months?" She sounded incredulous.

"It wouldn't be six months," Bentley said. "If the election goes the way we think it will, we're going to lose seats come November, and there's no way the bill will pass with a lame-duck Senate."

"So only five months." The words were doused in sarcasm. "That makes all the difference."

"Less than five," Thomas said. "Four and a half. Eighteen, nineteen weeks. A blink in the scheme of life."

"A *blink*? You consider five months *a blink?*"

Thomas held her eye contact. "I consider your life worth that and a lot more."

"That's because you're not the one being asked to leave everything behind."

"I would sacrifice that and more to keep you—"

"You're right." Bentley's words intruded like an armored tank. "I knew you wouldn't do it. Even if you did, Mitchell could find you no matter where you went. Unless you're willing to take your bodyguards with you—"

"And what would be the point of that?" Josie said "I have

them here. I'm just going to take my chances. Lake and Donley —and you guys… I feel safe with all of you."

"I knew you'd say that," Bentley said. "Which is why I told your father he should vote yes on the bill. It's the only real solution."

"He won't." Josie sat back, satisfied.

Bentley's lips slid to one side as he watched her. A moment passed before he reached out and took her hand.

Thomas clenched his fists to keep from knocking the guy away.

"Carlyle's on my side. Nobody wins if your father refuses to give in. Not you, not him, not the party."

She yanked her hand back. "The taxpayers win. Good wins."

"*Good* doesn't have a vote, and most of the taxpayers will never know the difference."

"If he votes in favor of it, he'll infuriate his constituents. He'll risk his seat."

"If he votes against the bill, the party's going to do everything in its power to make sure he loses his reelection bid. They can't let him get away with this. You know that. His political career will be over."

"That's up to Dad. His vote is up to him. I refuse to allow him to vote against his conscience in order to protect me. And I don't think he will."

Thomas didn't think so either, no matter what Bentley and Carlyle counseled him to do. Which meant there was nothing else to talk about.

Bentley regarded Josie for a long moment. But when Thomas expected him to concede her point and end the discussion, he only shifted.

"Then that leaves us with only one choice." He leaned

toward Josie, but she angled away as if she knew what was coming. "We have to go on the offensive."

"I can't." Her words were barely a whisper. "I won't do it again."

Everything in Thomas wanted to demand to know what they were talking about. But the way the color leached from Josie's face and the fear in her eyes kept him quiet.

Bentley stood. "Maybe you can't, but I can."

CHAPTER NINETEEN

Josie should have told Bentley to back off. She should have told him that she wouldn't have him using devious tricks in order to protect her. She should have told him that no vote, and no promise of safety, was worth what had happened the last time they'd played dirty.

But she hadn't said one word.

Because as much as she disliked alpha personalities, as much as she feared them, and as much as she distrusted them, they knew how to get the job done.

She'd forgotten that about Bentley. In her time in Coventry, sequestered away from all the people she'd been surrounded by all her life—Dad, Carlyle, Bentley, and others—she'd forgotten the simple fact that those on her side were no less powerful, no less willing to fight for what they believed in—using any means necessary—as those on the opposite side.

Just because she'd given up all those dirty tricks didn't mean everybody had. Jude Mitchell wasn't above playing them on her, and now Bentley had dived headfirst back into the game.

Which was why Josie had no plans, no desire, to ever reenter the world of politics.

It'd been nearly two weeks since Bentley had returned from DC. The conversation she'd had with Bentley and Thomas had been followed by one with her father, who'd assured her that, despite Carlyle and Bentley's recommendation, he didn't plan to capitulate to anybody's demands.

And then Dad had prayed for her safety right there on the phone, making Carlyle and Bentley incredibly uncomfortable. Which had been, honestly, a little amusing.

Unfortunately, it had also been nearly two weeks since Josie had enjoyed a good night's sleep, a night free of the nightmares she'd thought were behind her for good.

She'd spent those two weeks trying to find something, anything, she could use to connect the threats against her to Jude Mitchell. If she could prove he was trying to scare her to force her father's vote, she could threaten to go public with that information to get him to back off. If he didn't, then she'd be forced to call the newspapers.

That action would reveal her true identity to the people of Coventry, but if it meant she'd be safe and her father'd be free to vote his conscience, it would be a price worth paying.

The last two weeks had been difficult, no doubt. But they'd also been largely uneventful.

She hoped, prayed, that meant Mitchell had decided to back off. Maybe, when Dad hadn't capitulated to his demands, he'd realized he wouldn't be able to sway his vote. Maybe.

But Josie doubted it.

It was Saturday, the night before the first day of Liberty Fest, the last opportunity to get ready for Thomas's big announcement. Unfortunately, he'd been playing catch-up all day at work and wouldn't be able to come by until later.

Shelly lounged on the sofa in Josie's living room, back against the arm, one foot suspended above the floor, sipping a glass of red wine. Josie rarely drank, but her best friend was drinking enough for both of them lately, bringing a fresh bottle over every couple of days to enjoy during their dinners together. Despite their ongoing feud, when Bentley was there, he often poured himself a glass. When he wasn't, Shelly drank alone. Who knew how much she drank once she got back to Thomas's condo.

It was concerning. Josie fixed herself a glass of ice water and settled into the club chair adjacent to the sofa. "Does your new boyfriend like wine as much as you do?" Josie tried to ask the question as innocently as possible.

Shelly paused, glass halfway to her lips, and peered at her over the rim. By the look on her face, she knew what Josie was really asking but planned to let the question go unchallenged. She took a generous sip and swallowed. "He doesn't drink at all, which is probably why I'm going a little overboard now. He gives me a look"—she leveled a stare at Josie, who glanced away —"when he disapproves."

Obviously, that was not a line of questioning Shelly welcomed.

Lake sat on a kitchen chair she'd pulled near the door. No matter what they said—and Shelly had tested this theory often, spewing out the most outlandish remarks—Lake only reacted when she considered Josie's safety to be in question.

Josie changed tack. "What do you and he do for fun?"

Shelly's face lit up. "We don't get to spend nearly enough time together. When he's ready to introduce me to his kids, that'll change, but for now, we usually get together for long weekends when they're with their mother. We go to his vacation home sometimes, up in the Poconos. We spent a weekend on the beach once. Mostly, we just stay in, watch movies, sometimes go to dinner."

Though the guy claimed to be a Christian, if they were going away together, then he wasn't such a follower that it kept him from sleeping with his girlfriend.

Not that Josie should be throwing stones in that regard. Hadn't she claimed to be a Christian when she and Bentley were dating? Hadn't they moved in together after he proposed?

Talking the talk of Christianity was a lot easier than walking the walk.

"You two get to catch up very often?" Josie hadn't seen her friend talking on her cell much, but Shelly spent a lot of time tapping on the screen.

"We talk every night after he puts his kids to bed." Her eyes took on a dreamy look. "I miss him so much. I can't wait to see him again."

"When will he get back?"

"Two weeks," Shelly said. "His kids'll go to the ex's house, and he and I will have the second half of the summer to ourselves."

"What does he do for work that he can take so much time off?"

Shelly shrugged. "He owns his own business—something related to finance or investing. He works from home a lot." She swung her feet to the floor. "Enough about me, though. Let's talk about you and Thomas. You've been spending a lot of time together."

They had, an hour or so every afternoon, working through campaign issues. Shelly or Bentley or both generally attended those meetings, Shelly to help, Bentley to help protect her, or so he said.

Josie suspected his attendance was more about making sure Josie and Thomas were never alone.

What neither Bentley nor Shelly knew was that, every night after Thomas closed the office for the day—usually between seven-thirty and eight o'clock—he climbed her exterior staircase and knocked on her door. The first time he'd done it, the Monday after her false arrest, he'd said he wouldn't be able to sleep unless he knew Josie was safe for the evening.

The first few times, she'd been surprised by his knock.

By the fourth day, she'd found herself looking forward to it. Since then, she'd made sure to shoo Shelly and, when he was in town, Bentley out of her apartment early so she and Thomas could have time alone.

Not that anything had come of it.

She usually offered him something to eat. Sometimes he took her up on the offer, sometimes he didn't. He never stayed more than thirty minutes.

But those thirty minutes...

Just the thought of them had heat rising to her cheeks.

There was something incredibly attractive about a man who went out of his way to check on her every night. A man who'd moved out of his comfortable condo—and let a virtual stranger move in—in order to be available if she needed him.

A man who'd never once gone back on his vow to quit asking her out.

She wasn't sure what to think about that last one.

"Omigosh!" Shelly's shrill tone snapped Josie back to the moment. "You *like* him."

"What are you, twelve?"

Shelly giggled. "Oh, I don't think you like him the same way you liked Cody Finnegan in sixth grade."

"Wow." Josie sat back in her chair. "I haven't thought about Cody Finnegan in years." She pictured the middle school version of a tall, dark, and handsome bad boy. Cody'd been sent to the headmaster's office more than once for his antics. "I wonder what he's doing now."

"Computer programmer. He lives in Austin. Married with

three kids."

Josie laughed. "How do you know that?"

She shrugged. "I keep up with people. He's on social media. His wife's got a face for radio, but his kids are cute."

"You haven't changed one bit."

"You love that about me."

Josie smiled. Her friend knew her well.

Shelly drained her wine glass. "Don't think you've side-tracked me. What's the latest on you and Thomas?"

"There's no 'latest.' We're friends, that's all."

"Pfft." She stood and headed for the kitchen. "Whatever."

"Seriously."

Through the open door, Shelly called, "We both know he wishes he were more than a friend." She returned, her glass half full of dark red liquid. "Hasn't he asked you out yet? Because I can give him a little push."

"Don't even think about it." Josie leveled her friend with a look. "That's not what I want."

Shelly plopped back on the sofa. "Lie to yourself all you want, my friend, but I see that twinkle in your eye. Let me ask you this. If he were to ask you out, would you say yes?"

A fair question. Josie shrugged, but at Shelly's raised eyebrows, she said, "I would say yes. But it's not going to happen."

"I wouldn't be so sure about that."

"He promised he wouldn't ask me out again."

Her friend's already raised eyebrows practically disap-peared into her scalp. "Again? What is this?"

Josie shrugged. "He asked a few times over the last couple of months. But then, the night he carried me off the mountain, he promised he wouldn't ask again."

Shelly stared as if Josie'd just explained nuclear physics in pig latin. "You seriously made him promise not to—?"

"I didn't *make him*. He just did."

"Well then, I guess you're going to have to ask him."

Josie wasn't about to do that. She was a twenty-first century-woman and all that, but asking a man out felt desperate.

"Please tell me you're not letting Bentley stand in your way."

"No, not...really. I just..." How could Josie explain how she felt about Bentley to her friend? "He's working so hard to try to make things work with me. He even said he'd move here."

Shelly scrunched her face like the words had come with a rancid scent. "Do you want him to?"

She allowed herself to consider the question—seriously consider it.

If Bentley walked in the door at that moment and told her he'd bought a house in town, she would feel...

Trapped.

Stuck.

Because, the truth was, she didn't love Bentley, not anymore.

Now that she'd rededicated her life to Christ, she wondered if she'd ever loved him or if she'd just used him to fill a chasm of loneliness in her life that she now knew only God could fill.

"Where is the loser anyway?"

"Don't talk about him like that," Josie snapped. She'd had enough of Shelly's cutting remarks.

And his about her, for that matter. They'd never been great friends, but they'd tried harder before Josie had left DC, at least in front of her.

Josie went into the kitchen and started the water boiling for dinner. Thomas would be there soon.

Shelly stepped into the doorway and leaned against the jamb. "Sorry." A moment passed before she spoke again. "So, where is he?"

"He's spending all his spare time trying to keep me safe and protect my father. You might not like us together, but you can at least acknowledge what he's done, what he's doing."

Shelly's lips pressed together, and she looked away. "Fine." But then, she met Josie's eyes with a challenge. "He works for your father, so whether you two were together or not, he'd have to be doing what he's doing. It's his job. It's not for you."

"It's not *only* for me, Shelly. But it's also for me."

"Fine. Maybe."

"Why do you hate him so much?"

"I don't trust him. Never have. He's a gold-digging social climber, and you were an easy mark—daughter of a senator, wealthy and well-connected. He, meanwhile, came from redneck parents, went to college on a scholarship because they couldn't afford to send him otherwise."

"You don't like him because his parents are *poor*? Wow. Snobby much?"

"It's not that."

Tense silence stretched between them, but Josie wasn't about to fill it. Shelly'd dated her share of guys, many of whom hadn't come from their same social strata. Where did she get off judging Bentley? At least he wasn't abusive. At least he'd never attempted to empty Josie's bank account.

Could Shelly say the same about the yahoos in her past?

She added salt to the water, stared at it until tiny bubbles rose from the bottom, and admitted an ugly truth. She was judging Shelly as harshly as Shelly was judging Bentley. The two of them must have had a run-in, one neither had dragged Josie into. She didn't understand it, and maybe she was glad she didn't. She cared about them both. She didn't want to have to choose.

The water boiled, and she added linguine, then stirred to keep the noodles from sticking together.

"You know how guys like that are," Shelly finally said. "They're always looking for gain. Maybe Bentley came to love you, but he asked you out the first time because of who you are, not because of any feelings on his part."

Josie turned to face her. "You can't know that."

"I know, Jo. Trust me. I know."

"How?"

But Shelly just shook her head.

Her friend's refusal to answer—this woman who couldn't keep a secret to save a loved one's soul—had Josie's stomach turning.

Did Shelly know something about Bentley Josie didn't? And if so, why wouldn't she share it? Why not use it as ammo to get Josie to end things with Bentley once and for all?

Before she asked, a knock sounded.

Not that she wasn't excited for Thomas to arrive, but she wished she could question her friend, dig into that last comment.

She'd have to put that on her to-do list for another day. One way or another, she needed to figure out what had happened between her best friend and her ex, because the animosity between them was worse than ever. And there had to be a reason why.

Lake, the silent presence in the corner, peeked out the door. She turned to Josie. "Thomas."

Josie pretended her heart didn't get all aflutter at the sound of his name. "Let him in."

The bodyguard did, and Thomas stepped into the space. He usually wore a suit and tie, but tonight he had on a pair of jeans and a T-shirt that showed off all his muscles.

Not that Josie should notice such things.

"Sorry I'm so late. Someone called just when I was about to close up and wanted me to write a new auto policy." He shifted his gaze. "Hey, Shelly. Glad you're here."

"Oh, don't worry. I won't be staying long. I just wanted to hear your speech for tomorrow, and then I'll leave you two alone."

Thomas's gaze flicked to Josie, but she just shrugged. This was Shelly being Shelly. "The pasta will be done in a sec," Josie said. "What can I get you to drink?"

Ten minutes later, the three of them settled at the small kitchen table and shared linguine with fresh tomatoes, chunks of mozzarella, grated parmesan, basil, garlic, and olive oil. Josie had snagged a loaf of bread from the café, which rounded out the summer meal.

Thomas was four bites into it before he commented, his eyes wide when they met hers. "Wow. I was hungry, and this is delicious. Thank you."

Her cheeks warmed, and she lowered her gaze. "No problem." She turned to the bodyguard in the corner. "Lake, help yourself."

The woman crossed into the kitchen to make herself a plate, then returned to her chair by the door to eat.

Josie, Shelly, and Thomas talked and laughed throughout the meal, Shelly and Thomas trying to one-up each other with wild stories. Rather than participate in the verbal Olympics, Josie just listened, enjoying their easy comradery.

When the meal was over, they left the dishes for later and returned to the living area, where Thomas—obviously feeling self-conscious with the small audience—gave his announcement speech.

She'd never heard him speak in public, and though this wasn't *public*, per se, it was probably more awkward to speak in front of two than it would be to speak in front of a crowd the following day.

She'd been around politicians all her life. She'd heard some of the best, most well-trained public speakers on the planet, and yet when Thomas spoke, his tone was so genuine, his words so heartfelt, she wasn't sure she'd ever been as moved by a speaker.

When he finished, Shelly stood and clapped. "Omigosh, that was amazing!"

Shelly was the only person Josie knew whose dialog usually sounded like it should end with exclamation points.

"You were so good!" Shelly added. "How did you learn to do that?"

Thomas shrugged one shoulder, his gaze barely flicking to Shelly. He seemed to be waiting for Josie's reaction.

"That was outstanding."

Red crept up his neck, and his lips spread in a shy smile. "Really?"

"Oh, don't be so bashful!" Shelly rounded the coffee table to smack him playfully on the shoulder. "You know you're awesome."

"I'm sure I don't," he said, surprise clear in his wide eyes.

"I can't wait to see you in action tomorrow," Shelly added.

Thomas settled on the chair, and Josie didn't miss the worry in his expression when he spoke to her. "I think you should reconsider."

She leaned his way. "Be honest with me, Thomas. Do you not want me there because you're afraid I'm going to hurt your campaign?"

"No." The word came out fast, and she didn't doubt his sincerity. "Absolutely not."

"We covered that." Shelly focused on Josie as she settled beside her on the sofa again. "The best way to deal with bad publicity is to lean into it. It would be one thing if you were guilty, but no charges were filed. You did nothing wrong. If Thomas were to distance himself from you, it would make you look guilty, and him look guilty by association."

Josie knew her friend's argument. She hadn't been convinced until Bentley had tacitly agreed with her assessment with his offhand remark—*"Who cares if it's better for Thomas's campaign? This is about your safety."*

Thomas's expression, as always, broadcast no duplicity. "Of course I *want* you there, Josie. I just don't want you to put yourself in danger. It's not worth that."

"Except for church"—both Bentley and Shelly had gone, though neither had seemed particularly comfortable with it—"I haven't left this building since the arrest. Marcel's been managing the shopping. Kinsley won't even let me meet the delivery trucks. If I don't get out of this place, I'll go stir-crazy."

"There's the dinner tomorrow night," Thomas said. "It should be easier to protect you there." He looked at Lake for confirmation.

The woman said, "We can keep you safe at both events, ma'am. We've got it covered."

Thomas looked pleased, but like he was fighting it. The man really needed to work on those facial expressions.

"I'm going to see your big speech," Josie said. "No arguments."

"And you'll come to the fundraiser tomorrow night?" he confirmed.

"Oh, she'll be there, and she'll look fa-bu-lous!" Shelly stood. "You did a great job, Thomas. No kidding." She leaned down and kissed Josie on the cheek. "Thanks for dinner. Thomas, you'll help Josie with the dishes, right?"

"Of course."

"Good, good. See you tomorrow at the park. Break a leg and all that!" Shelly slipped out the door and closed it behind her.

Leaving them, aside from the silent bodyguard, all alone.

CHAPTER TWENTY

T homas stared at the closed door a moment while the air settled after the whirlwind that was Josie's closest friend. "She is a unique soul."

Josie was clearing the table. "That's one way to put it."

He chuckled and turned to Lake, whose plate was empty on her lap. "May I?"

"Thanks." The woman stood and handed it to him. She was as tall as Thomas and had a killer body, but she seemed to have all the personality of a jar of mayonnaise.

Or maybe it was her job to hide her personality behind that mask. He'd seen enough of Shelly's attempts to get a rise out of the bodyguard to know she was unflappable. Donley at least would crack a smile every now and then.

Thomas grabbed the rest of the dishes off the table and joined Josie in the kitchen, where she was already elbow-deep in soapy water.

"How do you survive without a dishwasher?"

She glanced his way. "It's usually just me, and I eat half my meals in the café."

He tore a paper towel from the roll and leaned beside Josie

to wet it from the spigot, trying very hard to ignore the way his every nerve buzzed at her closeness.

As he'd done a thousand times since he'd carried her off that mountain, he kicked himself for telling her he wouldn't ask her out again. Now that they were getting to know each other, he got the distinct impression she liked him.

And his admiration for her had only grown stronger.

But a promise was a promise. If they were ever going to move from friendship to dating, she was going to have to ask him out.

Would she, though?

He wanted to linger beside her, but he forced himself to return to the table in the living area to wipe it down. That task completed, he grabbed a towel and started drying dishes and putting them away.

He knew where everything went. He came over every evening to check on her, and more often than not, she offered him dinner. Not that he needed to eat her food, but he'd jump at any excuse to remain in her presence. He'd need to offer to bring dinner for her this week.

Josie handed him a wet plate. "You feel ready for tomorrow?"

"I do," he said. "If you and Shelly think the speech was okay—"

"It was perfect."

Her praise sent warmth to his neck that had nothing to do with the steam rising from her sink. "That means a lot coming from you."

She handed him the big pasta bowl. "What do you mean, coming from me?"

"I'm sure you've met and worked with great politicians and speakers. If you think I'm halfway decent—"

"You're much more than *halfway* decent, Thomas." She

handed him the pasta pot, shut off the water, and drained the sink before turning to face him. "You're completely decent, which is why your speech was so good."

"What do you...?" His words trailed, and he dried the item as what she'd said registered.

She took the pot from him and shoved it in the cabinet. "I've worked with a lot of slick politicians. You're right about that. I've seen my share of people who'll say anything and do anything to get elected. My father is a great man, but you don't survive in national politics as long as he has without making compromises."

"That's the job, though, right? To work with people, to find solutions. We all have to make compromises."

Josie leaned against the kitchen counter. "Yeah, it's the job. And when the stakes are as high as they are now, Dad sticks to his guns. I love that. But he hasn't always made the right choices. His party's asked him to vote for some pretty lousy legislation, and he's done it to keep the peace, to stay in office. And my grandfather, my great-grandfather..." She turned to wipe the countertop. "They were both politicians too. My great-grandfather voted against the civil rights bill. My grandfather fought busing as fervently as he fought the communists in Vietnam. He believed, wholeheartedly believed, that races shouldn't mix at all. That they should stay segregated. That interracial marriage was evil."

Whoa. That was ugly.

"They were good men in their own ways," Josie said, "but they were wrong. So incredibly *wrong*. They did a lot of compromising in their time—not all of it the aboveboard stuff you and I are talking about. Carlyle's dad worked for my grandfather, and he's told me a lot of stories—of corruption and secret deals..." She shook her head. "Anyway, my dad's not like them, thank God. He's done so much to try to make up for his family legacy. But it's not a great legacy."

"That's not you, though," Thomas said. "You're not like that."

"My parents raised Alton and me with high ideals. We had a lot of money, but they drilled into our heads that, since we were blessed, it was our job to bless others. They also taught us to see everyone as equal. They raised us to believe there are two races that matter, and those races have nothing to do with skin color. There are those who don't believe in Jesus and those who do. As Mom would say, 'seed of Adam and seed of Christ.' And whichever race a person belongs to, God loves him just the same. So those seed-of-Adam folks are only in that race because they don't yet understand Jesus's sacrifice."

"That's a unique way to look at the world."

"My dad agrees, but Mom's the spiritual rock in our family."

Thomas's parents were both strong believers, but Dad had always been the head of their household in spiritual matters. He hoped to be the same someday.

"I respect my dad so much," Josie continued, "but he's made a lot of compromises in his life, not just in the ways he votes but in the people he has working for him. The staff did things..." She shook her head and pasted on a smile. "Anyway, the point is that your speech was so good because you aren't just saying the words. You believe them. You mean them."

"I do. But the speech was also good because you helped me craft it and coached me on what to do with my hands and all the other little things I would never have thought of."

"That's just window dressing."

Department stores decorated their windows to get people to step in the doors.

Thomas was pretty sure the "window dressing" would be a huge reason why people looked beyond his suit to hear his ideas.

"Maybe so." He stepped a little closer to her in the small kitchen. "But I'm grateful to you for it. If I have any shot at winning this race, it'll be because of you."

"Oh. Well..." She blinked at him with those big, brown eyes, and the air shifted.

Something stretched between them like a band, drawing them together.

It took all his self-control not to step closer, to pull her into his arms. Because he loved their friendship, he did. But he wasn't satisfied with it. It was just the top layer of the depth of relationship he wanted with this woman.

Her lips parted, inviting. Her gaze held his.

He didn't move for a long moment, but she didn't step closer.

So he ignored the desire pumping in his veins, swallowed the words aching to be said, and stepped back. "Thanks for dinner."

She looked away. "Right. Sure. Of course."

"And for all your help on the campaign." He stepped out of the warm kitchen and into the cooler living area, thankful for the air conditioning pumping. Not that the heat he was feeling had much to do with the room's temperature.

He didn't turn to face Josie until he'd crossed to the far wall. The living room was safer than the kitchen. He probably wouldn't give in to the urge to kiss Josie with Lake there.

Probably.

Still, it seemed wise to leave before he did something stupid.

"Dinner was delicious, as—"

Someone knocked on the door.

Thomas started to open it, but Lake stopped him with a hand on his wrist.

"Who is it?" the woman asked.

"Bentley."

Thomas's heart sank. He should have kissed Josie when he'd had the chance. He should have kissed her and still been kissing her when the ex showed up. Because Bentley wouldn't have let a little thing like a promise stop him.

Lake turned to Josie, whose gaze flicked between them. She nodded, and Lake pulled the door open.

Bentley stepped inside, eyes squinted and focused on Thomas. "What are you doing here?"

Before Thomas could formulate a scathing reply, Josie said, "We were going over his speech for tomorrow."

"And having dinner." Thomas probably shouldn't have added that, but the words slipped out. Thomas waited for Bentley's cutting answer. What he saw surprised him.

Pain crossed his face so fast, Thomas would have missed it if he hadn't been studying him so closely.

Not for the first time since he'd met Josie's ex-fiancé, Thomas faced the fact that Bentley loved her. He loved her, and he wanted her back.

The problem was, Thomas wanted her too. He didn't have the same strength of feelings for Josie as Bentley did, not yet. But he knew the feelings were growing. He believed he and Josie could be happy together.

Josie could never be happy with Bentley again, not in his world, not with the life they used to have together.

Or maybe Thomas just wanted to believe that.

The two men stared at each other. Thomas didn't know what to say. Bentley didn't seem to either.

Josie crossed the floor. "Did you just get back?"

When Bentley turned to her, his whole face smiled. "I missed you."

"Oh. Um—"

"I'd better go." Thomas focused on her. "You'll be there?"

"Twelve o'clock. I'll be near the front."

"Wait." Bentley looked between them. "Be where?"

Thomas let Josie field that, not that Bentley shouldn't already know. He'd listened in on enough of their campaign meetings this week.

"Thomas is announcing his candidacy tomorrow at the opening ceremony of the Fourth of July celebration."

"You're not *going*, though, right?"

Josie straightened. "Of course. I'm going."

"What? No, no way." Bentley turned to Lake. "It's outside, right? How can you keep her safe?"

"We've got it worked out, sir."

"Worked out? Worked..." He rounded on Thomas. "You'd put her in danger just to—"

"I won't be in danger," Josie said.

Thomas didn't blame Bentley for his concern. "I suggested she shouldn't go."

Josie spoke to Lake. "Will you explain, please?"

"Nobody will expect it," the bodyguard said. "We'll be there less than thirty minutes. Donley and I will both be on hand to make sure she's safe, and I've alerted the local police about our plans. If someone were trying to assassinate her, we would play this differently, but that's not what's going on here. Whoever broke into her car and planted those drugs wants to embarrass her, maybe cause a scandal. We should be able to keep that from happening. We'll keep her safe."

Bentley listened closely, nodding. But when Lake was through, he stepped closer to Thomas. "If anything happens to Josie, I'll hold you responsible."

Thomas clenched his fists, fighting the urge to use them. "Back off."

"It's my choice," Josie said. "If anything happens to me, you should hold *me* responsible."

The man took a step back as her words registered, but he didn't look away.

Though tempted to smack that look off his face, Thomas nodded to the door. "I was on my way out. If you'll move aside..."

Bentley did.

Thomas aimed a smile Josie's way. "If you change your mind about tomorrow—"

"I'll see you there. You're going to do great."

He moved to pass Bentley, who *accidentally* shifted into his path. Thomas *accidentally* bumped the man's shoulder before he stepped out the door.

The perfect evening should have ended with a kiss. Instead, Josie would spend the rest of it with her ex.

Who was absolutely right about tomorrow.

Josie would take a risk to attend the speech. The dinner tomorrow night would be different, safer, and more easily controlled. But the speeches would be held in the park, in the open.

Anything could happen.

Thomas had tried to talk her out of attending, but had he tried hard enough? God help him, he wanted her there more than he wanted to do well on his announcement. More than he wanted to win the election. More than anything, he wanted Josie by his side.

But if anything happened to her, Bentley wouldn't be the only one to hold Thomas responsible.

He'd never forgive himself.

Thank God it'd cooled off now that the sun had fallen below the trees.

Thomas still felt overwhelmed by the support he'd received in response to his formal announcement for mayor that afternoon. His speech had been succinct and well-crafted, and his delivery...not bad.

Okay, he could admit to himself that it was the best speech he'd ever given in his life. Not that he'd done much public speaking, but he'd done his share. Thanks to the help of two very capable women—mostly Josie, but Shelly had done her part —he'd managed to hold the audience's attention, his own focus traveling over the crowd and more than once landing on the beautiful woman near the front. Whenever he'd locked gazes with Josie, he'd soaked up the confidence in her smile.

As important as that speech had been, this evening's was probably even more so. At the opening ceremony, he'd spoken to locals, business owners, and public employees. He needed their votes, no doubt. But tonight, he'd be speaking to a different kind of crowd, people who didn't hesitate to pull out their wallets for a hundred-plus-dollar-a-plate dinner. These were the people who could fund his campaign.

People who could make or break him.

And many of them might be leaning toward supporting Farley, who'd painted himself as a friend to business.

Thomas had memorized the speech he and Josie had written, but he'd jotted the high points on note cards, just in case he froze under pressure.

He stood at the edge of the stage, gazing out at the huge crowd in the clear tent on the grounds of the lakeside park. The decorating committee had done a great job. Each supporting pole was wrapped with garland, the flowers similar to those in the fancy centerpieces on each of the twenty-five tables that ringed the dance floor. White lights twinkled overhead, along with a disco ball that would surely begin spinning when the band got going.

None of that held Thomas's attention, though. He'd gotten pulled into conversations all day, which had made him late. He'd run home to shower and change into his tux for the evening festivities. He hadn't planned to meet Josie and Shelly before the speeches, but it felt weird that he hadn't greeted them when they'd arrived.

They were there, weren't they? Josie and Shelly, and of course Bentley, who was worried for her safety, along with the two bodyguards. They had to be somewhere.

Farley was onstage, and Thomas should really be listening to what the interim mayor had to say, but he was distracted, searching the crowd. The two tables he'd sponsored were supposed to be near the front. Thomas shifted to get a better angle, and...

There Josie was, at a table on the far side of the room, Shelly on her left, Bentley on her right. Lake stood a few feet away against one of the poles. All the tent sides had been pulled back to let the breeze in, so the enclosed venue he'd imagined wasn't as enclosed as he'd hoped. But Lake was scanning the crowd.

A perimeter rope had been set up around the tent to keep out anybody who hadn't paid for a ticket, so nobody should get in who wasn't meant to be there.

Donley stood near the entrance, his back to another pole. Other police officers ringed the area. Thomas was surprised to see Rich Fontier, Zack's partner and Thomas's old friend.

Josie should be safe.

He prayed so. If anything happened to her...

The audience clapped, signaling that the mayor had finished his speech. The emcee, Andrew Middleton, thanked him, made a few jokes, and then...

"I'd like to welcome Thomas Windham to the stage. Thomas, come on up."

Thomas's stomach filled with acid, but he sent up a quick

prayer, smiled at the crowd, climbed the steps, and shook Andrew's hand.

"Knock 'em dead." Andrew was new to Coventry, one of the guys who went to Braden's on Monday nights. He spoke the words low as he clapped Thomas on the shoulder.

"Let's hope nobody has to die," he responded just as quietly.

Andrew chuckled as he jogged down the steps.

"Ladies and gentlemen..."

Thomas launched into his speech, which was mostly an introduction to Cassidy Sullivan, the director of the youth center and another of his friends. He peppered his remarks with comments about Coventry, what was good for the town—and what wasn't. His speech was touching, he hoped, mentioning a few of the kids Cassidy's organization helped. It was challenging, encouraging the listeners to not just give money, but to give of their time and talents to the town's youth. And it was light-hearted, eliciting a few laughs. He painted a picture of the Coventry where he'd grown up and the Coventry where he hoped to raise a family someday.

Again, thanks to Josie, it was an excellent speech, and Thomas grew in confidence as he delivered it.

When he finished with, "It's my great pleasure to introduce Cassidy Sullivan," the crowd rose in applause.

Thomas stepped back and waited for Cassidy to join him on the stage. She looked gorgeous, the little bit of weight she still carried since the birth of her baby only enhancing her features. She joined him behind the podium, took his hands, and kissed his cheek. "Thank you." When she backed away, tears shimmered in her unusual blue-green eyes.

He squeezed her hands. "You got this."

The crowd was still applauding when Thomas descended the steps.

He should probably find his table, but he was too hyped to sit.

The speech earlier had been the best of his life...until tonight's.

That...that had been the best speech he'd ever given. And the crowd's applause, which had been polite for the mayor, continued. Of course they were applauding to welcome Cassidy, but still, his speech had elicited that support.

Thomas paced into the darkness behind the tent, thankful for the stage's backdrop that hid him, and whispered fervent thanks to God. The night breeze off the lake cooled his skin, though his heart continued to race. Pockets of people were gathered on the grounds. Scents of grilling food and the sound of laughter floated from the beach, where a couple of kids still splashed in the dark waters, their parents watching from the shore.

This was his town. These were his people. He'd never felt more a part of them. He'd never wanted to protect them more. And thanks to that speech, thanks to Josie, he might be able to do just that.

A figure came around the stage.

Josie.

He barely registered Lake a few feet behind.

Josie wore a silver dress with spaghetti straps, fabric resting on her upper arms in some new style. The dress fell over all her beautiful curves and skimmed the ground. The spiky silver heels were probably unwise after her sprained ankle, but she looked as at home in them as she did in the tennis shoes she wore for work. Most of her brown hair was pulled back, little wisps of it curling by her face. In her expression, he saw her joy. Her pride—in him.

Everything else faded away as she neared.

He opened his arms.

He'd only meant to hug her. That was what he told himself. But he lowered his head, and she lifted hers, and their lips met. She tasted sweet, like heavenly lemonade.

His hands slid against her cheeks, into the hair at her nape, hair he'd wanted to touch for months. It was soft, sliding silkily through his fingers.

The heat of her body warmed him through his tuxedo.

Everything about her spoke to everything in him.

He backed her closer to the stage's wall, shielding her from the view of passersby, and deepened the kiss, holding her against him until his body threatened to explode with desire.

And then he dove deeper.

He could keep kissing Josie for the rest of his life. Forever and ever and ever.

And Josie responded. Her hands sliding around his neck, pulling him closer.

This wasn't just a kiss. It was a connection. It was magic. It was everything.

Somewhere, firecrackers pop-pop-popped, and the spell was broken.

No, not broken. But he realized where he was, what he was doing. Who might be watching. Not that he cared, but she might.

He slowed down, gently ending the kiss, then held her against his chest, knowing and not caring that she'd be able to hear the racing of his heart.

He hoped she'd had half the reaction to that as he had.

Because that kiss had sealed it for him. He'd known he was attracted to Josie. Known he liked her.

But this...this was something new. Something different. Something...perfect.

CHAPTER TWENTY-ONE

Josie kept her ear pressed against Thomas's chest, listening to his racing heart.

She'd come to find him, to tell him what a good job he'd done.

She'd never expected...

She couldn't even name it. It wasn't the kiss that had rocked her world off-kilter.

It was...it was all of it. It was Thomas.

This man. This handsome, talented, wonderful man.

In the back of her mind, it registered that they were in public, though hidden in the shadow of the tent and the back of the stage.

Lake was probably just a few feet away, scanning the park for threats. Donley was somewhere nearby.

Somebody out there was plotting to use her to force her father's hand. Maybe plotting revenge, revenge she absolutely deserved.

But eclipsing all of those facts was the man who still held her close. The man who'd kissed her.

The man she'd wanted to keep kissing forever.

He chuckled, the sound low in his chest. "If you ever want to do that again…"

He let the words trail, and she leaned away to see his face. She couldn't make out much in the darkness besides the whites of his dancing eyes.

"What?"

"There's only one solution." He lowered his mouth to her ear, his words rumbling through her, sending tingles to her fingertips, her toes. "You're going to have to ask me out."

She shivered with pleasure and desire. "Am I?"

He straightened. "A promise is a promise, Ms. Smith."

"Maybe you shouldn't make promises you don't want to keep, Mr. Windham."

"Believe me, I've been telling myself that for weeks."

"Hmm." She settled against his chest again. "I'll take that under advisement. Meanwhile, we should go back before people start to talk."

He tightened his hold on her. "Let's just stay here until you work up your nerve. I'm in no hurry."

She leaned away again. "Now?"

"I'd love to, but I have a prior engagement. Maybe next weekend?"

She smacked his shoulder. "That wasn't what I meant."

"Okay." He pulled her close again.

"Thomas, we need to go inside."

"If that wasn't what you meant, then you'd better hurry up and ask."

She'd never asked a man on a date. And despite the mind-blowing kiss they'd just shared, she didn't feel comfortable doing so now.

What if…?

What if what? She knew how he felt.

As if reading her mind, Thomas whispered against her ear. "I have my answer ready. Spoiler alert—it's yes."

She swallowed her stupid, childish fear and leaned back to face him. "Thomas, will you go on a date with me?"

She expected a yes. Maybe a chuckle, or even a triumphant fist-pump.

She did not expect him to lift her off her feet and swing her in a circle.

She laughed. "Are you crazy? Put me down!"

He did, pulling her close once more. "Anytime, anywhere."

She wasn't sure about the when or the where yet, but she was pretty settled on the *what*.

A quiet restaurant with no Shelly and no Bentley, no talk of danger or politics or any of it. Just the two of them, together.

"One more thing," he said.

She felt very comfortable resting against his chest again. "What's that?"

"Will you let me off the hook on that promise? I'd like to be able to reciprocate."

"Consider the hook removed and tossed away."

"Good." He stepped back and held out his hand. "May I escort you to the dinner, Ms. Smith?"

She glanced at his hand, thought of Bentley.

Bentley, who wanted her back.

Bentley, whose heart would be crushed.

She rubbed her lips together, shook her head. "I need to talk to him."

Thomas didn't ask who she meant. The joy leached from his face, but he nodded. "Should we return from opposite sides of the tent? Are we pretending that—?"

"No, no. We can walk in together. I just... I don't want to hurt him."

She expected a smart comment from Thomas about her ex,

but he only nodded. "I understand. Why don't you return with Lake? I'm going to go for a quick walk, try to cool off. I'll see you in a minute."

"Fair enough."

But just when she was going to pull away, he took her hand. "I expect Shelly to relinquish her seat for me."

Josie giggled, sounding more like her friend than she usually allowed. "Don't worry. I'm sure that's her plan."

She swiveled and met Lake, who walked beside her silently around the stage and toward the table. She appreciated the woman's quiet disposition. The last thing she wanted at that moment was to chat.

Or to return to the party, but at least Thomas would be joining her soon.

Until then, she'd try very hard not to let on what had happened, though Shelly would guess within seconds.

Maybe Bentley too. Because a kiss that earth-shattering left signs. Josie could never un-experience feelings that Thomas's kiss had raised inside her.

Feelings she'd never experienced, not with Bentley, not with any man.

She wanted to explore those feelings. She wanted to explore a lot of things related to Thomas Windham.

CHAPTER TWENTY-TWO

By the time Thomas stepped beneath the clear tent, Cassidy had finished her speech and the band had assembled. Dinners had been served—though Thomas had missed that portion of the evening, pacing nervously behind the stage. But Josie'd held onto a couple of dinner rolls and ensured one of the pieces of chocolate cake remained on the table for him. He was grateful for the sustenance.

They'd enjoyed one dance, one perfect slow dance. Well, it would have been perfect if not for all the other people there.

He'd caught more than one person taking their photo, including a reporter at the local paper. With Josie outshining every other woman at the party in that dress, he had no doubt the photo would end up in the newspaper.

That she'd want to be with Thomas, that she'd kissed him... With all the good things—the two speeches, the applause, the feedback he'd gotten from townspeople—the highlight was Josie.

He wanted to dance with her all night long, but he needed to spend the evening visiting with guests, getting to know them, letting them get to know him. He already knew a lot of them, but he'd never spoken to most of them about the future of

Coventry. As he moved from table to table and talked with people over the music, he learned what locals wanted and hoped for, how they felt about the changing culture of their town. He filed away the ideas and worries and concerns to discuss with Josie later that week, hoping to address them in his campaign positions.

He'd reached the farthest corner of the tent and was seated at a table with a group of older folks. One woman was giving him an earful not just on local politics but about state and national concerns as well.

Not that he didn't care, but as the mayor of a small central New Hampshire town, he wasn't exactly sure how he could solve the immigration issue.

He caught sight of a certain gorgeous woman in a silver dress spinning on the dance floor with an irritating political strategist.

They looked good together. They looked like they'd danced together a lot. And not just the spin-in-a-slow-circle dancing Thomas could manage, but real dancing with actual coordinated steps.

Thomas did his very best not to watch. Or glare. Or growl under his breath

Josie could dance with Bentley. Of course she could. That didn't mean she loved him. That didn't mean she wanted him.

When they waltzed by a second time—was Bentley moving closer to make sure Thomas saw?—he noticed that neither of them looked particularly happy.

Hmm.

Maybe Josie was telling him...

"...have to stop the influx of drugs at the border," the woman was saying. "They're killing our kids."

Thomas forced his gaze back to the octogenarian who seemed to have more energy than he did. He was usually better about attending to the task at hand, not getting sidetracked. "You're absolutely right about that. I'm not sure—"

But she didn't need his input. She cut him off and kept going. He nodded and hmm'd at all the right places.

When another woman inserted herself into the conversation, Thomas shifted to speak with her. Ah, these were the Eatons, Tabby's parents. He'd known them as long as he could remember.

"You have my vote, Thomas," Mrs. Eaton said. "And not only for all those reasons Lola just mentioned. You've always been a really good boy. Why you and my Tabby never got together, I'll never understand."

"Good thing we didn't," Thomas said. "Fitz would be lost without her."

Mrs. Eaton waved that off. "You're right, of course. I wasn't sure about that one, moving my baby all the way to Rhode Island." Her tone dripped with derision, as if she spoke of terrorists or biological warfare. "But now that they're back, I guess he's all right."

Thomas worked hard not to smile, considering she was dead serious. Fortunately, Tabby hadn't let her mother's opinions drive her, or she'd never have taken that two-week vacation and met the love of her life.

"I'm supporting you because I trust you," Mrs. Eaton said. "That Farley fellow, he's got a wife and a couple of kids—and a girlfriend on the side, from what I hear. I know you'd never embarrass the town like that. You're never going to do anything to bring shame on us."

Beside her, Mr. Eaton, the quieter of the two, nodded. "If his own wife can't trust him, why should we?"

"Exactly," Mrs. Eaton said. "But you...you're an upstanding citizen."

"Thank you, ma'am. I try my best." Thomas had heard the

rumors about Farley and his mistress as well. He and Josie had worked hard to paint Thomas in an entirely different light, as a man everybody could trust. Despite the fact that he didn't have a family, they'd used language to hint that Thomas was a family-oriented, godly man.

She added, "You need to get yourself married, though. Post haste."

Thomas's gaze moved to where Josie and Bentley were exiting the floor—though the song still played. He couldn't help but grin. As he turned back to the older couple, he caught sight of Shelly and Rich chatting in the corner. Rich was in uniform tonight, acting as security for the party. Shelly didn't seem to mind that she was taking his attention off his duties.

Thomas forced his attention back to Mrs. Eaton. What had she said? Oh, yeah. "I'm working on securing the bride. Say a prayer for me, would you? I've got tough competition."

The woman nodded solemnly, as if he'd asked her to solve world peace. "I will be praying, for the election and the girl."

It was another thirty minutes before Thomas finished making the rounds, feeling buoyed by the promises for support and campaign contributions. It seemed all their work preparing for this event would pay off. Thomas had a shot, a real shot, at winning the election in November.

Somebody had closed most of the sides on the tent to keep out the cool night air, which made the area feel smaller, cozier—and more secure. He headed to the tables he'd reserved in the front. They each sat eight, so he'd offered tickets to his employees and their spouses and a few of his friends. Garrett and Aspen had joined them, as had Braden and Carly. Most had wandered off, though. A few danced, others huddled around the bar, talking.

All in all, the fundraiser seemed a rousing success. As happy as he was for the youth center, which would surely get its game room, and as happy as he was about all the promises of support he'd received for his campaign, his big win had come in the form of a beautiful woman in his arms.

And a kiss he'd never forget.

He felt the big, stupid smile on his face as he caught sight of Josie. She was seated at the table, alone. Lake stood a few feet behind her. Thomas glanced at the dance floor, where Bentley and Shelly were dancing.

Huh. Could they call a truce long enough to last an entire song? Shelly was jabbering, and Bentley may have been listening, though he didn't wear even a hint of a smile.

Interesting.

Thomas slid into the chair beside Josie. "I thought I'd never get back to you."

Her lips tipped up. But there was something...off about the expression. "Hey...you."

The words were drawn out, flirty, which wasn't like her at all.

"You all right?"

"I'm soooooo good." She leaned toward him, propping her elbow on the table. But it slipped off, and she fell toward him.

He caught her and settled her back in her chair. "Josie, what's wrong?"

"I've never felt better." Her words were slurred. "We should kish again. Let's kish..."

He gripped her shoulders and set her back so he could look in her eyes. "Have you been drinking?"

She waved toward a glass. "Jus' Dr Pepper. I must be drunk on you, Thomash." She giggled. "I mean Thomash."

He settled Josie back in her chair and sniffed the drink she'd indicated.

Smelled like Dr Pepper.

He got Lake's attention and waved her over.

The woman approached, the serious look she always wore morphing into concern. "What's going on?"

"Has Josie been drinking?"

"I jush tol' you..." Josie's words were coming too slowly, very slurred. "I only ha' pop."

Lake's eyes narrowed to slits. "I haven't seen her drink anything alcoholic."

Thomas took Josie's shoulders again. Her eyes were closing.

"Open your eyes, sweetheart."

She did. Her pupils were dilated. If she hadn't been drinking, then... "Somebody drugged her." Rage, hot and sticky, poured over him. While he'd been glad-handing supporters, somebody had...what? Slipped something into her drink?

Lake, Donley, Bentley, Shelly... None of them had protected her.

But neither had Thomas.

"Get the others," he snapped. "I'm taking her out of here."

"Don't move." Lake touched an earpiece. "Donley, we've got a problem."

Thomas drowned out the rest of the bodyguard's words. He crouched and slid a hand behind Josie's back. "Okay, sweetheart. We're going for a walk, okay?"

She stood, unsteady. "You're sho cute. You should wear tuxeses all the time." She tipped, swayed. "Whoa." She met his eyes. "Why is the room moving? I don't like it."

He held her close to his side. "Try to walk with me, okay?"

"Are we gonna kish?"

"We just have to get out of the tent. There'll be plenty of time for kissing later." He hoped. He prayed. But who knew what had been slipped to her. He helped her take a step, but on the second, she stumbled. He barely kept her from falling.

"Oooh!" The sound came out too loud, and people turned to look.

Thomas allowed himself a quick scan of the area. He saw friends with concerned expressions.

Others with disapproving ones.

A few were taking photos.

Photos.

Of course, that was what this was about. The man had to be out there, somewhere, the one who'd worn the red cap. Any minute now, the senator would receive evidence of this moment in a text message.

The exit was all the way at the opposite end. Thomas would take her out the other back exit, but he'd still have to cross in front of the stage—and the band playing there. And all the spectators.

"Try to stand up straight, sweetheart."

Josie turned to him, eyes wide and blinking. "I don't feel..." Her legs gave out beneath her.

Thomas scooped her into his arms, barely keeping her from landing on the grass. Forget the stage exit and the back exit. He locked eyes with Lake. "Move the plastic aside." Thomas knew where the ambulance was. He needed to get her there, now.

Because somebody'd slipped her something, a whole lot of something.

It might wear off.

It might kill her.

Lake slid aside the heavy plastic wall nearest their table, then stepped out and scanned the park, one hand held out to stop him from following.

Thomas wanted Josie to be safe, of course.

He also wanted out of the now-stifling air in the plastic tent.

He tried not to notice the people who'd stopped to stare. The cameras lifted. The murmurs that rose above the bluesy music.

He gazed down at Josie, whose playful expression had

morphed into something else—frightened and drowsy. "Wha's happening?" She'd lost color. Her skin looked pasty and moist. Her eyes were wide, her pupils unnaturally large. "I don' feel good."

"I know, sweetheart." *Please, don't let her throw up.* He didn't care about the tux. He cared about the images, the videos that were sure to be circulating all over town by morning. Josie didn't deserve the judgment she'd surely receive after this.

Donley appeared at Thomas's shoulder.

Thomas said, "Tell the police. Her glass—the Dr Pepper. Have them test the contents. We might need to know what she was slipped."

"Already talked to 'em. They're on it."

Thomas glanced back at the table, where Rich was snapping on plastic gloves. Good. Excellent.

"We're going out now," Donley said. "You got her?" At Thomas's nod, Donley stepped through the opening in the tent wall. Thomas slipped out into the chilly evening and jogged toward where the ambulance had been parked all day.

Except the ambulance wasn't there. Maybe they'd been called away. Maybe they'd only planned to stay until most of the events were finished. In any event, Thomas was on his own.

Behind him, Bentley shouted, "Hey, what happened?"

Thomas didn't slow his pace, but he yelled, "Find the guy taking the photos. You've heard the description—"

"You've *seen* him." Bentley fell in step beside him. "Let me take her. You go find the guy."

"You have medical training I don't know about?"

"I can take her to—"

"She's been drugged, Bentley, who knows with what. If her heart stops, you know how to do CPR? You know how to keep her alive?"

Thomas glanced long enough to see the color blanch from the man's face. "Right. Okay."

"Six feet, one-eighty. He's gotta be here. Blond hair."

Bentley turned back toward the party, but Thomas figured it was too late. The guy'd gotten the photos he needed. Now, he was long gone.

Shelly managed to catch up with them, her high heels dangling from her hand. "I'm staying with you."

"Maybe you could help look for—"

"I'm staying with her," Shelly snapped.

In his arms, Josie reached out toward the woman's voice. "My frien..." But her voice faded.

She passed out in his arms.

CHAPTER TWENTY-THREE

The world was spinning, sliding, swaying. Images were flashing too fast to make any sense of them. Faces of people she loved whose names she couldn't remember. They were talking to her. Angry and worried, all furrowed brows and tight lips.

What was wrong?

Why were they so upset?

If only Josie could pull herself out of her stupor, she'd help solve whatever problem had them so anxious.

But she could barely open her eyes, and when she did, everything was off.

Darkness, trees towering overhead.

White walls and long corridors.

Bright lights.

Concerned voices discussing things she couldn't wrap her mind around. Using words she didn't know.

She was smart, though. She could help.

"I went to Duke." In her head, the words were clear and sharp. But in her ears, they were slurred.

"I know, sweetheart." It was a man's voice, deep and tender.

"I'm smart."

"Very smart." Gentle fingers brushed hair away from her face. "Stay with us, okay?"

"Omigosh, is she going to *die?*" That voice was shrill, painful. "Josie! Josie, talk to me!"

"Shh." Josie was sure she'd made the quieting noise, but the shrill voice continued.

"Omigosh, what if she dies? Who would do this? Do you think they'll catch him?"

The deep voice said, "Let's try to stay calm. You're not helping." And the shrill one quieted.

Thank God.

God. There was a God. Where was He? "Are you here?"

"I'm right here," the man said.

"Me, too," the shrill woman added. "We're not going anywhere."

Not God, probably, though God would probably have a voice like that man's, soothing and kind.

He definitely wouldn't have a voice like the woman's.

Were they in heaven?

Where were they going? What was happening? But Josie couldn't seem to form the words to ask the questions.

"Just keep breathing, sweetheart," the man said. "Just keep breathing, and everything will be all right."

"Keep talking," Josie managed. "Your voice..." *It makes me breathe,* she thought. But she couldn't form the words because someone laid a heavy, heavy, suffocating blanket on her.

She wouldn't be able to keep breathing with it on top of her.

She wouldn't be able to do what the deep voice asked.

"I'm sorry," she said. "I'm sorry."

~

Darkness. So much darkness.

The world was black. But familiar.

Familiar soft sheets beneath her.

Familiar smells—a vanilla candle. Coffee.

She was cold. Why so cold?

Josie tried to kick her feet to feel for the blankets, but they didn't want to move. She struggled to sit up but couldn't manage it. The comforter had to be here somewhere.

But then something creaked.

Something pushed down on top of her.

She opened her eyes, and a figure leaned over her. "Are you with me?" he asked.

It wasn't the deep voice from before.

It wasn't any voice she'd heard.

"I need to make sure you're awake," he said. "Are you awake?"

She tried to nod but couldn't make her head move.

"Say 'yes, I'm awake.'"

This was another strange dream. She'd had them all night long, the visions, the spinning. She just wanted to go back to sleep until it stopped.

She ignored the phantom voice. She could sleep without covers. She was warmer now.

"I need you to say it, Josie. Say, 'Yes, I'm awake.'"

All she wanted was to fall back asleep. She tried to tell the apparition that, but what came out was, "Sleep."

Hands on her shoulders—how had she forgotten they were there? The fingers dug into her tender skin. "Are you awake?"

"Ouch." Maybe if she said what he asked, he'd go away. "Yes, I'm awake."

"Good." But the man didn't loosen his grip. "Can you hear me?"

How could she not hear him? His face was inches from hers.

She could smell his breath—onions and garlic. It was nauseating. She tried to turn away from the scent, but the man's hands tightened again. How did she keep forgetting them?

"You can hear me?"

"Yes."

"I have a message for your father. I'm going to say it, and you're going to repeat it. Okay?"

"Okay."

"No matter where she goes." He paused, then said, "Repeat it."

"No matter where she goes."

"No matter what she does."

Josie said, "No matter what she does."

"We can get to her."

A niggle of anxiety bubbled in her middle. This was the strangest dream.

"Say it," the man said.

"We can get to her."

"Vote yes."

Josie repeated, "Vote yes."

The pressure on her shoulders lessened, then disappeared altogether. A blanket was draped over her.

"Sweet dreams." Warm breath brushed across her cheek, that horrible onion scent filling her nostrils. Something bunched beneath her head. "See you soon."

Josie turned over and fell back into a deep, dreamless sleep.

CHAPTER TWENTY-FOUR

Thomas stepped into Josie's apartment and scanned the room. Bentley was in front of a laptop at the kitchen table. Lake, who'd let him in, sat in the chair she kept by the door. Shelly wasn't there. Donley, who usually slept during the days, had been on duty all night Saturday night, all day Sunday, and then all Sunday night. He must have gone to the hotel to sleep.

"Did she wake up?"

"Not yet." Bentley stood and stretched. Neither of them had slept. They'd been at the ER until the wee hours. Josie's blood pressure had dropped low enough that the doctors hadn't wanted to release her. Thomas had stood beside her bed in the Plymouth hospital, watching the monitor, knowing too well what all the numbers meant. They'd already been giving her fluids. If her pressure continued to drop...

People died from Rohypnol overdoses.

Thank God Josie hadn't been drinking. Alcohol increased the effects of the drug, and she'd been plenty affected by the laced Dr Pepper. A single glass of wine, and the drug might've killed her.

Maybe the attacker had given her too much. Maybe Josie was particularly susceptible.

Or maybe this had been attempted murder.

They'd assumed the enemy was trying to embroil Josie in a scandal, as they'd attempted when they'd had her arrested. But what if their plans had been darker this time?

At her bedside in the hospital, Thomas had kept up a steady stream of prayers, trying to ignore Shelly's steady stream of fears and Bentley's incessant pacing, until, finally, Josie's blood pressure inched up.

The ER had kept her another couple of hours, just to be sure, and released her at four a.m.

They got her home and into bed. After shooing Thomas and Bentley out of the room, Shelly had helped her get changed.

Then the three of them had sat, stunned and exhausted, in her living room, Shelly checking on her occasionally to make sure she was still breathing.

Everything in Thomas had wanted to skip the stupid Fourth of July parade, but Shelly wouldn't hear of it.

"We'll take care of her. We've all worked too hard on your campaign for you to blow it now." Shelly had been frantic at the hospital. That morning, she'd stood over him in Josie's living room. "This is the job, Thomas. If you want to be mayor, you need to show the town that you can be there, even when it's hard. Even when your personal life is messy. If you can't, then you have no business running for office."

She was right.

Thomas had gone next door, scarfed down food, showered, and put on his game face.

Thank God he'd gone to the parade. It seemed everybody in town had heard about what happened. Rumor was that Josie'd gotten drunk—apparently, one of the servers *remembered* her drinking multiple whiskey-and-Cokes—a fact the man had told both the police and a reporter.

How someone could remember something that hadn't happened, Thomas had no idea. He was working on getting that guy's name. Maybe it was their tall red-capped, photo-taking foe.

At the parade, Thomas was able to set people right, telling everyone who asked that Josie had been drugged, that they'd gone to the hospital, and that the police were investigating.

Some people believed him. Some people thought it sounded like an elaborate cover for a woman who obviously had a drinking problem.

Funny how what people believed depended largely on which candidate they were supporting.

When the parade was over, Thomas returned to Josie's.

Now, he moved deeper into the cool, quiet interior of her living room toward Bentley. "Where's Shelly?"

"She went for a walk."

"When was the last time she checked on Josie?"

Bentley glanced at his phone. "An hour probably."

Thomas stepped toward the hallway. "I'll just make sure—"

"You're not going into her bedroom."

"I'm just going to check her pulse."

"I can do that."

Bentley started down the hallway, but Thomas grabbed his wrist. "I'm the paramedic."

"Any idiot can check a pulse."

But Thomas didn't let up his grip.

He wasn't going to let Bentley go into Josie's bedroom. It was a matter of principle.

Bentley looked at Thomas's hand on his arm slowly, then at Thomas. "You know what the difference is between you and me?"

"I can think of a few things."

"Unlike you, I've been invited into Josie's bedroom before. Many times."

Thomas gripped the man a little tighter. "You know the difference between you and me?"

Bentley's eyes narrowed infinitesimally.

"She kissed me," Thomas said. "Last night."

Bentley yanked his arm out of Thomas's grip, stepping closer.

Lake inserted herself between the two men. "I'll check on her. She's probably sleeping. I recommend you two do the same."

Thomas barely heard the woman, glaring at the other man.

"I'll take you both down if need be," Lake said. "And don't think I can't."

Thomas's gaze flicked to the woman. She wasn't kidding.

He stepped back, turned away. Since when was he a kiss-and-tell kind of guy? Why was he stooping to Bentley's level? Josie would not be impressed. "Check her pulse, make sure it's strong, and check her color. If she looks pale or pasty, or if she's sweating, come get me." He amended with, "Get *us*."

Lake disappeared down the hall.

Bentley paced away and settled at his laptop.

Thomas plopped onto a chair.

Two minutes later, Lake returned. "She's fine. Pulse is strong, and her cheeks are pink."

"Thank you," Thomas said. "When was the last time you slept?"

"Donley will relieve me in a couple of hours. Until then, I'll be fine."

"You need anything?"

Lake shook her head. "Thanks for offering, though."

Thomas rested his head against the back of the club chair

and let his eyes close. There were so many questions that needed answers. Who was the man who'd told the police and the reporter that Josie had been drinking?

Why hadn't any photos been sent to the senator this time?

What good could come from drugging Josie? The truth about what happened would get out. Josie's reputation would be restored. Thomas had seen the photos in the newspaper of himself carrying her out of the tent the night before. Those pictures wouldn't hurt him. He'd been called a hero more than once that morning.

Except for scaring them all to death, what had been the point?

And how had someone gotten so close to Josie that they were able to slip Rohypnol in her drink without anybody—Shelly, Bentley, the others at their table, and the two bodyguards—noticing?

CHAPTER TWENTY-FIVE

J osie opened her eyes to a brightly lit room. Her room.
She was home. She stretched her arms and legs. Everything seemed to be in working order. Her limbs no longer felt like they were made of lead.

But when she pushed herself to a sitting position, her head pounded.

She stilled until the worst of the pain passed.

If Josie didn't know better, she'd think she was hungover.

She hadn't drunk anything, though, had she?

No. She would remember that. But something had happened.

She glanced at her phone for the time—it was almost noon— then stood, realizing she wore nothing but panties. She closed her eyes, vaguely remembering Shelly coaxing her to shift this way and that so she could slip off that silver gown. How humiliating.

Josie pulled open her lower bureau drawer and chose a pair of workout shorts and a T-shirt. She needed to brush her teeth, and then she needed water.

And then maybe coffee. And a shower.

And then she'd figure out what had happened.

She crossed the hallway into the bathroom, did her business, and then ambled barefooted toward the kitchen.

She stopped at the entrance to the living room.

She'd forgotten about Donley, but she wasn't surprised to see him.

Thomas popped up from the club chair, Shelly from the couch, and Bentley from one of the kitchen chairs.

"Oh." Josie had no idea what they were all doing there. She needed to ask, but the pulsing in her head, the confusion spinning in her brain, kept the words trapped inside.

Thomas gripped her arm as if to keep her from falling. "Are you all right?"

She nodded. "I need something to drink."

"I'll get it," Bentley said.

He disappeared into the kitchen while Thomas urged her toward the table.

"How do you feel?" he asked.

"Like I did tequila shots. What happened?"

"Somebody spiked your drink. Rohypnol."

Josie collapsed into a chair as his words floated around in her brain, looking for a place to land. "The date-rape drug?"

Thomas's lips pressed together in a look of fury. "They gave you a lot. What do you remember?"

She thought back, or tried to. "I remember trees. A white hallway. Your voice and Shelly's."

Shelly plopped down beside her. "We were so worried. Omigosh, I thought you were going to die."

"It wasn't that serious, was it?" She turned from her overly dramatic friend to Thomas, thinking she'd see amusement there. She didn't.

Bentley slid a glass in front of her and sat, looking as worried as the others.

Josie took a long sip of the cold water. It tasted so good, felt so good on her parched throat. After a second sip, she asked, "Was it really that bad?"

Her friends looked at each other. Thomas was the one to answer. "We took you to the ER. Your blood pressure was dangerously low, but they hooked you up to an IV and pushed fluids, and it went back up."

"Dangerously low, like...?"

"Like if we hadn't gotten you to the hospital," Bentley said, "you might've died."

"Or if you'd been drinking," Shelly added. "Thank God you weren't."

"Seriously?" She looked at Thomas, waiting for him to contradict them. He only nodded.

Their words, their worry... She tried to make sense of what they were saying. And then she realized... "You're saying someone tried to kill me?"

Thomas's lips turned down at the corners. "The ER doctor said there wasn't an inordinate amount of the drug in your system. You just responded to it drastically."

"Oh." It was taking her too long to process what they were saying. "If a bottle tells me to take two pills, I usually take a half. I've always been ultrasensitive to medication."

"That explains it." Thomas nodded to her glass. "Drink your water. The sooner you flush that poison out of your system, the better. I assume you feel a little hungover."

"A lot, yeah."

"You need a Tylenol? Food?"

"Toast?"

Shelly popped up and disappeared into the kitchen.

Josie sipped her water, recalling the strange events of the evening before, trying to discern the actual from the dreams. She'd kissed Thomas—that was real.

They'd danced. Also real.

She and Bentley had danced, and she'd told him she didn't think it was going to work between them. Bentley had looked heartbroken.

Very real.

And then things got murky. Had she asked Thomas to kiss her again?

Ugh. Hopefully Bentley hadn't been there for that. She'd already hurt him enough.

She remembered a car ride. Voices. And then...

"I had the strangest dream," she said. "Someone was in my room, telling me to tell my father...something. To vote yes, I think. I guess it was just my mind trying to make sense of what happened."

Thomas was nodding. Bentley was watching her. Neither seemed concerned, which made her feel better.

That had been a dream, of course. Only a dream.

She nibbled the toast Shelly brought for her, swallowed half a Tylenol, and then returned down the hall to take a shower. Her friends all looked exhausted, but they didn't seem ready to leave yet. Still, she needed to be alone, to wake up, to think.

The hot shower revived her a little.

She considered what her day should look like. The coffee shop was probably busy. She'd planned to get up and help with the preparations for the holiday. Hopefully, Kinsley and Marcel had managed everything without her. After she dressed, she'd go downstairs and check in with them. With the headache held at bay, she figured she might have a couple of hours of work in her before exhaustion overtook her.

Wearing her bathrobe, she crossed the hallway to her bedroom, hearing no voices from the living room, despite the fact that there were four people in there. What had the night been like for Thomas, Bentley, and Shelly as they hovered over her, worried for her? The three of them didn't exactly get along. She hoped it hadn't been too rancorous.

She yanked open her underwear drawer.

There, on top of her neatly folded panties, sat a small envelope.

With shaking hands, she lifted it. Pulled out a plain white note card. And read the words.

In case you forgot our conversation, here's the message to your father...

No matter where she goes, no matter what she does, we can get to her.

Vote yes.

A scream crawled up to Josie's mouth from the depth of fear. She tried to stop it, tried to clamp it down, but it escaped in a burst of sheer panic.

She had no more control over it than over the nausea that rose behind it.

She dropped the note and bolted to the bathroom, where she emptied the contents of her stomach into the toilet.

She heard her friends coming down the hall, knew when they were standing at the open door. One of them stepped in, closed the door, and crouched down beside her.

"What happened?" Shelly asked.

Josie couldn't say it aloud. Surely it wasn't real. Maybe she was hallucinating. Was that a side effect of the date-rape drug? Hallucinations after it wore off?

She prayed so. Hallucinating was better than the alternative.

When she felt able, she stood and brushed her teeth.

Shelly was uncharacteristically quiet beside her.

Josie nodded to the door. "Let me just get dressed." Maybe the note wouldn't be there. Maybe she'd imagined the whole thing.

Even if it was there, Josie would be better able to face it once she was clothed. A bathrobe didn't exactly dispel the feeling of vulnerability.

Josie crossed the hallway into her room.

The note was there, lying on the floor like a serpent ready to strike. She ignored it as she pulled on a pair of capris and a T-shirt. Only after she slipped her feet into sandals, sort of feeling like herself again, did she bend over and scoop up the paper.

Her friends were standing between the kitchen table and the back of the sofa, talking softly. They turned when she walked in, concern etched on their features. She ignored them and walked to Donley, who stood near the door.

"Did you hear me tell them about my dream? That somebody came into my room, told me to tell my father to vote yes?"

The man's eyebrows lowered. He nodded once.

Josie handed him the note.

Donley's face, always a mask of confidence, took on a hard quality. The bodyguard yanked his phone from his pocket, jabbed the screen, and said, "Lake, we have a problem. Get over here."

"What is it?" Shelly spoke, but it was Thomas who hurried across the room, his eyes boring into hers.

"What happened?" he asked.

Josie settled on the sofa, feeling weak as a newborn foal, and pulled a throw blanket over her. "Someone was in my room last night."

Thomas's eyes popped wide. He rounded on Donley, who stared back with an unreadable expression. "You and your partner have one job! One job—to keep her safe. Under your watch, she was drugged. And then someone snuck into her room..." His words faded, and he turned back to Josie. "Did he hurt you? Did he...?"

She knew what Thomas was asking.

Rohypnol wasn't called the "date rape" drug for nothing.

"I remember him crouching over me. He held my shoulders down so I couldn't move." She rubbed the spot, wondered if there were bruises where he'd touched her. She hadn't seen any, but she hadn't been looking. "He talked to me, told me what's on that note." She glanced at Donley, who had the phone pressed to his ear again. Who was he talking to? Lake? Someone else? "The whole thing felt...surreal. I didn't think... I should have screamed or something, but I thought..." She swallowed all her excuses. Truth was, she'd been high as the clouds. They all knew that. "Then he pulled the covers up..."

The blankets.

They hadn't been over her. She'd had on nothing but her panties.

Humiliation rolled over her, and she closed her eyes and hid her face from Thomas, from everyone. Not that she'd had any control over the events, but she couldn't have held that mortification at bay for anything.

She'd never understood why rape victims felt guilty, as if they'd done something wrong. Now, as shame heated her cheeks and burned in her middle, she understood.

A warm hand enveloped hers. "You're okay." Thomas's voice was deep, his presence beside her reassuring. "The Lord protected you."

Had He? It seemed, if He'd wanted to protect her, He might've alerted somebody to the fact that an intruder was in her room.

She opened her eyes to Thomas, kneeling at her side, Bentley and Shelly behind him.

Thomas leaned closer. He took her hands in his and rested

his forehead against hers. "Father, we come to You, knowing You know everything that happened, everything they're still planning. We thank you for protecting Josie from what could have been much worse. We ask You to continue to protect her. Keep her enemies at bay. Expose their deeds. Give her father wisdom. Give each of us wisdom to know how to fight these evil people, to accomplish Your will. We trust You with this, Lord." Thomas squeezed her hands, and she squeezed back, feeling slightly less afraid, slightly less off-kilter. Maybe that was the best she could hope for at the moment.

After Thomas ended the prayer, he leaned back, and Josie caught sight of her friends behind him.

Shelly looked bewildered.

Bentley had the same look he'd worn the night before when they'd danced, when she'd tried so hard to let him down easy. She'd told him the truth—that she didn't want to return to politics and couldn't imagine him being happy elsewhere, and that, even if he could, she couldn't imagine sharing her life with somebody who didn't share her faith.

He looked away, the dismay in his expression morphing into something else, something darker.

Before she could name it, a knock sounded on the door.

Donley looked out, then opened it to let Lake in.

A uniformed police officer followed the bodyguard inside. It was the one who'd responded after Josie's car alarm had sounded, after the first time she'd been threatened.

"Officer Tyler, ma'am. I understand you had trouble last night?"

She directed him to sit in the adjacent chair and explained everything that had happened from when she'd started feeling off the previous night until she'd discovered the note a few minutes before.

"We're already aware of the suspected drugging," he said.

"We're having the contents of your glass analyzed. There were three sets of prints on it, the bartender's, the server's, and yours."

"How do you have mine?"

"You were fingerprinted when you were arrested."

"Oh, yeah. What a red-letter month I'm having."

The cop's face softened for a brief moment. Then he pushed to his feet. "We'll just have a look around."

She considered getting up to follow him, but she didn't have it in her. Instead, she rested her head against the back of the sofa and closed her eyes.

The cushion shifted, and she turned to see Bentley beside her. Thomas was on the far side of the room, a phone pressed to his ear.

Shelly slipped out of the apartment, also on the phone.

"How you holding up?" Bentley asked.

"Tired."

"I bet." He sat there a moment, and she relished the silence. She wanted to shoo everybody out, turn on Turner Classic Movies—or maybe the Golf Channel—and take a nap. A long nap, maybe one that lasted until this horrible day was over.

"I'm going to have to call your father and update him."

"You told him about last night?" she asked.

"We talked when you were still in the ER. He's called me about twenty times today to find out how you're doing. He wants you to get in touch when you feel up to it. I didn't tell you before because..."

"I'm not really up to it."

"He wants to come here. He said your mother was ready to hop in the car and start driving last night. Your dad barely talked her out of it."

Josie could imagine the scene. Mom loved and supported Dad and his career, but her life had been devoted to raising and protecting her children. Now, she spent hours every week with

Alton's kids, reveling in the role of grandmother. If Mom thought her daughter might be in danger...

Josie hated to think of her parents fighting about Mom coming to New Hampshire, or fighting about Dad's vote on the bill. Dad had to do what was best, even if it was hard.

Some things were worth fighting for. Some things were worth dying for.

Part of her wanted her mother to come. Mom would wrap Josie in her arms, comfort her, protect her. Mom would lay down her life to protect Josie.

Which was why, though Josie might want her mother close by, she wouldn't ask her to come. The last thing Josie or her father wanted was Mom in the line of fire of these horrible people.

"You could always go there," Bentley said. "Your father's hired an entire team of bodyguards. You could hang out with your mother until the vote is called."

"They're not going to bring it to the floor until they know they have the votes. And they're not going to get the votes unless Dad changes his mind. I'd have to stay there until November, and that's only assuming they wouldn't bother to get it passed with a lame-duck Senate. Which assumes our party loses the majority."

"Fine, then. You'd stay until January. At least you'd be safe." Bentley shifted to better face her. "Which I don't think you are here. I don't know how they got to you at the party last night, or how they got in, but these people are relentless. Your plan to hide out in this town isn't working," Bentley said. "They know where you are, and nobody here seems able to protect you. You have to see that."

She did see it. She did.

But she didn't want to leave Coventry. And would she really be safer at her parents' townhouse in Georgetown? Or back at their family home? "This is about Dad's vote." She lowered her voice and leaned in. "And we both know it's about more than that. Mitchell's been biding his time, waiting for the perfect opportunity to repay me for what I did."

"What *we* did," Bentley said.

True, they'd been in on the scheme together. But, though Bentley was an important member of Dad's staff, to the outside world, he was a typical staffer, interchangeable with any number of well-educated, hard-working political wannabes. Josie, though... Josie was the senator's daughter.

Hers was the name Mitchell would have recognized, the face he would have remembered from countless events over the years.

Josie was the one he held responsible. And she *was* responsible. That Bentley was, too, was irrelevant.

"The real question is, would I be safe there?" she asked. "Or would I just put the rest of my family in more danger?"

"You're too vulnerable here." Bentley ignored the second part of her question. "This apartment isn't secure. Josie, if last night had turned out differently... If you hadn't survived, your father would never forgive himself. And your mother might never forgive him. This isn't just about you. Your entire family depends on you staying safe."

Did they, though? Because, though Josie knew her parents loved her, she also knew they were strong people, people of principle. If the worst happened, Dad would do the right thing, and continue to do the right thing.

Josie's parents would rise to the challenge, no matter what happened.

But Josie didn't plan to be a casualty in this war. She just had to figure out how to fight back.

~

"Ma'am."

Josie dozed on the sofa, though not nearly long enough. Had she really thought she'd be able to work today? She could still barely think straight. She'd called downstairs. Marcel had been full of questions and concerns—apparently, everybody in town had heard some version of the events of the night before. Once she'd convinced him she was recovering, he'd assured her that he and Kinsley had the shop in hand.

Officer Tyler stepped into her line of vision, the other officer behind him, the one who'd arrested her. Fon...something. Fondue? No, he wasn't dip. Fontaine?

Officer Tyler crossed to the far side of the coffee table and stood in front of the television. "You remember my partner, Officer Fontier."

Fontier. Right.

"Yes. Hi."

Fontier spoke. "You have a trellis against the back of your house. I'm guessing somebody climbed that to your bedroom window."

That old wooden thing? "Is it really strong enough to support a man's weight?"

Fontier nodded. "Tested it myself. It's sturdy."

"But how did they get inside?" Bentley had left her alone to sleep and now stood behind the couch. "The window was locked."

"Maybe," Fontier said. "There are markings on the wood that tell me somebody used a tool to get in. Those old windows aren't exactly secure."

Bentley's gaze snapped to Josie. "I thought you got a security system."

"I did, but I didn't have the second-floor windows wired. I thought..." Her gaze skimmed the room. "It never occurred to me that someone would break in that way. And with the body-guards here…"

Bentley glared at Donley. "The bodyguards who weren't doing their jobs."

Before Donley could respond, Josie said, "Don't do that. This wasn't their fault. It was just—"

"It was somebody's fault!" Bentley's shout reverberated in her brain. "You have hired bodyguards who did nothing to stop this."

"Sit down," Officer Tyler said in his no-nonsense cop voice.

Bentley rounded the sofa and settled beside her.

The police officer spoke over their heads. "You too, Windham."

Thomas came around the opposite side of the sofa and sat in the club chair. From the look on his face, he was as furious—and concerned—as Bentley.

Officer Tyler focused on Fontier. "You're sure it was forced open?"

The younger cop said, "Not a hundred percent, no. Some-body definitely used a pry bar to lift the bottom sash, but that might have been necessary regardless. It's hard to lift a window without a handle."

"But the lock?" Tyler asked.

The other cop shrugged. "It's possible to stick a tool between the two sashes and jimmy the lock open. Either that or it was unlocked."

"We check the locks every time we come," Lake said.

Officer Tyler turned to Josie. "Who had access to your apartment yesterday?"

Josie looked around at the people who'd worked so hard to protect her. Was one of them her enemy? She couldn't believe it.

She wouldn't.

"Lake and Donley," she said, nodding to her bodyguards. "And Bentley and Shelly."

Officer Tyler looked around. "Shelly is...?"

"I'm right here." She stepped into the apartment. "I was on the phone." She lifted her cell. "I didn't want to interrupt. Bentley, Josie, and I were all here yesterday afternoon. Josie and I were getting ready for the fundraiser. Bentley was just hanging around."

"I was your escort," Bentley said. "I wasn't just *hanging around*. I'm trying to keep her safe."

"Well done," Shelly said. "Really, fine job."

He might have retorted, but Josie laid a hand on his forearm. She didn't have the patience for their sniping today.

"I can't imagine either of them working against me," Josie said. "Maybe somebody broke in the front door while we were out and unlocked the window."

Tyler said, "You have a security system. Did your alarm go off?"

"No."

"Did you set it?"

"I always set it."

"She did," Bentley added. "I remember distinctly."

"You were standing right behind her." Shelly said the words slowly, as if working something out in her head. She moved into the circle, standing between Fontier and Lake, but her focus never left Bentley. "You watched her set it. You must know the code."

"I knew the code anyway." Bentley waved Shelly's words off like an irritating fruit fly. "It's the same one we used at our place in DC."

Our place. She wished he hadn't said that. What would Thomas think? She didn't have the courage to look his way to find out.

Not that she didn't have more important things to worry about.

"You disappeared during Thomas's speech, Bentley, and for much of the next one." Shelly blinked twice, then shook her head slowly.

"I got a phone call," he said. "What do you think? I jogged back here in my tuxedo? I don't even have a key. Come on." He looked at Josie. "She's not making sense. Even if I could have gotten in, I was gone for like five, six minutes."

Before Josie could respond, Shelly spoke again. "It was longer than that. And I don't... I don't want to say this." She looked away from Bentley, meeting Josie's eyes. "Last night, Bentley and I danced. He was pretty upset about..."

Josie shook her head quickly, hoping her friend wouldn't tell the entire room that Josie'd broken his heart the night before. Nobody needed to know about their conversation.

Shelly looked at Bentley. "I'm sorry. I have to tell her. Tell them."

"Even if I'd come back here and broken in, Lake and Donley check the windows whenever they get here." He turned to Lake. "Were the windows locked?"

The woman nodded, but the motion was slight.

"You're sure?" Tyler asked.

She opened her mouth, cringed as if pained, and said, "I think so."

"You *think* so?" Donley asked. "You aren't sure?"

Lake turned to Josie. "You were pretty out of it. Ms. Sanders and I helped you back to your room. I was out of my routine. I can't remember if I checked the locks or not."

Shelly turned back to Bentley. "So you could have unlocked them."

"I didn't."

"I have to tell them."

Bentley gave her a hard look. "That has nothing to do with anything."

"What?" Josie asked. "What are you two talking about?"

Shelly shifted to face Josie. "He bought a house in Fairfax."

Bentley's head dropped forward.

Shelly kept talking. "A really expensive house, for you. He thought you'd like it there, out of the city. He thought maybe—"

"Okay," Josie said. "I'm not sure what that has to do with—"

"He also bought a new car. Right, Bentley? That one outside. A Mercedes or—"

"It's a BMW," Bentley said. "What about it?"

Josie's empty stomach churned. She caught up, and she didn't like where Shelly was going with this line of thought.

"It's just..." Shelly's gaze flicked around the room. She seemed uncertain. "Where did you get the money for those things?"

"I work," Bentley said. "Most of the world does. They trade their time and talents for money. It's called a job. You should try it sometime."

"I have a job, Bentley. But I couldn't afford a house in Fairfax on what I earn."

"Maybe you should get a better job."

Shelly ignored his jab and gave Josie an imploring look. "I'm just saying, he's not exactly wealthy. Would his income cover a new car and a three-bed, two-bath in Fairfax?"

Before Josie could answer, Bentley shifted to face her. "You remember Aunt Bernie, the one in Louisiana? The one who owned all the land?"

"I remember," Josie said.

"She died last winter. She left me an inheritance. I didn't tell you about the house because I wanted to surprise you. I thought, when you came home with me..." His Adam's apple bobbed, and he turned to Shelly. "This is what I get for trusting you."

"Somebody's working against her." Shelly focused on the cop. "I'm not saying it's Bentley, but you need to check out his story. Because the guy doing all of this is well funded, and maybe he paid Bentley to—"

"To what?" Bentley shot to his feet. "Do you really think I'd hurt Josie? She almost *died* last night."

"Okay, let's settle down." Officer Tyler's words were calm and firm.

Bentley sat again and gave Josie an imploring look. "I would never hurt you."

She didn't respond. Couldn't think of anything to say.

He'd driven the BMW to New Hampshire, so she'd known about it. She'd figured purchasing the luxury car had put him pretty deep in debt.

Bentley's great-aunt was a widow whose husband had died early in their marriage. They hadn't had children, so Josie wasn't surprised to learn she'd left Bentley money. But enough to buy a luxury car and a house in a market where a typical single-family home would cost well over half a million dollars?

"You don't believe me." Bentley's tone held incredulity and no small measure of hurt. "You really think I'd do this to you?"

"I don't know what to think." She stood, needing space. Needing air. She scooted past Thomas and rounded the sofa. "You show up here out of the blue years after we broke up."

"*You* broke up, not *we*." Bentley stood and talked over the back of the sofa. "I missed you. I wanted you back."

"That's what you said."

"I *love* you, Josie." He didn't seem to care who heard him say it.

The two cops, the two bodyguards, and Shelly were watching.

Thomas sat with his forearms propped on his thighs, gaze on the floor. She wondered what he was thinking. Maybe he was judging her, judging all of this, and realizing he'd been an idiot to have gotten involved with her.

Or...maybe he was praying. She hoped so.

God knew they needed all the help they could get.

"I bought the house for you," Bentley said. "I thought maybe... I bought it before I came here. If I'd realized how much you love Coventry, I wouldn't have done it. I've already put it on the market. Hopefully, I can sell it for a profit, or at least get my money back. I didn't understand how much you loved it here. I didn't understand the life you'd built here. I'd hoped..." His voice faded. After a moment, he said, "Please tell me you believe me."

"I don't know, Bentley."

Shelly stepped around the sofa. "I believe you want her back. No question." She slid her warm fingers over Josie's arm. "He never thought he was good enough for you. After you left him, and left the city, he confided to me that he thought you deserved someone from your... How did you put it, Bentley? Her 'station.'"

Bentley's face paled. "Please. Don't."

"She needs to know."

"That has nothing to do with this."

"I never wanted to..." Shelly clamped her lips closed. Then she swallowed. "I think you'd do anything you could to win her back, even if it meant getting in bed with the worst kind of people. You and I both know—"

"Don't." Bentley's voice lost the imploring tone. Now, it was hard, his brows low, his glare threatening. "Don't."

The two stared at each other for a long moment.

Josie's heart thumped wildly. She needed to sit, but there was something passing between her ex-fiancé and her best friend, something she couldn't comprehend. Something she needed to understand.

Finally, Shelly tore her eyes away from Bentley and faced Josie again. "After you left, we were both..." She licked her lips, swallowed. Her eyes filled. "It was hard on us when you left. He was heartbroken, and...and so was I. You and I have been best friends our whole lives, and all of a sudden, you just wrote me out of your life."

"I didn't," Josie said. "I moved away. People do that."

"Fine." Shelly snatched her hand off Josie's arm and swiped at her tears. "Okay, people do that. But the way you did it, the way you turned your back on me..." She looked at the floor, shook her head. "I was hurt."

"I never meant for that to happen. You had your own life. I didn't realize..." Josie looked at her friend a long time, then at Bentley. Neither would meet her eyes.

And she knew.

"You two...?"

"Just for a couple of months." Shelly's gaze snapped up. "We were both lonely. We commiserated."

"Bentley?"

When he looked up, it was to glare at Shelly.

"When we were together," Shelly said, "we both knew it was about you, about missing you. He admitted to me that he'd do anything to get you back. I think...I think..." She pulled her phone from her pocket and turned it over in her hands a couple of times. "I have a friend who works for Mitchell. She told me Bentley's on their payroll."

Bentley took a step toward Shelly. "That's a lie. I would never..." He turned to Josie. "I would never do anything to hurt you. I love you."

"But you thought she rejected you because you're not rich,"

Shelly said. "Because you come from—your words—redneck roots."

Defying his stoic expression, red crept up his neck and into his face.

"You can't really believe that about me," Josie said. "What happened between us had nothing to do with your family."

Bentley's lips pressed closed.

"So I think…I'm guessing you agreed to work for Mitchell," Shelly said the words fast, as if forcing them out. "You came up here, figured you could play protector and win her back all while trying to encourage her father to vote for the bill. You could make the money you felt you needed to be worthy of her. One stone, lots of birds."

Bentley *had* suggested her father should vote for the bill.

He turned his back on Shelly and reached for Josie's hands.

Josie crossed her arms.

But his eye contact never wavered. "You know where my loyalty lies. I would never work against your father—or you. And Mitchell…" He shook his head. "After everything he did, after everything *we* did, he wouldn't trust me any more than I'd trust him. Think it through, Josie."

That was the problem, though. She couldn't think anything through.

She couldn't think at all. She'd been drugged. Bodily threatened. Her space and her privacy, violated.

And now she'd learned Bentley and Shelly had had an affair.

Her best friend and her former fiancé.

Not that they owed her anything. She'd left them both. Shelly was being overly dramatic, as usual, claiming Josie had abandoned her. But that was probably how Shelly felt, even if it wasn't true.

And Josie'd broken Bentley's heart.

Still. They'd had an affair, and they'd hidden it from her because...because it wasn't okay.

How could she believe anything either one of them told her now?

At least Shelly had fessed up. At least Shelly had been honest. Right up until Josie had guessed the truth, Bentley was trying to get Shelly to keep quiet.

He stepped closer, tears in his eyes, his voice low. "I love you. I would never do those things she said."

"But you did have a relationship with her."

His eyes closed. Moisture leaked out of them.

Despite the air conditioner pumping cold air into the space, the room felt sticky and stifling.

"Mr. Kent." Officer Fontier crossed the space. "We need you to come down to the station with us."

Bentley stepped back and turned to the cop. His eyes were red-rimmed, but his voice was strong. "Am I under arrest?"

"We just want to ask you a couple of questions," Fontier said. "Maybe you can clear up a few things."

Bentley took two steps closer to Josie, stopping when they were close enough to touch, but he didn't reach for her again. "I would never hurt you. I might not be religious like your new... whatever"—he aimed a glare at Thomas, though the other man didn't look up—"but even I have my limits."

She didn't know what he expected her to say. She had nothing.

He watched her a long moment.

"Sir?" Fontier said.

Bentley broke eye contact and crossed the apartment.

Lake opened the exterior door, letting bright afternoon light in, and Bentley stepped out, the cop on his heels.

The door clicked shut.

Shelly said, "I'm so sorry. Josie, you have to know—"

"You need to leave."

"Oh." Shelly blinked, wide-eyed. "Josie, you have to forgive me."

"I will. Eventually. But right now, I need peace, and having you here is anything but peaceful. You need to go."

Her best friend looked crestfallen as she gathered her purse and followed Bentley and Officer Fontier out the door.

Only after it closed did Thomas stand and round the sofa. He opened his arms, and Josie fell into them.

CHAPTER TWENTY-SIX

Thomas savored the moment.

Josie was curled up beside him, sound asleep. After Bentley and Shelly had left, he'd urged her to the couch, where she'd wept on his shoulder. Afterward, to distract her from the cops coming and going, bodyguards having hushed conversations in the corner, and CSI people rifling through her bedroom, Thomas turned on Turner Classics. About five minutes later, she'd drifted off.

But Zack—Thomas should probably call him Officer Tyler as long as the guy was in uniform—had already asked him once to step outside, and now he leveled that low-brow cop look that meant, *do what I say or pay the consequences.* So Thomas eased Josie onto the sofa and laid a blanket over her.

He followed the cop to the small stoop at the top of the stairs outside her apartment. The sun was falling behind the trees, and the evening air was cooling. The park was only a few blocks away, and the sounds from Liberty Fest carried. Somebody was already setting off firecrackers a block or two behind.

He'd forgotten about the holiday.

"Tell me what you did last evening," Zack said.

Maybe Zack and he hadn't been friends in school because Thomas bested him in just about every contest. Maybe because sophomore year, Serena Kane, Zack's big crush, had asked Thomas to the stupid Sadie Hawkins dance. He'd only said yes because he hadn't known how to say no without hurting her feelings.

Zack and Serena had been dating by the time of the junior prom. Now they were married.

The whole thing was ridiculous. Surely Thomas and Zack could get past high school rivalries now.

"What time exactly?"

"They left here about six-thirty, so from then on."

"I was at Liberty Fest all day, mostly at my campaign booth. The fundraiser began at six-thirty—cocktails and appetizers— but I didn't have to be there until seven."

Zack jotted something on his notepad.

Thomas hadn't done anything wrong. There was no reason for him to feel nervous.

On the other hand, Josie had sent both Shelly and Bentley away, and Bentley had been carted down to the station. Thomas would prefer not to be a suspect.

A uniformed police officer stepped out of Josie's apartment, Lake at his side. She didn't meet his gaze as she walked past.

"What's that about?" Thomas asked.

Zack's expression didn't change. Apparently, the cop didn't feel the need to explain anything to Thomas. Which made sense, he supposed.

"I'd planned to head home around six," Thomas said, "but it was almost half past by the time I got away. I didn't have my car —you know how parking is at Liberty Fest—so I walked back to my office. I let myself into the apartment upstairs, where I've been staying, and—"

"Why?"

Thomas wasn't sure what Zack was asking and waited for clarification.

Before Zack could offer it, his phone rang. He glanced at the number, then connected the call. "Tyler here."

Though Thomas strained to hear, he couldn't pick up anything.

Other noises didn't escape him, though. The stage from the night before would still be set up, though the tent would have been broken down. There were usually performances all day. At that moment, it sounded like an Irish band was playing. The show would continue until the fireworks began after sunset.

Zack ended the call, a grim look on his face.

"What?" Thomas asked.

"The lab won't get to Josie's glass and its contents for a few days at best, maybe a few weeks. But there's a quick test for Rohypnol, and one of our people got her hands on a kit. It's not official, but from what I understand, it's very accurate."

"And?"

"And there was no trace of the drug in her drink."

"How can that be?" Thomas hadn't meant for his volume to rise and tempered it. "I don't understand."

"At this point, there's zero evidence that anybody drugged her. Are you sure she didn't just—"

"Drug herself? Is that something people use recreationally?"

Zack shrugged. "You'd be surprised what people do."

"She doesn't even drink alcohol, and you think she gave herself the date-rape drug at a public event? Come on, Zack. Why would she do that?"

Another shrug. "You tell me."

Thomas took a long, slow breath to keep his frustration from leaking out. "She wouldn't. Somebody drugged her. We just don't know how."

Zack watched him a long moment. "Or you drugged her."

Thomas met his old classmate's eyes. "I didn't. And if you question the people from the fundraiser, you'll know that, after Josie and I danced, I left the table and didn't return until she'd already been drugged."

Zack glanced at the adjacent building that housed Thomas's agency and current home. "Why have you been staying there?"

"After those two guys threatened her, I wanted to be close."

"You always did have a hero complex."

"Says the guy in the uniform with the gun."

That elicited not so much a chuckle as a loud exhale. "Okay. Go on."

"I let myself into my apartment, took a shower, put on my tuxedo, and then drove back to the park."

"Why drive when you'd walked earlier?"

"The parking wasn't as bad late in the day"—which Zack should already know—"and unlike earlier, I was wearing a tuxedo."

Zack gave him a go-on nod.

"By the time I parked and walked to the tent, it was a little after seven. Andrew was introducing the mayor."

"Did anybody see you?"

"Well, I was onstage, so yeah."

"Before that, I mean."

"Sure." He rattled off the names of the people he'd waved to during his walk from the car to the tent, thankful for his good memory.

"Before you left your apartment, you didn't stop by here to see if they were ready?" Zack asked. "Maybe see if you could give them a ride?"

"We'd planned to meet at the park, and I knew they weren't here because Bentley's BMW wasn't parked in the driveway."

For the first time in their conversation, Zack perked up. "So you knew the place was empty?"

"I don't have a key, and unlike Bentley, I don't know the alarm code, so I couldn't have broken in. Also, I barely made it back in time."

"Did anybody here see you when you left? Maybe Josie's customers?"

"Yeah, I saw a couple of families I knew." He named a few locals he'd greeted, then mentioned Kinsley, Josie's employee, whom he'd waved to as he was driving away. "You can ask all of them."

Zack made notes, then snapped his notebook shut.

"There's one more thing," Thomas said. "The newspaper said a waiter claimed Josie had been drinking whiskey all night. That was a lie. Her medical records showed zero alcohol in her system. Did you get the same story?"

"We did," Zack said. "When we called him on it, the server claimed he had her confused with somebody else."

"Who?"

"He said someone at your table."

"Nobody at my table was drinking whiskey."

"How do you know?"

"Because they're my friends, and I know what they drink." He spouted off the names of everybody who'd sat with them. "Bentley was drinking scotch on the rocks. Shelly was drinking red wine. As far as I know, nobody else at our table drank anything alcoholic. Ask them."

Zack's eyes narrowed. "Gosh, is that how it works?"

Thomas's blood pressure ticked up. "That server lied to you, and he lied to the reporter, who printed a story that was either intended to make Josie look bad or me look bad—or both."

"I'd hate to see Mr. Perfect's reputation smeared."

"Don't be an..." He swallowed the word dying to escape. "I'd never seen the waiter before, but he was young—maybe twenty. The point is, he was really quick to make up a story about Josie, somebody he didn't even know. Why would he do that?"

Zack said nothing.

"That server could very well have been the person who slipped the Rohypnol into Josie's drink."

"Assuming someone did, which at this point we can't prove."

"Someone drugged her. Maybe she drank the Dr Pepper, and the waiter brought her a fresh one. He should be a suspect. If he didn't do it, he was working for the one who did. I think if you find the server, you'll find the person who did this."

"Hold on while I write this down," Zack deadpanned. "If only I had your investigative skills."

"We'd all be better off," Thomas snapped.

Zack took a step closer, getting into Thomas's personal space. "Believe it or not, I've actually investigated crimes before. We already know what happened."

Rather than be irritated by Zack's aggression, Thomas asked, "What?"

"We put a little pressure on the kid, and he admitted that somebody paid him to say she'd been drinking."

"Who?"

"He doesn't know. Got a message on Snapchat to tell anybody who asked that she'd been drinking whiskey-and-Coke, and the guy would pay him a thousand dollars."

"And did you—?"

"We checked out his story. The message was gone. The waiter remembered the guy's name, but the guy had blocked him. We've contacted Snapchat. Our tech guy said somebody probably just opened a dummy account. We're probably not going to find him."

"And the money?" Thomas asked.

"The thousand dollars was left in an envelope in the waiter's mailbox. And yes, we dusted it for fingerprints. And no, there were none but the waiter's. And yes, we charged him with obstruction of justice."

"There's no way to trace who the money came from? No cameras or—"

"Nope. The newspaper plans to print a retraction. I wouldn't look for it on the front page."

The publisher was an old friend of Farley's, so Thomas didn't expect fair coverage.

He was more concerned about Josie. "What's your theory about what happened?"

Zack backed to the far side of the landing and leaned against the railing, looking up at the building. "I don't know what to think. Whether the window was unlocked or not—"

"I doubt it was," Thomas said. "Donley and Lake seem pretty competent."

Zack met his eyes. "Unless you unlocked it."

"I didn't, and you know it."

A moment passed. "Yeah, I do."

That was something. Zack might give Thomas a hard time, but at the end of the day, the men knew each other. Thomas knew Zack was a good cop who'd do his best to get to the bottom of what happened.

Zack knew Thomas wouldn't knowingly put anybody in harm's way.

"What's your take on Bentley and Shelly?" Zack asked.

Thomas allowed himself to consider the question carefully before answering. "I don't like Bentley. He's an arrogant, elitist jerk. To be fair, though, maybe my opinion is jaded."

"You've got that love-triangle thing going on."

"But the guy's been doing everything in his power to not only win Josie back, but to protect her. And he works for her father. I don't see him risking either his relationship with her or his job to fill his bank account."

"So you don't think he's behind any of this?"

"No. I don't."

"And Shelly?"

Thomas smiled. "She loves Josie. As far as I can tell, she's completely devoted to her. Unlike Bentley, Shelly's got all the money she needs. What would be her motive?"

"I don't know any of these people. How about the bodyguards?"

Thomas shrugged. "I thought they were competent, but somebody drugged her drink, and Lake was standing right there." The words brought another idea. "Did you check out the bartender?"

"It was Shelby McCaffrey."

"Oh." Thomas hadn't glanced that direction all night. Shelby was the younger sister of Thomas's friend Fitz. "What did she say?"

"She just made the drinks. The servers delivered them. A few people came straight to the bar after the music started, but Josie wasn't one of them. For the most part, Shelby didn't know which drinks were for which guests, so even if she'd wanted to drug Josie, she wouldn't have been able to."

"And why would she?" Thomas asked.

Zack flipped through his notes briefly. "Who was Bentley talking about earlier? Someone named Mitchell?"

"You need to ask Josie about that. Suffice it to say, there are other elements involved."

"Things we need to know about."

"I don't disagree," Thomas said.

Zack studied him. "But you won't tell me." When Thomas said nothing, Zack asked, "Who will?"

Josie could share the story, but she needed to rest and

recover. "I can give you a number for Josie's father's chief of staff, Carlyle Nichols."

"Carlyle..." Zack flipped through his notebook. "He's the one who hired the bodyguards. Chief of staff?"

"Oh. Yeah. Josie's father... She doesn't want anybody to know this."

"Someone could have killed her last night. Tell me who he is."

Maybe he shouldn't. But finding whoever did this was more important than Josie's anonymity. "Senator Davis Harrington."

Zack jotted the name in his notebook.

"I don't know how much Carlyle will tell you, if anything, but he'd be the guy to ask." Thomas found the number in his contacts and showed it to Zack, who copied it down.

"Good, good," Zack said. "We need to talk to him anyway. The bodyguards... My understanding is that Donley escorted you back here last night and then went to their hotel room to sleep. Lake stayed. Is that right?"

"Yeah."

"You ever seen either of them back in her room?"

"I know they both check all the windows and doors when they first arrive."

"Who did that last night?"

"Lake. Donley just got us to the door and left."

"Other than that, have you seen either of them in her room?"

"Lake went back there a few times. Shelly, too. We were all worried, but neither Bentley nor I felt we ought to go into her bedroom."

"That's the same story I get from them. By all accounts, Donley was nowhere near your table at the fundraiser, and he wasn't in the apartment last night either. We checked with the hotel, and the clerk saw him arrive at about four-thirty and leave again at about eleven. He's been cleared as a suspect."

"Okay, good. You're looking into Lake?"

He nodded. "And you'll be sticking close? Your girlfriend's obviously a target."

"She's not my girlfriend."

Zack rolled his eyes. "Whatever. Has she considered moving to a more secure location?"

"She can be pretty stubborn."

"Can't they all?" Zack cracked the first smile of the day, but he covered it fast. "See if you can talk her into going to a hotel, preferably one outside of Coventry."

"You don't think there's a safe one in town?"

The cop's lips tipped up again. "I just want her out of my jurisdiction. We've got enough to manage without having to chase her ghosts."

"Sorry to keep you from your holiday cookout."

"Don't lie." Zack clapped him on the shoulder. "You're not one bit sorry."

Josie was still asleep when Thomas stepped back inside. He was looking for something to make for dinner—she didn't have much—when his cell rang. It was a local number he didn't recognize. "Thomas Windham."

"Mr. Windham, this is Rebecca St. Cyr, *Coventry News*. Do you have a minute?"

He returned to the living room and looked over the sofa at Josie. Her breathing was steady. She'd be all right alone for a few minutes. Besides, Donley was standing watch at the door.

"Are you there?" the woman said.

"Just a sec." He stepped outside. "Sorry about that. What can I do for you?"

"I understand we got the story wrong last night, that Josie Smith wasn't drunk but drugged. I wanted to give you the chance to set the record straight."

"Have you tried contacting Josie?"

"Oh, I'll do that, but it's you the readers are most concerned with. She's not running for mayor, after all."

"What do you want to know?"

"We were told, and the police were too, that the woman you were with, Josie Smith..."

The trailing words sounded like a question, so Thomas said, "Josie's a friend."

"If you say so." The woman's laugh sounded about as authentic as techno-music. "I wondered because there's a rumor you were seen kissing—"

"You wanted to ask me a question?" He wasn't going to discuss their kiss.

"Right, so you were with her, and the rumor was that she got drunk, so drunk that you had to carry her out of the tent. But we have now heard from a source at the police station that they analyzed the contents of her glass, and she was drinking Dr Pepper. Do you want to explain what happened?"

"Somebody slipped her Rohypnol."

"Somebody *roofied* her?"

"I'm afraid so. We took her to the hospital because she had a really powerful reaction to the drug. She's fortunate she survived."

"Someone slipped her the *date* rape drug." Rebecca emphasized the word. "Weren't you her date?"

Thomas started to speak, then stopped and considered her question. This woman was trying to pull him down a rabbit hole he figured would be filled with well-hidden snares. "Like I said, we're friends."

"Of course you are!" False enthusiasm if he'd ever heard it.

Thomas's guard was rising fast.

"Everybody saw how you carried her out of there like a superhero," Rebecca said. "I didn't mean to imply anything else. Do you have any idea where the drug came from?"

"The police are working on that."

"Interesting. Interesting. I wonder if..." She lowered her voice conspiratorially. "I don't know if you've heard," Rebecca said, "but people are saying that Farley has a woman on the side, a very young woman. What do you think about that?"

"I prefer not to speculate about other people's relationships."

"So you agree that he is in a relationship with another woman?"

Thomas laughed, though it sounded about as genuine as the woman who heard it. "I have no idea what Farley does in his spare time, and I don't spend time worrying about it. I'm focused on getting elected and how to be the best mayor for Coventry that I can be. I'm sure Farley is doing the same."

"Maybe." She batted the word like a tennis ball. Thomas let it fly out of bounds. Finally, Rebecca continued. "I just wondered if maybe Farley was behind what happened to your girlfriend, trying to make you look bad. I mean, I know you would never stoop to anything like that, but Farley..."

"She's not my girlfriend." Thomas closed his eyes, shot up a quick prayer for wisdom. "Did you have a question?"

"Of the two of you, you have to admit you are the more moral of the candidates, right?"

"Like I said, Rebecca, I prefer not to talk about—"

"Okay, okay. But you attend church every Sunday. You're

not the kind of guy to have a wife and a little something-something on the side."

"I haven't been blessed with a wife, but if I am, I certainly have every intention of being faithful."

"Unlike Farley."

"I didn't say that."

"But you agree that having a mistress isn't exactly moral, right?"

"Listen, Rebecca, I'm not sure what you're getting at."

The door opened, and Josie stepped onto the porch. She looked sleepy, but she smiled at him.

Donley stood behind her, scowling as if it was Thomas's fault she'd come outside.

"Oh, come on," Rebecca said. "You can't really be afraid to answer that question. Even you can admit, if Farley is having an affair, that would make you the moral choice, don't you agree?"

"I want what's best for Coventry—"

"I know, of course..." She continued talking, saying how she knew Thomas was a great candidate, how she trusted him, laying it on thick. He put the phone on speaker so Josie could hear.

Her smile faded, and she stepped closer.

"...and what's best for Coventry," Rebecca said, "is a candidate with a strong moral backbone, don't you think?"

"Yeah, of course. But also—"

"Which makes you the moral choice."

"Sure, I guess, but—"

Josie yanked the phone from his hands. "Mr. Windham has nothing further to say on the matter."

"That's okay." The reporter's voice, laced with glee, was loud enough that he could still hear it. "I got what I needed."

Josie ended the call and closed her eyes.

"What?" he asked.

"She was trying to get you to proclaim yourself the moral candidate."

"Yeah." He replayed the conversation. "I figured she was doing something like that, but I can't figure out why."

Josie's eyes opened. "Where does she work?"

"The local paper."

"You have any contacts there?" At his nod, she said, "Reach out, see if you can find out what that was about."

"I will, but I haven't done anything to be ashamed of."

Her head bobbed, but not as if she agreed. "There was a reason for that phone call. We need to find out what it was and get ahead of it."

They were in the backseat of Donley's SUV that evening. Thomas sneaked a look at Josie beside him. She looked tired but otherwise no worse for wear. He'd been against this, but Josie had insisted she needed to get out of the house.

They were on their way to a restaurant a half-hour from Coventry, a place where neither of them should be recognized. A place that should be pretty quiet on the Fourth of July.

"You sure you feel okay?" Thomas asked.

"Better than I've felt all day."

"You'd be safer if we'd stayed at your place or gone to my office."

She gave him a look he was coming to recognize—head tilted down, brows up, closed-mouth frown. It meant *I can take care of myself* and maybe, *quit worrying.*

He could do that. If it meant he'd get to spend an evening with Josie, just the two of them—not counting the bodyguard in the front seat—he wasn't going to complain.

The oversize vehicle twisted and turned through the thick

forest toward Campton, a little town north of Coventry. The road was mostly deserted. Donley's gaze flicked to the rearview often, but he looked unconcerned.

They traveled in uncomfortable silence for a few minutes. The SUV was big, but not big enough for the elephant seated between them. Thomas was tired of pretending it wasn't there. Might as well start small and work his way to it. "What do you think about Bentley being questioned?"

She glanced his way. "At first, it seemed ridiculous, the idea that Bentley could be trying to hurt me, going against my father."

"At first?"

"Shelly's right about him, about how he sees himself. His family wasn't poor, but they were definitely working class, a far cry from mine. His dad's a heat-and-air technician. His mom's a school secretary."

"Both noble professions," Thomas said.

"Definitely. But when you rub shoulders with the kinds of people we did in Washington, it can make people feel...less than, I guess."

"You don't have that problem."

One shoulder lifted and fell. "An accident of my birth, nothing more. My family's wealth is certainly not anything I can take pride in. But Bentley doesn't understand that. He always felt like he had to compete, to measure up to some imaginary line."

"You think it's possible he switched sides in order to reach that line?"

She considered the question a long moment. "I wouldn't have. But the new car, the house... It's suspicious."

"The inheritance—"

"I know he inherited something. How much, I have no idea. The police will get to the bottom of that."

"What does your gut tell you?"

She smiled. "I'm not in the habit of consulting my gut."

"Sometimes, we pick up on things instinctively that we don't understand intellectually."

She shifted to face him better. "Interesting. So what does *your* gut tell you about Bentley?"

He chuckled. "Waltzed right into that, didn't I?" She didn't answer, just waited. So, fine. "Honestly, I can't see it. Bentley cares about you, and he obviously loves his job. Would he really risk both for money?"

"I've known people to do worse. And we'd be talking a *lot* of money. I wouldn't have thought it of him, but now that I know about his relationship with Shelly, I feel like I don't know either one of them."

Since Josie'd finally brought it up, Thomas asked the question that had been dogging him for hours. "You say you don't want to get back together with Bentley, but when you found out he and Shelly dated, you had a pretty strong reaction." He remembered those moments as he'd held her close while she wept against his chest. Though he'd enjoyed the *holding* part very much, he hadn't loved that she'd been weeping for Bentley.

"It's just... You think one thing, and then you find out the truth is a totally different thing."

He waited, sensing she needed time to figure out what she was trying to say.

She shifted in the seat, facing forward again. "For a while there, you seemed to be...pursuing me." Her gaze flicked his way but didn't linger.

He wasn't sure what he was supposed to say to that.

"Let's say for argument's sake you were still pursuing me," she said.

He grinned, thinking of their kiss. "I'll allow that...for argument's sake."

Her lips twitched at the corners. "Let's say you'd continued to ask me out consistently, making me feel like you really wanted to date me."

"Okay."

"And let's say maybe I start to think, you know, 'Thomas might really like me.'"

"Sure. Let's say that."

"And let's say I started to think maybe you were onto some-thing when you suggested, if you had"—she shifted to face him, gesturing back and forth between them—"that we might be good together."

"I like this line of thinking."

"And then let's say maybe I decide that, the next time you ask, I'll say yes."

"Which could happen—in your theoretical world—now that I'm off the hook on the whole *not asking* thing."

"Exactly."

He smiled and waited.

She seemed to lose her train of thought, just watching him for a long moment.

"So, let's say all of that," he prompted.

"Right. And then let's say I'm in the café one day, and you walk in with a woman on your arm, maybe a friend of mine."

"Shelly?"

Her expression darkened. "Let's not use Shelly in this scenario."

"Another friend of yours then."

"And you start dating her. How do you think that would make me feel?"

He shrugged. "In your scenario, I don't really owe you anything. I mean, in your scenario, maybe we danced."

"Maybe."

"Maybe we shared a mind-blowing, life-altering kiss."

"Don't get ahead of yourself." At his raised eyebrows, she said, "But maybe that, yeah."

He chuckled. "But a kiss isn't a commitment. We haven't even been on a date. We're friends, and all we've promised to be is friends. So I can date anyone I want."

"Exactly. And if it hurts me, well, that's my fault for not saying yes when I had the chance."

"Let's hope you've learned your lesson."

"But with Bentley..."

Thomas barely managed to contain a growl. He'd forgotten they were talking about another man.

"Bentley and I were engaged. When I ended our engagement, he acted like he was devastated. He tried to change my mind for months. I moved away, but he called me all the time. And then he came up here, trying to reconcile with me. He's been here for weeks. He's told me multiple times that he still loves me. He claimed he wants me back."

"And you've been considering that." He didn't phrase it as a question.

"No. Yes. Maybe, for a little while. I mean, here was this man who was willing to give up everything for me. He offered to quit his job, to move here to Coventry. You have to understand, politics is his dream. He loves it. He *thrives* in it. But he said he was willing to give it all up for me."

"What a hero." Thomas couldn't help the sarcastic undertone. Fortunately, Josie didn't seem to pick up on it.

"And all that time... It's not as if they dated. I would have heard if they'd been seen together around town. So they didn't go out together in public. They didn't tell anybody. They had an affair, a secret affair. My fiancé and my best friend. During those months when he was calling me, begging me to take him back, he was sleeping with Shelly."

"But you weren't together."

"I know that."

"So, what's the problem?"

She sighed, the exhale long and tired. "The problem is, he never would have told me, though how he thought Shelly would be able to keep that secret indefinitely, I have no idea. Telephone, telegraph, tell Shelly. But the point is, he would have gotten back together with me. He would have *married* me, knowing all the while he'd betrayed me."

"But—"

"I know, Thomas. I know. We were broken up. Under the current rules of society, he should be able to do whatever he wants if we're broken up. It's like that old sitcom."

"'We were on a break,'" Thomas quoted.

"Exactly. Except I understand now how the woman felt. If he really loved her, how could he sleep with someone else?"

Thomas didn't know how to answer that question. He'd never been in love, so he couldn't speak to that aspect of it. But he'd been that guy once. Not that he'd been a player, picking different women every weekend. But he'd slept with women he'd only marginally cared for. He'd slept with women he'd known he'd never fall in love with, never marry.

In college, he'd learned the damage that kind of behavior could do to a soul. He'd repented. But he knew very well how a man could sleep with someone he didn't love.

And he'd known his share of women who could do the same. He was happy to learn Josie wasn't one of those.

Thomas doubted Bentley had felt much of anything for Shelly. In fact, he seemed to loathe her, and the feeling was mutual. How they'd put up with one another, he couldn't fathom. Maybe they'd kept the talking to a minimum.

"I shouldn't have moved in with him," Josie said. "I shouldn't have been intimate with him. We're connected because of that, and now that I know he was with Shelly, it feels like the worst kind of betrayal."

"The fact that you feel so deeply about it," Thomas said, "makes me wonder if you and Bentley are really through, or if maybe I should bow out." He almost added "gracefully." But if she asked him to quit pursuing her, he'd do so kicking and screaming. There'd be nothing graceful about it.

Josie shook her head. "I don't love him. I don't want to be with him. I just feel like he lied to me. I'm hurt. But my heart isn't broken."

"And Shelly?"

She released another sigh. "Oh, Shelly. I don't even know. Why should she be off the hook? I've known her almost all my life, but I'm not surprised by her behavior. She's always been pretty weak-willed. Gullible. I'm sure Bentley seduced her."

Thomas didn't know if he agreed with Josie's opinion of Shelly. The woman was a little ditzy, but that didn't make her stupid. In fact, helping with his campaign, she'd proved herself to be insightful and talented. Maybe Josie was the smarter of the two, but that didn't make Shelly a simpleton.

"I'll forgive her," Josie said. "It'll just take time."

"So, thinking about what happened last night," Thomas said, "do you think one of them changed sides?"

"There's no reason to believe that. Anybody could have broken into my bedroom."

True. And yet...

There had been four people in that apartment besides Josie. As far as anybody outside knew, one of them could have been sitting with her all night.

Maybe one of them *should* have been.

Yet, somebody felt confident enough to climb the trellis, take a pry bar to the window, and climb in. Which led Thomas to believe that somebody had given the intruder the go-ahead.

That could have been any of them, not just those who had access to her bedroom—meaning both Thomas and Bentley would be included on the list.

Had Lake been keeping Donley informed of everybody's whereabouts in the apartment? If so, Donley could be on the suspect list.

Except Zack had confirmed that Donley had been at the hotel all night. Donley had been cleared.

Thomas hadn't been in contact with anyone, but Shelly had been on her phone more than once. To whom?

And Bentley...Bentley had been on his phone throughout the night.

"What are you thinking?" Josie asked.

Nothing he needed to share with her. Josie had enough worries without adding more reason for her to suspect the people she'd trusted to protect her. But Thomas would be giving Zack Tyler a call when he had a chance.

Because it was very possible one of the people closest to Josie was working against her.

CHAPTER TWENTY-SEVEN

Josie sat across from Thomas at a little restaurant she'd never heard of. "What is farm-to-table fusion?"

Thomas studied his menu. "I think it means they can't decide what kind of restaurant they want to be. They have French food, Italian, Greek, Asian... Maybe 'fusion' is another word for 'befuddled.'"

It felt good to laugh. "Smells good, at least."

Donley stood near the door, gaze flicking around the room. The modern place, with its shiny light hardwood floors and square tables and black chairs, was mostly empty. She figured a lot of folks were preparing to watch fireworks or flipping burgers on a grill. Farm-to-table fusion wasn't exactly traditional Fourth of July fare.

"We should ask Donley what he wants," Josie said. "We can get it to go."

Thomas popped up from the table and approached the bodyguard, menu in hand. Donley didn't look pleased, but after they chatted a minute, he glanced at the menu.

Thomas slid back into his chair. "He told me he didn't need anything and refused to choose until I threatened to order him a chickpea salad. He'll have the steak."

Josie studied the menu, reminding herself that this wasn't a date, just two people sharing a meal, chatting, acting like all was well. Not that she wouldn't gladly go out with Thomas. In fact, she looked forward to it, but she didn't want this to count as their first date. She hoped that could happen when they didn't have a bodyguard in tow.

They'd decided not to talk about what had happened the night before. This was to be a break from the drama, not a continuation of it.

After they ordered, Thomas told her what it was like growing up in Coventry, about skiing in the winter and boating in the summer, about his parents and his siblings. His folks still lived in Coventry, but his siblings had moved away after college, two to southern New Hampshire, one to the Boston area.

"I see them a few times a year," Thomas said. "I miss them, of course, but I don't blame them for leaving. Small-town life is great, but the employment options aren't like they are in the city. If you don't want to work in the tourism industry or at HCI, there's not a lot of opportunity here."

"You made a way for yourself, though," Josie said.

"I'm lucky."

Blessed, she thought. And a hard worker. And he loved people and treated them with dignity, especially important for someone in sales.

How had she ever thought him disingenuous, a typical politician? She used to trust her first impressions, but she'd been way off about Thomas.

And if he was an alpha male, he was the best kind—a leader, but a sacrificial one.

Meek.

In modern language, meek equated to weak, but she'd heard a sermon once that delved into the origins of the word in Greek.

The pastor had explained in great detail what the word would have meant to Jesus's listeners when he'd said, *"Blessed are the meek, for they shall inherit the earth."*

Josie didn't remember all of that sermon, but she remembered the phrases the pastor had used to define meekness: strength under control, a willingness to take on others' burdens.

Thomas was a beautiful image of meek. Strong and eager to use his strength to bless others.

An alpha male submitted to God's authority.

It was...beautiful.

He set his drink down, head tilted to the side. "What are you thinking?"

Warmth filled her cheeks, and she dropped her gaze. She hated to think of the adoring look she must have had on her face. "Nothing, nothing." She took a bite of salad and chewed slowly, wrestling her thoughts back in line.

When she did, she told him about her growing-up years—long, humid summer days, evenings decorated with brilliant sunsets and flickering fireflies, so many afternoons sitting in the stands to watch her brother's baseball games.

"You didn't play?"

"You've clearly never tossed me a ball. If you had, you'd see I don't so much *catch* as *duck and pray*."

He chuckled. "You get that from your mother?"

"Dad, actually. Mom was an all-star softball player. Dad was captain of the debate team. How about you? Sports?"

"I played a few in high school. Even played football in college for a couple of years."

"College ball? I'm impressed."

"Don't be. Plymouth is a D3 school."

Her facial expression must have clued him in that she didn't understand because he chuckled. "You went to Duke, right? That's a Division 1 school. We weren't in their league."

"How did you know I went to Duke?"

His smile was quick, very amused.

"What?"

"You mentioned it last night. A couple of times."

Her cheeks flared for the second time in a few minutes. "Oh, no. What else did I say?"

"Nothing to be embarrassed about." But the way he was still smiling told her different.

"What?"

"You told us you're smart. You wanted us to explain what we were so worried about. You were sure you could help, which is why you said you went to Duke. The doctor was very impressed."

She touched her cool hands to her burning cheeks. "How embarrassing."

Thomas was *still* smiling. There must be more to the story. "What?"

He shrugged. "Nothing."

"Not nothing. What?"

He leaned forward and lowered his voice. "You might have suggested you and I should kiss again."

"Oh, no. I hope I didn't say that in front of Bentley."

Thomas's expression dimmed. "You didn't." He speared a few bits of penne pasta.

She'd definitely ruined the moment. She ate a few bites of her meal and then set her fork down. "You said you played football a couple of years in college. How come you didn't play the whole time? Did you tire of it?"

If she'd hoped to revive Thomas's mood, she'd failed. Thomas took another bite.

She could let him off the hook, but she was curious, so she kept her mouth shut.

He set the fork down. "It's an ugly story, one I don't like to talk about. Or think about, actually."

"You don't have to tell me."

He studied her a long moment. She wondered what he saw in her eyes. Hopefully acceptance and friendship, and maybe more.

She was starting to feel the *more*. And it wasn't just the kiss. It was the way he'd stuck by her despite the conflicts swirling around her. The way he'd pursued her friendship as ardently as he'd once pursued her as a date.

It was his kindness and generosity. His meekness. It was...everything.

"December, junior year," he said. "I was at a frat party. Most of my teammates were there, along with what seemed like half the women on campus. I was dating this girl, Amber, and she came. We'd been out a few times, nothing serious. Except, you know college kids... Maybe you weren't like this. You probably weren't." He swallowed. "Anyway, we'd been...you know."

"I'm not sure I do."

"We were sleeping together." He seemed to cringe at the words. "Which to me felt like...no big deal. I was young and stupid, and girls seemed to like me."

She could imagine Thomas as a college kid—handsome, strong, popular. Also, charming, kind, remembering everybody's name. Of course the girls liked him.

"Anyway, Amber was at the party, but I was with my buddies, drinking. I wasn't paying attention to her. I sort of wanted her to leave. I guess I wasn't as into her as she was me. Which makes me the biggest jerk."

"What were you, twenty?"

"Yeah."

Josie picked at her salad until he continued the story.

"She asked me to take her home. She was mad that I'd been ignoring her, demanding I stop what I was doing. It was about nine-thirty, and I didn't want to leave. I was playing ping pong, and I was winning. The guys were razzing me about being henpecked, which ticked me off. I told her I'd take her home later, but she got huffy and stormed out. I should have gone after her."

"She could have waited until you were done with your game."

Thomas nodded, sipped his drink.

Josie had a bad feeling about where this was going.

"She was attacked," he said. "After she left the party. A guy grabbed her, dragged her off the road into the woods. Raped her."

"Oh, my gosh. Thomas, that's awful. I'm so sorry."

"Didn't happen to me." She heard not defensiveness but something else in his tone. If she had to guess, she'd name it self-loathing. "I was drinking beer and having the time of my life."

"What happened to her wasn't your fault. She made her choices."

"So it was her fault?"

"I'm not saying that. The person who attacked her—it was his fault. I'm just saying she decided to walk home alone. She didn't have to do that. Did they catch the guy?"

"He went to prison."

"How about Amber?"

"A stranger got her to the hospital and called her parents. She left school and never returned. We talked once after that. I told her how sorry I was, and she said the same thing you said, that it wasn't my fault. But I should have been there for her. After that, I had no desire to play football. Or go to parties or do any of the stuff I'd been doing. In that respect, what happened to her was good for me. I got my act together, returned to God."

"And Amber?" Josie hoped her story ended as well.

"By all accounts, she recovered physically. She'd been a

recreational drug user, but they prescribed her painkillers in the hospital, and she got hooked. When they proved hard to come by, she graduated to heroin. Last I heard, she'd checked herself out of rehab and relapsed."

"Oh. Poor thing." Josie leaned toward him, wishing there weren't a table between them, wishing she could comfort him as he'd comforted her earlier. "It wasn't your fault. Maybe you should have walked her home, but you didn't attack her. And you certainly didn't force her to use drugs."

"I know." He tipped up the corners of his mouth as if trying to force a smile, but the rest of his face wasn't on board.

Why was the world such a horrible place?

What kind of men lurked behind bushes and attacked defenseless women?

What kind of people slipped drugs into women's drinks?

What kind of people made their living killing unborn babies?

She knew there was a God and knew that He didn't condone any of that. He sent people—people like Josie's father, like Thomas—to fight evil.

Her gaze snapped up. "That's why you're so protective."

One of his shoulders lifted, dropped. "I just think... I know I wasn't the person who attacked her, but I could have prevented it. I could've been there. So now, I guess I just always want to *be there*. I never want to be the guy who's sitting at home drinking a beer while somebody's trapped in a burning building or suffering a heart attack."

"Or stranded on a mountain with a broken ankle."

A glimmer lit his eyes. "That worked out well for me."

"Me, too. I'd still be sitting there if not for you."

"Beta would've gotten you out of there somehow."

She gave him a look intended to convey disapproval, and he

chuckled. "You asked me to stop calling him that, and I did...to his face."

"Very big of you."

"I'm nothing if not kind." He regarded her across the table for a long moment, and she felt a connection between them, a stirring deep in her soul. There was something here with this man. There was something new and different, something she'd never felt before.

She couldn't define it, not yet. But maybe, with time...

"So," he said, "now I've told you my big, bad secret. What's yours?"

Everything she'd been feeling twisted inside her along with the salad. What was she thinking? He was only attracted to her because he didn't know the truth about her.

When he did...

"I'm guessing it has something to do with Mitchell, right?"

She looked around at the restaurant. Not that there were many diners there, but some people had better hearing than others. Shelly'd taught her that.

She didn't want to tell Thomas. She didn't want to tell anybody. But Thomas had confided in her, and he'd proved his devotion over and over. And by staying by her side, he'd likely made himself a target.

Yes, if anybody deserved to know the truth, it was Thomas. Maybe after he knew everything, he'd distance himself from her.

Because Josie could only bring trouble into his life. She had very little else to offer.

∾

Josie hadn't told Thomas her story in the restaurant. And, seated in the backseat of Donley's SUV, she didn't want to share it. Donley could be trusted not to tell anybody her secret.

Probably.

But Josie didn't trust anybody except Thomas at the moment. She'd tell him her story later, when they were alone.

And maybe she was full of excuses. Who could blame her for wanting to hide the worst thing about herself from this good and kind man?

The scent of Donley's take-out filtered back from the front seat, making her wish she'd eaten more of her salad, or at least a few bites of the cheesecake Thomas had ordered for them to share. As they wound along backroads toward Coventry, fatigue was pressing in.

Thomas slid his arm around her shoulder and urged her closer. She settled her head against his chest and closed her eyes, drifting off.

The shrill sound of her phone ringing jarred her from sleep. She pulled it from her purse and glanced at the screen. Dad.

Thomas shifted away and pulled his arm back. "You'd better get that."

She was surprised her father had left her alone for a couple of hours. She'd been talking to him off and on all day. Steeling herself, she connected the video call. "Hey, Dad."

His face filled the screen. "Where are you?"

"On our way back from dinner."

He didn't have to speak his disapproval. It was written on his features. "Someone almost killed you last night."

"I know, but—"

"Your bodyguards shouldn't have let you—"

"They don't tell me what to do," Josie said. "Did you need something?"

Mom leaned into view. "We're worried about you, sweetheart."

"I'm being careful, Mom. Nobody knew where we were going—"

"Who's we?" Dad asked.

She angled the phone to Thomas, who said, "Senator, Mrs. Harrington."

Thomas hadn't spoken to Josie's mother yet. Mom's eyes brightened. "You must be Thomas. It's nice to meet you."

"You too, ma'am."

She smiled. "Look at that. A Yankee with manners. I didn't think they existed."

Thomas laughed. "We're a rare breed."

Before Mom could respond, Dad said, "Josephine, you need to come home where you'll be safe. I've gotten you a flight out of Manchester tomorrow at—"

"I hope it's refundable," Josie said. "I'm not leaving."

"Josephine Maria Harrington," her father said, "this is no longer negotiable. Your mother is worried sick."

Mom nodded, all amusement fading away. "We're both worried. Won't you just come home for a visit until we can get this sorted out?"

"I own a business here," Josie said. "It's bad enough I've been AWOL all day. I can't leave my employees to manage the place while I'm gone."

"Then hire better employees," Dad snapped. "If you lose the business, you can start another—"

"Easy for you to say." She took a breath and infused calm into her voice. "I've built a life here, Dad. This is my home."

"It would be temporary," Mom said. "Your safety is more important than your business."

She glanced at Thomas, whose lips were pressed in a grim line.

He said, "Marcel and Kinsey could keep the business running."

"Et tu?"

"Your safety is—"

"Listen to the man," Dad said. Then, "Hold on…"

The screen went black a moment before Carlyle's face popped up. "Hey, Josie."

She suppressed a sigh. "Carlyle, are you here to bully me too?"

"Was that on the agenda?" the older man asked. "I'm not prepared, but I can get caught up."

She scowled at him, and he grinned.

Dad was not amused. "We're explaining why she needs to come home."

"And?" Carlyle asked. "Are you going to?"

"No," she said.

"Definitely," Dad said.

"Precious girl," Mom said. "It would be so nice to have you home."

Donley pulled the car into the driveway beside Josie's house and turned to her, a no-nonsense expression on his face. "We need to get you inside."

She'd never liked the bodyguard more. "Sorry, y'all, but I have to go." Before they could argue, she ended the video chat and rounded on Thomas. "Thanks for backing me up."

His eyes widened. Before he could come up with a response, Donley opened her door, and she climbed out and stomped up the exterior staircase. She stepped inside her apartment, and Thomas and Donley followed. Donley locked the door, and she and Thomas stood against the wall, silent, while the bodyguard searched the apartment. A moment later, he returned from down the hall. "It's clear."

Josie crossed the room and collapsed on the sofa. Though

Thomas wasn't her boyfriend, she could imagine it. She liked the idea of it, but if he didn't back her up on the important things...

"I just want you to be safe." He settled beside her on the couch. "You'd be safe there."

"Would I? Or would I just put my mother in danger?"

"Isn't she already in danger?"

Josie shrugged. "My brother and his family haven't been targeted. Mom hasn't been targeted."

"Any chance that's because they have better protection?" Thomas's gaze flicked to Donley. "No offense."

"You could be better protected," Donley said. "I can call my agency tonight, get more guys up here."

Assuming she could trust them. She shifted to face the man by the door. "Did you get an update on Lake?"

His eyes didn't react to the question, but his lips hardened. "She's been taken off the case. The agency's sending someone else."

"Someone you trust?"

He dipped his head.

"You thought Lake was trustworthy."

"Lake *is* trustworthy." Donley's tone dared her to argue. "I don't know what they found, if they found anything, or if they're just being extra cautious, but I'd trust Lake with my life."

"Can you call and ask her what happened?" Josie asked.

"I've been told to have no contact with her."

"Can *I* call her?"

The bodyguard regarded Josie a long moment. She didn't know what she hoped to learn from Lake, but she'd trusted the woman. She didn't want to believe Lake had betrayed her. Maybe if she understood...

Donley yanked his phone from his pocket and, stepping

closer, tapped the screen. He held it so Josie could see the number there.

Josie dialed her own phone, putting it on speaker.

It rang four times, and she was preparing to leave a message when it connected. "This is Lake."

Did the woman ever use her first name? Come to think of it, Josie didn't even know her first name. "It's Josie. How are you?"

There was a long pause before Lake said, "Fine. Are you safe?"

"Yeah." She waited a beat, hoped Lake would say something else, but the woman didn't. "What happened?"

"A sizable deposit was made into my bank account yesterday."

Thomas shifted closer. "Sizable like...?"

"Fifty thousand dollars," Lake said. "I have no idea where it came from."

"How was the deposit made?" Thomas asked. "In person, online, or—"

"By mail."

"I didn't know you could make deposits by mail," Josie said. "Is that how you usually deposit your checks?"

"It's the twenty-first century, ma'am. I have an app for that. I've never mailed a check, but the bank didn't think to flag it as unusual. They don't question deposits like they do withdrawals. The authorities are investigating the origin of the check."

"Do you know what they've learned so far?" Josie asked.

"They're not in the mood to share." For the first time, Lake's voice held a tinge of bitterness. "I knew nothing about that deposit until the chief there in Coventry—"

"Cote?" Thomas said.

"Until Cote told me about it. I was not working against you."

Donley stood by the door. A glance at his face told Josie he was satisfied with his partner's answer. She wasn't so sure. She'd known people to do things they'd never otherwise consider for less money than fifty thousand dollars.

Thomas said, "Do you have any theories, Lake?"

The question was met with silence that stretched for ten seconds, twenty, thirty. Then Lake said, "Ms. Smith?"

"I'm here."

"Donley's on your side. I'm on your side. Your family's on your side. I wouldn't trust anybody else."

Josie turned to Thomas, who glared at the phone.

"Thomas was nowhere near my room last night."

"I'm not saying he has anything to do with this. I'm saying... I'm saying you were smart to send your other friends away. Maybe you're right to trust Thomas. Maybe you're not. I don't know. I do know this is bigger than we first understood. Whoever's behind this... They're not playing games. You're not safe."

The words made Josie's heart jolt. She breathed through the fear. "Okay. Thanks for talking to me. I'm sure they'll get to the bottom of this, and you'll be cleared."

"Thank you, ma'am." Three beeps told her Lake had disconnected.

The momentary relief Josie had enjoyed during dinner was long gone. She turned to Donley. "This new agent, you trust him?"

"It's a woman, and I don't work with people I don't trust. But two people can't protect you like a team can. If I were you, I'd either hire more protection or do what your father suggests, assuming he and your mother have better protection than you do."

The problem was, Donley and Thomas—and her father, for that matter—didn't know what Josie knew, that Mitchell had reason to target her. That if she went home, she might be safer, or she might be putting her family in more danger.

Staying here, though, she was likely putting Thomas in danger.

Maybe a team of bodyguards wasn't a bad idea. It was better than the alternatives.

Her phone rang.

She'd sort of hoped they'd take her not having called back as a hint, not that her father'd ever been great at taking hints. She connected the video call and angled the phone so Thomas was on the screen.

Carlyle's image popped up first, her dad's a moment later. Both the images were tiny on her phone. "If you're not going to come home," Carlyle said, "then we need to consider our options."

"There are no options," Dad said. "I'm not voting for the bill."

Josie had known Carlyle for as long as she could remember. She'd worked with him for years. So when he shifted, when his cheeks puffed out, she knew he had something important to say, something he didn't think her father would want to hear.

Dad knew it too. "Spit it out, Carlyle."

"Talked to Parker," Carlyle said. "She said they'd be willing to make changes."

"We've been down this road." Dad's voice held a level of frustration he rarely allowed voters to hear.

"They've put more on the table," Carlyle said. "They're willing to cut the overall cost by half. That's a heckuva concession."

Her father glared at the screen, but she knew the anger wasn't directed at her. "Are they still going to fund new clinics?"

For his part, Carlyle didn't squirm, just looked dead into the camera. "They won't budge on that."

Dad crossed his arms. "I won't either."

Carlyle sat behind his desk in his office, despite the fact that it was nearly ten p.m. "You'd put your daughter in danger?"

Dad ran a hand through his hair. A single word escaped his mouth, filled with anguish. "Josie."

She wanted to tell him not to worry about her, that she'd be fine.

But these people, whoever they were, had gotten to her not once, not twice, but three times. They'd threatened her. They'd drugged her. They'd broken into her bedroom.

And that wasn't even counting the time they'd had her arrested.

How far would Mitchell go to get what he wanted? As far as she and Bentley had gone to get what they'd wanted? Maybe just a little bit farther.

Maybe a lot farther.

"Sir?" Carlyle and Dad had been friends for years. Carlyle rarely called him sir.

Her father lifted his hand in a *let me think* motion.

Nobody spoke for a long moment.

Then Dad said, "Josie, please, darlin'. Please come home."

She didn't want to. But this wasn't about her. It was much, much bigger than one small-town coffee-shop owner.

Her employees could keep Cuppa Josie's open. She could hire more staff, if need be. Not that the business was raking in the cash, but she had money.

Thomas took her hand and squeezed. His voice was low when he said, "It wouldn't be forever."

When she looked his way, his expression was pleading. He didn't want her to leave—she knew that. But he did want her to be safe.

"Okay. Tomorrow, I'll talk to my employees. I'm not willing to lose my business over this."

Dad's shoulders relaxed. "You just tell us how we can help."

"In the meantime," Carlyle said, "you need to keep me informed about where you go and what you do. I need to know what's going on up there, who you're spending time with, that sort of thing."

"I have a bodyguard, Carlyle. I don't need a keeper."

He leaned toward the camera. "Look, I know you're mad at Bentley right now..."

Mad wasn't the right word.

"...but he was my eyes and ears there," Carlyle said. "Now that he's gone, I feel like I'm flying blind."

"There's nothing going on here you need to know about," Josie said.

He stared into the camera. "You're wrong. I need to know everything. Where you go. What you do. Who you talk to. The more I know, the better shot we have of getting to the bottom of this. You and I both know what this is about."

The words hung between them.

So Carlyle knew.

The realization churned her stomach.

"What does that mean?" Dad asked.

Thomas gave her a curious look but said nothing.

Carlyle ignored the other two men. "I expect you to keep me in the loop."

Dad's eyes flicked back and forth, studying them both. But neither of them would tell Dad what Carlyle was talking about. And fortunately, Dad had been in politics long enough to know when he ought not to press it.

Finally, Josie nodded. "Will do."

"Better yet," Carlyle said, "give your bodyguard the go-ahead to alert me about your plans, and you won't have to worry about it."

She glanced at Donley, expecting him to nod or give her a gesture of approval.

But he didn't. He shook his head.

What did that mean?

Rather than get into it, she focused back on the screen. "I'll keep you informed." Before either man could speak again, she ended the call.

She'd been tired before the conversation. Now, she felt wrung out.

She turned back to Donley. "Do you not trust Carlyle?"

His gaze flicked from her to Thomas and back. "Bentley was keeping Carlyle informed last night. I don't know what he told him. I do know somebody felt pretty confident climbing in your window. So...no. I don't trust anybody right now. Not even the man who hired me."

CHAPTER TWENTY-EIGHT

It was just after ten o'clock when Josie said goodnight. Thomas watched as she padded in bare feet down the hall to her bedroom. How she thought she'd be able to sleep with the fireworks going off at the park just a few blocks away, Thomas had no idea.

After she disappeared into her room, Thomas stretched out on the sofa. "I know you're not thrilled I'm here."

Earlier, when the cops were still there, Donley had wedged a two-by-four on top of the double-hung window in Josie's room to ensure nobody would be able to break in again. Still, he'd asked her to keep her door open and warned her he'd be popping his head in occasionally to ensure she was safe.

Josie hadn't argued, though she'd looked so tired, Thomas thought maybe she hadn't had the energy to care.

Now, Donley leveled his gaze at Thomas. "Can I look at your phone?"

"Come again?"

"All the rest of us—myself, Lake, Bentley, Shelly—had our phones checked. But you didn't."

Thomas crossed to where his phone was plugged in, disconnected it, and handed it to the bodyguard.

Donley lifted it to Thomas's face, and the phone unlocked. Then the man tapped the screen.

Thomas had nothing to hide, so he returned to the couch. After dinner, he had run home to change and brush his teeth. He was struggling to keep his eyes open.

He wasn't sure how Donley was holding up.

"When will your partner be here?" Thomas asked.

"Couple hours. She was on another assignment." Donley barely glanced up from his perusal. "When she gets here, I'll head back to the hotel and rest." He lowered the phone. "No calls or texts from the time we left the hospital last night until this morning."

"I know."

"Unless you deleted them."

"Lake was here. You can ask her. I got my charger from my apartment, plugged it in right there"—he nodded to the TV console—"and never touched it again."

Donley returned it to the charger. "I had to make sure."

"Somebody alerted the intruder that it was safe to break in."

"Possibly."

"You don't think it was Lake."

"Assuming that's what happened, I know it wasn't Lake. Was she on her phone?"

Thomas thought back. He'd never seen either bodyguard look at a cell phone while on duty except to talk to one another. But she always had that earpiece in her ear. Somebody could have called her. Maybe there'd been some super-secret signal through her earpiece.

At this point, anything was possible.

"If you're right," Thomas said, "then that leaves Bentley and Shelly."

"Both of whom were questioned and released," Donley said. "But that doesn't mean they're innocent. It just means they weren't caught."

"Or maybe the intruder just took a chance she'd be alone."

"Also possible." Donley stared ahead, but his eyes narrowed. He shook his head. "This guy has managed to avoid getting caught. Would he take the chance last night? Unless... I can see somebody well trained. He might try to see if anybody was awake in the room."

"How?"

"Toss pebbles against the glass, get somebody to glance out. If he was really good, he could climb the trellis without being heard and peek inside. Her curtains have gaps."

"Maybe nobody alerted the intruder," Thomas clarified.

"Maybe."

"So, we've got nothing."

Donley's frown reflected Thomas's frustration. "It's good she's going to her parents' house. This place isn't secure at all. I assume she'll be safer there."

Thomas was about to agree when he remembered something Donley had said earlier. "You don't trust Carlyle?"

"I don't trust anybody."

Carlyle had seemed to be trying to convince the senator to vote for the bill, and according to Bentley, he'd been on board with that plan since the weekend Josie was arrested. Did that mean he was working for Mitchell?

Or was this typical politics—fight for what you believe in until it gets hard, and then give in?

Thomas hoped that, when his own back was against the wall, he'd stand strong like the senator was doing. He hoped he'd be able to place the people he loved in God's capable hands.

Right. Because he'd done such a good job of that.

Since Amber's attack, he'd struggled to trust God with other people's safety. His own life—no problem. But with anyone else? That was one reason Thomas so often stepped into the role of protector. God hadn't looked after Amber. How could Thomas trust Him to protect Josie? Or anybody else?

That was why he was running for mayor. Maybe somebody else would have stepped up to protect Coventry from Farley, but Thomas hadn't been willing to risk the people he loved on a *maybe*.

He needed to learn to trust God in that area. But it wasn't going to happen tonight.

"And what about you?" Thomas asked. "When she leaves, will you get another assignment right away?"

"Probably."

"Is this one typical?"

The man almost cracked a smile. "Most of our clients are rich, often famous, and either paranoid that somebody's after them or trying to make themselves seem more important than they are."

"So the opposite of Josie."

"Yeah."

"This must be a nice change of pace."

The bodyguard scowled. "There's nothing good about it. And the fact that we've failed to keep her safe doesn't sit well. We need more resources. More information."

"Or just to get her to her parents' house. Then you'll be off the hook."

And Thomas would be alone with all the time in the world to devote to his campaign. That should feel like a good thing, but it didn't.

Thomas settled back on the sofa, yawning. He was just drifting off, despite the fireworks booming outside, when his phone rang.

Should he ignore it? All things considered, probably not. But when he crossed the room to glance at the screen, he almost rejected the call.

"What do you want?"

Bentley said, "I need to talk to Josie."

"You have her number."

"She didn't pick up, but this is important."

"I don't know what to tell you, man."

"You're still there, right? Is she"—Bentley swallowed audibly—"right there with you? It's okay. I mean, she and I—"

"She's in her room. I'm on the couch. Not that it's any of your business." Thomas didn't want anybody, including Bentley, getting the wrong idea.

"Okay." Bentley's tone was considerably brighter. "Good. That's... Anyway, I need to talk to her."

"Obviously, she doesn't need to talk to you. Why don't you tell me what you need, and I'll pass the message along."

"We don't need a go-between."

"Do you want my help or not?"

"I'm not working against her. I would never hurt her. Or her father, for that matter. The man means everything to me. *She* means everything to me."

Bentley sounded sincere. Thomas took a chance and asked, "Where'd the money come from?"

"My great-aunt. I don't have the will, but when her lawyer's office opens tomorrow, I'll have a copy sent over to whoever wants to see it. She had a lot more money than anyone in the family knew. I get that it looks bad, but I haven't done anything wrong."

Maybe. But Bentley had urged the senator to vote yes on the bill. Did that mean he was working for Mitchell? Or did it mean his care for Josie overrode his convictions?

Assuming he had convictions.

"Maybe that's true," Thomas said, "but it doesn't change anything."

"You could put in a good word for me."

Thomas didn't bother to respond to that.

"She doesn't belong here," Bentley said. "She'll never be happy here."

"It's possible she knows herself better than you know her."

"Maybe she does. But one thing's for sure—I know her better than you do."

Not for long, not if Thomas had anything to say about it. But he wasn't the type of guy to pour salt into wounds. "You said you had something important?"

"I've been working on finding a way to get Mitchell to back off. Rumor has it he's involved with another mistress, this one older than the last, and well-connected. Unfortunately, that angle probably won't work because Mitchell's at his summer home with his family, so we won't be able to catch him with this woman anytime soon. I have people trying to hack his phone, but—"

"I don't want to know this, Bentley, and I'm sure Josie doesn't either."

Bentley's laugh was short and humorless. "Proving what I said earlier, that I know her better than you do."

Surely Josie wouldn't condone such behavior. Right?

"Until we get something solid," Bentley said, "I've started rumors in his organization to try to get a little "Me Too" action going. The rumors are vague. I'm just trying to get someone to go on the record, someone not afraid of backlash."

Though that still didn't sit well, if Mitchell was the pervert a few of his female employees suggested he was, he needed to be removed from a position of authority, possibly prosecuted. "How will that help?"

"If Mitchell thinks we can keep the truth about himself and his behavior from coming out, he'll back off."

"So what will that look like? A woman gets the courage to come forward with allegations, and then Mitchell leaves Josie alone, and then what? You shut that woman up?"

"We incentivize her to keep quiet."

"And all the other women, assuming there are others and you haven't just made that whole angle up, are taught that coming forward ends with...what? What would happen to the one who came forward? She'd get fired, probably. She'd be publicly humiliated."

"We can't save the world here, Thomas. We're trying to protect Josie."

"By putting other people in harm's way."

"Not harm. Just—"

"Because a man who almost killed Josie wouldn't harm a woman who spoke out against him."

"You're getting way ahead of yourself."

"No. I'm taking your actions to their logical conclusions. Do you ever do that? Or do you just run ahead, full-bore—"

"I'm a strategist, Thomas. This is what I do. And yes, I know the consequences. I also know that the senator won't vote yes. I'm trying to protect him, my boss. And Josie, the woman I love."

That line hit its mark.

Thomas cared about Josie too. Was it love? Maybe not yet, but it could be. Still, he wasn't willing to destroy other vulnerable women to protect her.

Arguing this point with Bentley felt fruitless. "What if Mitchell doesn't capitulate?"

"Then we bring him down, hard. We destroy him, destroy his reputation, so that even if the senator votes for the bill, Mitchell doesn't profit—"

"But he still will. He owns all that property. He owns the

abortion mills. Maybe he'll back out of the public eye, but we can't exactly force him to sell his clinics."

"Fine, but he's a public figure." Bentley's tone was that of a patient teacher speaking to a dull-headed student. "Famous people want to be loved. He'll do anything to keep the truth from coming out."

"So you're planning to destroy him to punish him? Not to stop him but to…what? Make yourself feel better, knowing you got the last word?"

"You have a problem with that? Don't you want him to pay?"

"Not like this. If he's behind what happened to her, then we should prove it. We should bring what he's done to light. We should have him arrested. Have charges—"

"That's not how the game is played. There's no way he'll ever face criminal charges."

Was that true?

Could Mitchell truly threaten a woman, drug her, nearly kill her, and get away with it?

Or was this all really just a game to Bentley and people like him, a game they preferred to play outside the boundaries of the law?

"Look, man, I get it," Bentley said. "This is too much for your small-town mind to comprehend—"

"If by small town, you mean honest, forthright, and above-board, then yeah, I guess it is too much for me."

"Which is irrelevant. I'm just asking you to tell Josie what I told you. Tell her I'm working on a solution. If she goes home and stays out of the public eye, stays safe for a couple of weeks, I can bring him down."

Outside, the booms of fireworks became more frequent. Maybe they were getting to the finale.

Maybe, once the booms stopped, Thomas would be able to

rest.

But in life, unlike in fireworks, the most damaging attacks didn't come with booms. They came with drugs being slipped into drinks. Intruders creeping through windows.

Powerful people pulling strings, bringing down enemies and damaging the innocent along the way.

"You'll pass the message along?" Bentley asked.

"She's sleeping."

"Maybe she'll rest easier knowing I have a plan."

Thomas hoped not. Bentley scheming—trying to expose Mitchell's mistress, paying to hack a phone, spreading false rumors in hopes of bringing out some version of the truth, no matter who got hurt—should not lead to improved sleep.

"I'll tell her when I tell her, Beta."

"What is with that name?"

Finally, the man had asked. Thomas had waited for this moment, the opportunity to explain the difference between being the alpha and being the beta. But he didn't have it in him. "It's too much for your big-city mind to comprehend." He ended the call and plugged his phone in again, silencing it before padding back to the sofa.

Donley gave him a long, hard look, but Thomas wasn't about to recap the conversation. The bodyguard had overheard enough.

Thomas closed his eyes and put the conversation with Bentley out of his head. Instead, he thought about something Donley had said. There was nothing good about Josie's life being in danger, except that the situation had given Thomas the opportunity to get to know her. He'd been attracted to her from the first time he'd seen her. That attraction had grown to something else, something much stronger. Because of that, he'd be grateful for this difficult situation, as long as Josie came through it unscathed. He prayed, when this was all over, when she returned to Coventry and picked up her life again, she'd still want Thomas to be a part of it.

But she had a secret, a big one she hadn't wanted to share at the restaurant. One that he was beginning to believe involved Bentley and the kinds of tactics the man had seemed so proud of.

A secret she hadn't shared with Thomas.

Thomas was up and down all night, replaying that conversation with Bentley and worrying about Josie. More than once, he wandered toward her bedroom and peeked inside, always to find her sound asleep and safe.

He'd been aware when Donley's replacement had arrived but hadn't opened his eyes. He had plenty of time to meet her later.

Even when he'd slept, his mind had been churning with all he'd learned. It wasn't exactly a restful night.

He awoke to Josie's voice. "Dad, calm down."

Thomas opened his eyes. Light was peeking through the curtains, though not very much. It was either very early or very cloudy outside. He sat up as Josie entered the living room, hair messy from sleep. She wore blue cotton pajamas and walked on bare feet. As adorable as the picture was, her expression told him something was wrong.

He stood and stretched.

Josie stared at him, eyes widening, speaking into the phone pressed to her ear. "What pictures?" She settled in a chair at the table, pulled her laptop from its bag, and opened it up.

Thomas sat beside her, not sure what was going on or what to do. He got a glimpse of the clock in the kitchen. It was just after five in the morning.

Josie set the phone on the table and hit the speaker button. She lifted her finger to her lips, telling Thomas to keep quiet.

Senator Harrington's voice came through loud and clear. "...gonna have that man drawn and quartered, and don't think I won't do it. It's one thing you living with Bentley. I didn't like it, but—"

"Dad, it's not what—"

"But this is unacceptable. I don't even know this fellow. Here he's acting like he's trying to protect you, and all the while—"

"Stop, or I'm hanging up."

Silence.

"Just let me catch up with you, okay?" Josie asked.

"I'm waiting."

Thomas mouthed, *What happened?*

She shook her head and clicked on her laptop screen. Her eyes widened.

A flush crept up her neck and into her cheeks, and she dropped her face into her hands.

Thomas angled the laptop toward himself.

And the bottom dropped out of his stomach.

It was a photograph. Josie lying on her stomach, her head to the side, her face pressed against the pillow, her eyes closed. A sheet covered her bottom half. Her top half was bare. No pajamas. No bra. Just skin.

On the far side of the bed, a man was standing over her.

Thomas looked at the man's face.

It was his own.

He was wearing nothing but a towel.

Looking down at her.

He stared at the photo, but he couldn't make sense of it.

He'd never been in Josie's room. Never.

Certainly never in a towel. Never when she was in bed. Unclothed.

Josie met his eyes. She mouthed, *I'm so sorry.*

He opened his mouth, but her quick head-shake silenced him.

"You up to speed now, darlin'?" the man asked.

"It's not real, Dad. It has to be photoshopped."

"Or maybe your Thomas isn't the hero he pretends to be."

Thomas wanted to speak, to defend himself. Why were they pretending he wasn't there? They'd done nothing wrong.

"It has to be photoshopped, Dad. Thomas and I are just friends."

"Is that so?" The man's voice held more than a hint of doubt.

"I can date anyone I choose. Why would I lie?"

"I just sent you another photo," the senator said. "I'll wait."

Josie angled the laptop back to herself and clicked a few times. Then her eyes closed.

Again, Thomas shifted the screen.

He scrolled down to see there were ten photos. They captured Thomas and Josie's kiss from the first, fervent moments to when he'd backed her against the stage wall to when they'd ended the kiss and embraced.

His body remembered that moment and longed to revisit it.

But his mind registered the awful truth. Somebody had been watching.

Josie took a deep breath and opened her eyes.

She avoided looking Thomas's direction.

"Dad, I need you to listen to me. Thomas and I kissed just one time, after his speech at the fundraiser. Is there an attraction between us? Definitely. Is it more than that? Certainly not."

Wow.

Jab a little knife in his back to go along with the nausea and crumbling dreams.

"The photos of us kissing are real," she said. "The photos of us in my bedroom are photoshopped. That kiss…that's as close as Thomas and I have gotten to the bedroom."

"And this paragon of goodness just waltzes around in a towel?" The senator scoffed into the phone. "Or in less, if the threats are real."

What threats?

Josie looked at Thomas to explain the image. He lifted imaginary barbells.

"They were probably taken at the gym," she said.

He grabbed her laptop, opened a note, and typed, *SAR, fire department, paramedic.*

"And he's a volunteer with search-and-rescue. Remember how I told you he was the one who carried me off the mountain?"

"Mm-hmm." The senator didn't sound impressed.

"He also volunteers with the fire department and the local ambulance service. I'm guessing all of those places have showers and locker rooms. Lots of opportunities for someone to take his photo without his knowledge. And then they plopped his image into the picture of me, making it look like he was there. But Dad, he wasn't. It's not real."

"If that's the case," the senator said, "someone did a heckuva job faking it."

"Get Carlyle on it. He can find someone to prove—"

"You think I want to show this to Carlyle? It's not fittin'." The man's Southern accent was more pronounced than Thomas had ever heard it.

Josie said, "I know, but—"

"And for all we know, Thomas set the whole thing up.

Maybe you were sleepin', and he let himself into your room. It could've happened weeks ago. Maybe—"

"That's not what happened. Listen to me."

"So you can defend him?"

"He doesn't need me to defend him. He hasn't done anything wrong." Josie shot Thomas a tortured look. "That photo had to have been taken the night before last, when I was drugged."

"You don't know that."

"I do because I sleep in pajamas. Every single night. You woke me from a dead sleep this morning. Shall I take a selfie so you can see what I wore to bed? They're blue, and they have little yellow flowers on them."

The senator was quiet for a long moment. "Okay, you sleep in pajamas."

"Which means the intruder did more than just relate that message to me the other night." She swallowed, and horror filled her features. "He took these pictures when I was drugged."

"You weren't in pajamas because—?"

"Because I was so out of it from the drug that it was all Shelly could do to get my dress off. We thought...you and Bentley and I all thought they slipped me the drugs to make me look bad. We thought they broke into my apartment to prove they could get to me. But this was their real objective." Her gaze snapped to Thomas, and her mouth opened in a little O.

But Thomas had already put it together.

This was what the reporter's phone call had been about. Either she'd already had these photos, or she'd been told they were forthcoming.

While Josie and her father discussed the many terrible possibilities, Thomas crossed the room and grabbed his phone, barely registering the bodyguard standing against the wall. He unlocked it and maneuvered to the local paper's website.

No photos. Nothing about him.

Huh.

He settled beside Josie and showed her the paper's home screen.

She nodded. "Dad, have any of them been released?"

"They scheduled the vote for later today. If I vote yes, the photos will be destroyed. If I don't, these and others that are much more graphic will be released all over the country."

"They can't be more graphic," Josie said. "Not unless they photoshop our faces on other people's bodies. They might have more revealing photos of me"—a flush filled her expression, but her words remained calm—"but there won't be any with me and Thomas. It's not possible."

"With today's technology," the senator said, "anything is possible."

The senator was right. Who knew what other evil deeds these people had up their sleeves?

"Dad, get Carlyle on it. Have him get in touch with Shelly. She works with professional photographers all the time. She'll know who to call. Meanwhile, I need to contact Thomas."

"You need to keep your distance from that man."

"Dad." Josie gave Thomas an apologetic look. "He's just as much a victim as I am. Remember, he's running for mayor. He's got a reputation in this town, a very good reputation. This could ruin his candidacy."

"Right." The senator sounded slightly less angry when he added, "I see what you mean."

"Not only that, but he owns an insurance agency. If this gets out, it could ruin him."

The senator sighed, long and resigned. "These people have gone too far. I don't have the stomach to see you hurt by them anymore. I'm just going to—"

"Don't make any decisions. Call Carlyle. I'll talk to Thomas and get back to you."

"Isn't Shelly there? Talk to her in person. The fewer people who see this—"

"I would prefer if the request came from Carlyle."

The senator's words shifted from angry to concerned. "What's going on, darlin'? Did you and she have a falling out?"

"It has nothing to do with this."

"So you sent her away like you sent away Bentley?"

Bentley. The man was like toe fungus. Would they ever be rid of him?

The conversation from the night before came back to him. While Bentley was spreading rumors at Mitchell's company, Mitchell was altering photographs.

They were all playing ugly games. Mitchell was just better at it.

Josie said, "I had a falling out—"

"We trust Bentley to keep an eye on you," Senator Harrington said. "Shelly and Bentley are your friends. I know the police up there questioned them, and they were both cleared. Did they question Thomas?"

"They did, and he was—"

"Doesn't matter. He probably shoots pool with the chief. You don't understand how small towns work. Can you really trust the authorities in Coventry?"

Thomas pushed back from the table and stood. This was beyond frustrating, not being able to speak.

She met his eyes. "I trust Thomas."

"More than you trust your oldest friend in the world?" the senator asked. "And the man you almost married?"

"As a matter of—"

"If that Thomas fellow is trying to separate you from people you know you can trust, then he might be the problem."

"Thomas had nothing to do with my decision to send Bentley and Shelly away. If you knew why I did it, you'd understand."

That statement was met with a long silence. Then the senator said, "So you found out about them."

"You *knew*?" Her voice was too loud in the small room. "You knew they were together?"

"I heard a rumor. I didn't know for sure. And anyway, that was between them. You were out of the picture."

Josie propped an elbow on the table and massaged her temples. "Okay. Fine. It doesn't matter now."

"You're going to have to let it go," her father said. "Bentley's still there, and we trust him. He'll stay close by until you're safely home. I expect you on a flight today."

"But if they've scheduled the vote for this afternoon—"

"No matter what happens today, your mom and I need to put eyes on you. All right?"

Thomas nodded, encouraging her to agree. He hoped it would all be over today, and maybe it would. But maybe it wouldn't. Maybe it was all about to get a whole lot worse.

If those pictures were released, would Josie ever want to return to Coventry? Or would whatever this was between them be crushed under the weight of rumors and ruined reputations?

"Josie, darlin'," Senator Harrington said, "I went a little crazy, thinkin' about somebody hurtin' you, takin' advantage. Maybe I shouldn't have..." He seemed flustered. "I just...I worry, and..."

For the first time since Thomas had woken up, he saw the slightest smile on Josie's lips. "I love you, too, Dad. And I understand. But Thomas is my friend, and I trust him. If you trust me—"

"I understand. I'll try."

She ended the call and collapsed against the chair back. It

took a long moment before she met Thomas's eyes. "I'm so sorry."

"You didn't do this."

"I know, but if those pictures get out... This is all my fault."

"You're less to blame for this than I was to blame for what happened to Amber."

"You weren't at all to blame for that, so..." She nodded slowly. "Okay. Okay, you're right."

"I am ticked, though."

"You have every right to be. This could ruin—"

"That too." He tried to temper his frustration, but it carried in his words. "What you and I have is 'certainly not' more than attraction? Maybe on your part, but on my part—"

"It seemed more expedient to downplay this"—she gestured between them—"than to tell him everything."

"And expediency is more important than honesty? Or are you employing expediency now to avoid telling *me* the truth?"

She sat forward. "What are you asking?"

"You either lied to your father or you're lying to me."

"I didn't lie. I just didn't—"

"Tell him the truth. Which is the same thing. Or do you have a different definition?"

"Are you seriously angry with me?"

Rather than retort, he took a breath. How did he feel?

Shocked. Exposed. But the cause of those couldn't be laid at Josie's feet. He also felt hurt, which could. "You didn't tell him I was here. Why the secrecy?"

"Why does it matter so much?"

"Because I don't lie to people I love."

She stood and stepped into the kitchen. "I didn't lie. I just didn't tell him everything."

"That's where you draw the line? Because from where I'm sitting..."

"What?" She returned to the doorway, facing him. "From where you're sitting, what?"

"Maybe you don't think I'm good enough for you. Or maybe you believe he'll think I'm not good enough for you. Maybe you're embarrassed to tell him you're falling for a small-town insurance agent."

"Why would you even suggest something like that? Have I ever given you that impression?"

"Besides the twenty times I asked you out and you turned me down?"

"I didn't know you then."

"What you knew about me didn't impress you enough to take a chance on me. I'm just saying...maybe you *did* tell him the truth." He stood. Maybe he should walk away. Maybe he should give her space to think.

Instead, he approached her, half expecting her to back up.

The new bodyguard inched closer as if to step between them if necessary, but Thomas ignored her.

Josie held her ground.

"Maybe this thing between us is all in my head." He stopped inches away from her. "Is it? Because you don't owe me anything. If you didn't tell your father about us because I'm imagining the *us*, then that's...fine. But you need to tell me because...because maybe we're just friends who kissed that one time." He hoped, prayed, that wasn't how she felt. But he needed to know. He stepped closer, wanting more than anything to wrap his arms around her. But her flimsy pajamas had him keeping his hands to himself. "Friends who kissed. Maybe that's all we'll ever be. But I need to know, because I'm already in a lot deeper than that."

He angled nearer, setting himself up for another rejection. This would be the last one. If she backed away, he'd leave.

He'd keep protecting her as best he could, but he'd do it

from a distance. Somehow.

She licked her lips.

Was that an invitation? He held still, a breath away. Inviting her into the space between them but not taking anything for granted.

She rose to her tiptoes and pressed her lips against his.

Fireworks all over again, only these booms were much more powerful than the ones in the park the night before.

He pulled her close and deepened the kiss, wrapping her in his arms. He could feel the warmth of her body through the thin fabric. All the emotions he'd endured in the ten minutes since he'd been pulled from sleep mixed and shifted into one strong feeling of desire. He dug his fingers into her long hair, relishing the silkiness, loving the feel of her in his arms.

Wishing they were alone.

It was good thing they weren't.

He ended the kiss and took a sizable step back, breathing heavily.

Her smile, when it came, seemed shy. "I was just trying to get through the conversation with Dad as fast as I could. That's all. In case you haven't figured it out, there is *certainly more* between you and me than simple attraction. I just know my father, and I didn't want him to get sidetracked. Okay?"

He paced to the sofa and gripped the back of it, trying to bring his rogue thoughts in line.

He wasn't imagining her feelings. She cared for him. And he cared for her.

"You and I haven't done anything to be ashamed of." She spoke to his back. "If you want me to tell him you were here last night, or that you and I are...whatever we are...then I'll tell him. But right now, we have more important things to worry about. Because if Dad doesn't vote for the bill, those photos are going to be released."

Right.

He turned and leaned against the couch.

Josie crossed the room and took his hand. "You have a decision to make, Thomas."

"Me?"

"Dad will do whatever I ask him to do. If I ask him to vote for the bill in order to protect my privacy and your candidacy, he will."

"I won't be the reason—"

"Think it through. Pray about it. I know you want to do the noble thing here, but wanting to run your town well, to fight corruption, is also noble. Keeping those pictures out of the press..."

"I'd do anything to protect you from that," he said.

One delicate eyebrow quirked. "Anything?"

She made a good point. Because he could protect her, but at what cost?

She squeezed his hand. "Dad wants to protect me too. But is it the right thing?" Her shoulders lifted, dropped. "There are no easy answers."

While Josie started a pot of coffee, Thomas tried to figure a way out of this mess. Even if they could prove the photo was doctored—*photos, if the threat of others was real*—that would take time. Once the pictures were released, the damage would be done. Would it destroy his candidacy? Coventry was a pretty conservative town, and Thomas's voters were the most conservative of the lot. Many of them were older, most churchgoers. Sure, some people wouldn't be shocked to learn their local insurance agent wasn't as pure as the driven snow, but to see images of it?

Would he be able to overcome it?

What had Tabby's mother said at the fundraiser. *"You're not going to do anything to bring shame on us."*

Her concern was valid. Brent Salcito's arrest and conviction had thrust the town into national news. He'd been one of the perpetrators of a thirty-year-old unsolved murder. Wasn't exactly a glowing endorsement of Coventry.

The town needed somebody they could trust.

He wanted to be that somebody.

A few of his supporters wouldn't let the photos affect their votes. But he'd never believed he'd win the election by a landslide. If he had any shot at all, he'd be squeaking out a few more votes than Farley.

If just a few of his voters couldn't get past the images, what would they do? Vote for Farley, who at least had the decency to keep his sins hidden, or stay home.

Either way, Farley won. Thomas would lose. Coventry would lose.

And his business would take a hit. He'd always painted himself as an upstanding guy. He attended church faithfully. He led Bible study. He rarely dated. He didn't sleep around. His clients trusted him. They believed in him.

His business—his livelihood—would suffer. He might have to let employees go, which meant they'd suffer. He'd have to do more of the work himself, which would keep him from volunteering, keep him from being the protector he'd once vowed to be.

But the other option was to ask Senator Harrington to vote yes on the so-called health care bill, a bill that would fund more abortion clinics and ultimately lead to thousands more abortions every month.

If he believed life began at conception...

Which he did.

Then that option was unconscionable.

There really was no choice here.

Which meant...Thomas was about to lose everything.

CHAPTER TWENTY-NINE

"You're absolutely certain?"

Josie shifted to watch Thomas's reaction to her father's question. They were once again seated at the kitchen table, but this time, she hadn't hidden Thomas's presence. Earlier, he'd gone home to shower and change clothes—and pray for wisdom—while she'd done the same. It was just after seven o'clock in the morning. She felt like she'd lived an entire day in two hours.

"I refuse to be the reason you vote yes on this bill, sir," Thomas said. "If you decide to do that for Josie's sake, I'll understand. But don't do it for mine."

Dad stared at the screen for a long time before he spoke again. "You're willing to give up your political aspirations for this?"

"I don't have aspirations. Our current mayor's corrupt, and I wanted to stop him from doing any more damage to my town. But if he gets elected... I have to leave that in God's hands."

"And what about Josie?" Dad asked. "What are your intentions toward my daughter?"

Thomas glanced her way, one side of his mouth tipping up.

"I intend to date her if she'll let me. I intend to get to know her better and take it from there."

"Are you the marrying type, Thomas?"

Heat rushed into Josie's cheeks. Dad had never shied away from difficult or awkward conversations, but really?

Thomas didn't fidget or squirm. Instead, he spoke with confidence. "My parents have been happily married for forty-five years. I was fortunate to have an example of a solid, love-filled marriage. I've always wanted that."

"That's a good answer, son."

Son? Seemed Dad's low opinion of Thomas was growing by the second.

Dad shifted his attention to Josie. "You're getting on a plane today, right?"

"We need to come up with a plan for Thomas to deal with the fallout, should those pictures be released. I'm not going to abandon him here without a strategy."

"You can do that and be on a flight by the end of the day."

She calculated the distance to the airport, the flight schedules she'd studied. Even if they spent all day strategizing, she should be able to make the latest one back to DC. She'd rather be going to her childhood home, but both her parents were in Washington. "I will."

"Thomas, you'll get her to the airport safely?"

"I will. May I ask what your plan is at this point?"

"They called the vote. I'll be there."

"You know Parker is going to ask," Josie said. "What will you tell her?"

"Lying to the majority leader is akin to political suicide." Dad blew out a long breath. "But so is going against her on her pet projects. Either way, I have no future in the party. If they ask, I'll say, 'I don't see where I have any choice' or 'I'll do what I have to do.' But I will not tell her my plans. That way, the bill will be defeated on the floor, which should kill it permanently."

"Do you think she knows what's going on?" Thomas asked.

"Not the details, but I'm sure she's aware Mitchell's pressuring me."

Thomas made a low noise in his throat, like a growl of disapproval. "When you cast your no vote, is there any chance they'll accept defeat gracefully?"

"None." Dad's single word hovered in the room like smoke in a house fire. "Which is why we need to keep this circle very small. You two know how I'm voting, and Carlyle, of course. Nobody else. Keep it that way."

"We will, sir." Thomas slid his arm around Josie's waist and pulled her closer, kissing the top of her head, seemingly unconcerned about her father watching.

Dad sighed. "I'm sorry it's come to this, darlin'. I never wanted you to get hurt. I wish..." His Adam's apple bobbed. "I wish I could protect you"—his voice cracked, and he swallowed again—"protect you from this."

Were those tears misting his eyes? She'd never seen her father cry. The thought of it had her own eyes stinging. "I know, Daddy." Her voice squeaked.

"The thought of anybody seeing that picture..."

"It's okay. I'll be okay."

"Maybe they won't publish it." Hope infused Thomas's voice. Josie hated to pop that optimistic bubble of his, but Dad's enemies would not accept his defiance. The pictures would be published as retribution.

Josie would be embarrassed.

Thomas might lose the election.

But the bill wouldn't pass. For that, this would all be worth it.

"We need to go, Dad. We need to figure out how to handle

this." After Josie ended the call, she faced Thomas. "I'm so sorry."

He leaned forward and touched his forehead to hers. "You don't have to apologize to me. But I do want you to promise me two things. First, that you'll leave today, no matter what happens. I want you to be safe until the backlash of your dad's decision blows over."

She'd already been downstairs to talk to Kinsley and Marcel, and they were prepared to run the shop until she returned. She'd given Marcel the go-ahead to hire someone else to pick up the slack. "I'll leave today. I promise."

"Second..." He took a strand of her hair in his hand and slid his fingers down it, sending chills into her scalp that somehow reached her toes. "Promise me you'll return."

How had she come to depend so much on this man? He'd been her friend and confidant and champion. In the space of a month, he'd become one of the dearest people in her life.

She slid her palm along his jaw, reveling in the smoothness of his freshly shaven face and realizing that this man, this handsome, kind, self-sacrificing man, suddenly meant everything to her.

"Josie?"

"I promise."

They stared at each other a long moment. Her lips tingled, anticipating what was coming.

A knock on the door shattered the sacred moment.

The bodyguard, a stocky brunette with short-cropped hair, said, "Who is it?"

"It's Shelly." Her shout came through the door. "You need to let me in!"

Thomas's lips spread into a slight smile. "To be continued."

She liked the sound of that. Turning to the bodyguard, she said, "It's fine."

The woman opened the door, and Shelly burst inside. "Omigosh! Thank you!" She took in the sight of the stranger and said, "Who are you?"

"Greta Wagner. Security."

"Oh." Shelly approached Josie at the table. "I just got off the phone with Carlyle. He told me what's going on. This is unbelievable! Somebody actually took photos..." Tears filled her eyes and dripped down her cheeks. She fell to the floor in front of Josie and grabbed her hands. "You have to forgive me, Jo. I've screwed up the only friendship that means anything to me. I'm so, so sorry. Will you please forgive me?"

Josie glanced at Thomas, who said nothing.

Josie had already promised she would. God expected her to forgive as He did.

She hadn't completely managed it yet, but He'd help her with that, in time.

Meanwhile, they had a situation to deal with. As much as she might have wanted to send Shelly away, she needed her expertise. "Of course I'll forgive you." Eventually.

Shelly couldn't read her thoughts and took the words as Josie had known she would—as complete and immediate absolution. She threw her arms around Josie and hugged her tight.

Josie couldn't help but smile at her old friend's exuberance.

Then Shelly sat beside her. "I've got a guy analyzing the photo. If it's fake, he'll know."

"It's fake." Thomas's serious tone didn't faze Shelly. "And in the end, maybe they won't release it."

Shelly turned to Josie. "Your dad's voting yes?" Her smile spread across her whole face. "I knew it. I knew he wouldn't put you in this position. That's great news."

Josie wasn't sure what to say to that. She didn't want to lie to her friend, but Dad had just told her not to tell anybody his plan.

How could they strategize if Shelly thought the photo wouldn't be released? Before she could come up with a plan, Thomas jumped in.

"The thing is," he said, "the photo is out there now." He told her about the call he'd received from the reporter the day before. "I have a bad feeling she has it, and if she does, the paper will publish it, not to use against Senator Harrington but to use against me."

Shelly nodded, studying him through squinted eyes. "I see what you're saying. It makes sense to get ahead of it."

"What are you thinking?" Josie asked.

"You two should release the photo, along with my expert's report. That way, you get to control the news cycle. I mean, you're the strategist here, Jo, but isn't that what you'd recommend?"

If it weren't Josie herself in the photo, maybe.

Probably.

"If you release it," Shelly said, "you can blur anything you don't want the world to see. If somebody else releases the original or other pictures, well, that's what was already going to happen. Right? At least you'd have a modicum of control."

"That's a good idea," Thomas said.

"No need to sound so surprised." With a hand on her chest, Shelly feigned offense. "I've been known to have my share."

Thomas smiled at her, but the expression faded when he faced Josie. "What do you think?"

Releasing the most revealing photo ever taken of herself to the public wasn't exactly high on her bucket list. But if she grayed out her body, if she released it with an explanation...?

"How would you go about it?" Shelly asked. "Would you just send an email, or—?"

"No." Josie took herself and her embarrassment out of it. If this were a stranger, what would she do? "A press conference.

You can take questions, Thomas. It signals that you have nothing to hide."

"You too," Shelly said. "If you're at his side, then you both show you have nothing to be ashamed of."

Thomas studied Josie a long moment. "You really want to do that?"

"I want your campaign to not fall apart."

"Me, too. But...this feels drastic. And humiliating."

Shelly popped to her feet. "Sometimes, drastic is the answer. And because it's humiliating, more people will tune in —and believe you. This is the perfect solution."

Easy for Shelly to say. It wasn't her unclothed body in those photographs.

But, though this would certainly embarrass Josie—and expose her to the whole town as the daughter of a senator—it was the only idea that made sense if they were going to salvage Thomas's campaign and reputation.

Because when Dad voted no, that photo and possibly others were going to be released. Mitchell and his people weren't exactly paragons of mercy. And if what Bentley said was true, Mitchell was dying to get his revenge.

It was one thing for that revenge to cost Josie. For what she'd done, she deserved whatever came. But Thomas had done nothing wrong.

Josie would do anything in her power to shield him from her moral failures.

Josie followed Greta into the police station through the back entrance, Thomas at her side, and Donley bringing up the rear. It was just after one o'clock. The press conference was scheduled for one-thirty and would be held right next door.

It had been no easy feat to schedule it, even harder to get the mayor to agree to have it on the steps of the town office building. According to Shelly, who'd made the request, Farley had flat-out denied them.

But Shelly was proving more adept than Josie had ever given her credit for. She'd argued that the town offices actually belonged to the town, not the mayor, and if Farley refused to let them have the press conference there, she'd make sure everybody knew the man was scared of his political opponent.

She'd also explained that if Thomas messed it up—implying it was highly likely he would, him being a political novice and all—all would work out well. "After all," she'd told Farley over the phone, "why not give him a very tall platform from which to tumble."

In the end, the mayor had agreed—though probably at least in part because Thomas had called on a few of the members of the town council to help persuade him.

Josie's estimation of Shelly had jumped a few notches.

The report had come back from Shelly's friend showing that the photograph had indeed been altered. They had a link to his report that would be made public for the reporters to peruse after the press conference.

While Donley and Greta waited in a conference room, Josie and Thomas met with the chief of police, an older, heavyset balding man named Cote, who brought them up to speed on what they'd uncovered about the intruder and everybody they'd questioned so far.

He explained that Shelly had made a few calls the night of the incident to her boyfriend, whom they'd spoken to. Shelly was not on the suspect list.

The police were looking into the deposits made into Lake's account.

"She's still a suspect," Cote said, "though her phone registered no unusual calls or texts. We aren't sure how she was communicating with anybody outside. Maybe she wasn't. Maybe they'd set it all up from the beginning."

"Maybe nobody was communicating with anybody," Josie said. "Maybe the intruder just got lucky."

Thomas said, "Donley seems to think somebody well trained could have learned Josie was in the room alone." He explained Donley's theories on that subject.

"Maybe," the chief said. "Or maybe the guy just doesn't want to believe his partner was taking bribes."

That seemed equally likely.

The chief continued. "Bentley Kent's story checks out. His aunt's attorney forwarded her will. He inherited a sizable amount of money, enough for the new car and the down payment on the house in Fairfax."

Bentley wasn't working against her. That didn't change the fact that he'd had an affair with her best friend, but at least she didn't have to suspect him of being complicit in all the horrible things that had happened to her.

Thomas had told her that morning that Bentley'd called the night before and updated him on what he was up to. Though Thomas obviously wasn't impressed, weeks before, Josie had given Bentley the go-ahead to dig into Mitchell's life to try to find something to use against him.

Tactics she'd sworn she'd never sink to again.

She was thankful Bentley's efforts would be for naught. This drama was going to be over today, as soon as Dad cast his vote, which should happen at right about the same time as the press conference. Tomorrow, they'd deal with the fallout.

Dad would either have to switch parties or resign from the Senate altogether. His party would never get past what they would see as betrayal. As hard as it would be him, he'd served a lot of years. It might be good for him to go home and turn his attention to other endeavors. He'd always dreamed of being a college professor. Now would be a great time for him to start a second career.

Whatever happened, Dad would be all right.

Hopefully, after today's press conference, Thomas's campaign would be back on track.

And then after she assured her parents she was healthy and happy, after this story was replaced by the latest juicy news, Josie would return to her coffee shop and the life she'd built in Coventry, the life she loved.

Everybody would know she was the daughter of a senator, but she didn't think the townspeople would treat her much differently. Maybe, when she came home, life would be better than before. She'd be able to build friendships without worrying about revealing who she really was. And she'd have Thomas.

When the chief was finished bringing them up to speed, they moved as a group—the chief, Officers Tyler and Fontier, Donley, Greta, Thomas, and Josie—through the police station and into the attached town offices, where they met Shelly, who practically squealed with delight. "You wouldn't believe the crowd out there!"

Josie and Thomas, flanked by Donley and Greta, waited just inside the wide double doors of the old building while reporters listened to Chief Cote and Officer Fontier explain Josie's drugging Sunday night and the intruder who broke into her house.

It made sense to have them speak first, to give the background of the case before she and Thomas told everybody about the blackmail photograph.

Officer Tyler stood on the far side of the room wearing his ever-present scowl. The chief had asked him to answer questions from reporters, but he'd flat-out refused.

The man was decidedly unimpressed by the whole thing.

Josie and Shelly had sent the press release to all the major media outlets between Coventry and Boston. On his own, Thomas wouldn't have gotten nearly as good a response, but Josie had crafted the message to hint at a political conspiracy "that reached the highest levels of government."

Reporters had come in droves.

Any minute now, she would tell the world her real name and who her father was.

Meanwhile, Dad would cast his *no* vote.

She kept glancing at her screen. The vote should happen soon. Carlyle would text her when it was done.

Beside her, Thomas swallowed hard, staring out the window. He wore a dark-blue suit with a white shirt and a blue tie and looked handsome and trustworthy. His strong jaw was tight with worry, his brown eyes intent as he stared outside. He wore spicy scented aftershave that had her wanting to lean closer.

He glanced her way, worry clear in his dark eyes.

"You've got this."

"I don't know. It's not like Sunday's speech. I had days to prepare for that." He flipped through the index cards in his hand. "I could royally screw this up."

She faced him, adjusting his arrow-shaped tie clip, which had tilted ever so slightly. Maybe. Or maybe she was making up excuses to touch him "What's with the arrow?"

"Gift from my dad, a reminder to keep walking the path, even when life is hard."

"I like it." She smoothed his shirt. "You aren't going to screw it up. If I feel like you're floundering, I'll jump in. But I doubt you'll need me."

He kissed her forehead. "If I make a complete fool of myself, will you still stand by me?"

"I will."

"Promise?"

"I promise."

His smile, when it came, transformed his face. It softened his strong jaw, lit his dark eyes. "I'm willing to lose my reputation, my business, and my run for mayor, as long as I don't lose you."

A blush warmed her cheeks. "I'm honored."

"You're worth it."

It was as if the solid ground beneath her crumbled, and she fell. It wasn't scary, though. No, it was the most surprising, joyful feeling in the world. Not a fall to an unknown and dangerous landing, but a fall into the arms, into the heart, of this good man.

Was it love? Maybe not yet, but it could be.

Thomas was focused on her as if nothing else mattered, as if they were the only two people in the room, as if hordes of journalists didn't stand outside. In his eyes, Josie saw her future.

A squeal had her backing up, remembering where she was.

Shelly had been looking out the window on the other side of the double doors. Now, she hurried their way, beaming. "My gosh, can you see that? I just saw another van pull up. It's crazy. There're like hundreds of people out there! They're gathering all along the street and on the other side. I think the whole town is here!"

Thomas groaned.

"You're not helping." Josie squeezed his hand.

Shelly giggled. "Sorry. You two ready?"

Thomas swallowed hard and then nodded. A moment later, the doors swung open.

Josie wasn't accustomed to being in the public eye. That was Dad's sweet spot, and Carlyle's, and even Bentley's. Josie'd always been more comfortable behind the scenes. But she stood beside Thomas on the steps facing the street, the reporters, and the town she'd come to love. She listened as Thomas explained the photograph that had been sent to them that morning, how it had been doctored, and what the sender's goals were.

"Someone, we aren't certain who, is trying to manipulate Josie's father, Senator Davis Harrington, into voting a certain way on a certain bill. We aren't at liberty to discuss which bill or which way he was being asked to vote. That aspect of this is between the senator and his constituents, not to mention law enforcement."

Thomas went on to explain the photoshopped picture, promising to make available the expert's report. When asked if he would release the original photograph, Thomas smiled. "I will not. If somebody else releases it, there's nothing I can do about that. But I'm not about to expose my friend to such humiliation." He smiled at Josie, and she smiled back.

Which brought on a whole new barrage of questions about their relationship, which had been the plan and which they answered honestly. Thomas, for all the nerves prior to stepping out there, managed it perfectly. He was honest and humble. He was funny and charming. He even had the hardened reporters smiling as they took their notes and snapped their pictures.

By the time they were finishing up, Josie was convinced they'd gotten ahead of what could have been a career-ending story for Thomas. The people of Coventry would stand by him after this. More of them could even swing to his side.

He could win this race.

All of this drama would be over, and they'd be able to go on with their lives.

Assuming Dad had cast his vote.

CHAPTER THIRTY

Thomas's heart was pounding as Shelly stepped to the microphone. "That's all for now," she said. "Thank you for coming."

Thomas followed Josie back into the municipal building. The press conference had gone well. Really well, at least from his perspective. He thought he'd handled himself skillfully. Josie had fielded the questions lobbed at her like the professional she was. But would it be enough?

Once they were inside and the doors behind them closed, he glanced at her.

Her smile carried unmistakable triumph.

They'd done it. They'd actually done it.

The sight of a very angry Mayor Farley on the edge of the old building's wide entrance sealed the deal.

Thomas could barely contain his glee.

"Come on, come on." Donley's serious tone belied Thomas's mood as the bodyguard ushered them back through the door connecting to the police station. They followed him, flanked by Zack on one side and Rich on the other. Greta was bringing up the rear.

Shelly had driven her own car. She planned to hang around, try to overhear what the reporters had to say when it was all over.

Thomas and the bodyguards would escort Josie to the airport, where she'd fly to DC and spend time with her parents. But she'd be back. She'd promised.

The group walked in silence. Thomas couldn't stand it. Fireworks should be exploding. Bands should be playing. They'd defeated their enemies, protected their reputations, and stood up for their principles. This should be a moment of celebration, not fear. Right? He slid his arm around Josie. "What did you—?"

"No time to chat," Greta said. "Get to the car."

Josie glanced his way, her smile still in place. She kept her voice low when she said, "You nailed it."

Donley had lectured them about getting out of there as fast as possible after the press conference. The man was paranoia on steroids today. But Thomas couldn't stop himself.

They entered the hallway leading to the back door. It was dim and cramped, but he didn't care.

He turned and swooped Josie off her feet, spinning her in a half circle. "We did it!"

She giggled like a schoolgirl, and the sound did weird things to his brain. "Put me down." But there was laughter in her voice, in her eyes.

Holding her against his chest, Thomas planted a kiss on her beautiful, kissable mouth, and she welcomed it. She tasted of vanilla and victory.

"That's enough," Donley said.

"Fine, fine." Thomas put her down, smiling at her as he took her hand.

When the back door opened, light spilled in.

Donley's SUV was parked right by the exit, so they just had to cross a few feet and climb inside, and then Thomas would kiss Josie again. Maybe he'd kiss her all the way to the airport.

He and Josie followed Donley into the light.

A loud pop broke into his thoughts.

Donley stumbled.

Thomas reached out instinctively, but he missed the bodyguard, and the man fell.

"Get down. Get—" Zack's words were cut off, and he went down too.

Before Thomas's brain caught up, his instincts sprang into action. He forced Josie down and covered her with his body. He needed to get her back inside. He looked up, toward the door, expecting to see Rich or Greta there, beckoning him.

The door was closed. Someone was down just outside it. Someone whose body would have to be moved in order to get it open.

It was Rich. Rich was down. Shot? Was he dead?

Another pop. Another.

Something fell against him. A body.

A body. Greta?

Were they all down, all their protectors? This was a police station. Where was everybody?

The pop-pop-pop of gunshots didn't let up.

And then a strong hand gripped him and yanked him up.

Before Thomas could react, a black hood was pulled over his head and cinched around his neck. The material was thin enough that light came through the weave.

Something hard pressed into his back. A gun. "Move." A hand on his arm propelled him forward.

He was shoved into a vehicle. A van or something with a big cargo space.

Doors slammed shut.

The vehicle lurched forward.

The sounds of gunshots faded into the background.

Someone held Thomas down, reached in his pocket.

Took his phone.

He didn't fight. He didn't care what happened to him, as long as Josie was safe. *Please let her be safe. Please let her not be shot. Let her not be* here.

But someone struggled beside him. He tried to remove the sack over his head.

A strong hand gripped his wrist. "Leave it, lover boy." It was a man's voice. A deep voice he didn't recognize. "Stop struggling, princess. I just want your phone."

Thomas said, "Josie?"

"Thomas." She said the word on a sob. "I'm sorry. I'm so, so sorry."

"Silence!" The man's voice echoed in the small space, and the vehicle careened around a corner, away from the police station, the bodyguards, and safety.

They weren't allowed to talk.

The vehicle had only driven for a couple of minutes—plenty of time for the man to handcuff Thomas's hands behind his back, and probably Josie's, too—before it stopped. He heard a garage door closing. When the rumble silenced, the rear door of their vehicle opened. The same man who'd spoken before said, "Slide this way and stand."

He did as he was told. With no way to see his surroundings, no hands to defend himself, he had little choice.

He listened intently. Josie was behind him. Her breaths were shallow. She was sobbing softly.

At least one other person was breathing, maybe the driver.

Then a commotion—a door opening, feet scuffling. Heavy breathing. Two people at least had entered the garage.

The man who'd spoken before said, "Were you followed?"

Silence, but somebody was probably nodding or shaking a head. He hoped it was a nod, but then the man said, "Good."

There were at least four people, maybe more.

The man said, "Move, princess."

Thomas heard her footsteps, felt when she stood near him. He leaned toward her, hoping to infuse her with courage he didn't feel. "It's going to be okay."

"No talking." The fist came fast, a blow against the side of Thomas's skull that left him off-balance, head throbbing. "Keep your mouth shut. Got it?"

Thomas nodded.

"Don't move." The man must've been speaking to Josie, because he gripped Thomas's upper arm and pulled him to the side. "Get in and be quiet."

His head was shoved down, and his face bumped into a cold, metal surface. His legs were lifted behind him, and he was pushed inside the vehicle.

"As far as you can go," the man said.

Thomas managed to sit up and scooted backward until he bumped something hard. He sat with his back to what he assumed was one of the seats.

A moment later, Josie was herded toward him. She settled beside him, shoulder to shoulder.

Neither of them spoke, but just having her beside him, warm and alive, alleviated a modicum of his terror.

Just get her out of this, Lord. Show me how I can protect her.

Never in his life had he been so afraid. Never in his life had he felt so helpless.

Doors closed all around.

The garage door opened.

The vehicle backed out, then lurched forward.

It was so quiet. Were they alone? He wanted desperately to speak to her, but he held his tongue and bumped her shoulder.

"You okay?" she asked.

A hard blow landed on the side of Thomas's knee, and he sucked in a breath.

Josie gasped.

"Here's the deal," the man said. "You seem to have trouble taking direction. If you tick me off, princess, your boyfriend gets hurt. If you give me trouble, lover boy, she gets the punishment. You fight me, the other one pays the price." There was shifting, and when the man spoke again, his voice was much closer. "If you escape, princess, I'll put a bullet in his head." More shifting, and then, "I don't want to hear either of your voices again, so nod if you understand."

Thomas nodded. He assumed Josie did the same.

"Settle in. We've got a ride ahead of us."

These people were smart, too smart. They didn't have to worry about being spotted or caught since they'd changed vehicles.

Nobody would be following them.

Nobody would find them.

Thomas thought maybe thirty minutes had passed, thirty minutes of winding roads that, thanks to the lack of seats—and hands—had him struggling not to crash into the wall on one side or Josie on the other.

Then the vehicle left the pavement and bounced along what felt like a dirt road, or maybe it wasn't a road at all. They traveled on that for a little while, but they couldn't have gone more than a mile or so when they jerked to a stop.

Doors opened and slammed. And then the door that led to the cargo area opened. Through the black hood, Thomas saw daylight.

He started to inch toward that light, but the man said, "Don't move."

He stilled, and Josie nestled beside him.

And then came the electronic sound every phone makes when a photograph is taken.

"Okay," the man said, "Come."

Come. Like they were trained dogs.

But Thomas wasn't about to protest and cause Josie pain. His head was throbbing, his knee smarting. The last thing he wanted was for Josie to pay for his defiance.

He scooted forward, reached the edge of the vehicle, and hopped down, soft bracken beneath his feet. With a rough grip on his arm, he moved in the direction he was propelled. Up a few wooden steps and inside a room that smelled old and musty. He was guided across a wooden floor.

A door creaked, and Thomas was pushed forward again.

The world got darker on the other side of the hood.

"Careful," the man said.

Thomas tapped his foot forward and bumped into something. A step. It was a very narrow staircase, and steep. The man pressed a hand to Thomas's back as he went up slowly, feeling his way and counting. There were twelve steps. They entered a hot, stale space that stank of age and death. The floor was wooden and creaky. He was pushed across the room. "Turn around and sit."

He did.

"Lean forward."

Again, he did.

The man reached behind him, pulled at the handcuffs around his wrists. Thomas felt something cold and hard. Metal. When the man backed up, Thomas realized his handcuffs had been attached to something else—maybe other handcuffs?—which were attached to a metal pipe.

"Your girlfriend will be right up. If you two behave yourselves, you should be out of here by the end of the day."

Thomas wasn't sure he believed that. On the other hand, he had no idea who these people were, or where they'd taken them, or even how many there were. There'd only been one voice.

Theoretically, if Thomas and Josie were let go, they wouldn't be able to lead anybody back here or to identify their captors.

But the police had ways. Maybe their captor had left a hair, a fingerprint somewhere. Maybe they could be found. And if this guy was caught, Thomas would remember his voice.

He'd never forget the man's voice.

A few minutes after he left, footsteps sounded again on the wooden staircase, and then Josie sat beside him.

Probably cuffed to the pipe, just like he was.

More footsteps on the stairs, these getting quieter.

A strange creaking noise was followed by a thump.

And then silence.

He strained to hear. Beside him, Josie cried softly. Her shoulders shook against his side.

Was there anybody else there?

He needed to know. But he wasn't about to risk her getting hurt.

He nudged her shoulder.

She nudged him back.

But then nothing. He needed her to say something to see if they were alone. If not, then he'd be the one they hurt.

He decided to try to force her to speak. He started coughing. Hard. Gasping as if he couldn't breathe.

Finally, she said, "You need water?"

He stilled, waiting for a blow.

But nothing happened.

"I think we're alone," he said.

"You faked that?"

"Did they hurt you?"

"No. I'm okay." He heard tears in her voice. "I'm so scared."

He was, too, but saying so wouldn't help. "It's a good sign they haven't let us see their faces. Maybe it means they're going to let us go when they're done." He hoped, anyway.

"Not until they've forced Dad's vote. You heard the camera shutter, right?"

"Shouldn't the vote have already happened?"

"Right before you kissed me, I got a text from Carlyle. The vote was postponed for this afternoon."

A curse word slipped out. Everything they'd done had been for nothing. And that kiss... Had he made everything worse? If they'd left the building a few seconds earlier, would it have made a difference?

Was this all his fault?

Maybe. Maybe not. Whoever'd done this had been one step ahead of them all along.

But something didn't sit right. "Your father gave the majority leader, Parker, the impression he was going to vote in favor of the bill, right? Even if the press conference made them suspicious, how could they have set this all up in time? I mean, we were behind the microphones for what? Fifteen, twenty minutes? There's no way this operation was set up that fast."

"Maybe they knew before then how Dad planned to vote," Josie said.

"How? Who else knew? You, me, your father. Do you think he told Bentley?"

"Dad said just the four of us, remember? Him, you, me, Carlyle..."

The name fell between them.

"Carlyle?" Josie sounded equally shocked and dismayed. "Oh, my gosh. He's my father's oldest friend. I can't believe he'd do this to Dad. To me! I've known the man since I was a child. As long as I can remember."

Thomas didn't know what to say. "I wish I could think of another possibility, but all indicators point to him."

"Why? Why would he do that?" She sounded so defeated as she rested her head on Thomas's shoulder.

"Money? Power?" Thomas guessed.

He thought back to those terrifying seconds at the police station. Donley had been shot. Though he hadn't seen it happen, Greta must have been, too, and Rich, whose body had blocked the door. If not for that, they might've been able to get back inside.

What had happened to Zack? Had he been shot as well? Thomas prayed for the bodyguards and the officers, his friends.

Even if Carlyle had figured out the senator was going to vote no, how would he have known Thomas and Josie's plan to leave after the press conference? Though the municipal office building and the police station shared a wall, there was a stockade fence separating their parking lots. Wouldn't the shooters have assumed they'd exit from the municipal building, not the police station?

Had someone seen Donley's SUV? Except it wouldn't have been moved until the very last minute. Donley had given the keys to a uniformed police officer and told her to move it when the press conference ended. How many minutes had passed between that moment and when they'd stepped out the back door? Two, three?

More because of the kiss, but not *that* much more.

Had Carlyle known the plan? About the press conference, of course, but about their escape route?

Thomas had been with Josie all day, and he never remembered her going into that level of detail with her father. But somebody...

Shelly? No. Donley hadn't told Thomas and Josie the plans until they'd been in the SUV. Shelly had driven separately.

Donley and Greta? He couldn't imagine either of them turning against Josie. And both of them had been shot, right?

Who else knew?

Rich and Zack had helped Donley set it all up.

But Thomas had known both of them most of his life. They were both married, both small-town cops. Surely they wouldn't have betrayed Thomas and Josie.

Or maybe they had. Somebody had. Somebody Thomas trusted. "I'm sorry I didn't protect you." That was all he'd wanted to do, protect her. And he'd failed. Miserably.

Lord, what do I do now?

He'd taken it upon himself to protect the people he cared about a long time before, but now... Now, he couldn't do anything to save Josie. He couldn't even save himself.

Help us, Father. Do what I can't do.

Do what only You can do.

"This isn't your fault," Josie said. "This is my fault. This is entirely my fault."

He shifted toward her, wishing he could see her face. "What are you talking about?"

She sighed. "That secret you asked me to tell you last night...it's the reason Mitchell is willing to go to such lengths. It's the reason I deserve exactly what I'm getting."

Thomas pressed his shoulder against hers again, wishing he could wrap her in his arms. He wanted desperately for her to tell him, but he wouldn't ask again. He pressed a kiss through the hood onto her head. "Whatever happened, I'm sure it wasn't that bad."

She sighed, the sound long and low, and his heart raced.

What could be so terrible that it would justify this?

CHAPTER THIRTY-ONE

When Josie had decided to tell Thomas the truth, she'd never imagined she'd do so from beneath a hood, her hands cuffed behind her back.

She'd never imagined this scenario in a million years.

Jesus, Jesus... She'd been sending up a steady stream of prayers, not that she deserved God's help.

Deserved? Certainly not, but in God's economy, who *deserved* anything good?

She might not deserve His help, but she'd shamelessly ask for it anyway. It wasn't about what she deserved, after all. God was all about grace. Jesus had been sent not to save the well but to save the sick.

Not to rescue the righteous but to redeem the lost.

She'd been lost, and God had pursued her and drawn her back to Himself. He loved her, loved her enough to let His Son die for her. That was a depth of love Josie didn't understand and probably never would.

So, maybe God would rescue her and Thomas.

But maybe He wouldn't. Maybe this would end with them

walking hand-in-hand into eternity. Tears stung her eyes and dripped down her cheeks.

She didn't want to die. That small, faithless part of her was afraid of it. But she knew, she *knew,* that God had a place for her in heaven. And a place for Thomas.

Her death might kill her father. But Mom's faith was strong, maybe strong enough for both of them.

God could hold all of them in His capable hands. She was afraid, but she could face it.

And she could face Thomas's rejection. He deserved to know what he'd stepped into. He deserved to be prepared for whatever would come.

"It was during Dad's last reelection campaign," she said. "Our state's been moving steadily toward the other side for some time, so we already knew it was going to be a tough general election. This was back when our party had a true majority in the Senate, so his vote didn't matter as much, and he was able to vote his conscience—and his constituents' will—without so much pushback from the leaders. Now, of course, the senate is evenly split, so Dad's vote is often critical. We have a functional majority because the vice president always votes—"

"I know how our government works, Josie." Thomas's voice held a hint of amusement. "You can skip the civics lessons."

"You'd be surprised how many don't understand this stuff. Anyway, Dad had voted against one too many bills Mitchell supported, and Mitchell was tired of it. From his perspective, whether Dad or the other party's candidate won the election, both would vote against the bills he supported. But if Mitchell got lucky and his candidate won, he'd gain a strong ally in the senate."

"That makes sense," Thomas said.

"Dad had a strong pro-choice opponent, and Mitchell's organization started donating heavily to him. Dad is very popular in our state, and we thought he'd win the primary despite the opponent, but only after spending a lot of money and taking a lot of hits that would hurt him later. He'd be much weaker going into the general election. We tried to get the party to put pressure on Mitchell to stop donating to his opponent, but that didn't work. So, we decided to find another way to get him to back off."

This was where the story got bad.

She was tempted to stop.

Thomas's voice was gentle when he said, "What did you do?"

He would despise her for this.

"We needed leverage, so we started digging into Mitchell, his company, and all his various entities—the nonprofit, the lobbyist, all of it. We started hearing rumors of an affair. Mitchell's rather notorious for always having a woman on the side. As far as anybody can tell, his wife never believed the rumors. So, we set out to prove them. We got the woman's name —she was a twenty-year-old intern—and we hired somebody to hack her social media accounts. In a private message, she posted, 'SSB and me are going to Aruba.' She gave the details, even where they were staying."

"What's an SSB?"

"My guess is 'super-secret boyfriend.'"

"Oh." Thomas didn't sound impressed. "Wow."

"Remember, she was only twenty. As in, a few months before, she'd been a teenager."

"How old is Mitchell?"

"Late fifties."

"Gross."

"Yeah," she said. "I know. So, we hired an investigator, who followed her to Aruba. The next day, Mitchell showed up. They had a private villa, a private beach, which they took full advantage of."

"Meaning... Oh, wait."

"Yeah. Our guy got lots of pictures, revealing pictures. We blew up the shots, had them FedExed to Mitchell's office the day of his return, and added his candidate's campaign photo with a note on the back that simply read, 'Back off.'"

"I bet that was effective," Thomas said.

It was, and they should have left it at that.

"Just to be safe, though..."

This was the part she didn't want to share.

She barreled forward. "We sent the same pictures to the girl with another note. 'Tell your SSB to back off or everybody will find out.'"

Thomas said nothing.

"It was awful. She was a child. We should never have... We just got so caught up in winning that we forgot there was a person behind those glossy photos, a young woman with parents and siblings, with dreams and desires. We just...we forgot."

Thomas was quiet for a beat. When he spoke, his voice was still gentle. "What happened?"

"We can only speculate at this point. Maybe she was distraught and didn't know what to do next. Maybe she showed the note to Mitchell, and they fought. If she showed it to him, then he would have asked about the SSB comment, right? He would have known she was the reason he'd been caught. So maybe they fought, and he dumped her and broke her heart. Or maybe..."

She let her voice trail. She didn't want to think about the third option.

"A few days after we sent her the pictures, she swallowed a bottle of sleeping pills." The pitch of Josie's voice rose on the last words, squeaky and filled with emotion. She couldn't stop that emotion for all the money in the world. "Her little brother found her the next morning. It was too late."

"Oh, Josie." Again, Thomas leaned in, pressing his shoulder against hers. "I'm so sorry. I'm so sorry that happened."

"Don't be sorry for me. Be sorry for that little boy, for her parents and her other siblings. For her, a woman at the very beginning of her life who decided it wasn't worth living because of what I did."

She waited for Thomas to tell her it wasn't her fault. But he was quiet for a long time.

Because it *was* her fault.

"You started to say something," Thomas said finally, "like you have another theory about what happened to her."

"There were things that didn't make sense. A few of the pills were in her throat, which could mean they'd been forced into her mouth. Or it could mean she passed out before she swallowed them. There were marks on her bedroom window, like maybe somebody had broken in, but that was inconclusive. And she had bruising on her neck. Light bruising, though. The photographs weren't there. Of course, she might have hidden them or burned them. Anyway, despite the questions surrounding her death, the coroner ruled it a suicide. Bentley always thought..."

Josie had always secretly hoped Bentley's theory was true. It would let them off the hook for what they'd done. But what was happening now changed the game. If Bentley's theory was true...

"Thought what?" Thomas asked.

"She talked too much," Josie said. "She was the reason we found out about their affair. Through social media, she'd told most of her friends about her so-called SSB. If Mitchell hacked her accounts like we did, then he knew her lack of discretion had been his downfall. Bentley believed that...that Mitchell had her killed."

"Oh." There was a long silence, and then Thomas said, "So maybe he's a killer."

"He's an abortionist. He's definitely a killer."

"It's not the same, though. Abortion providers don't believe they're committing murder. They find ways to justify it. But to murder someone you cared about, someone you knew... I assume you told the coroner and the police about the photos?"

She closed her eyes, not wanting to answer. But it was too late for that now. "I wanted to, but Bentley said we shouldn't, that it would blow back on Dad."

"A woman was dead, Josie. I can't believe your father would condone—"

"Dad didn't know about any of it."

"Huh." There was a long silence before he spoke again. "Forget law enforcement. Maybe the guy killed somebody, but he gets away with it because that's how the game is played."

She swallowed the knee-jerk defense that rose to her throat. He was right. Of course he was right.

"The game," Thomas said. "Bentley told me that last night. I suggested we should try to prove Mitchell was behind all the things that happened to you. He seemed more interested in getting revenge than getting justice."

"I care about justice, Thomas," she said. "I quit the game. That's why I'm not in politics anymore. That's why I live in Coventry, not DC. When this is all over, if we make it out of here, I'll be seeking justice."

For herself. Because Mitchell and his cronies had harmed her. But what about that young intern? Did Josie care about her, about her family?

If she'd cared more about that woman and less about her own reputation, maybe none of this would be happening now.

She'd gone along with Bentley and Carlyle, but she knew in her heart that, if her father had known what happened, he'd have urged her to tell the police everything.

Dad wouldn't thank her for what she'd done.

It was time to do the right thing.

She pulled in a breath of faith, of courage. "I'll go public with everything that happened back then. The story makes me look bad, but my public image is nothing compared to the grief that family has endured. They deserve to know the truth."

"I think..." Thomas paused a long time before he spoke again. "I think that's a good idea. I wish I didn't. The last thing I want is for you to be hurt, but as hard as telling the truth will be on you, I think it's your only path to freedom from what happened."

Maybe it would destroy her reputation, but the people who loved her before, truly loved her, still would.

Even if nobody else did, God's love would never change. She felt His pleasure even then.

"When we first started working together," Thomas said, "you told me that I needed to beware of people doing under-handed things on my behalf. This was what you were thinking about."

"I'm always thinking about it."

A moment of silence, then, "Carlyle knows what Mitchell has against you."

"I think so. Maybe not all of it, but enough."

"And still, he helped set this up?"

"Oh." Josie couldn't believe it was true, but nothing else made sense.

"Okay," Thomas said. "Okay, that's a lot of information to take in." She expected him to distance himself from her, emotionally and physically. Instead, he nuzzled closer. She shut her eyes and breathed in his warmth, his presence, wishing she could see him, wishing she could make out his scent over that of the musty space and the scratchy fabric over her head.

"Hey, Josie?"

"Yeah?"

"You and Bentley never meant for that girl to get hurt."

Emotion closed off her throat, preventing her from responding.

"You didn't want that to happen any more than I wanted Amber to get attacked. Any more than you wanted to hurt Shelly when you moved away. We can't know all the consequences of our decisions. Maybe you and Bentley went too far."

"Maybe?"

"That's between you and God, sweetheart. But you didn't put those pills in that girl's mouth. Maybe she killed herself. Maybe Mitchell killed her. Either way, it wasn't you."

The emotion in her throat escaped on a sob. It had been four years, and she'd thought about that girl every single day. She'd thought about the girl's parents, her siblings, that poor little eight-year-old boy who'd never be the same after finding his sister's body.

Every single day, she'd begged God to forgive her.

Maybe it was time to accept that He already had.

She wept against Thomas's shoulder, wept for that family. Wept for the woman she used to be, so focused, so determined to win, that she hadn't cared who got hurt in the process.

She wasn't that person anymore. She was forgiven. She was a new creation.

That didn't mean she would escape the consequences of what she'd done. Not in this life, anyway.

～

Josie had spilled more tears than she'd known she had, and then she'd spilled more.

Now, she felt spent, exhausted.

But nothing had changed. They were still trapped. Still blind with hoods over their heads. She wore a sleeveless dress, but the room was stifling. She hated to think how hot Thomas must be in his suit and tie.

They were just waiting, waiting, waiting.

Would this wait end with freedom, or death?

Come to think of it, either way it would end with freedom.

Thomas had been uttering a constant stream of prayers beside her, and even through her tears, she'd silently joined him. They needed help, and they needed it desperately.

That strange creaking noise she'd heard before was followed by someone tromping up the steps. She braced herself as the man crossed toward them. A light hit her. It was blinding even through the hood.

And then, suddenly, her hood was yanked off.

She winced in the brightness.

She could barely make out the image of a man behind the flashlight he shined in her face. In his other hand, he held a phone. "Say cheese."

The camera clicked a series of shots, rapid-fire. When he was done, he tapped his screen, then reached the phone toward her. "Say something."

"What do you want me to—?"

"Josie!" It was her father. "Are you—?"

"That's enough." The man yanked the phone back. "She's alive, for now. Do what you have to do, and she'll stay that way." He turned and climbed back down the stairs. A moment later, the creaking sounded, and then the loud thump.

Leaving her and Thomas in silence.

That was it. Dad would vote for the bill, going against everything he believed and all the promises he'd made to the people who'd voted for him.

Even if he survived politically, making that compromise would destroy him.

Maybe Dad could go back and undo it. Maybe, if they got out of this mess, they could go public with what happened. Forget playing the game. They could just tell the truth, all the truth. Surely people would demand that the president not sign the bill—assuming he didn't sign it today.

Either way, they could bring Mitchell down.

If they survived.

Beside her, Thomas asked, "You okay?"

She turned to him, blinked as his form came into view, and realized what it meant. "He didn't put my hood back on."

"Oh. Good, good. Look around. What do you see?"

It was dark, very dark. They were in an attic. Rafters angled overhead beneath a steeply pitched roof. A little bit of light came through where the roof joined the floor. The floor was plywood. On the far side of the room, she caught sight of a trunk and a few boxes. She explained all of that. "I see nothing we could use, certainly nothing within reach."

"Maybe a stray nail or something?" he said. "I think if we could get something skinny and hard, we could maybe pick the locks on the handcuffs."

She studied the floor all around them, but it was clear of debris. "I don't see anything." She turned back to him, and something on his chest glinted in the dim light.

"Your tie clip."

"Yes! Can you reach it?"

There was only one way to get it—with her teeth. She bent toward him, but the clip was too far away. "Sit up higher and angle toward me."

He did, and she tried again. "A little more toward me?" He turned, grunting, straining against the handcuffs.

She did the same, pressing her mouth against his chest.

"I have to admit, I've had a few, uh, thoughts about you and me and..." He chuckled. "This is definitely not what I pictured."

She wasn't about to join him in that laugh, no matter the giggle that tickled the back of her throat as she found the clip with her lips.

She clamped her teeth on it and pulled. She sat up and tried to say, *Got it*. But with the clip in her teeth, it came out, "Ghhh..."

He angled away. "Drop it between us, as far back as you can."

She did, and it fell to the plywood.

Thomas shifted, lifted his rear end, and sat on the tie clip. He slid back toward his hands. He did it a couple of times. Grunting, he tilted up, pressed his hands down. "Got it."

"Yes!"

"Now just to figure out how..."

It took a long time, a *long* time. She waited silently, trying not to rush him, praying, praying, praying that he'd be able to pick the lock on his handcuffs. And then...

"Done." He slid away from the wall, hands still behind his back. He'd picked the cuff that held him to the pipe. He leaned her way. "Can you get my hood with your teeth?"

She bit the thick canvas, and Thomas pulled back. It took some wrangling, but finally he freed his head.

He looked around at their prison and then turned to her. "Uh, you can drop it now."

She opened her mouth, and the hood fell to her lap. "It's good to see you."

"It's good to see. Move as far forward as you can. I'll get your hands free, and then you can pick mine."

It was a torturous process, him trying to unlock her handcuffs with his hands bound behind his back. But he did it, and then she took the clip and got his open.

Finally, they were unbound.

But still trapped in the attic.

She felt like they'd managed the first step of a very long journey. A lot stood between them and freedom, not the least of which were a couple of men with guns on the floor below.

CHAPTER THIRTY-TWO

Thomas moved, and the plywood creaked. Unless they were very, very careful, their every movement would register downstairs.

There were no windows in the attic, so the only way out was through the house. But suddenly the creaking thump made sense. It was attic stairs, the kind that pulled down from the ceiling. Even if they could cross the attic without anybody hearing, there was no way they could lower those stairs without getting caught.

Sweat dripped into his eyes, and he desperately wanted to remove his jacket and loosen his tie. But he couldn't. If their captor came back, they'd have to pretend nothing had changed.

"What are you thinking?" Josie whispered.

"The only way we can get out of here is by luring someone up and overcoming him."

"Okay. But how?"

"They must have heard me coughing before. Maybe I can cough again, and then you can yell and ask for water. You and I will pretend to still be handcuffed. You'll have your hood off. I'll have mine on. When the guy comes close, I'll attack. I'll have the element of surprise."

"But you'll have the hood on."

"He'll have to take it off me to give me the water."

"Oh, right. What if he's carrying a gun?"

"He thinks we're bound. Did he have a gun out last time?"

"Not that I saw."

"If he does this time, you'll tell me."

"How?"

"Just say it. Like, 'What's with the gun?'" Though they kept their voices low, he spoke with a high pitch that almost made her smile. "Or sound panicked, maybe, 'Oh, my gosh, are you going to shoot us?' Whatever feels right."

A short laugh, and she said, "Panicked feels right."

Thomas took her hand. "We've got this. We can do this."

"What happens then?"

"Hopefully, I can take the guy down, find a gun in his pocket, and then..." And then it got murky. There'd be another thug downstairs, at least one. He'd just have to improvise. "And then I'll get us out of here."

"What if he's not armed?"

Thomas didn't have an answer for that. "We'll figure it out, Josie."

Her mouth closed tight. She nodded, but she looked far from convinced.

"Our only other option is to wait here until the vote is over, at which point, maybe they'll let us go."

"Or maybe they'll kill us."

He didn't want to say that, but it seemed as likely. Thomas leaned close, rested his hand against her neck, his forehead against hers. "Here's the truth. Alone, there's no way we can get ourselves out of this. But we're not alone. We've got God, and He's with us. Do you believe that?"

"I do."

He kissed her lightly. "Let's pray, and then let's do this."

Five minutes later, back in the positions their captor would expect, Thomas started fake coughing again, silently cursing the stifling black canvas over his head.

After a moment of that, Josie yelled, "Hey! Hey, can we get some water up here?"

Nothing happened. No response. No noise from downstairs.

Thomas kept coughing, stomping on the floorboards to get their attention.

Josie yelled again.

Finally, the creaking and thump of the stairs being lowered, then the man's footsteps.

Thomas's heart pounded. All this fake coughing wasn't exactly making him stronger. If he screwed this up, he could get them both killed. But if his guess was right, their captor didn't plan for either of them to walk away.

It wasn't a risk Thomas was about to take with Josie's life.

Thomas kept coughing as the man climbed.

"Thank you." Josie sounded so relieved, telling him the man wasn't carrying a weapon. Hopefully, he had one in a holster or in his pocket. If not...

One step at a time.

Thomas felt the boards give as the man stomped toward them.

"What happened to your hood?" he asked.

"You didn't put it back on," she said. "I was enjoying the air so much. Oh, don't, please..." There was movement as the guy put Josie's hood back on her.

Then he took Thomas's off.

As soon as he could see, he yanked his hand from behind his back and punched his captor in his most sensitive spot. This wasn't a man who should reproduce anyway.

The man *oomphed* and pitched forward.

Thomas punched him in the face, and the guy fell to the side.

Thomas lunged on top of him and hit him again, but he recovered fast, kneeing Thomas in the ribs, hard, twice, three times. Then aimed a punch at his face. The first one hit his chin.

"What's going on up there?"

The sound came from below.

Thomas couldn't think about that as the man aimed another blow.

He angled to the side, and the fist hit his ear.

He shifted and landed an elbow in the man's chest. He levered up and throat-punched him. The man gasped, and Thomas hit him hard in the nose.

Moisture filled their captor's eyes, blood poured from his nose. He gasped for breath.

Thomas hit him again, and the man lost all fight.

Thomas searched his pockets, beneath his shirt.

Stifled a swear. No weapon.

Someone was coming up.

Thomas turned that direction, ignoring the burning in his ribs, the pain in his face, preparing to fight.

But Josie was there, on the opposite side of the opening for the stairs, holding something in her hand. It was dark, but...was that a vase?

Where in the heck—?

The man's head popped up, and she whacked him with it, hard.

He tumbled back down.

Thomas scrambled down behind him.

The man hit the ground, reached to his back.

Had to be a gun.

Thomas dove, tackling him. The guy fought hard, but Thomas was fighting for his life, for Josie's life. Maybe he was stronger. Maybe he just wanted it more.

He ignored the man's punches, hitting him over and over.

When the guy curled in on himself, groaning, Thomas checked his pockets, grabbed his phone and his gun. He checked to make sure it was loaded and the safety disengaged before pushing himself to his feet. Everything hurt. The room was spinning.

Where was Josie?

Holding onto the back of a chair, he turned in a slow circle, taking in the rustic cabin. Old plaid couch. Dingy yellowing shades. It was shabby-chic without the chic.

It looked familiar.

He heard footsteps and braced himself, lifting the weapon as he turned toward the noise.

Josie halted in the entry between that room and the next and held up her hands. She had a phone in one. In the other... "It's a walkie-talkie," she said. "They just said they were on their way. Maybe we can prove who they're working for with the phones."

"Maybe." It hurt to talk. To breathe. "You didn't happen to find keys anywhere, did you?"

"I didn't see any cars here."

As she spoke, the sound of an engine reached them. Coming closer.

"Come on." She led the way through the house to the back, pushed open a door, and burst outside.

He followed, braced for gunshots, for somebody to yell at them to stop.

Nobody did.

"Give me the walkie-talkie." He had no idea if it could be traced, but he didn't want to find out. She handed it to him, and he turned it off.

They ran into the thick woods, kept running until they were out of sight of the cabin.

And then, Josie stopped and bent over, heaving breaths. "I'm sorry. I can't—"

"It's okay. I need to rest." He leaned against a tree, scanning behind them, all around. He pretended he wasn't in terrible pain. Pretended his lungs were working properly.

They weren't. Something was wrong. If he had time to put on his paramedic hat, he might be able to figure out what.

Where were they? Where should they go?

There'd been something familiar about the cabin. He thought back, remembered a 911 call, a father and son on a hunting trip. The man had had a stroke, and Thomas had been one of the first responders.

The son had told him he'd had to drive a mile to get cell service to call for the paramedics.

"I know where we are," he said.

She swiveled to face him. "You do?"

Before he could answer, he heard someone shout, "This way!"

Thomas groaned. He'd taken too many hits. His ribs ached. His head pounded. He was running through the woods in a suit.

Josie wore a dress, and her little heels were even less practical than his leather shoes. At least she wasn't one of those women who thought stilettos were all-occasion footwear.

He was so tired, in so much pain. He didn't know if he had it in him to run. But the other option was a gunfight, and he definitely didn't have that in him.

He dropped the walkie-talkie onto the bracken and handed her his jacket. "Run that way about twenty yards and drop this, then come back."

He appreciated that she did it without question. When she returned, he grabbed her hand and started moving to the left. If his memory served—and it usually did—town was south of them, and they'd find a dirt road to the west. If they could get to it, maybe move in the woods alongside it, it would lead them down the mountain until they got phone service. At least if he could get her to the road, she'd have a shot at escaping, even if he couldn't go any farther.

Help me get her out of here, Lord. I just need a little more strength.

By the sound of the ruckus their pursuers were making, at least Thomas wouldn't be taken by surprise if they got close. Unlike the men behind them, Thomas picked his way quietly, and Josie followed suit.

Beneath trees, around bushes, up little hills and back down. They didn't need speed, as long as none of those guys were trackers, which felt likely. They were thugs, not hunters.

Thomas hoped.

They doubled back, giving the cabin a wide berth.

Nausea churned in his middle. He was hot and tired and dehydrated and injured. Maybe those things were to blame for the nausea. Maybe he wasn't badly injured, just weak.

Thomas was a lot of things, but he wasn't weak.

"You all right?" Josie asked behind him.

"Yup."

Every breath brought agony.

He checked the phone often. So far, no service.

There wasn't a path, and the woods were thick and overgrown, slowing their progress. The only consolation was that their enemies didn't have it any easier. And Thomas had grown up in the woods. He'd spent years of his adult life rescuing people from the woods.

If anybody could get them out of there, he could.

Assuming he could stay on his feet.

CHAPTER THIRTY-THREE

Thomas was not okay.

Josie watched with growing alarm as he led them through the thick woods. He seemed to be falling forward from one tree to the next, one support to the next.

How many hits had he taken while she'd searched for a weapon? She'd ripped open a box in the attic and found a crystal vase, and she'd been about to aid Thomas in stopping their captor when it seemed he'd bested the man.

But not after taking a whole lot of blows.

The vase had come in handy when the guy's partner came upstairs. If only she'd hit him harder, Thomas wouldn't have had to fight him too.

He was hurt, very hurt, but he kept going. Determined to get them both to safety.

There were no sounds of their pursuers. They'd probably taken the bait—the walkie-talkie and the jacket—and kept going in that general direction.

She checked the phone she'd taken. No service. It was after seven. The sun had fallen behind the trees, but it would be another hour or more before sunset.

Ahead, there seemed to be a break in the trees. Was that the road?

Something glinted in the twilight.

In front of her, Thomas lifted his hand, telling her to stop as he did the same.

After staring a long moment—or maybe resting—Thomas crept forward.

It was a car, a blue car. It looked like...

"Is that Shelly's?" Thomas whispered.

Before Josie could answer, Shelly yelled, "Thomas? Is that you? Josie?"

It was Shelly? She was here?

Josie bolted past Thomas and onto the dirt road.

Shelly swept her up in a hug. "Thank God you're okay!" She held her tightly, sobbing into Josie's shoulder. "I was so worried."

Josie backed away. "How are you here?"

"I heard somebody mention this road. I told the police, but they didn't believe me. Nobody gets my hearing. You wouldn't believe it. Everybody's going crazy in town. Those two cops were shot, even the young, cute one. Ricky?"

"You need to be quiet," Josie said.

"Oh, sorry."

Thomas reached them, moving much more slowly.

He held the gun in his hand. "His name is Rich. Is he okay?"

"Yeah, but the other one was pretty bad off, the older, cranky one. They were both taken to the hospital. The bodyguards were hit too." She turned back to Josie. "I was so scared you were shot. Come on. Let's get out of here."

But Thomas leaned against the skinny trunk of a birch tree, and he didn't look ready to move. "I'm sorry. How did you find us again?"

"Somebody said the name of this road."

"Who?"

"In the crowd, after the press conference and the shots. I overheard—"

"Who said it, Shelly?" Thomas wasn't moving, and he wasn't kidding.

"I don't know. I didn't see the person, I just overheard—"

"She's lying."

The words came from a familiar voice, though Josie couldn't see him and couldn't imagine how he could be there.

"Bentley?" she called.

Thomas lifted the gun. He aimed it at Shelly, then at Bentley when he stepped into the clearing.

"What are you doing?" Josie asked. "Put the gun down. Have you lost your mind?"

"How are they here?" He shook his head, his skin pasty and pale. "Doesn't make sense."

"He's right, Josie," Bentley said. "It doesn't make sense."

Donley stepped into the clearing beside him.

"You're okay." Josie stepped toward the bodyguard who'd tried so hard to protect her. The sight of him, standing, seemingly safe and sound, sent grateful tears to her eyes. "Thank God."

"Bullet grazed my thigh."

"More than grazed it," Bentley said.

Must have, considering he'd gone down.

Shelly's gaze flicked to the men. "How did you get here?"

"We followed you." Bentley glared at her. "It had to be you."

"What are you talking about?" Her voice was shrill, loud.

"Quiet." Josie hissed the word. There were still men looking for them.

"However it happened, I'm glad you're here." Shelly reached for Josie. "Come on. Get in, and let's get out of here before somebody finds us." To Bentley, she said, "My car only seats four, but you two can follow us back to town."

"I don't think so." The words came from Thomas. He still held the gun, and it was aimed Shelly's way.

Josie looked between them. "Thomas, what are you doing?"

Shelly lifted her hands. "What is wrong with you? Let's go before they come!" Her voice was too loud, almost as if she wanted them to be found.

Shelly could be a little thick, but she wasn't *that* dumb.

Bentley walked closer to her. "Why don't you give Josie your keys, and she can drive Thomas to town? You can ride with us. Donley's SUV is just down the road."

Shelly's gaze flicked between Bentley and Josie. "Just get in, Jo."

"The man's about to collapse," Bentley said. "If you really care about them..."

Shelly was wearing a jacket, a long-sleeved windbreaker, even though the temperature had to be in the upper seventies. It didn't make sense.

Until she stuck her hand in the pocket.

Josie got a glimpse before chaos erupted.

Thomas yelled, "Gun!"

Bentley and Donley rushed across the space.

Bentley tackled Josie, landing on top of her.

A gunshot rang out.

There were sounds of a struggle.

Josie squirmed out from beneath Bentley and peered over him.

Donley was lying on top of Josie's oldest friend.

Her best friend.

Shelly turned her head and met Josie's gaze. She didn't look afraid. She didn't look hurt. She looked furious. She fought the man on top of her. "Get off me. Get off me!"

Donley held her down, shoved a hand in her pocket, and came out with keys. He tossed them to Josie. "Go. Get Thomas to the ER. We'll take care of her."

"But that gunshot—"

"Went wide," he said.

Thank God, but... "The men will be coming."

Donley held her eye contact. "We got this, Josie. Go."

Go.

She turned toward Thomas. He'd collapsed.

Before she could process it, Bentley was at his side, helping him up. He maneuvered him into the passenger seat of Shelly's car while Josie climbed in the driver's seat.

Thomas groaned, held out the gun he'd taken from the cabin. "Just in case."

Bentley took it and looked across the seat at Josie. "Call 911 as soon as you have service."

Before she could respond, Bentley slammed the door and jogged to Donley to assist with Shelly.

Josie would have plenty of time to think about what just happened. Later. At that moment, Thomas needed medical attention.

She did a three-point turn and headed down the mountain, glancing at Thomas as she hit the gas.

He'd passed out.

Josie hadn't been alone in the waiting room for ten minutes before Thomas's friends started pouring in, people she'd seen in her café, people who, before the dinner Sunday night, she'd only known by their drink orders. The blonde who preferred tea got there first, hugged her, and then reintroduced herself as Grace. She came with two brunettes, Tabby and Cassidy. Cassidy carried a little baby, while Tabby rubbed her expanding belly. Her usual order had changed from Americano with an extra shot to water with lemon a few months before.

Grace's husband, Andrew, was the first man to join them, but not the last. Within an hour, the waiting room at the hospital in Plymouth was full of people whose faces had become familiar but whose names she mostly couldn't remember. She'd met Aspen, the blonde from Hawaii. Josie'd given her a ride one night, and when she walked in the door with Garrett, she hugged Josie tight. "We're praying for Thomas—and for you. Is there anything else we can do?"

They'd all asked her a version of that question. But there was nothing these kind people could do, nothing but pray.

And be support for her.

As she sat beside them, the truth hit her. She hadn't known how badly she needed support, needed community, until Thomas had nudged his way into her life. She'd been going it alone in Coventry for too long, content with her long-distance relationships with her parents and Shelly. After the intern's death, Josie had felt she didn't deserve friends, didn't deserve a good life.

What foolishness was that? Jesus hadn't come to punish her. He'd come to give her abundant life. To deny herself that life wasn't selfless or good. It was arrogant, as if she alone knew what she deserved.

God had forgiven her. Jesus had *died* for her, so she could live—free, happy, glorifying Him.

Instead, she'd been hiding.

Scorning the life He'd died to give her.

No more.

Soon, she'd tell the world what she and Bentley had done. She'd tell the world what Mitchell had done. She'd come clean about all of it, and then, she'd live.

Even if everybody rejected her...

But Thomas wouldn't. Her parents wouldn't. And these Coventry folks seemed like the loving, forgiving type.

Maybe, when this was all over, she'd be freer than she'd ever been before.

As long as Thomas survived.

Please, God. Please.

The doctor had explained that he'd been bleeding internally and that all the fighting and then walking after that had only made it worse.

Everything he'd done to save her. How much pain must he have been in? How weak must he have felt?

He would be undergoing surgery any minute now. The surgeon had seemed confident.

Thomas should come through this alive. But what if he didn't?

Please, I can't lose him now.

Aspen squeezed her hand from the chair at Josie's side. "He's going to be okay." The woman smiled at her, and that expression infused confidence. "Did they say how long?"

"The surgeon wasn't sure. She said it depended on what they found when they went in."

"Well, we'll all be here, however long it takes."

One of them—the tall man with the little girl, the one married to the redhead—called above the murmur of voices. "Hey, let's pray together."

Aspen stood and reached for Josie. "Come on."

She joined the circle of friends and prayed silently as they lifted their pleas to God. She'd heard sermons delivered by some of the most skillful pastors in the world. She'd been in beautiful cathedrals and heard world-renowned choirs, but never in her life had she felt the Spirit move like He did in that room.

These people, this little group of friends, had power Josie

could only marvel at. All the power in the Capitol, in the White House, in Washington, was nothing compared to the power Josie experienced in that waiting room. Not human power, but God's power.

Her fears dissipated. God was in this. He could be trusted.

When the prayer ended, Josie accepted hugs from Thomas's friends—she really needed to learn all their names—and started to return to her chair. But movement in the doorway caught her eye.

Chief Cote waved her over. Thank God he was there. A detective had met her at the hospital, but he'd had no information about what had happened on the mountain with Shelly, Bentley, and Donley, and he had shared very little about how the two cops and Greta were doing after the ambush. She was desperate to know.

She followed the police chief into the hallway.

"How's Thomas?" he asked.

"In surgery. How are the others?"

"Donley you know. The bullet grazed his leg, but a paramedic treated it on-site. He refused to go to the hospital. The other bodyguard, Greta Wagner, was hit in the side of the head."

Josie gasped.

"She's all right." Chief Cote pressed his huge palm against Josie's upper arm and squeezed before dropping it again. "If she'd shifted one inch to the side, it would have killed her. As it was, it took off her ear and a chunk of her skull. Though she'll need plastic surgery, she'll recover."

"Thank God," Josie said.

"Officer Fontier—Rich—was shot in the shoulder. He's

stable. Officer Tyler's wounds are the most serious. The bullet went through his middle, hit his intestines. He had surgery, but..." Cote's voice hitched. "It doesn't look good."

He could die.

"There were two shooters," Cote said. "They'd set up in a vacant house across the street from the parking lot. They kept firing until you guys were gone, then took off. We believe they must've run through the yards to the block behind. We're not sure how they escaped yet."

Josie had already given a statement, but she'd been so distracted by Thomas's injuries. She couldn't remember what she'd said. To be safe, she told the chief what happened right after they'd been taken, how they'd been transferred to a different vehicle right away, how someone, maybe two people, had entered, breathing heavily, and how she'd thought they'd all left in the one vehicle.

"That would explain how we never found the shooters or the van. We've already got a team searching homes near the police station. Right now, we have five people in custody. Two men were found in the cabin. Two more were detained by your bodyguard and your friend, Mr. Kent."

"Seriously? How did they do that?"

"That Donley's got skills." Cote seemed impressed. She guessed that didn't happen often for the hardened cop. "Was he special forces?"

"No idea. I wouldn't be surprised."

"Anyway, none of the thugs are talking. We detained Miss Sanders, but she refuses to speak to anybody but you."

The words brought a fresh jab of betrayal. Surely Shelly hadn't been working against her all this time. But Bentley and Donley had both seemed convinced. And she had the gun.

And gave Josie that scathing look.

"What do you think? Did she...?"

His face softened with compassion. "I'm sorry. I know she was your friend."

"I don't understand. She really does have excellent hearing. Maybe she did hear someone mention that road. Did she tell the police about it?"

"Not as far as I've heard. Besides, it's a dirt road. The locals call it 'the pass' because you can use it to get from one highway to another, but it's not a real road. In other words, she might have overheard someone mention it, but she wouldn't have been able to find it on a map. Not only that, but it's miles long, yet somehow, she just happened to have stopped a few hundred yards from the cabin. The story might have worked to get you and Mr. Windham in the car, but beyond that... It doesn't hold water."

Shelly had betrayed her.

Josie's oldest friend, her best friend in the world.

Josie asked, "Do you know why?"

"She'll only talk to you. I know Mr. Windham is in surgery, but the sooner we do this—"

"Now? You want me to come *now*?"

"We transferred her to a local police department, so you don't have to go all the way back to Coventry. She's about five minutes from here. Normally, we wouldn't do it this way, but someone hired the guys we detained. We need to know who's behind all this."

Josie knew exactly who was behind this. If Bentley and Carlyle were here, they might be conniving a way to use this as a winning play in the political game. But Josie wasn't playing that game anymore.

She wanted justice.

"How long will I be gone?"

"Depends on her, I guess."

"If something happens with Thomas—"

"I'll bring you right back."

"Okay. Let me just tell them where I'm going."

Fifteen minutes later, Josie followed Chief Cote into a drab, squat building the shape of a mini-mall. Tabby had insisted on joining her and walked at her side. Josie hardly knew the woman, but that didn't keep Tabby from holding her hand, squeezing it for support.

How had she not realized before how wonderful the people of Coventry were?

She didn't want to think about everything she'd been missing by hiding behind her coffee counter.

They stepped inside, and a familiar man walked their way. He drank his coffee black and always ordered a scone to go with it. He had longish hair and wore a suit, and he greeted Tabby with a kiss before holding his hand out to Josie. "Fitz McCaffrey."

Tabby nudged Josie's shoulder. "My husband."

"Oh. Nice to meet you."

"Sorry it's under such terrible circumstances. How's Thomas?"

"In surgery. The doctor seemed optimistic, but..." She didn't want to end the sentence.

Fitz's voice was gentle. "He's a fighter." He turned to Cote. "Ready?" He led the group to a conference room set up with video monitors. Just as Josie was about to follow Fitz out, Cote gripped her upper arm. "Don't tell her about Zack or Thomas's injuries. We don't want her to know attempted murder is on the table. Right now, she thinks it's just kidnapping."

"But they shot at us."

"We think they weren't shooting to kill. If she learns that two people might die..."

Josie cringed at the words, and Cote's voice softened.

"Sorry. I'm sure Thomas will be all right. The point is, we don't want her to clam up. Got it?"

At her nod, Fitz escorted Josie to a smaller room with a table in the center and chairs on both sides.

Shelly was seated on the far side, hands cuffed and resting on the laminate top. Her usually perfectly curled blond hair was disheveled, her makeup smudged. The windbreaker was dirty, one sleeve torn.

But what surprised Josie most was the look in her oldest friend's eyes.

She'd expected to see hope, regret, maybe pleading. She'd expected to see tears.

But her friend held the same expression she'd worn on that dirt road. Josie had thought it was anger at the time, but now she named it rightly.

Loathing.

Josie glanced at the uniformed officer in the corner, but he didn't acknowledge her.

She slipped into the chair facing Shelly. "You wanted to talk to me?"

Shelly lifted her bound hands, let them drop. "I'm sure you're wondering about this." When Josie didn't respond, Shelly flashed her signature smile. "Didn't think I had it in me, did you?"

"I never would have believed it, not in a million years."

"You always did underestimate me."

Josie wasn't sure how she should play this. What she wanted to do was scream at Shelly to hurry up and tell the truth. What she wanted was to get back to the hospital, to check on Thomas.

But people had been shot. Two men could die. And this woman, this *friend,* had been involved in it all.

"Did I?" Josie asked. "I think perhaps I overestimated you. I thought you were kind and good and trustworthy. Come to find out, you're none of the above."

"You think I'm 'a lot to take.' At the thought of spending time with me, you said to Thomas, 'Pray for me.'"

Josie cringed at the quotes, knowing she'd said both things about her friend in the previous few days.

"At least Thomas just referred to me as ditzy. I can own ditzy from a practical stranger. But you're supposed to be my friend."

"You're right. I love you—you know that. But sometimes, you do tend to barrel in. You're a tiny package with a huge personality."

"One you feel like you have to apologize for."

"Not apologize, just..." There was no defense for saying hurtful things about her friend.

"It's not like it's new," Shelly said. "I've been hearing your opinions of me as long as I've known you. I mean, I expect it from other people, but you... Do you have any idea how hard it is to hear *everything*? To walk out of a room and hear what people say about you as soon as your back is turned?"

"I'm sorry. I have no excuse."

"I'm shocked. Little miss perfect apologizes."

"I'm far from perfect, as you well know."

A smile spread on Shelly's pretty face. "Far from it."

"Why don't you just tell me all the things I'm guilty of so we can be done with this conversation." She made a show of checking her watch. "Believe it or not, I have other places to be."

Shelly's smile didn't fade. "I know what you did."

"Unfortunately, my sins are myriad. You're going to have to be more specific."

Shelly leaned close and whispered. "She was twenty years old, and you killed her."

Josie sat back. "Are you talking about Mitchell's...?"

And then Josie understood.

The new boyfriend, the one who was at a summer house with his children. The one she'd claimed was named Jay.

His name definitely started with J.

And he wasn't at a summer house. The new boyfriend was out of the country on a family vacation.

And the part about him being divorced...that was a lie too.

Because the new boyfriend was Jude Mitchell.

"How long have you been seeing him?"

Shelly shrugged. "We're in love."

"He's married."

"He's getting a divorce."

"You're a fool, Shelly." Josie shook her head. "A foolish, foolish pawn in a game you don't even understand."

"That's it, isn't it? You think I'm stupid."

"I think..." She paused to take a breath, to consider her answer. She lowered her voice. "That *girl* he was seeing, do you know how she died?"

"Suicide, because *you* sent her those pictures."

"Maybe suicide. But Bentley never believed it, and frankly, I'm not convinced."

Shelly's eyes narrowed the slightest bit. "She took a bunch of pills. She killed herself."

"Or Mitchell had her killed. There were markings on her window indicating someone might have broken in—you know, like somebody broke into my house the other night. There were signs of a struggle. There were bruises on the woman's neck. Oh, and the pictures were nowhere to be found. Sure, it looked like a suicide, but maybe it was made to."

"You're lying."

"I have the police report. I'll be happy to show it to you."

Shelly stared, and for a brief moment, Josie thought she

might soften, tell the truth. But then her friend's countenance hardened. "He would never do that."

"If you think Jude Mitchell is going to leave his wife for you, then you're stupider than I thought." Josie's heart was pounding in her chest, but she forced her breathing to even out. "The worst kind of stupid. He got you to betray your best friend for a promise that, mark my words, will prove as solid as vapor. Just tell me what you wanted to tell me. I don't know if you noticed, but your thug-friends really did a number on Thomas. I'd like to get back to the hospital."

A hint of regret crossed her features. "I'm sorry he got hurt."

"Sure you are. What do you want, Shelly?"

"I wanted to tell you that I didn't do anything wrong. I overheard the name of that road in town. I asked around until I found somebody who could tell me where it was, and I drove up there."

"And just happened to be parked in that very spot."

"No. I stopped the car every so often and got out to listen and look. I thought maybe I'd hear voices that would lead me to you or see a house or something. Instead, I heard what sounded like someone moving through the woods. So I waited. And then Thomas whispered, and I knew I'd found you. I wasn't a part of any of this."

"Except you lied to us. You said you tried to tell the police what you'd overheard, but they wouldn't believe you."

"I knew they wouldn't. It was utter chaos there. I figured I'd find you and then call them."

Josie might have believed the story, except Shelly was in a relationship with Mitchell, and Mitchell was the mastermind behind all of this.

And there was the matter of the gun she'd pulled from the windbreaker.

Shelly had been sitting at Thomas's table at the fundraiser. She could have drugged Josie's drink.

Shelly was the one who'd gotten Josie's dress off and left her unclothed, which worked very nicely for whoever took those photos. If not for her memory of that man in her room, she might have believed Shelly took the photos.

Shelly could have unlocked the window.

But Shelly hadn't known about Dad's plan to vote no.

Except...she'd shown up moments after they'd hung up with Dad. If Shelly had been outside, with her super hearing, she could easily have overheard.

It didn't explain how she'd set up the ambush at the police station, since she hadn't known Donley's plan. Maybe he'd discussed it with somebody when Shelly was nearby.

She'd known, somehow.

Josie stood. "Good luck with that story." She tried the door, but it was locked. She turned to the cop in the corner.

"Bang on it," he said.

She did. If Shelly wasn't going to confess, there was no reason for Josie to be there.

"I would never hurt you." But Shelly's words were flat, emotionless. If Josie turned toward her, she figured she'd see that same loathing in her eyes.

She didn't want to see it, but she turned anyway. "I always believed that. I might have said less than kind things about you over the years. For that, I am sorry. Next time somebody gossips about you, I recommend you call her on it, not conspire to have her kidnapped." She knocked again, and the door swung open.

Cote glowered at her, whispering, "Maybe you should go back in and try again."

If she thought Shelly had any intention of confessing, she would. But this was all a game to Shelly, a pathetic game with a pathetic prize—a man who would use her and then spit her out like a chewed piece of gum.

"No sense whispering, Chief. She can hear everything you say. It's her superpower." Josie brushed past him.

Behind her, she heard Shelly say, "Hey, Chief."

"Sit tight," he said.

"No, I need to say something."

Josie stopped in the long hallway to listen. Maybe Shelly would confess. Maybe she'd ask him to talk Josie into going back in there so she could explain.

The police chief stood in the open door. "What?"

"Lawyer."

CHAPTER THIRTY-FOUR

Thomas opened his eyes and glanced around, looking for Josie. It seemed like she was always there. She'd taken to sleeping on the chair by his bed. When he'd told her to go home the night before, she'd just laughed him off. "If the tables were turned, you'd be here."

He couldn't argue with that.

He pushed the button to raise the head of his bed. The slight movement sent stabbing pain to his abdomen. He had three broken ribs. One of them had nicked a blood vessel, which had caused internal bleeding. The day before, the doctor had explained that, if he hadn't gotten to the hospital when he did, he very well could have died.

The Lord had chosen to spare him. For that, he was so thankful.

He was also surprised to find he was alone.

He didn't think he'd been alone since he'd arrived at the hospital two days earlier. Josie was always there, along with one or more of his friends, or his parents, or his siblings, who'd driven up when they'd heard the news. He hadn't had a moment's peace.

Not that he was complaining, but the only one he'd wanted was Josie.

Where was she?

The clock in the corner showed ten a.m. He'd been awakened by the nurses early but had fallen back asleep. Maybe Josie had gone for breakfast or coffee. Maybe she'd gone home to get a shower.

The doctor, a pretty brown-haired woman who was even tinier than Josie, stepped into the hospital room. "Knock-knock."

"Morning, Dr. Crighton."

She turned to the computer in the corner. "How you feeling?"

"Better. Much better."

"Really, or are you just saying that because you want to go home?"

She could see right through him. "I am better. Just maybe not *much*."

After she gave him a quick examination that involved her stethoscope and his deep, painful breathing, she said, "You've improved."

"Told you. That means I can go home, yes?"

She laughed. "Let's see how you do moving around today. It won't kill you to stay another night."

"It might, doc." He wore his most serious expression. "You don't know."

She shook her head, unimpressed. "You up for visitors?"

"Always."

"They were waiting for me to finish."

She left, and a moment later, Josie stepped in, followed by a crowd of people.

Bentley and Donley were first, Chief Cote behind them.

Then a pretty woman with dark blond hair walked in beside an older, distinguished gentleman.

Oh.

Thomas pushed his bed up higher.

"Don't sit up on our account." Senator Harrington approached and shook his hand. "Davis Harrington."

"Thomas Windham. It's an honor, sir."

The man turned to his wife. "You've met Marie."

"Nice to meet you in person, Mrs. Harrington." Thomas shook her hand too. The movement only hurt a little.

She smiled, the expression so like Josie's it made his heart expand. "A polite Yankee." Her Southern accent was almost lyrical as she shook her head. "I continue to be amazed."

They stood at the end of the bed.

Bentley and Donley rounded to the far side. "How you doing?" Bentley asked.

"Sorry to say, it looks like I'm going to make it."

The man chuckled. "I'll somehow survive the disappointment."

Donley barely cracked a smile. He'd been by the day before but hadn't said much, just hovered in the corner, continuing to protect Josie, even though most of their enemies were in custody.

"How's the leg?" Thomas asked Donley.

"Just a scratch."

It had been much more than a scratch, but the man had proved tough and fearless under pressure. Despite the bullet wound, he'd managed to apprehend Shelly and then both the men who'd been following Thomas and Josie through the woods.

And okay, maybe Bentley had helped. A little.

The two guys Thomas had beaten had still been at the cabin when the police got there. Seemed the four had all been using the single van—a Mercedes van painted to look like an Amazon delivery truck. No wonder they'd moved through town without being stopped.

Josie approached the other side of the bed and leaned down to kiss Thomas's cheek. "The doctor seemed pleased when she left."

"I might get to go home today."

Josie's smile faded, but she didn't argue. If it were up to her, he figured he'd be trapped in that hospital bed until he was well enough to run a marathon. He took her hand and squeezed. "I'm okay, sweetheart."

She lifted their joined hands and kissed his knuckles.

She held his gaze a long moment.

Senator Harrington cleared his throat. "We wanted to thank you in person."

"All I did was not die." Thomas tore his eyes away from Josie to look at her father. "It's possible our escape only made everything more complicated. I mean, if they'd planned to let us go…"

His words faded as the people surrounding his bed cast each other knowing glances.

"What?"

Cote fielded the question. "We're not sure that was the plan. We've been able to put most of the pieces together. Dr. Jude Mitchell's phone linked us to one of the thugs. His name is Leo Richards, and he seemed to be in charge."

The chief paused, so Thomas said, "Never heard of him."

"He's been arrested multiple times down in Mass. Spent time in prison."

"He was the tall one the night my car alarm went off," Josie said. "The guy who took the pictures when I was arrested. And the man who kidnapped us."

"You identified him?"

She nodded. "I barely saw his face, but his body style matched what we'd seen. And I heard his voice. It was him."

"So he was the one who did this." Thomas patted his wrapped ribs.

The chief answered. "That's what Josie told us. When faced with all the evidence, Miss Sanders finally started talking. She admitted to drugging Josie's drink. She loosened the lock on the window so Richards could more easily break in."

"Apparently," the senator said, "she overheard when we were on the phone discussin' my vote. She must've passed that information along, setting this all in motion. If she hadn't heard that, then I think our plan would have worked."

Thomas squeezed Josie's hand. "I'm so sorry, sweetheart."

Tears filled her eyes, but she didn't say anything.

When Thomas looked forward again, he caught Mrs. Harrington's curious—maybe calculating—gaze.

He'd gladly tell her everything, if there weren't so many people in the room. If things worked out as Thomas hoped and prayed, he'd have plenty of time to tell Josie's mother exactly how he felt about her daughter.

Donley said, "Only thing we still don't know is how they knew where to set up the ambush after the press conference."

"I still say it was obvious." Bentley turned to the man beside him. "You weren't going to go out front, and you'd gone in through the police station. If somebody was watching—"

"We could have gone out the front," Donley said. "We could have gone out the back door of the municipal building. We seriously considered using the side door. Somebody had to know."

"Then you must've said the plan when Shelly was nearby."

"I didn't." Donley glowered at Bentley.

Thomas had the feeling the men had had this conversation before. "I have a theory."

Everybody turned to him.

He hated to say this. He hated to even think it. The thought had come to him in the middle of the night, and he hadn't been able to shake it. In fact, the more he thought about it, the more sense it made.

He turned to Chief Cote. "Have you looked into Rich Fontier?"

The man blinked, narrowed his eyes. "Why?"

"Just... I hope I'm wrong. But the night of Josie's alarm, there was a second man. Shorter and stockier. He was about the same size as Rich."

"A lot of men are that size," the chief said. "And you said you didn't see his face."

"I didn't. But Zack responded to the call alone that night. He said Rich was home with a stomach bug. But when I asked Rich about it the day Josie was arrested, he seemed confused."

"He probably didn't realize you'd known he was sick," the chief said.

"That was what I thought at the time. But..." He turned to Josie. "It was Rich who found the drugs in your car, right?"

She nodded slowly, turning to the detective beside her. "He went straight to the trunk."

"He got a tip." Cote's words didn't hold the confidence they had earlier.

"*He* got it?" Thomas asked.

Cote's chin dipped, his lips pressed tight. "Said he did."

"Okay." Thomas swallowed and shook his head. "The night of the fundraiser, I saw Shelly and Rich talking. I thought it was strange because Rich was supposed to be acting as security for the party, but he seemed pretty engrossed in the conversation."

"Say what you want about her," Mrs. Harrington said, "but Shelly's an attractive woman."

"Sure," Thomas said. "But Rich is married with children."

The woman's expression darkened. "Not that that would have stopped her."

"It was Rich," the chief said, turning to Josie, "who bagged your glass that night."

"The glass that had no sign of Rohypnol in it," Bentley added. "Son of a—"

"All right." Senator Harrington turned to the police chief. "This is one of your officers?"

"One of my best. And he was shot."

"In the shoulder," Donley said. "And he was involved in all the planning."

Josie's eyes widened. "He fell in front of the door, blocking our way back into the building."

"Because of a *shoulder* injury." Donley didn't look impressed. "A through-and-through."

The chief drooped as if a very heavy weight had fallen on him. "I'll get to the bottom of this."

"See that you do," the senator said. "I want everybody involved in this behind bars."

"You and me both." the chief said. "Speaking of which, I understand the FBI has arrested Mitchell."

"Shelly cut a deal in exchange for everything she knew," the senator said. "Once she realized the true endgame, she turned on him."

"Wait." The *true endgame?* It reminded Thomas... "You said something about how maybe they weren't going to let us go."

Cote rubbed the back of his neck. "I just can't believe Rich..."

"We played ball together," Thomas said. "We were friends." He looked at Josie, realizing he must be feeling only a tiny portion of the betrayal she was dealing with.

"The FBI checked all their bank accounts," Cote said.

"Richards had received an electronic transfer of two hundred grand the day of the shooting. Considering that happened before the kidnapping, we can assume there was another payment coming after it was finished."

"Whoa," Thomas said. "That's a lot of money."

The chief held his gaze. "More than the going rate for a kidnapping."

Oh. *Oh.* "You're saying—"

"I'm saying he was probably going to kill you. He's been suspected of contract killing in the past, but the police down in Lowell hadn't been able to make those charges stick."

"Then why keep us hooded?"

"To keep you from fighting." It was Donley who spoke. "To make you think there was hope. As long as you had hope that they'd let you go, they figured you wouldn't try to escape. But they pegged you wrong."

"Probably more dumb luck than anything else," Thomas said.

Josie gripped his hand. "We haven't put our faith in luck, Thomas. The Lord led us out of there."

She was right. God had been there.

The chief patted Thomas awkwardly on the shoulder. "Glad you're improving."

"Thanks for everything."

The chief's lips pinched at the corners as if he might be trying to smile. "Good chance you're going to be my boss come January, so I figured I'd better do my best work."

His boss? Thomas wasn't so sure about that. "You always do your best work, chief."

"That I do."

"How's Zack?"

"They thought he wasn't gonna make it. Your friends had some kind of a prayer thing at the hospital on his behalf last night. Probably not related, but he turned a corner. Looks like he's going to survive."

"You might consider," Thomas said, "that it *is* related."

Cote shrugged. "Doubt he'll be able to stay on the force, but at this point, I think his family just wants him home. If I find out Rich was involved..." The chief shook his head. "Anyway, I'll be in touch." He walked out the door.

Thomas settled back against the pillows as the information they'd discussed settled into place in his mind.

For two days, he'd been thanking God that he hadn't gotten Josie killed with that stupid escape plan. Now he knew the truth.

"You saved our daughter's life," Senator Harrington said.

Thomas swallowed and waited until he could speak without emotions leaking out. "We did it together."

Josie squeezed his arm. "You did it, Thomas. You almost died saving us." She kissed his cheek. "I owe you my life."

"You swing a mean vase, though."

She shook her head, her small smile telling him she thought he was being ridiculous but didn't plan to call him on it.

He loved that smile. And those eyes that so freely expressed her feelings. He'd seen disgust in them, amusement, and terror, but at that moment, he only saw love.

He wanted to stare into those eyes for the rest of his life.

The senator cleared his throat. "Anyway, I just wanted to say how sorry I am all this happened to you two."

Josie's voice cracked when she answered. "It wasn't your fault, Dad." She and Bentley had confessed the incident involving Mitchell and his intern to her father the day before. She'd been tearful when she'd told Thomas last evening about the disappointment she'd seen on her dad's face.

Maybe he'd been disappointed, but he'd also flown to New

Hampshire, and the look he was giving Josie now held only affection.

The senator said, "I dragged you into a very ugly business. You have a gift for strategy, but if I were any kind of a father, I'd have steered you to a different career."

"I wanted to work for you."

"That's because you were young and idealistic. You didn't understand the world where I live. Where my family, for generations, has lived. I wanted to do good. I've tried to do good."

"You *have* done good, Dad. Look at the bill. It was defeated because of you."

Her father had told Parker and the vice president what was going on. They'd pulled in the minority leader, and the four of them had decided on a plan.

The senator had voted yes.

And the vice president had voted no.

The bill had been defeated, and Parker, horrified at what had been done on Mitchell's behalf, had agreed it wouldn't be brought to the floor again in any form.

"This is a corrupt business," the senator said. "We try to do the right thing, but there are always deals being made, palms being greased. My dad and granddad..." He shook his head sadly. "I loved those men, loved them fiercely, and they did some good. But a lot of ugliness remained because of them. I wanted to be different."

"And you have been."

"Maybe," he said. "But pulling you into the whole mess of corruption and deceit." He slipped past his wife to Josie's side and took her hand. He lifted it and pressed their joined hands against his chest, facing her alone.

Thomas felt like an intruder in a private moment. He turned away.

"I'm glad you got out," Senator Harrington said. "It's time

for me to do the same. It's time for someone young to step into the role, someone without all the baggage, someone idealistic who can take on the powers that be."

"You're not resigning," Josie said.

"I'll finish my term."

Mrs. Harrington studied her husband's back, a look of pure pride on her face.

Someone knocked, then a woman said, "Oh." They all turned, and Josie stepped aside enough for Thomas to see the nurse, Trish. "I need to get the patient's vitals."

The senator clapped Thomas's shoulder, which felt like the only thing uninjured on his whole body. "We'll see you later, son."

His wife added, "I do look forward to getting to know you better."

Thomas could only smile at the twinkle in the woman's eye.

Josie said, "Be back in a few," and walked out with her parents.

Bentley watched her leave, then scowled at Thomas. "Glad you're not gonna die."

"You ever leave politics, you could write condolence cards."

Bentley pressed his hands to his chest. "I'm just a warm-hearted kind of guy." He turned for the door, and Thomas had the distinct impression he was hoping to catch Josie. But Thomas wasn't worried. Josie seemed to know what she wanted, and it wasn't to return to DC. It wasn't Bentley.

Miraculously, it was Coventry...and him.

Bentley glanced back at Thomas. "I guess I'll see you around."

Thomas held out his hand.

Bentley looked at it a long moment before he shook it.

Thomas met his rival's gaze. "Thank you for being there. I don't know what we would have done if you hadn't been."

Once again, Bentley's eyes flicked toward the door. "Don't screw it up. I'll swoop in and steal her back."

Thomas tightened his grip, ignoring the ache in his ribs. "I wouldn't expect anything less."

After Bentley left, Donley shook Thomas's hand. "Headed back to Boston."

"I hope your next assignment is dull as dirt."

"You and me both." The man cracked a rare smile, but it didn't hold. "Glad you were there for her. I'm sorry I wasn't."

"You were shot. I think you get a pass. Besides, in the end, if not for you and Bentley, we'd have been delivered right back into the lion's den."

Donley shook his head. "Not sure I could have lived with that."

Thomas understood exactly how he felt.

If anything had happened to Josie, he wasn't sure he could have lived with it either.

But they'd both survived. Thank God, they'd both survived.

CHAPTER THIRTY-FIVE

Josie stood at the edge of the ice-skating rink that had been set up in the park. The lake wasn't frozen yet, but the little man-made rink was solid as granite, proved by the people who were enjoying it so much. Children laughing. Parents teaching their toddlers how to navigate the rented skates. Couples gliding hand-in-hand, all while Christmas songs played overhead.

It was the Saturday after Thanksgiving, and the locals had gathered for the annual festival. The ice-skating rink was the biggest attraction. Thomas had told her about his plans to bring in snow-making machines the following year—assuming there wasn't snow on the ground already. He'd clear out an area for sledding. It would require bulldozers to take out a few trees on a nearby hill and maybe to move dirt to make the slight incline a little steeper. Apparently, he'd given Farley the idea, but the current mayor hadn't been impressed.

Lame ducks didn't like to work that hard.

Once Thomas took office in January, he'd be able to enact a lot of his plans, and not just for the Christmas festival. He'd told her about his strategy to get new hotels—not big resorts, but small places, both family-oriented and posh—on the lake. As it stood, folks who visited Lake Ayasha had to drive straight through Coventry to get there. Thomas's idea was to put in a highway that would circumvent downtown, and then build a road from the resort area to link them. That way, people could still enjoy the shops and restaurants in Coventry, but it wouldn't add an undue amount of traffic.

The resorts themselves would help pay for the road.

It was a brilliant idea. Josie was proud of him. So proud.

She checked on her food truck. She'd purchased it used, figuring it would come in handy for town festivals. It seemed the locals found reasons to gather at the park about once a month, and if the truck did a decent business, it would be paid for within two years.

Sure enough, people waited in line to buy coffee and hot chocolate, sandwiches and pastries.

James, owner of The Patriot, ambled close. "I used to get a lot of customers on festival days." His voice was wistful.

James was a friend of Thomas's—now a friend of hers, despite the fact that they were business rivals. "Too bad you didn't have that idea, huh?"

He gave her a smirk. "It's all right. Not everybody wants to freeze their fingers off to eat dinner. I bet a good share of them will wander by my place, now that I've got that fire going."

He'd built a stone fireplace in the back of his restaurant. It'd probably cost a pretty penny and taken up the space of a couple of tables. But man, in the winter, people loved it. "If Thomas does what he plans to do, I think we'll both have more business than we can handle."

James's expression turned to a full-blown smile. "I believe you're right. Where is he, anyway?"

She searched the crowd and caught sight of Cassidy, James's wife, chatting with Tabby and Fitz, who were bent over a stroller, no doubt doting on their baby. Beyond them, Reid walked beside Jacqui, Ella between them, toward the playground. They'd announced Jacqui's pregnancy a month or so before.

Other friends were scattered among the people at the park that day. People Josie had only known by their drink orders six months before but who'd become her dearest companions. Grace, Aspen, Carly... She loved these women. She felt connected to them in a way she hadn't felt connected to anybody in a long time.

Zack Tyler and his wife were seated at one of the picnic tables. Zack had recovered, though he still moved slowly. As Cote had feared, he hadn't been able to return to the force. Rumor had it, he'd bought a storefront that faced the lake and planned to open a bar and grill with alfresco dining.

She hated that he'd been injured, but looking at him now, a wide smile aimed at the two kids who looked like little mini-Zacks, she decided he looked happier than he ever had in uniform.

Josie had gone public with her part in Mitchell's young mistress's death. Unfortunately, there was insufficient evidence to prove she'd been murdered. But after both Shelly and Leo Richards, the would-be hitman, had turned on Mitchell, he'd been convicted of enough crimes to send him to prison for the bulk of his life.

Josie hadn't outed Bentley for his part in the scheme. She'd taken all the blowback, and she'd survived. Sure, the media had been rough on her at first. But of course, they'd moved on. They'd forgotten her.

And the people in this town had been supportive, and they continued to be supportive.

Finally, she caught sight of Thomas, chatting with people

she'd never seen before but whose names he no doubt knew. Because that was the kind of man he was.

They'd been dating officially for almost five months. Five months of laughing, sharing stories, and kissing. They'd been together a month when Thomas first told her he loved her.

He'd repeated the sentiment every single day since then, and still, her heart fluttered like birds' wings when she heard the words.

This man, this exceptional man, knew all the ugliness of her past, but he saw beyond it. He loved her anyway.

She watched as he crossed the park. Though the little snow that had fallen that month hadn't stuck, the grass was squishy with moisture, so most adults stuck to the gravel paths, Thomas included. It took time because so many people stopped to greet him. Everybody loved him. The horrid photograph had never been released, and even if it had been, these people would have believed in Thomas. He was so kind, so obviously *good*. How could anybody doubt him?

Finally, he reached her side and leaned in to kiss her. "Good afternoon, beautiful."

"Mr. Mayor."

His smile faltered. "You're going to help me, right? What if I—?"

"You're going to be wonderful. I have no doubt."

He greeted James with a handshake. James gave him a nod. "You two have fun." He walked away, heading toward his wife and child.

Thomas nodded at the ice-skating rink. "Shall we?"

"Oh, I'm not very good."

"Don't worry." He faced her, taking her hands and giving her his full attention. When he looked at her with those smoldering eyes, it was all she could do not to melt into his arms.

"I'll be right beside you." He leaned down, kissed her lips so softly, so tenderly. He backed away enough to see her face. "We'll be together. We'll hold each other up."

And she knew, she *knew*, he wasn't talking about ice skating. There wasn't a ring, and it wasn't official. He'd be taking office in six weeks, and he needed to focus on the job.

But she also understood that, while it might not be official, it was real. They would be together. They would hold each other up.

Tears prickled her eyes. "Always."

"And forever."

The End

~

I hope you enjoyed Josie and Thomas's story. This was my first shot at writing a love-triangle story, but I enjoyed it so much, it won't be my last.

Turn the page to find out what else was going on at the park that day. You'll meet an old friend, Denise Masters (Ella's mother, Reid's ex-wife) and a new friend you'll recognize from this story, Jon Donley. You're going to love this one!

Amanda Series

Chasing Amanda

Finding Amanda

Standalone Novellas

A Package Deal

One Christmas Eve

Faith House

My Book

ABOUT THE AUTHOR

Robin Patchen is a *USA Today* bestselling and award-winning author of Christian romantic suspense. She grew up in a small town in New Hampshire, the setting of her Nutfield Saga books, and then headed to Boston to earn a journalism degree. After college, working in marketing and public relations, she discovered how much she loathed the nine-to-five ball and chain. After relocating to the Southwest, she started writing her first novel while she homeschooled her three children. The novel was dreadful, but her passion for storytelling didn't wane. Thankfully, as her children grew, so did her writing ability. Now that her kids are adults, she has more time to play with the lives of fictional heroes and heroines, wreaking havoc and working magic to give her characters happy endings. When she's not writing, she's editing or reading, proving that most of her life revolves around the twenty-six letters of the alphabet. Visit robinpatchen.com/subscribe to receive a free book and stay informed about Robin's latest projects.